Praise for The Best Girls Series

"If you enjoy a rollicking good romance story, you'll love Best Dating Rules as much as I did."
        Carol Marrs Phipps, Author
        The Heart of the Staff Series

"The line between smut and puritanism has rarely been tweaked so enchantingly, with just the right amount of yearning and heat applied in all the right places that makes the Best Girls books suitable for young-hearted romantics of any age."
        Jan Hawke, Author
        Milele Safari: An Eternal Journey

"Dearen elicits laughter, gasps and even tears. The emotion which she imbues to her characters is enchanting."
        Scotty Shepherd

Books by Tamie Dearen

Sweet Romance

The Best Girls Series:
The Best is Yet to Come
Her Best Match
Best Dating Rules
Best Foot Forward
Best Laid Plans
Best Intentions

Sweet Romance

A Rose in Bloom

Christian Romance

Noelle's Golden Christmas
Haley's Hangdog Holiday

The Alora Series
YA/Fantasy

Alora: The Wander-Jewel
Alora: The Portal
Alora: The Maladorn Scroll

Best Dating Rules

The characters and events portrayed in this book are fictitious. Any similarity to real persons, living or dead is coincidental and not intended by the author. To the extent any real names of individuals, locations, businesses or organizations are included in the book, they are used fictitiously and not intended to be taken otherwise.

Best Dating Rules
by Tamie Dearen

All rights reserved. Except as permitted under the U.S. Copyright Act of 1976, no part of this publication may be reproduced, distributed, or transmitted in any form or by any means now known or hereafter invented, or stored in a database or retrieval system, without the prior written permission of the author.

Copyright © 2014 Tamie Dearen

ISBN-13: 978-1975846268
ISBN-10: 1975846265

Best Dating Rules
The Best Girls Series
Book Two

By
Tamie Dearen

To Mom and Dad, who have been happily married for sixty-three years. You taught me the meaning of true love and happily-ever-after.

Acknowledgements

I want to thank all of my beta readers: Bruce, Nancy, Heidi, Alyssa, Emily, Wesley, Kay, Kitty, Mom, Courtney, and Carol. Your excitement over the story and love of the characters inspired me, and your feedback was invaluable. Thanks to Avery for guiding me through this publishing process. I also extend heartfelt apologies to all of my family, especially my sweet husband, Bruce, for all of the times I ignored you while writing about my imaginary family and friends. I love you!

*****

All characters are fictional except for my cameo winner, Rachel, who is exactly as described.

Chapter One

EMILY BEST ALWAYS DID the right thing. The smart thing. The safe thing. So why on earth had she moved to New York City? She'd had a nice, secure job in Fort Worth, Texas. She'd had a small, but comfortable apartment and a few good friends. Granted, she didn't have a lot of excitement in her life. But that's because she didn't want excitement, not because she couldn't find it. She'd had no good reason to move to New York City.

She was stubborn and independent; no one told her what to do. But her new stepdad was adept at getting into her head. He'd argued how her mom would be so happy to have her in the city. And he'd reasoned his company, Gherring Inc., could provide a lot more intellectual challenge than the small tax firm where she was employed in Fort Worth. He'd also flattered her, exclaiming over how smart she must be to have her Master's degree and a CPA by the age of twenty-four. Now, on her way to her first day at Gherring Inc., she was second-guessing her decision, and that wasn't like her, either. She obviously wasn't herself today.

A quick stop in the ladies room on the first floor revealed nothing out of place. Her long brown hair was confined to its usual braid. Dark lashes, unadorned by makeup, framed her large, blue, almond-shaped eyes. She had on a skirt, blouse, and sandals with a low heel. At five feet nine inches, she didn't need heels to make her legs look long. She was dressed stylishly, but not too trendily, since she didn't like to waste money on clothes that would go out of fashion quickly.

Satisfied with her inspection, she squeezed onto the crowded elevator full of Gherring Inc. employees. Most of the occupants chatted together, but Emily remained quietly to herself. She was never pleased when people labeled her as shy; she preferred to describe herself as quietly observant. She learned a lot about people by listening instead of talking.

Emily arrived at her cubicle, which was about the same size as the one she'd had in Fort Worth, but it looked sad and mundane. She'd never be satisfied until she'd put her personal touch on it. She began to organize her things, adding photos and paintings. Most of the artwork was her own, although she never signed it. Soon the cubical walls were decorated with wistful watercolors in pastel shades, hinting of imaginary worlds. In painting she found her adventure, letting inspiration take her to places no one had ever seen. With paintbrush in hand she found adventure and explored new realms—all from the safety of her home. Not that she was unwilling to take a risk—she simply needed an extremely good reason to do it.

"Hey, Sweetie," said a willowy attractive woman with a thick mane of brown hair. Her brown eyes crinkled in a broad smile as she regarded Emily.

"Hi, Mom."

"I'm so excited you're here. It's too bad we have to work so we can't just visit all day."

"Shhhh! You don't have to talk so loudly."

"Oh, it's okay. No one's actually started working yet; it's still early. Do you want me to introduce you to everyone? I don't know all the people in Accounting, but I do know a lot of them. Sam works in this department." Emily recalled Samantha as one of the Gherring Inc. employees her mom had successfully matched with a boyfriend—now fiancé.

"No, that's okay, Mom. I don't really want to meet a lot of people all at once. I'll meet them all eventually."

"Hey, Anne." A cute young woman with perky blond curls joined them at the cubicle.

"Sam," said Anne, "We were just talking about you. How's Tanner?"

"He's great—just great." Sam smiled, holding out her hand to admire the diamond sparkling on her hand. "And how's married life, Anne? I can't believe you're still working, to be honest."

"Married life is wonderful, if you're married to the most wonderful man in the world, like me. And I'm working because I like it. I told Steven, 'Work brought us together, so now it can keep us together.'"

"Mom, where's your engagement ring? Why are you just wearing your band?" Her mother's hand sported a simple eternity band, encircled with small round diamonds. The ring was beautiful, but not what you'd expect for the newly married wife of the billionaire owner of Gherring Inc.

"I just can't get used to that huge diamond he bought. I prefer the simple band. But I wore the engagement ring every day for five months, and today's the first day I left it off." Anne's face reddened as she hid her hand at her side. "I was hoping no one would notice."

"Are you excited about your first day?" Sam asked Emily.

"Uhmm, sure."

"Are you going to let your mom find a match for you, like she did for me?"

"Absolutely not." Emily cast a stern look toward her mother. "I know we've teased about that in the past, but I really don't want you to interfere in my love life."

"I'll try not to, but it goes against my nature."

"Mom, I mean it. Anyway, I have no time for the complications of a relationship right now. Maybe in a couple of years..."

"Oh no—I want to be a young grandmother. And Gram wants to be a great-great grandmother before she dies."

Gram had claimed great-grandmother status with Emily and her sister, Charlotte, upon her grandson's marriage to Anne. At the age of ninety-six, Gram was a feisty force of nature.

"We can discuss this another time, Mom. I really want to get to work. I need to make a good impression so the employees won't accuse Mr. Gherring of nepotism."

Sam chuckled. "No worries, Emily. We can't accuse anyone of that—we don't even know what it means. But I'll take your mom away, and let you get to work. Let me know if you have any questions."

Emily had all of her things arranged and her workspace decorated with five minutes to spare before her workday officially started. She considered getting a cup of coffee, but opted to simply plunge into her work. Her mind was engrossed in figures on an Excel spreadsheet when she heard a man's voice beside her.

"Hey, Emily. What are you doing here?"

A smiling face peered over the top of her cubicle. It was him. He was the last person she wanted to see in New York City and one of the few she actually knew. She'd met Spencer Marshall at a rock-climbing gym while visiting her mom in the city in the fall. He was everything she wasn't. He was an outgoing, adventurous, adrenaline junkie. He'd be a perfect match for her audacious sister, but instead, he'd chosen to pursue *her*. Calling. Texting. Skyping. Emailing. He was incredibly persistent, despite her discouraging hints. She hadn't mentioned her move to the city, knowing he would be even more tenacious.

It's not that he was unattractive. Merely looking at his face made her blood start pumping faster. He had deep penetrating brown eyes; he kept his dark brown hair cut short on the sides and a little longer on top. He smiled at her with even white teeth and dimples to boot. His youthful face contrasted with the strong jaw line and rugged look that said he was all man. And she knew from watching him climb he had a body to go with it—tall, with broad shoulders and lean muscles. No, the problem wasn't with his looks. The problem was... The problem was... He was overwhelming. That's what the problem was. After every encounter or conversation, her mind quit working, and she couldn't think straight. He had a sort of aura or presence that interfered with the proper function of her brain. That simply wouldn't do.

She'd jammed dating at the bottom of her extensive agenda for her new life in New York City. But if she ever decided to date again, she needed someone different. Someone calm. Stable. Conservative. Even-keeled. Unexcitable. She needed a rock she'd be able to anchor her life to. Not someone who was unpredictable and daring—even if he was heart-stoppingly handsome.

"I *work* here. And what are *you* doing here?"

"I work here, too. Your stepdad gave me an internship this summer. This is great. We can get together... I mean, we could do some fun things together. Would you like to go climbing again?"

"Uhmm, I'm not sure. I think I need to concentrate on getting settled—you know, moved in and unpacked and such." She mustered her most discouraging tone.

"Great. I'll come help you unpack tonight. What time? And I need your address, too."

"I don't know about tonight. I still need to stock my pantry. I don't have any food yet. So tonight will mostly be grocery shopping. Nothing I really need help with, but thanks—"

"Even better. I'm a wiz at shopping and a great cook. I'll get you set up." He answered his vibrating cell phone. "Hi, Olivia... No, not tonight. I've got plans. Maybe Wednesday? Awesome—see you."

Without blinking an eye, he turned back to Emily. "So tonight? I'll come about six thirty? Sound okay?"

Emily shook her head in disbelief. She knew from her mom's description he was popular with a lot of girls. But had he actually made a date with another girl on the phone while he was in the process of making a date with her? He was way too much of a player.

"Spencer, it sounds to me like you've got too much on your social calendar to squeeze me into it." She poured on the sarcasm. "Maybe tonight's not a good idea."

"I'll never have too much going on to squeeze you in. I'd tear up the whole calendar and throw it away to make room for you. See ya tonight."

He turned on one heel and left her standing with her mouth agape. She was in big trouble.

Returning home from her first day at work, Emily felt bone-tired. She'd successfully negotiated the subway system, but her commute still took her about forty minutes. Of course, she'd been offered a ride home with her mom and stepdad, but she'd steadfastly refused. She had to prove she could do this on her own. Her stepfather had convinced her to move into one of the apartments owned by Gherring Inc., but only until she could find a place on her own. Steven Gherring had explained the apartment was merely a part of the initial job offering rather than a special favor for a family member. But it felt like favoritism to her. She couldn't help but worry the employees at Gherring Inc. would secretly resent her. After all, she was the youngest person in the Accounting department by at least five years, with most being in their thirties and forties. Well, except for Spencer, who was only twenty-five; but he was an intern.

A merry tone sounded on her cell phone.

"Hey, Charlie."

"Hey, Sister. How was your first day?"

"I'm pooped, but everything went pretty well. Mom only embarrassed me a little bit, and I managed to talk her out of introducing me to the entire office."

"You'd sit in your cubicle and never meet a soul if you had your way about it. I'm glad Mom's there to do my job for me."

"I'm quite happy without either of you interfering in my personal life. I've got enough trouble already."

"What? What happened?"

"You won't believe my bad luck. Spencer Marshall is working a few cubicles down from me."

"That's awesome. I didn't know he worked at Gherring Inc."

"It's not awesome—he's pushy and overbearing. He's an intern for the summer, so I only have to make it for three months or so. Then he'll be gone, and I can have my quiet, private life back."

"He's not going to mess up your life by working next to you. Think of it as a bonus. He's improving the scenery at the office. You have to admit, he's pretty hot."

"He *is* messing up my life. He invited himself over here tonight to help me unpack and stock up on groceries. The problem is I've already done all of that. I told a little white lie about it as an excuse for why we couldn't get together." Emily rubbed her forehead. "Now what am I going to do?"

The sound of Charlie's giggles echoed over the phone.

"Stop it—it's not funny."

"You've always been so good at telling those little lies, and you always got away with it. But not this time… And Spencer's coming to your apartment. He really does like you, doesn't he? You've been denying it all this time, so now you've been caught in another little lie."

Emily had been skirting the truth about Spencer's relentless pursuit since their meeting in the fall. Both her mom and her sister had quizzed her about him repeatedly. But Emily didn't want the complication of a relationship right now. And she certainly didn't want the complication of a meddling family.

"Stop it. You're my sister—you have to be on my side. You have to help me. What am I going to do?"

"Well, you could always tell the truth and admit you lied to keep him from coming over."

"I can't do that. It would hurt his feelings. Although… Maybe he deserves it. Do you know he made a date with another girl on the phone while he was making this date with me?"

"So we're calling this a date?"

"No, it's not a date. It's a friend coming over to help a friend. It's only a date if they spend money on you or kiss you. You know the dating rules. He's not spending any money, and he's definitely not gonna kiss me."

"Whatever you say…"

"Charlie, help me."

"Okay, okay… Knowing you, you've already completely unpacked and thrown away your boxes and decorated the entire space, right?"

"Of course. I did that the night I got here."

"So, go get your suitcases out and take stuff off your shelves and put it in the suitcases."

"What about the groceries?"

"Just tell him you were really hungry, so you went by the grocery store on the way home from work. Honestly, he's a boy, so all you really need to do is feed him. If he smells food cooking when he gets there, he won't ask any questions or be suspicious at all."

"Right. Good idea." Emily relaxed a little. "How is it you know so much about boys, but you don't have one of your own?"

"There's plenty of them hanging around all the time. I can ski and climb and raft and hike and bike with them without having one guy tied to me. They're so needy. All the girls I know with boyfriends can't ever do anything fun because they have to be with their guys all the time."

"Awesome, Sis. Thanks for your advice. I hate to take my stuff off the shelves. But maybe if I'm really organized about it, it won't be so bad."

Emily scurried to follow Charlie's advice before Spencer's arrival. She decided to make spaghetti because the aroma would be really strong. She chopped up half an onion and bell pepper and sautéed it, before adding ground turkey. The smell was working on her as well—she noticed her stomach gurgling.

Spencer knocked on the door at six thirty on the dot. "Wow—what smells so good?" He waltzed in the door and proceeded straight to the kitchen. "I thought you didn't have groceries yet?"

"I stopped on the way home from work. I didn't want to wait for a late dinner."

"Awesome. Spaghetti? Want me to make garlic cheese bread? Let's see what you've got." He perused her totally stocked and well-organized kitchen and raised his eyebrows. "Wow, you've got everything, even the spices. I can't believe you did all this after work."

She cringed, but his face split in a sincere smile. "I just love a girl who's smart and efficient." He found the supplies needed for his bread and started working.

As relief flooded her body, she hurried to finish preparing dinner. Spencer chatted about his excitement at getting the internship at Gherring Inc. He expressed admiration for her accomplishments, never suggesting Steven Gherring had given her a job she didn't deserve.

His manner was friendly and platonic. She began to wonder if she'd only imagined his forwardness. Maybe he was simply an extremely amicable person. Maybe he only wanted to be good friends. After all, he'd never actually said he wanted to date her. That would explain why he felt comfortable making a date with another girl while talking to her. Emily knew she wasn't good at understanding guys. She'd probably misinterpreted his intentions from the start. Surprisingly, her heart gave a little pang at this thought. Not that she liked him or anything. But he was really cute, so she was flattered by his attention. Realizing he probably gave the same sort of attention to everyone, she was a little letdown.

Soon the sauce was stewing and the water boiling for pasta. Her own stomach growled again at the scent of Spencer's garlic cheese bread in the broiler oven.

"I guess it's a good thing we're eating earlier." He chuckled as he spooned a sample of the sauce.

"How'd you get to be good at cooking? Most guys I know can barely boil water."

"The same's true for most girls I know, as well. But I've been cooking since I was a kid. Momma and Papa both worked, so I helped out as much as I could. Grocery shopping and cooking became my job."

"So you were the oldest?"

"Yep, oldest of five. My youngest sister is seventeen. She'll graduate from high school next year, and every one of us are going or have gone to college," he said proudly. "That was their dream. Neither of my parents got to go when they were young, but they've both gone back to school and earned their degrees."

He stopped to pull his bread from the oven. "Tell me about your family. I know you've got your sister, Charlie. When did you lose your dad?"

"I was eight years old, almost nine. But I'm glad Mom's got someone now; she was alone for a long time."

"Yeah, I have to admit those two look pretty happy together. It's funny... I see them less since I'm working at Gherring Inc. instead of the restaurant next door."

"The restaurant next door? Are you talking about Papa's Place? The one Mom's addicted to?"

"Yep, my Aunt May and Uncle George own it. I worked for them until I started this job. They're great, and they really helped out raising the five of us."

Emily was increasingly relaxed as dinner progressed. When Spencer got up and started washing the dishes, she took a moment to admire the view he presented from behind. She'd seen him in shorts before, when they'd gone climbing together, but she'd forgotten how nice his muscles were. His calves flexed even when he was simply standing at the sink. And she could see his shoulders straining against his t-shirt.

What was she doing? She shouldn't be looking at him like that. Still, it was harmless—she was merely enjoying the show.

"... Hello? Emily?"

"I'm sorry. I was... Uhmm... I was daydreaming. What did you say?"

"I said we should go for a walk. You could change into shorts." Then he glanced at the suitcases. "Or did you want me to help you unpack?"

Her mind churned. Unpacking would mean close contact. Walking was safer.

"A walk sounds good. I'll go change."

Outside, they strolled at a fairly nice pace. Emily was glad. She hated walking slowly—it felt like a waste of time, even if you didn't have any particular place to go. She was afraid Spencer would try to hold hands or put his arm around her or something dreadful like that, but he kept his hands to himself. He carried the conversation, explaining all the things the city had to offer in the summer.

But Emily thought this was her chance to be proactive. Her mom had gotten herself in trouble by not speaking clearly about what she was thinking. With Spencer being so... What was he? *Assertive*—that's what he was. Since he was so assertive, she needed to be up-front about her intentions.

"You know, Spencer. I don't want you to get the wrong idea. I really don't want to date anyone right now. I want to concentrate on my career."

"I totally agree. I don't want to date anyone either. I don't know why people think you have to date. Why can't people just do things together as friends? Most girls think if you have dinner together, you've become a couple. It's such a relief to meet someone who thinks like me. I really don't have time to date right now."

"Really? You don't want to date? You don't want to date *anyone*?"

"Not now."

"But I thought you were sort of a player. I mean, Mom said there are girls hanging around you all the time."

"I don't know why she said that. I mean, I have a lot of friends, and some of them are girls. But I'm not dating anyone." Red crept up his face as he spoke.

"It's hard to believe you aren't dating anyone. Do these 'friends who are girls' know you aren't dating them?"

"Why would it be any harder to believe I'm not dating anyone than it is to believe you're not dating anyone?"

"I'm sorry... Fine. So you're in a non-dating phase. If you say so, I believe you."

"Here, let's get a gelato. I love this place." He led her across the street.

Emily reached into her pocket for money, but Spencer objected. "I'll get it. It was my idea."

"No! You can't buy me anything."

"Why not? Not even an ice cream?"

"No. If you pay for something, it's a date."

"Says who?"

"It's our rules—me and my sister and my mom—the Best Dating Rules. It's an official date if the guy pays for something for you or if he..." Her voice trailed off and she felt her face flushing.

"If he what?"

"Nothing. But you can't buy me anything. Okay?"

"Whatever you say. So... Let's go hike the AT this weekend. There's a group going; it's an intermediate hike, about thirteen miles."

"Uhmm—"

He grinned as he opened the door to the gelato shop. "Okay. So we're officially not dating. Awesome."

"Yeah, great." What had just happened? It seemed they were in an official relationship, albeit non-dating.

*****

Spencer strolled down the corridor toward the break room to grab a cup of water. As he passed Emily's desk, he watched from the corner of his eye, but she never even glanced his direction. His shoulders slumped. He'd employed every possible excuse to walk past her cubicle, but she remained intent on her work. He was so full of water and coffee he was about to bust.

Leave it to him to fall for a workaholic. But really, it was better this way. She thought he was a player—what a joke. She'd be shocked to know he'd never even kissed a girl, though not for lack of opportunity. But he had this weird thing about wanting his first kiss to be special, and no one had seemed special enough.

He had a lot of female friends, but he'd always made sure he was never alone with them. He wasn't sure how he'd gotten his reputation as a playboy of sorts, but all the girls seemed to believe it. They made suggestive comments and dressed in low cut shirts and flirted audaciously. For his part, he appreciated the scenery, but he'd had no trouble turning down what was offered. Until he met Emily.

She was different from all the other girls. She was beautiful, no doubt. She was taller than most girls, and she had long sleek muscles. She didn't look as if she starved herself to be thin. Her hair was dark brown and shiny, always in a long neat braid. And her eyes—they were the most beautiful he'd ever seen, blue with little gold flecks in them. Her skin was amazing, and the most incredible thing was he didn't think she wore a speck of makeup. She was naturally beautiful without any adornment.

But it wasn't her looks that captured his attention. It was... It was... What was it? Her brains? Her wit? Her accomplishments? No, it was her smile. The first time he'd spoken to her and she'd rewarded him with that genuine smile, he'd melted inside. He knew he'd do anything to make it happen again. He could happily spend the rest of his life simply making her smile. Not that he was in love or anything. He merely liked her. Well... He liked her a lot.

It's a good thing she doesn't want to date. If she ever kissed me she'd be disappointed. She thinks I'm an experienced lover. Ha! What a joke. It would probably be the worst kiss of her life. But what can I do about it now. I read one time you could practice on a coke bottle— maybe I can try that. But I guess it doesn't matter anyway, since I can't even get her to notice me when I walk by.

He finally gave up on his waiting game, stopping to peek over her cubicle wall.

"Hi, Emily."

She glanced up, rather dazed.

"Hi, Spencer. I was just, uhmm... I'm having trouble with my computer."

"Want me to take a look?"

"Sure, I guess. It's probably me. I'm sure I'm doing something wrong."

Spencer leaned over her to examine her work. He reached out to access the keyboard and brushed against her shoulder. She jumped as if he'd burned her, and his heart fell. She didn't even want him to touch her. He'd thought she at least liked him a little. No wonder she'd ignored him. He might as well give up on ever dating Emily Best.

"Look, you're just in the wrong entry mode." He tapped on her keyboard. "That should fix it. All you have to do is choose this option."

"Thanks. I didn't want to ask anyone because I'm supposed to know what I'm doing. But, I've been wasting the whole morning trying to make this work."

She smiled.

His heart lurched. There it was—that smile. And it was only for him.

"Uhmm... No problem. Any time. I've worked with this program before."

"So, uhmm... Do you want to go to lunch at Papa's? I'm going with Mom and Steven."

He tried to hide his surprise. Why was she asking him to go with her? He thought she wanted to avoid him.

She looked down as color rose to her cheeks. "Uhmm, you don't have to go. I mean... If you have other plans..."

"No, I don't have plans—I'd love to go."

"Okay." She lifted her huge blue sparkling eyes, peering through her lashes. "And, thank you."

She smiled again, and his heart turned a flip inside his chest. He was in big trouble.

Chapter Two

ANNE COULDN'T STOP SMILING. Having lunch with her daughter brought such joy, and this would likely be the first of many. She'd missed Emily so much since she left Texas to move to New York. They were sitting at their usual lunch spot—a table in the private room at Papa's Place. Papa George and May gladly accommodated Steven Gherring so he could dine away from the public eye. She and Steven had dined at this table numerous times since they'd gotten married. But today Emily was with them, and Anne was excited. She gave her husband an appreciative glance. He'd been instrumental in convincing Emily to make the move to New York. Now, if she could only get Charlie to move here as well, everything would be perfect.

Emily had brought Spencer along to lunch. Anne attempted to tamp down her curiosity. Did their relationship involved more than friendship? She thought she'd seen him glancing at her daughter with rather adoring eyes, but she couldn't be certain. They spoke as if they were simply buddies. She really wanted to question Emily, but she'd been warned not to interfere in her love life. Since she'd been matching up couples for a number of years, Anne found it quite difficult to resist the temptation to intervene a little.

"You're not eating your lunch, Mom," Emily observed. "I thought pot roast was your favorite."

"I know, but I'm not hungry."

"And I think it's becoming a trend," said Steven. "Are you losing weight?"

Steven was getting worried—she had to distract him.

"I don't know. I haven't gotten on a scale. I get like this when I get stressed." She pinned him with a playfully stern look. "Like when I thought you were sleeping with Ellen."

"Will you never let me forget that little incident?" His lips curled in a guilty smile before he turned, clarifying to Emily and Spencer. "I was only trying to make her jealous. And nothing happened at all."

"You called me up to your apartment with some made-up excuse, and you had Ellen lounging on your couch with a glass of wine. And you had your shirt unbuttoned. And you had soft music playing…"

"But I was only pretending to do what you said you wanted me to do," he protested in a playful tone. He defended himself again. "She was trying to get rid of me by pawning me off on another woman."

Spencer's eyes were the size of saucers, but Emily was chuckling.

"I admit it," Anne grinned. "I asked for it. But don't you remember I could hardly eat for four days."

"But this has been longer, hasn't it? And what are you stressed about?" he asked.

"I don't know. Maybe it's because you look so good today. I'm probably worried some girl is going to steal you from me." She winked, hoping her flirtatious remark would throw him off his pursuit.

"You do look a little thin, Mom," Emily countered. "You should try to eat. Maybe the meat is too much. Try your salad."

"Fine. I'll eat something."

Anne forked a piece of lettuce and transferred it to her mouth. She ignored the wave of nausea and forced herself to swallow. If it had only been nausea, she could have handled it. But the nagging pain seemed to be there even when she wasn't eating.

"Maybe you should see a doctor."

Her ploy had failed—Steven was still watching her pick at her food.

"I'm not going to the doctor every time my appetite changes a smidgeon. I promise you I'm fine. But I don't want everyone to watch me while I eat. Can we change the subject please?"

Spencer obliged. "Well, I'm going with a group to hike the Appalachian Trail this weekend. I invited Emily, but you guys are welcome to come along."

Anne watched her daughter's reaction. Her eyes were a little wide. Had she really agreed to go on the hike? She didn't usually go for outdoor activities, except for skiing.

"Thanks Spencer," said Steven. "We'll get back to you on that." He looked back to Anne and indicated her food with his eyes.

Her mind wandered while Spencer explained about the upcoming hike and the group that was going. She took another bite of food and suppressed a shudder as she swallowed. Maybe Steven was right. She'd tried to ignore the symptoms that had plagued her off and on over the past month or so.

After she married Steven Gherring, she'd felt more relaxed and stress-free than she had for years. Her appetite had been great. But recently she'd had stomach pain and nausea. She hadn't been on a scale, but her pants were hanging loosely on her hips. She'd estimate she'd lost at least ten pounds, probably more. But she'd tried not to think about it, because she had a nagging fear. Would she meet the same fate as her mom?

Her mother had lost a battle to stomach cancer when Anne was only three years old, and her father had never married again. She tried to tell herself her symptoms were different, but they matched the information she'd found on the website. She knew she shouldn't wait. It was important to diagnose cancer as early as possible. But she couldn't bear the thought of Steven suffering through what her father had. It wasn't fair. Steven had been alone for fifty years. She couldn't leave him alone again. On the other hand, it might only be an ulcer. She berated herself for assuming the worst.

She gazed at her husband as he chatted with the kids. He was so handsome. His dark hair was peppered with grey, his blue eyes intense. His face was chiseled with a strong jaw, but softened with deep dimples that appeared even when he wasn't smiling. She loved him so much. She couldn't tell him until she knew for sure, because she didn't want him to be worried if it wasn't true. But she wouldn't put it off any longer—she'd see a doctor right away. If it was cancer, she'd fight for her life. And she'd beat it somehow. She wouldn't leave him alone again.

Determined to call the doctor and make an appointment as soon as lunch was over, she pushed the food around on her plate to make it appear emptier.

"Anne?" All the levity disappeared from Steven's voice. "What aren't you telling me?"

She blanched at his words and the severity of his tone.

"Nothing. Nothing, I just... uhmm... I was trying to remember something." She rose from the table, scrambling for an excuse. "I remember what it was. I forgot to mail our RSVP for the wedding. You know Sam and Tanner's wedding? I've got to get it in the mail before it's too late."

"Anne!" Steven rose from his chair and pinned her with his glare. "Stop avoiding my question. What is it?"

"Nothing. I don't know what you're talking about. I was just..."

She watched in confusion as the sides of the room turned black and closed in on Steven's face. Then she saw the floor coming toward her. Then she saw nothing.

As she struggled to open her eyes, she gradually focused on Steven's worried face.

"You're in an ambulance. Stop trying to push the mask off your face. It's oxygen."

An ambulance. She was going to the hospital. She had to tell him—he couldn't find out from the doctors. He'd be so angry. She struggled to speak, her words muffled by the mask.

"She's trying to say something," Steven told the paramedic. "Can she move the mask?"

"Sure, we can take it off for a minute."

How could she break the news to him? Her eyes filled with tears, and she sobbed out the words.

"I th-think it m-may be cancer."

"No, sweetheart, no." He soothed her, pushing a stray strand of hair off her face. "It's not cancer. It's probably not a big deal. Maybe it's appendicitis."

"No. M-my mother died from it—stomach cancer. And now I have the symptoms. I didn't want to tell you..."

"No! That's not it. You have something else wrong with you. It's not serious." His brows creased, and his jaw flexed.

"But, my mom..."

"No! It isn't cancer!" He blinked rapidly and rubbed at his eyes. "It isn't—it can't be. Not now, when I've only just found you. It can't be that..." He kissed her all over her face, saying, "No, no, no, no..."

Anne sobbed even harder and grasped his neck in desperation. "I'm sorry. I'm so sorry. I didn't want to do this to you."

"Stop. You didn't do anything, and we don't know anything. We'll just do tests and see what the doctor says. It's going to be okay. Everything's going to be okay."

Anne knew the words he repeated to comfort her were his futile attempt to convince himself.

*****

Anne and Steven sat beside each other in tense silence. Their hands were clasped between the two upholstered armchairs in the doctor's office in front of the empty desk.

"But what exactly did she say on the phone? Did she sound upset?" Anne asked for probably the tenth time.

"She said she wanted to talk to us together in person. That's all. And she didn't sound upset... And you're squeezing all the blood out of my fingers."

"Sorry." She forced a weak smile, attempting to pull her hand away.

"I'm only kidding. I don't want you to worry so much. Everything's going to be fine. No matter what, everything's going to be okay. Whatever it is, we'll face it together. And you're assuming it's something really bad."

"But if it wasn't serious, wouldn't she tell us on the phone?"

"Not necessarily—"

A creak behind them announced the doctor's entrance through the office door.

"I'm so sorry to keep you waiting. Thanks for coming in." She shook their hands and sat behind her desk, opening her laptop. "Let me bring up your reports here... So." She smiled at the nervous couple. "I know you're worried about the possibility of cancer. And we haven't totally eliminated that, but it's highly unlikely."

"Why haven't we eliminated it?" Steven asked. "Can't we do an x-ray or CT scan or something?"

"Well, we don't like to use radiation during early pregnancy." She smiled again.

"Pregnancy? I couldn't possibly be pregnant. How could that happen?"

The doctor raised her eyebrows. "I think you know how it happens. Isn't it possible?"

"Well it's... It's... I guess it's possible. But I'm too old—I thought I was starting menopause." She felt blood rushing to her face. "And I've lost weight, not gained weight—"

Steven came out of his stupor. "She's pregnant? We're pregnant? Are you sure?"

"Oh, it's very certain you're pregnant. We did a blood test. Now, at your age, this is a high-risk pregnancy. If you carry to term, you'd deliver at age forty-six."

"What does that mean? Is it dangerous for her to be pregnant?" Steven was gripping her fingers so tightly her knuckles were white.

"No, but there's a high chance of miscarriage or, barring that, chromosomal abnormality." She leaned forward to emphasize her words. "You might choose to terminate the pregnancy."

"No!" Steven almost shouted the word. She saw him flinch and turn toward her with a weak smile. "I mean, I'm sorry... I should have asked what you thought—"

"No, I agree." She squeezed his hand. "That is, if it's really true. If I really am pregnant, I wouldn't want to terminate."

"Oh, it's really true. Now, we'll need to help you manage this nausea so you can start eating..."

*****

Anne stared with unseeing eyes out the limousine window as the New York City streets passed by, silence hanging heavy in the air. She glanced at Steven.

"What're you thinking?"

"I think I'm in shock." One corner of his mouth kicked upward, and he took her hand, raising it to his lips. "I wasn't planning this, but now I want it to happen. A *baby*."

"If I'd known you really wanted a baby, I'd never have married you. You should have a younger wife like I said all along."

"You're not going to start trying to find a different wife for me again, are you? I don't think I could handle another of your crusades." He chuckled, leaning over to kiss her cheek. "And anyway, I didn't even want to have a baby until I thought I could have one with you."

"Okay, I promise I won't try to find you a new wife. Believe me, I've finally admitted to myself I never want you to be with anyone else. But can we keep it a secret for now? The doctor says I'll most likely miscarry in the first trimester. I don't want to tell everybody and then... You know..."

"No, we don't have to tell anyone unless you want to. But you don't even want to tell the girls? You'll have to tell them something—Emily's really worried."

"No, I think I'd be embarrassed. And, I think they might be embarrassed, too."

"They love you. They won't be embarrassed."

"I don't know."

"And you know you won't be able to keep it a secret for long. Especially since the doc gave you medicine for the nausea." He patted her thin tummy. "I can't wait until you start getting all fat."

"I'll tell you right now if you ever call me fat, you'll be sorry."

"Okay. I promised to call you skinny the whole time, even if you look like a whale." His adoring smile brought on another surge of tears. "What's wrong now?"

"I don't know..."

He scooped her into his lap. "This is just hormones making you weepy."

"But... What happens if our baby has something wrong with him?"

"Him?" He smiled. "Do you think we're having a boy? Maybe I might like a little girl." He hugged her close, kissing her hair. "And we'll love our baby no matter what. Right? And we can't change anything by worrying about it."

"But what if I have a miscarriage? The doctor said it would probably happen." A single tear rolled down her cheek, and he wiped it off with his thumb as he caressed her jaw.

He chuckled a little. "You know, two hours ago, we didn't even know we wanted a baby. And now you're crying because we might not have one."

"I know, it's silly—"

"No, it's not silly." He pressed his lips to her forehead. "If we lose this baby, maybe we can figure out another way to have one. We could even adopt."

"Okay... A baby..." She gave him a weepy smile. "But it's a secret. We won't tell anybody, right?"

"We'll do whatever you want. But won't you start showing soon? The doctor said the ultrasound showed you're already at least seven weeks—she could see a heartbeat. And she said you could be as much as ten weeks according to when the nausea started."

"I don't know. I didn't show very early with the girls. I can probably hide it until I'm about sixteen weeks."

Steven's face fell. "Oh really? That long?"

"You want to tell people?"

"Of course I do—I'm excited."

"I'll make a deal with you. If you'll wait until I'm starting to show, I'll let you be the one to tell everyone."

"Hmmm. And perhaps we could add something else to the deal?"

"What's that?"

"I think we should keep you in bed as much as possible."

"No. The doctor specifically said bed rest wasn't necessary, and it wouldn't prevent a miscarriage anyway."

"Who said anything about resting?" He began to nuzzle her neck.

"Steven," she squeaked, and they both dissolved into laughter.

"What are we going to tell everyone for now?" asked Anne.

"I don't know. You're the one who looked up the differential diagnosis when you thought it was stomach cancer." Then his face was suddenly stern. "And by the way, we're not through with the discussion about why you kept that from me for so long."

"I know it was wrong. We'll talk about it later. Okay?"

"No fair flashing those big brown puppy dog eyes at me. We'll drop it for now. But we *will* discuss it, because it will *never* happen again."

"But as for what to tell the others... hmmm... Let's go with stomach ulcer. It explains the loss of appetite and weight loss. So here's the plan. You tell everyone it was only an ulcer and I'm embarrassed about it. Then no one will ask me about it, and I won't have to lie."

"But I'll have to lie."

"But you're so much better at it than I am. Please?"

"Fine, I'll do it. But you know this could backfire on you."

"No it won't. I feel better—everything's settled for now."

"But one more thing." His bright blue eyes twinkled. "Let's go home and celebrate before we go to work."

"I don't know. What if the boss finds out?"

"I'm willing to bet he'd approve."

*****

Emily regarded her mom with suspicion. Something didn't quite add up. She'd come by her cubicle to assure her everything was fine, but she'd brought Steven along to be her mouthpiece.

"So, you have an ulcer? And you passed out because of an ulcer?"

"She passed out because she was dehydrated," Steven clarified. "But she'll be fine since they've given her medicine."

"And have you called Charlie to explain? She's worried out of her mind."

"I thought you could call her," Anne suggested in a pleading voice.

"Why wouldn't you call her yourself?"

"Oh... I could... but I thought you'd be better at making her not worry. You've always been able to calm your sister down."

"And where is this ulcer?"

"What do you mean?"

"You can have ulcers in different areas. I know that because my boss in Fort Worth had an ulcer and explained it to me. At the time I thought it was too much information, but now I'm glad I know. So where is your ulcer?"

"Uhmm, in my stomach?"

"So it's a peptic ulcer?"

"Uhmm." Anne glanced at Steven. "That's right. Isn't it honey?"

His lips pulled back in a grimace. "Sure, that's what the doctor said."

"And what tests did they do to confirm it?"

"Oh, I was so out of it, I don't remember." Her mom studied the water bottle in her hands. "What tests did they do, sweetheart?"

"Of course, I don't know what tests were performed, since I wasn't allowed to be with you." Did Steven sound annoyed?

"Y'all didn't get much information from the doctor this morning," Emily observed. "What—"

Spencer's arrival interrupted her question.

"Mrs. Gherring, I'm glad you're okay. You really scared us yesterday. What happened?"

Anne pressed her lips together, glancing at Steven.

"She has a peptic ulcer. They gave her medicine, and she'll be perfectly fine." The tone of his voice closed the subject from further discussion.

Spencer nodded. "My dad had one of those. He takes medicine, and he's great. I think it's only dangerous if it's a bleeding ulcer."

"Is yours a bleeding ulcer, Mom?"

"No. It's just a plain one. No blood. It's nothing to worry about."

"Hey! Since you're okay, do you guys want to go with us on the hike this weekend?" Spencer's eyes were bright and eager.

"Sure." Her mom smiled.

"No, I don't think it's a good idea." Steven pinned Anne with narrowed eyes. "It might hurt your *ulcer*."

"My *ulcer* will be fine. It's only a hike."

"But what if you fall? It might be dangerous. It might... It might turn into a bleeding ulcer."

"I won't go if you don't want me to. But it would be fun." She added in a quiet voice. "We should have fun together while we can."

"Can we have a word in private?" He grabbed her hand, dragging her down the hall.

"Do you have hiking boots?" Spencer broke Emily out of her reverie.

"Me? Hiking boots? Why would I want hiking boots?"

"Oh... I thought you were going on the hike this weekend."

"Well, you assumed I wanted to go. I never actually said I was going. It's not really my thing."

His face fell.

"I'm sorry... I understand. It's only a bunch of people going as friends. But I didn't mean to push you into something you didn't want to do. I thought... You know... It could be fun."

He patted her shoulder and she jumped at the tingle that shot through her. He jerked his hand away, blushing furiously. Her heart was racing. What was it about him that affected her like that? Granted, she wasn't a real touchy person, but she didn't usually feel electricity from casual contact. He made her feel out of control, and she didn't like it. Or did she? She considered the warmth that had spread through her. It wasn't entirely unpleasant.

Steven returned without Anne.

"Hey, Spencer. We're going on the hike after all. Okay? Call us with the details."

"Okay, Mr. Gherring. That sounds good."

Steven hurried to catch up with her mom. Perhaps she should go on the hike, simply to keep an eye on her mother. Not because she wanted to spend more time with Spencer, of course. She'd simply have to sacrifice for the good of her mother.

"I'm going. What do I have to do?"

"Well," Spencer's eyes revealed his bewilderment. "I probably need to take you shoe-shopping."

"Ughh! I hate shopping!"

"A girl who hates shopping? One thing's for sure... You're not predictable."

Emily called Charlie after work. "They said Mom has an ulcer, but they were acting pretty weird. Mom was letting Steven do all the talking. And they didn't seem to know much about her condition. Wouldn't you think they'd ask a lot of questions about a condition that put Mom in the emergency room?"

"Yeah, I agree. Mom might not ask detailed questions, but Steven would for sure. Do you think it's more serious than they're letting on?"

"I really do. Maybe it's a really bad ulcer, a bleeding ulcer, and Steven's lying to cover it up."

"Or maybe it's something else. Did she look bad?"

"No, she looked okay today. But she looked awful yesterday. And she's really thin—I bet she's lost ten pounds." She chewed her lip. "And Steven's obviously still worried about her. He can be overprotective at times, but I'm not sure if that's it. And Mom said something to him about doing things together *while they can*."

"Well surely it's not something really bad," Charlie reasoned. "If she was going to die, I think she'd tell us. Wouldn't she?"

"I think so, but maybe she might wait for the right time. Like, she might not tell us until after your birthday."

"You're right. That does sound like Mom. So, I know you've probably already researched this. What do you think she might have?"

"I looked up all the possible causes of weight loss. There are all kinds of things, including ulcers. The things that seemed most likely were Crohn's Disease, Ulcerative Colitis..." Emily hesitated before she said the scary word. "And cancer."

"Cancer? She wouldn't keep that from us."

"I don't think so either, but as long as they're lying to us, we can't be sure. And surely they wouldn't be going hiking this weekend if she had cancer."

"They're going hiking? Man, I wish I could be there."

"Actually, *we're* going hiking."

"You're going hiking? Ohmygosh—hell is freezing over. Why on earth are you going hiking?"

"I'm going to keep an eye on Mom."

"Really? And who else is going on said hike?"

Emily felt herself turning red. Thank goodness her sister couldn't see her—she'd tease her without mercy. "Look. Spencer's going. Okay? But that's not why I'm going."

"Hmmm... If you say so."

"Charlie, I'm telling the truth. I'd pretty much told him I wasn't going when I found out Mom and Steven were going."

"Okay. Okay. Don't get so defensive, Sister."

"And now I have to go buy hiking boots because I don't own any. You know how I hate shopping. And Spencer's taking me. In fact he'll be here in ten minutes to pick me up."

"Oh? So Spencer's going to help you try on shoes?" Amusement crept into Charlie's voice. "And have you shaved your legs for the shopping trip?"

"Oh no—I forgot. And I have ape legs. Gotta go. Bye, Sis."

"So what type of shoes am I getting?" Emily asked Spencer as she puzzled over the myriad of choices on the wall. "Boots? Do they need to come up over my ankle?"

Spencer frowned as he considered her question, his eyes wandering down her freshly shaved legs.

"I think boots would be overkill for this hike. You don't really need the protection. And having boots come over your ankle doesn't necessarily provide ankle support. Boots are more for guarding against abrasion. Also, I think you're more likely to get blisters from boots if they rub your ankles."

Emily blushed as he continued to stare at her legs. She glanced down. What was he staring at? Had she missed something when she shaved?

"I think we should get you in a good trail shoe with a stiff sole and heavy tread. You probably won't be doing water crossings..." He turned to the shoes and started picking a few possibilities. Emily released the breath she'd been holding. At least he'd finally quit staring at her legs. She studied the pile of shoes in his arms.

"I like those with the turquoise. The ones with the brown and orange are ugly, and they won't match anything I have."

Spencer raised an eyebrow. "Really? You're going to pick a shoe based on the color? You need to pick one that feels comfortable and supportive."

"That's fine. I'll pick a comfortable and supportive shoe, but I want them to be cute, too."

As the salesman took the samples and disappeared into the stockroom, Spencer turned back to Emily.

"You probably need good hiking socks, too." She opened her mouth, but his quelling look stalled her protest. "Don't argue about this. I don't want you to get blisters. Don't you wear special ski socks when you go skiing?"

"Yes," she admitted, feeling a distinct loss of control. She should have researched hiking shoes and hiking before she went shopping. Could you learn to hike by studying it? She wasn't sure, but she would try. That was how she handled every aspect of her life. She studied situations in advance, preparing for every contingency. She didn't like surprises. Depending on others led to certain disappointment. The only person Emily Best trusted with utmost confidence was Emily Best.

The salesman returned with an armload of shoeboxes, and she sat down to try them on. He opened the first box, offering her the distasteful orange and brown striped shoe. Reluctantly, she slid her foot into the shoe.

"I don't know... It rubs on my heel," she lied.

"Hmmm."

Spencer knelt down next to her, probing his fingers around the heel of her foot. Overcome by a sudden light-headedness, she closed her eyes and gripped the chair. He was touching her foot. His arm was pressing against her leg. Tingles were shooting up from where his skin contacted hers. She closed her eyes and tried to slow her pounding heart. Still he continued to examine the fit of the shoe, oblivious to her reaction. At least she hoped he was oblivious. Unable to bear the sensations any longer, she used the toes of her other foot to wrench the offending shoe off, flinging it up in the air in the process. The tumbling brown and orange streak narrowly missed the salesman's head as he ducked.

Spencer jumped back along with the shoe salesman, both staring with wide eyes.

"Are you okay?"

Emily felt the blood pounding in her face. "I... I don't like that shoe."

They stood frozen for an eternity before Spencer spoke to the salesman from the corner of his mouth. "She uhmm... She doesn't like that one. I think we should try another style."

"Is there a pair here you *do* like?"

"The turquoise ones."

His hands were shaking as he searched through the boxes, murmuring quietly to Spencer, "Which ones are turquoise?"

"She's talking about these shoes with the blue on them."

He handed the selected box to Spencer. "I'll... I'll let you guys try these on. I need to... uhmm... I need to check something in the stockroom." He dumped the other boxes on the floor beside Spencer and fled.

Emily jerked the chosen box from his hands. "I can do it. I don't need any help."

"Okay." He held his up his hands and backed away.

She slipped her foot into the cute shoe, but immediately noted a seam rubbing on the side. Pulling the shoe off in disgust, she stuffed it back in the box. "Let me see the others. Maybe there's one that isn't too ugly."

Spencer handed her the boxes, one at a time. She peered inside two boxes and immediately rejected them. The third box held a black pair with small flashes of lime green.

"These are pretty cute." She slipped her foot in and rejoiced inwardly. Nothing was rubbing—it felt comfortable. "Great. I'll take these."

"Wait. Let me see where your toe is and how they fit around your heel." He knelt down and reached toward her foot.

"No need." Emily stood, clomping awkwardly in one shoe, avoiding his scalding touch at all costs. "This one fits great. It doesn't rub anywhere, and it's not too loose."

"You should at least put the other one on and walk around for a while."

"Fine!" she growled, flopping back into the chair. She picked up the shoebox and fumbled with the other shoe, struggling to free it from its plastic shape-holder. After a few seconds and a few frustrated grunts, Spencer reached out to help her. When she saw his hand approaching, she dropped the shoe on the floor like a hot potato.

His eyebrows lifted as he retrieved the shoe. Removing the shoe's plastic form, he held it toward her, keeping a careful distance. Her lack of self-control not only embarrassed, but also irritated her. She had to get over her fear of touching Spencer. She simply needed to ignore the sparky thing that always occurred.

She laced up the ties, obediently walking in both shoes for several minutes until Spencer seemed satisfied. He insisted she try the shoes on with hiking socks, and she complied despite her impatience.

"It's just a sock. It won't make a difference."

"Don't you try on your ski boots with your ski socks?"

"Maybe... But this is taking such a long time. And I'm hungry."

He shook his head, but his face had a broad grin. "I'm gonna take a lot of snacks on the hike Saturday. You're pretty grouchy when you're hungry."

Emily couldn't suppress a begrudging chuckle. When she checked out, she winced a bit at the cost.

"These are good shoes," he soothed. "You'll be able to wear them for a long time. I'm sure you'll get your money's worth out of them."

"You're assuming I'll go on more than one hike."

"Okay, we'd better get some dinner into you right away." He winked, as his dimples peeked out.

"It's too late for dinner; I think I need some chocolate in an IV."

"Finally, you're smiling. I was about to give up."

"Sorry to be so difficult."

"It was worth the wait."

She pondered his words as they walked. He'd certainly been patient with her. Her mom and sister always complained when they took her shopping, saying she spoiled the experience. And they hadn't even had to put up with her spasmodic episodes in response to random skin contact. He was pretty nice—for a guy. And he was nice to look at, too. Of course, she only liked him as a friend.

She caught his eyes and flashed him a sincere smile. He snapped his face away, but she still noticed his ears reddened. Was he blushing?

Spencer felt his face heat up, and quickly turned his head to the side. She'd given him one of those full-on devastating smiles. He'd really had to work hard for this one. She must really, really hate shopping. She'd been acting awfully strange—jumping, dropping things, tossing shoes into the air. And she was really stubborn, even more stubborn than his four sisters. And that was saying a lot. He hated to be so demanding, but he knew he'd feel responsible if she got blisters on the hike. After all, he'd talked her into it when she obviously didn't want to go.

He wasn't quite sure how he'd accomplished it. He guessed he'd convinced her by emphasizing they'd be going as friends. That seemed to be her main concern. Just his luck... Girls had thrown themselves at him for years while he'd insisted on remaining friends.

But since he'd met a girl special enough for his first kiss, she had instituted the *friends policy*. God must have a sense of humor.

He felt really protective of her, the way he felt about his sisters. No. Nothing like the way he felt about his sisters. He never thought about kissing his sisters, and he thought about kissing Emily all the time.

He turned his face toward her again. "You want to try the best pizza in New York City?"

"Oh, yeah—that sounds great."

Her smile was radiant. He needed to remember that. Pizza made her smile. Shopping did not.

"It's in the next block."

She nodded her head, picking up the pace almost imperceptibly. She must be really hungry. He observed her without turning his head. She was chewing on her bottom lip the way she always did when she was thinking about something. Her lips were so full and soft-looking. He could imagine how they would feel against his own. She continued to worry her lip, as she turned to look at him. He darted his eyes to the sidewalk.

"I'm buying my own pizza."

"But it was my idea. It won't make it a date just because I buy you a slice of pizza."

"Yes it will. It's our house rules."

"Then don't tell your mom and your sister. If they don't know, it won't be a date."

"But I'll know, and Charlie will know. She always knows. I can lie to Mom, but Charlie always knows."

"Fine. You can buy your own pizza. But just so you know, that's not how I was raised."

"What do you mean?"

Spencer hesitated. "You'll probably think this sounds chauvinistic, but my dad taught me to respect women. You know, to treat them with deference. To open doors and speak politely, to protect them, and... He taught me to pay for their dinner."

"He didn't really tell you to pay for every woman's dinner, did he?"

"Well, not exactly. But he did teach me if I asked someone to go eat with me, I'm offering to pay for the meal. That would be true even if you were a guy. It's especially true since you're a woman."

"Because I'm the weaker sex?"

"Because you're the fairer sex. Nothing weak about you."

She chuckled. "Okay, I don't think you're a chauvinist. But, I can afford to buy my own pizza, and there's no reason for you to pay." Her face took on a determined look to which he was growing accustomed.

"You know, that pride of yours is going to get you in trouble someday."

Chapter Three

SPENCER PACED AND FUMED, his face creased with worry. He really wanted this hike to go well, especially since Emily had been so hesitant. But the rest of the hiking club had decided to tackle a more strenuous hike that would take over seven hours. Emily might flat-out refuse to go, or she might insist on going because of her pride. Either way, it wouldn't be a good first hike experience. Plus, the Gherrings were going. Steven Gherring was in amazing shape, since he was constantly training for Iron Man competitions. Emily's mother seemed fairly fit as well, but she'd recently visited the emergency room for her ulcer. A seven-hour hike seemed like a bad idea for someone who'd been in the hospital earlier in the week.

He planned to suggest an alternate hike, but that meant it would only be the four of them. Emily seemed diametrically opposed to anything resembling a date. Would she think he was trying to trick her into going on a hike without a big group of friends? He'd considered asking one of his sisters to come along to make Emily feel more comfortable, but he didn't want his sisters to meet Emily. They would pick up on his feelings for her and tease him mercilessly, and with good reason. He'd done the same to them numerous times.

He walked into the lobby of the apartment building to find Steven Gherring waiting alone. "The girls aren't coming?"

"Oh, they're coming. Anne's in Emily's apartment, trying to talk her into leaving some of her supplies at home."

"Supplies?"

"Yes, her backpack weighed about fifty pounds. She researched all the things that can happen on a hike, and she stocked enough supplies to last all four of us if we were stranded for a week."

"Why would she do that? I told her I'd have all the supplies we needed in my backpack. She only needed to bring water."

"So you are now learning the Best women are stubborn and like to think of themselves as self-sufficient." Gherring grinned. "Especially Emily. I don't think I've seen her accept a single thing from me without a fight. Not since she moved to New York on a mission to prove herself."

"I'm glad to hear it—I thought it was only me. Hey, I need you to help me figure out a little problem with the hike."

"What's that?"

"Well, the club decided to change to a seven-hour strenuous hike. So I think the four of us should go on a shorter hike. Do you think Emily would be okay with that?"

"Why wouldn't she?"

"She doesn't want to do anything that looks like a date. I'm afraid she'll think I'm trying to trick her or something since I told her there was a big group of friends going."

"Well, I'm no expert on relationships—it took me fifty years to finally get married—but I think Emily likes to be in control. Why don't we let her make the decision? Just leave it to me." He spotted Anne and Emily emerging from the elevator.

Emily's brows sunk low over her eyes. "I still think I should've brought the canned ham."

The face Anne turned to her husband showed desperation. "Steven, would you please give your expert opinion on supplies here."

"Well, first we've got to make an important decision about the hike. The hiking club has changed their destination. They're headed for a strenuous seven-hour hike. So we could join them as planned, or pick another hike that's shorter and more moderate."

Emily brightened. "I've been researching all the hikes on the AT near here. I found one that sounded really good—Silvermine Lake Loop. It's only rated moderate and it's a four-mile circuit." She pulled out her phone and quickly retrieved the route information.

"This looks good, Emily," said Spencer. "I've always wanted to do this one."

"This will be much better for Mom. She doesn't need to go on a seven-hour hike."

Anne rolled her eyes at Gherring, but he nodded. "I agree. I don't want her to do anything so strenuous. So we're all in agreement? And as for supplies, we won't need so many since we're doing this hike. We'll never be more than an hour from the car, and there will be plenty of people on this trail if we have an unforeseen problem."

"Let's go." Emily led the way out the door.

Spencer hung back. "Thanks, Mr. Gherring. You're really good with women."

"Sometimes I get lucky. I've screwed up plenty of times."

"That's the truth," agreed Anne.

Emily paced outside the apartment building as she waited for the others to emerge. She realized she hadn't thought this whole thing through. She'd suggested they go on this alternative hike, but that meant they wouldn't be going over in a group. With only the four of them, would it be like a double date? And she was still worried about her mom's health. Steven had readily agreed her mother shouldn't strain herself. Yet she'd done extensive research on ulcers and found no evidence physical exertion was harmful. Maybe he was simply being overprotective, but she still thought they might be hiding something.

Spencer came out with his phone to his ear. "Hi, Becca. Yeah, I know I said I was coming on the hike. But I'm with some friends who weren't prepared for a seven-hour hike. Yeah. Yeah, we decided to do Silverman Lake Loop instead. Uhmm, I don't know. Who's 'we'? Just you and Candace? Remind me—who's Candace? Oh yeah, I remember. Well, I guess you guys could come with us, but I don't know if there's room in the car for two more."

"Hey Spencer, my car will hold six if we get cozy." Steven pointed to a shiny black SUV, parked and waiting on the street.

"Uhmm, okay. There's enough room. I guess you could come. But I heard you were one of the ones who pushed for the long hike. Oh... Oh... Well, sure. I guess we can pick you up on the way. We're leaving right now. Fine. See you in a few."

"So, it looks like we're taking Becca and Candace along. I hope you really don't mind," he said to Steven and Anne, with a sidelong glance at Emily.

"Of course we don't mind. Why should we mind? We were planning to go with a huge group before." Her mom climbed into the car.

"Well... I think they heard I was bringing Mr. Gherring, and maybe that's why they decided to leave the big group and go with us. They might be weird around you. You know what I mean?"

"I really don't think it'll be a problem. The star status wears off pretty quickly in these situations." Steven leaned inside to fasten Anne's seatbelt, kissing her cheek.

"I'm gonna make sure your shirt stays on around those girls. And you'll have to keep your eyes on the trail." Anne poked his arm with her finger to emphasize her words.

He lifted her hand and pressed his lips to her fingers. "I only have eyes for you."

"Get a room," Emily teased. "So who's going with us now?"

"Becca and Candace are two of the girls from the hiking club."

Two extra people would prevent their outing from becoming a date. So why did this information annoy her?

Emily tried to like the two girls who joined them in the car. She tried for about two minutes before she gave up. She sat in the middle of the back seat next to Spencer. Becca sat beside her, but barely paid her any attention. Instead she leaned forward and across Emily's legs while talking to Spencer. She seemed to feel the need to reach over and touch his leg with every sentence. And she spoke a lot of sentences. Leaning over also provided a startling view of her generous cleavage. For his part, Spencer did a remarkable job of not staring at the displayed goods. Maybe they bored him, since he was such a player—he'd probably seen plenty in the past. Emily glanced down at her own meager endowment. She certainly didn't have anything that could compete, not that she wanted to compete in that way. Since she and Spencer were only friends, there was no reason to worry about whether he was attracted to her assets. Right? And he'd insisted he wasn't interested in dating anyone right now. But evidently Becca hadn't heard that... she was certainly sending an open invitation.

She might have liked Candace better since her shirt wasn't so revealing. But she was so ridiculously perfect she looked like a model headed to a fashion shoot. Her long blond highlighted hair was pulled back in a fancy French braid. Her face was flawless under meticulous make-up. Her skin was tanned and smooth. Emily felt her white skin glowed in comparison, and as usual, she wore no makeup at all. In contrast, Candace looked chic and sophisticated. She was even more annoyed Candace was friendly and outgoing. She chatted easily with her mom and Steven when she wasn't giving her attention to Spencer in the back seat. Both girls managed to completely ignore her existence—at least, that was how it felt to Emily.

Arriving at the trailhead parking lot, Emily's cell vibrated.

"Hey, Charlie." Emily moved away from the group to speak more privately.

"Hey, Sister. Are you hiking yet?"

"We're fixin' to start."

"I'm sooooo jealous you and Mom are having fun without me. I wish I could be hiking with y'all instead of leading this group of thirteen and fourteen-year-olds on this rafting trip."

"Well, I wish I was there with you."

"What's wrong, Sister?"

"We'd decided to go on a shorter hike, just the four of us. And I guess that could've been weird. But now we've been joined by Betty Boobs and Polly Perfect, and they're putting the moves on Spencer, big time."

Charlie's peals of laughter rang through the phone.

"Stop it—no laughing. What am I going to do?"

"Why do you care so much? I thought you and Spencer were just friends."

"We *are* just friends. But now I have to spend two hours hiking with these two bimbos."

"Really? Are they that bad?"

"One has like double-D's absolutely spilling out of her top, and the other girl is charming, tanned and beautiful."

Charlie giggled again. "Em! You're the only person I know who can say 'charming, tanned and beautiful' like a horrible insult."

"Arghhh! You're not helping."

"Come on. What's wrong with you? Since when do you compare yourself to anyone else? Especially not a couple of bimbos. And you know you're beautiful. You must be—people tell us we look alike all the time, and I know I'm beautiful."

"Interesting argument, Sister. But you're right. I don't know why I'm comparing myself to these girls. That's not like me."

"Have you figured out anything else about Mom? How does she seem today?"

"She seems fine. Steven's really attentive and protective, but maybe no more than normal. It could just be my imagination."

"Well, let me know what you find out. Have fun on your first hike."

Spencer called, "Hey, Emily. Ready to go?"

"Coming." She smiled down at her new hiking shoes and her matching lime green top. She didn't really care much about clothes, but she liked her colors to coordinate. It soothed her artistic sensibilities. She was determined to have a good time. She detested pouty people who spoiled the fun, so she wasn't going to be that person.

Steven and Anne took the lead as Spencer motioned Emily to follow, falling into stride beside her on the broad path.

They hadn't gone twenty-five yards when Becca said, "Hey Spencer. I think my Camelback has a pinched hose. Could you check it for me?"

Emily continued on behind her mom, while he dropped back with the other two.

"You need to keep drinking the whole time," Steven told Anne. "You can't risk getting dehydrated."

"I will and I am. I'm practically floating. I'm sure I'll have to pee numerous times on the hike."

Emily's stomach constricted. She hadn't considered what type of restrooms would be on the hike. "Where do we use the bathroom, anyway?"

Her mom smiled. "There was a bathroom at the parking area. Out on the hike, you have to make a little side trip into the trees."

Emily gasped in horror. "Outside? On the ground? With people walking by?"

Steven laughed. "Hopefully you'll get far enough away from the path you'll have some privacy."

"No way—the hike's only two hours long, so I'm holding it."

Anne chuckled. "I expect you will."

Candace appeared beside her. "Hey, Mrs. Gherring. Don't you have some good stories to tell about Mr. Gherring? You know, things we'd never hear about in the magazine articles?"

"Oh I've got lots of stories, but if I start revealing things about Steven Gherring's personal life I might lose my job."

"You work?" Candace asked in surprise.

Steven answered for her. "We work together now. We make a great team, and I like spending time with my wife."

"Wow, that's really romantic. It's just not what I'd expected to hear after all the stuff they say in the tabloids."

"What stuff?" A concerned frown creased Anne's forehead.

"Nothing, sweetheart." He reached out to take her hand. "We don't care what they say in the tabloids."

"Oh, I know it's not all true," said Candace. "Especially the stuff about Mr. Gherring having a love child and all that."

"A love child?" Anne voice became a bit shrill. "They said that in the papers? Can't you sue them or something?"

"If it were a legitimate paper, I might sue them; but it's not worth the trouble with the tabloids." He sent a cold look in Candace's direction. "I could really care less about the opinions of the type of people who read the tabloids, anyway."

Candace's face blanched, and she stepped off the trail, mumbling about trying to find her lip balm before falling in behind Becca. Emily chuckled inwardly. Her stepdad could be truly intimidating if he wanted to be.

Spencer moved into stride beside Emily. "How're the shoes doing? And the socks? I'm a little worried about you getting a blister. It's not a good idea to hike in brand new shoes—it's better to break them in first."

"No problem. I brought moleskin with me in case I get a blister." She was proud of her thoroughly researched preparation.

"So you're not much of a hiker?" Becca's voice sounded behind her. "I've been hiking with Spencer for a long time. How many hikes do you think we've done together, Spencer? I mean the group hikes, not our private ones."

"I've been on a lot of hikes with the club, Becca. I really can't remember which ones you were on."

Emily noted he didn't address the private hikes, but she wasn't about to ask for clarification.

"You haven't forgotten that overnight hike have you?" Becca grabbed Spencer's arm, pulling him back to walk beside her. He slowed with Becca, speaking to her in low tones.

"Comin' through." Emily passed her mom and Steven, taking the lead and distancing herself from Becca and Spencer as the trail narrowed, entering the woods.

"Follow the yellow blazes," directed Steven.

Emily set a slightly faster pace to prevent any possible criticism from the two experienced hiker girls. The trail became a bit steeper, but she managed to maintain her speed. She'd always been extremely disciplined about exercise, so she was undaunted by the cardiovascular challenge. Back home in Fort Worth, she'd managed to squeeze in a ballet class once a week. But the other days she followed a vigorous workout routine that included thirty minutes on an incline treadmill. After pushing her speed for about fifteen minutes, she realized she'd forgotten about her mom. She glanced behind her.

"Hey, Mom. Is this pace okay? And are you drinking plenty of water?" She took a swallow of her own water to encourage her mother, who'd always resisted drinking.

Anne made a face. "Yes, I'm drinking. Yuk! I'm not enjoying it, but I'm drinking."

"How're you feeling, anyway?" Her mom didn't look as perky as when they started.

"Maybe a little queasy, but I'm okay."

Steven announced, "We're stopping for a second."

Anne mumbled her objection, but he forced her to sit on a log, take sip of water and eat a few bites of a granola bar. One look at her mom's chalky face confirmed his wisdom. He whispered something in her ear, and she shook her head forcefully.

By this time the entire group was sitting down. Emily noted with a bit of satisfaction Becca was breathing heavily and Candace's mascara had started running from the sweat on her face. Then she scolded herself for her malicious feelings toward the girls who'd done her no actual harm.

Spencer caught her attention. "Emily, I thought you'd never been hiking. You're sure setting a blistering pace on the climb."

"Sorry. I was in the zone, I guess."

"How're your feet doing?"

"Great." At the obvious relief on his face, she added, "Thanks, Spencer. I'm sure I would've been slipping all over on the steep part without my new shoes."

His face lit up like she'd given him an amazing gift. "I was glad to help."

Becca sat with a sullen expression beside Candace, whose eyes were darting nervously toward Steven. Emily couldn't help feeling sympathy for the two girls and attempted to make them more comfortable.

"I really like your hair, Candace. Did you do it yourself?"

She smiled, fingering her hair to check the condition of the beautiful braid. "No, Becca did it for me."

"Really? Becca, you did that? It's amazing. How'd you learn to do it?"

Becca shrugged. "It's nothing really—I just like doing it."

Spencer inspected Candace's hair. "Wow. It's pretty cool, Becca. You have hidden talents." Becca beamed at his praise.

"Well, Candace has such beautiful hair, but I'd love to learn how to do it. I always do this plain braid." Emily indicated her own hair. In truth, she knew a variety of braiding styles, but usually didn't bother with them. Still, none of her braids had ever approached the intricate design woven into Candace's hair.

"I could show you." Becca's smile seemed genuine enough.

"I'd love that."

"Your shoes are really cute, Emily," said Candace.

"Thanks. They're new, and I thought this might be the only time I used them. But hiking seems pretty fun, as long as I don't have to pee in the woods."

Candace and Becca both giggled and followed up with hilarious tales of hiking disasters. When Steven stood up with Anne to start the group moving again, Emily let them stay in the lead. Nothing she'd observed on the hike had bolstered her confidence in her mom's claims about her health. She resolved to research ulcers a bit more. Was nausea a symptom?

Now the group moved up and down the trail in single file. But Spencer was behind the Gherrings, followed by Candace, then Emily and Becca. Candace and Becca chatted with Emily about inane topics. Emily discovered Candace had done ballet in the past and knew of a barre-based fitness program in the city. They stopped a few times to take pictures in the scenic spots. By the end of the two-hour hike, the three girls were conversing with animation and making plans together. Emily couldn't see Spencer very well, but he didn't look too happy.

Spencer brooded as he hiked. He ought to be glad the girls were getting along. At first, Becca and Candace had been rude to Emily. Then he'd had to fuss at Becca for intimating they'd spent the night together on a hike. Technically they had spent the night together, since the whole group of twenty-eight slept in one giant campground. He'd slept in a hammock, while Becca and two other girls had been inside a tent. Of course, that wasn't what it had sounded like to Emily. Becca had pretended innocence in the comment, but he wasn't convinced.

She'd always been flirty, but he'd laughed it off in the past. Had he led her on somehow? Ordinarily, he wouldn't have cared whether someone had misunderstood such a comment. But this time he was upset both Emily and her mother had heard Becca. Mrs. Gherring had already told Emily he was a player, and he wasn't even sure what she'd seen or heard to base her comment on.

But since the girls were acting chummy, Candace and Becca were monopolizing Emily. He'd barely gotten to speak to her on the entire hike. He frowned as the three broke out in laughter over some comment Candace made about leotards. What on earth was a leotard?

"We're almost back," Spencer said to Anne.

"That's good," Anne's voice seemed bit shaky.

"Beautiful hike," said Gherring. "Usually, even when I'm running or riding outside, I don't really get to enjoy the scenery."

"When's your next Iron Man?" asked Spencer.

"Well, I'm signed up at the end of July." He hesitated, glancing toward Anne. "But I'm thinking of backing out because of all the training time."

"I don't mind you taking time to train," argued Anne.

"But, what if I'm off on some seven hour bike ride and... And something happens?"

Anne gave him a tiny shake of her head, pursing her lips. She asked Spencer, "Have you ever thought of doing triathlons?"

"Possibly someday... But not until after I graduate next December—the training is intense."

Nearing the end of the hike, Anne grabbed her husband's hand and whispered in his ear.

"Go on ahead. We're making a quick potty break." Gherring disappeared into the woods with Anne.

Spencer wondered why she couldn't make it the ten minutes back to the parking lot. But he kept his thoughts to himself. Emily cast worried looks into the woods where they'd disappeared.

"Come on, Mr. Gherring said it would be a quick potty break. They'll catch up." He led the way down the end of the trail.

They waited at the parking area almost fifteen minutes before the Gherrings returned. Anne was attempting to smile, but her expression was forced, her face ashen. She was grasping onto Gherring's arm for support, and he didn't bother to hide his concern.

"What's wrong with your mom?" asked Candace.

"She's... She got severely dehydrated earlier in the week. She probably shouldn't have come today."

"I feel bad for talking them into coming." Spencer debated offering to help Gherring get her back to the car.

"It's not your fault," said Emily. "He tried to talk her out of it. She can be very persuasive when she puts her mind to it."

The Gherrings made their way to the group, stopping once on the way for Anne to rest. Gherring looked like he was about to pick her up and carry her, but she stepped away and began to walk again.

"I'm fine. I just got a little overheated. I should have worn shorts." True to her statement, Anne's forehead was beaded with sweat.

Gherring was quiet while everyone climbed into their seats and buckled up. He drove back a little faster than the speed limit, glancing at his wife frequently to check her condition. The ride might have been interminably quiet, but for Candace and Becca gossiping about all the people in the hiking club and forecasting potential hookups within the group.

Spencer noticed Emily was smiling and nodding her head in response, but kept watching her mom in the seat in front of her. From his vantage point, Anne appeared quite grey. Gherring made it back in record time and unceremoniously deposited Candace and Becca where he'd picked them up. They were still trying to talk to Spencer through the window when he drove away.

"Where would you like to be dropped off?" he asked Spencer and Emily. "We're going to the hospital."

"No, we're not," Anne protested.

"I'll go with you," said Emily.

"No!" Anne's alarm was evident in her voice.

Gherring said, "Right now, it would be easier to go by ourselves to the emergency room. I'm sure she won't be admitted. They'll probably give her another IV and let her go. But if they admit her, I'll call you."

"Okay, but I want you to call me as soon as you know what they're going to do with her."

"Hello," said Anne. "I'm in the car. Stop talking about me in third person."

"Do you think she's just dehydrated again?" Emily disregarded her mother.

"Yes, she's definitely dehydrated, and she's not eating enough. I don't think her medicine's working," Gherring replied.

Spencer cleared his throat. "Why don't you drop us off at Papa's Place? We'll grab a bite to eat. It's walking distance to the hospital if you call."

They hopped out on the curb next to Papa's and watched Gherring speed off. Emily was obviously worried, but at least he finally had her to himself. The morning hadn't gone well, but lunch at Papa's ought to be a slam-dunk.

Emily tried not to worry about her mom. Hopefully she'd hear from Steven by the end of lunchtime.

"This hike turned into a bust," said Spencer. "Sorry about that."

"It's not your fault. I have a feeling she'd have been back at the hospital today whether or not she'd gone on the hike."

"Well, I'm also sorry about Becca and Candace."

"There's no need to apologize for your friends."

"They're not my friends—not really. They're just part of the hiking club."

"Just part of the club? Even Becca?"

Spencer's frown was severe. "I never dated Becca. We didn't spend a night together camping, and we didn't go on any private hikes."

"It's okay. It's none of my business, anyway."

"It's the truth. I never dated her."

Spencer held the restaurant door open for Emily. She was about to respond to his declaration when they were suddenly bombarded.

"Spencer!"

"Hey look, there he is!"

"Spencer!

"Who is this? Is this your new girlfriend?"

Four attractive girls surrounded them, pulling Spencer inside. Emily was immediately overwhelmed. Three were as tall as her, but one stood about chin-high at five feet two inches. The taller girls were lean and lanky, but the short girl was curvaceous. She was evidently the spokesperson for the clan, because she held up her hand for silence.

"Spencer, you can have lunch with us and introduce us to your girlfriend," she spoke in a commanding voice.

Spencer's eyes were apologetic. "Emily, these are my sisters. And this is Emily, my *friend*." He looked pointedly at the shorter girl. "Not my *girlfriend*."

"You didn't tell me you had four sisters."

He shrugged. "I told you I had four siblings."

"Why didn't you tell her about us?" asked the short one. "Hi, I'm Grace, by the way."

"*Gracebytheway*—that's a funny name," she quipped.

Grace linked her arm around Emily's and led her into the restaurant. "Ah—a sense of humor. We're going to be best friends. Spencer, why did you keep this one from us?"

"Does he usually bring lots of girls to meet y'all?"

"*Y'all*? How cute—she has a southern accent. No. He never brings a girl to meet us. I can't imagine why not."

"Can we use the back room today, Aunt May?"

"I don't have it reserved... Unless your mom and dad are coming?" May gazed expectantly at Emily.

Emily shook her head in answer, but Grace asked, "Who are your mom and dad? They get to sit in the back room?"

The blood rushed to her face—she hated attention. And she especially hated the kind of attention Steven Gherring garnered. Spencer came to the rescue.

"Grace, please. Can we sit down before you grill Emily further? And maybe you shouldn't be quite so nosey."

"Me? Nosey? Surely you've gotten me mixed up with Olivia."

"Hey," objected one of the tall sisters with long, brown hair hanging in a mass of curls. "I'm not nosey." She pulled up a chair next to Emily. "But I'm great at keeping secrets. So you can tell me anything, and I'll go to my grave with it."

"Right, Olivia," teased Grace. "But on your way to your grave you'll tell your secrets to anyone who asks."

"That's a lie... Don't listen to her."

"Where did you two go today?" asked a tall girl whose curly hair looked similar to Olivia's, but auburn. She had fair skin and rosy cheeks. She reached across the table to shake Emily's hand. "I'm Hannah."

"On a hike," Spencer answered.

Grace frowned. "She's one of those hikers?"

"You don't like the people in the hiking club?" Emily asked.

"How should I know? I never get to meet them. He doesn't bring anyone over."

"I don't live at home anymore," Spencer defended. "And why would I bring a friend to the house so you could grill them?"

The tall sister with shoulder-length brown hair spoke up. "We don't grill them, and you know it. You're afraid we'll tell them stories about you. We have lots of stories, and most of them are true. I'm Claire, and I keep secrets better than Olivia."

"I'd love to hear a story." Emily grinned, while Spencer buried his face in his hands.

"You want to hear about Spencer's Senior Prom?" asked Claire.

"Oh, no. Tell her about his Superman underwear," said Hannah.

"Hannah!" Spencer lunged for his sister.

Emily laughed. "Don't worry, Spencer. I'm sure you don't still have that underwear. You've probably moved on to Spiderman."

Grace hooted. "I like you, Emily. Want to come to family dinner on Sunday?"

"No!" Spencer exclaimed.

"Why not, big brother? We promise to play nice." Grace batted her eyes.

"I'd love to come, but can I let you know tonight."

"Sure. Give me your cell number."

"So how do you know Spencer?" Claire asked.

"She's a friend from work," Spencer explained.

"I didn't ask you," teased Claire. "If you wanted to tell us about her, you should have done it a long time ago."

"So, are you in the hiking club? I don't really have anything against them," said Grace.

"No, this was actually my first hike. I don't hike or anything like that. My favorite exercise is ballet dancing. At least it used to be."

"She's also an artist," said Spencer.

"How did you know that? I never tell anyone."

His face reddened. "I... I just saw the watercolors in your cubicle and assumed they were yours. I'm sorry if I wasn't supposed to tell people, but I thought they were really good. Grace does watercolors, too. I didn't know it was a secret..." His voice trailed off.

Grace said, "Oh, would you like to take a class with me? There's a great summer class with a fantastic teacher. He's amazing—you'll love him. It's on Tuesday nights."

"Actually, it sounds fun."

She glanced at Spencer, who sported a rather miserable expression. "It's okay, Spencer. I was only surprised you knew about my painting. That's all."

All four sisters observed the small exchange closely. Grace considered Spencer with narrowed eyes.

"I'm really looking forward to getting to know you better, Emily. We've got a lot of things to talk about."

When Steven called during the middle of their lunch, Emily sent a tense glance toward Spencer before stepping away from the table to answer.

"Steven? What is it?"

"They put her on an IV again, and now they're sending us home. They told us to come back tomorrow if she still can't eat or drink, and we're seeing the doctor on Monday. I think we need to try a different prescription."

"So what do they have her on now?" asked Emily.

"Uhmm... I can't say exactly. But it isn't working."

"Do they have her on an antibiotic?"

"An antibiotic? For an ulcer? Uhmm, no I don't think so."

"Maybe that's the problem. Most ulcers are caused by infection, so they usually prescribe an antibiotic. I wonder why they didn't give one to Mom."

Steven heaved a heavy sigh. "I wish I could answer that one for you, Emily. Maybe Monday I'll be able to give you a better answer."

"You're worried, aren't you?"

"I... I'm not... Yes. I am. But, your Mom's going to be fine. I promise. I'll make sure she's okay."

She wanted to believe him. At least he'd admitted his concern, but she knew from her research things didn't make sense.

She walked back to the table, avoiding the probing eyes of the Marshall sisters. She had to say something. "Good news... Mom's fine. She's just dehydrated again."

Grace started to ask a question, but Spencer caught her eyes. When he shook his head almost imperceptibly, she forked a spoonful of salad and chewed with relish.

Spencer asked Emily, "Are you finishing lunch? Or do you need to go?"

"No, I'm good. I guess I'll be available for dinner on Sunday as well," she told Grace.

"Six o'clock, as usual?" asked Spencer.

"Did we invite you, Spencer? I thought this was a girls' night." Hannah stuck out her tongue.

"Fine," he smirked. "Are you cooking?"

"Hey, Spencer. Can we have shrimp scampi this week? You know, since Emily's coming?" asked Claire.

"But that's *your* favorite, Claire. Maybe Emily doesn't like it."

"I like everything. Well, except for liver. And eggplant. And mountain oysters. Other than that, we're good."

"Too bad," Spencer chuckled. "I was really hoping to do mountain oysters."

"What's mountain—" Claire began.

"Don't ask," said Olivia. "I'll tell you later."

"I'll bring dessert. Do you like Hello Dolly Bars?" asked Emily.

"Do they have chocolate in them?" asked Hannah.

"Of course... Dessert has chocolate by definition."

"This is fun, isn't it, Spencer?" Grace's eyes were twinkling. "You should have introduced us to *all* your many, many female friends."

Emily watched as he glared at Grace, the muscles in his jaw clenching. But he didn't respond to her provoking comment. How many female friends had he had over the years? He was awfully good-looking—of course he'd had a lot of girlfriends. Perhaps she could find out at dinner tomorrow night. In fact, she might learn a lot at the Marshall family dinner.

Chapter Four

ANNE FELT LIKE warmed-over death. And she looked like it, too. She stared at her drawn face in the mirror. She pulled out her concealer and dabbed it under her eyes to camouflage the huge dark circles. Then she rummaged through the back of her drawer, searching for powder blush to lend an appearance of color. Inspecting her work, she told herself she looked halfway normal. Hopefully, she looked good enough to pass the inspection of her daughter who was on her way up. Her husband had already seen how bad she looked. He was getting a full-blown trial of the "for worse" part of his recent wedding vows.

Why did she feel so terrible with this pregnancy? Her first two had been easy, and she felt terrific the whole time. Of course, she was in her early twenties when she had Emily and Charlotte. She'd had a little morning sickness, but nothing like she was experiencing now. The nausea meds prescribed by the doctor provided little relief for her severe symptoms. She had hoped fervently she'd eventually adjust, praying each day her symptoms would improve. But so far, she found it almost impossible to keep anything in her stomach.

She spied her husband behind her, watching her in the mirror, his face clearly exhibiting the emotions warring inside him. Whoever said men don't have any feelings had never met her husband. He had them in droves, and most of them were intense.

"I look bad... I'm afraid for Emily to see me."

"If you'd tell her the truth, it wouldn't be a problem. I really don't like lying to her, and I'm having to do it a lot. Have you considered how angry she'll be when she finds out the truth?"

"I know, but I'm just not ready."

He sighed. It seemed like he was doing a lot of sighing these days. "Have you had anything to drink today?"

"I liked those ice chips you brought me. And I ate a cracker."

"And they stayed down?"

"Well... Not exactly." She felt tears forming, and she turned away, blinking rapidly.

She found herself enveloped in his arms. "Don't worry. We're already planning to go back for an IV this afternoon; you'll feel better soon."

"I'm really worried the baby's not getting enough nutrition."

"I'm worried about *you*. If something doesn't change, there won't be anything left of you." He gave her a squeeze. "But Monday, something's going to change. We're not going on like this. So why do we have to keep lying about it, even to our family?"

"It's... You won't understand."

"I will. Please tell me." He lifted her face toward his, so she could see the promise in his eyes.

"I'm... I don't want to go through this in public—in the newspapers, in the tabloids. I'm just not used to it. I know it doesn't bother you, but I was even embarrassed over all the press stuff when we got married. I can't imagine what they'll say when they find out I'm pregnant at my age. And then if I lose the baby..." She couldn't stop a few tears from rolling down her cheeks.

"I didn't know the paparazzi upset you that much. I guess I'm used to it, so I can ignore it. But if it matters to you, it matters to me." He kissed a few stray tears off her face. "Couldn't we at least tell the girls and Gram?"

"But then they'll have to lie about it."

He heaved out another weighty sigh. "Okay, we'll wait as long as we can. And I'll see what I can do to keep the media out of it. Truthfully the best way to fight the tabloids is to be very open with the mainstream press. It'll be hard to keep it a secret for long."

She managed a little smile. "Maybe you could simply buy all the tabloids."

"I'm considering it." He grinned, and her heart leapt in her chest. He was so handsome. Sometimes she still had a hard time believing he could love her.

"Help me get dressed and ready for when Emily comes. I want to look really normal."

"I'd rather help you get undressed." He kissed the back of her neck.

"You've got to be kidding. Me throwing up ten times a day hasn't turned you off?"

"Na! I'm used to it. I've always had that effect on women."

Emily's mom lounged on the couch. Her color was better, but she looked thin—like she could easily snap in two.

"So you're feeling better?"

"Yes, much better. Tell me about Spencer? Are you sure you're only *friends*? He's such a nice boy."

"Yes, we're friends. So what medicines are you taking for your ulcer?" Emily had done a thorough Internet search on ulcers. She was prepared to catch her mom if she was lying.

"Are you *really* sure you're only friends?"

"Yes, we're just friends. And what medicine did you say you're taking?"

"Some type of antacids. Uhmm, I forget." She fidgeted with a button on her shirt, refusing to make eye contact. "I wanted to know if you were really only friends, because his Aunt May wants me to match him with someone."

"May asked you to match him up?" Something heavy fell to the bottom of her stomach.

"Yes. You know, she wants me to find a wife for him."

"Mom, maybe Spencer doesn't want you to find someone for him. Maybe he's not ready to get married. Have you thought of that?"

"No, he told me a while back he'd love for me to find someone for him. In fact, before y'all came to visit me in New York, I showed him a picture of you and Charlie. He told me he'd take either one of y'all."

"Either one?" Why did that bother her?

"I think he meant he thought y'all were both cute," Anne clarified.

"Well... If Spencer wants a wife, I guess you should find him one. Do you have someone in mind?"

"No, I actually thought you could help me look. I don't know him that well, and I don't meet a lot of young people."

"Sure, I guess. You know, he told me he wasn't even interested in dating anyone right now. Are you sure he still wants a wife?"

"I guess he could've changed his mind, but to be honest, most guys don't know they want a wife when they find one."

"That's true." Steven walked in and sank onto the couch next to Anne. "I was determined to remain single for the rest of my life."

"But Spencer's still in grad school," Emily reasoned.

"Doesn't he graduate in December?" asked Steven.

"I guess that's true," said Emily. "Still, he doesn't seem to be in a hurry to settle down."

"What do you think about Becca? She seems interested in Spencer." Her mom blinked wide innocent eyes.

"Oh, you mean Betty Boobs?" Emily asked sarcastically.

Anne giggled. "I thought y'all were getting along well by the end of the hike. You have something against her besides her significant endowment? I thought y'all were becoming *bosom* buddies."

"Ha, ha. Very funny. I was only trying to make them feel comfortable. Becca's okay. But she's not good enough for Spencer. She's too... too..."

"Busty?" Steven grinned.

"No—too shallow. Becca and Candace were both too shallow for him. He can do better."

"All the girls I know are too old for him," said Anne.

"I'm having dinner with his family tonight. Maybe I should ask his sisters."

"That sounds fun. Have you met his family?"

"I met his four sisters yesterday at Papa's. They were crazy—you'd love them."

"And you're having dinner tonight? Are you supposed to bring something?"

Emily clapped her forehead with the heel of her hand. "Ohmygosh! I almost forgot. I said I'd bring Hello Dolly Bars, and I haven't even been to the grocery store yet."

She jumped up to give her mom a hug, cringing at the feel of her gaunt shoulders and the weakness of her embrace. "I'm sorry I have to run. I hope you're better soon, Mom. I'm really worried about you, and so is Charlie."

As she left, she realized her mom had never answered her question about medications. She'd have to pursue her investigation tomorrow. She wouldn't stop until she knew the truth.

"That went well." Anne relaxed against her husband on the couch.

"Yeah, that story about finding a wife for Spencer was really distracting."

"That wasn't a story—it was true. May's been after me to find him a wife for a while. But I think Emily likes him more than she's letting on, don't you?"

"Really? She hardly talked to him on the hike. It's not like they ever touch each other, even accidentally."

"Exactly. Emily makes up her mind about people pretty quickly. She likes you, or she dislikes you. One or the other. Black and white. She'll always try to be polite, even if she doesn't like you. But, she won't ever be around you voluntarily. So I know she doesn't dislike him. And she's so awkward around him—almost as awkward as he is around her."

"If you say so. I didn't notice all that. I was probably distracted by all the cleavage."

She punched him in the chest, chuckling. "Watch out buddy. When I get my strength back, I'll make you pay." Then she grimaced. "Ugh. Help me up, will you?"

"Where to? Do you feel nauseated again?"

She nodded, before her feet buckled under her. He scooped her up and carried her to their bed, handing her a basin. Anne stared at the plastic tub, thinking once again there was nothing inside her to throw up. She felt like crying, but she was so dehydrated no tears emerged.

"That's it—I'm calling the doctor. I don't care if it's Sunday."

"No." Anne spoke between dry heaves. "Let's wait. We'll go get an IV and call her tomorrow."

"I think she'd want us to call. She doesn't even know you've gotten worse instead of better. We haven't talked to her since Wednesday."

"I don't want to bother her on the weekend."

"Well, you're not going to bother her—I am." Gherring stalked from the room.

Anne could hear his voice, rising and falling. She felt the room start to spin and closed her eyes against the sensation. Then she was blissfully asleep.

*****

Spencer was nervous, and with good reason. His sisters couldn't be trusted. Even while he was cooking he observed them whispering and plotting. Occasionally they'd glance his direction, laughing out loud. True, they were aware of his observation, and they were probably egging him on. But they seemed to function together as an enemy organism whose sole purpose was to embarrass him. And tonight, he really didn't want to be embarrassed.

Emily was special. She was a really good friend. He knew they were only friends, and it's all they'd ever be. She'd made that perfectly clear. He knew it in his head, but his body kept thinking about other possibilities. Last November, when she was visiting her mom in New York for the first time, he'd actually hugged her. He'd had a great excuse, sharing his warmth by wrapping her inside his coat on a windy water cruise. But he'd enjoyed it immensely. Now, all these months later, he could still remember exactly what it felt like to hold her tight, as she snuggled against him. The tingle of her arms around his back. The clean scent of her hair. The awareness of her soft areas pressed against his firm muscles. If he closed his eyes, he could almost feel it like it was happening now. He imagined her huddling against him. He sensed her body relaxing against the warmth of his chest. He remembered how his heart swelled with the knowledge he was protecting her.

"Spencer. Are you listening?" His mother's voice invaded his mind.

"Oh, sorry. What did you say?" His face flamed.

"I was telling you the back burner isn't working any more."

"Okay, thanks. I'll work around it. Are you getting it fixed?"

She groaned. "Maybe after I get a job. I've had several interviews, but new RNs get the worst schedules. Everything I've been offered has been working nights. I'd never get to see your dad."

He gave her a hug with his arm, holding his shrimp-covered fingers away from her. "I'm so proud of you, Mom, for finally getting your RN. Surely you'll find a good job soon."

"So… Tell me about this girl who's coming to dinner."

Grace grinned. "Yes, Spencer. Tell us about Emily."

He glared at Grace. "You invited her. Why don't you tell us about her?"

"Oh. I'm confused. Hannah told me she was Spencer's new girlfriend." His mother scratched her head.

Spencer switched his glare to Hannah. "She's just a girl I work with. She's a friend."

"Maybe," said Grace. "But I don't think so. At least, I think you like her more than that. I'm not sure how she feels, but I intend to find out."

"Grace, I'm warning you. If you do anything to—"

"I'm not going to do anything. I'm merely going to observe."

"Grace—" Spencer began.

"Well," his mother interrupted. "I'm just glad your friend is coming to dinner. You've dated all those girls, and you've never brought a single one to the house before. I was beginning to think you were ashamed of us."

"Mom, please don't say stuff like that around Emily," pleaded Spencer.

"Like what?"

"Stuff about me dating so many girls. I don't want her to think I'm a player."

"What's a player?" she asked.

Olivia jumped in. "But you *are* a player. Aren't you, Spencer? At least you've never minded us saying it before."

"You may not bring them home, but every time we see you, you're with a different girl," said Claire. "What are we supposed to call you?"

"The important thing is he doesn't want us to call him a player around *this* girl. Like I said, Emily is different. Sorry Bro, you can't hide anything from me." She whispered in his ear, "Even if you're hiding it from yourself."

"And this," said Spencer, "is why I've never brought a girl to dinner."

*****

Anne woke up once when Steven was carrying her. But her head hurt, and she squeezed her eyes closed again.

When next she opened her eyes, she was staring at a fluorescent light. She considered the unattractive fixture. One of the bulbs was dark at the end. What did that mean? Maybe she needed to tell Steven to change the light bulb. Would he do it himself? Or would he call someone from maintenance? She opened her mouth to call out his name, but no sound emerged. Was she dreaming? Maybe this was one of those nightmares where you try to call out for help, but you can't make anyone hear you.

"She's awake."

Anne turned her head toward a woman's voice.

"Do you want me to explain it to her? Or do you want to tell her?"

She heard Steven say, "I'll tell her."

Steven, the light bulb is going out. He couldn't hear her. Or he was ignoring her. He was talking to that woman.

"I'll be back tomorrow morning, early, before I go to my office. And we'll decide our next step. Okay? And now you have my cell number. You will call me if anything changes. Do you understand?"

"Yes. And thank you."

Anne drifted back to sleep.

*****

Emily's palms were sweating. Why was she nervous? She was simply going to dinner with a friend. In fact, she was really going to dinner with a female friend. Grace was the one who'd invited her to dinner. Spencer was only a guy who was going to be at the dinner. Not that she had any reason to be nervous about dinner with Spencer anyway. And even it she wanted to date him, she wouldn't, because he was a player.

And besides that, she wasn't a risk-taker, like Spencer. He liked every adrenaline-pushing sport that existed. He'd be bored with her in a week. No, tonight she was simply going to dinner at Grace's house. In fact, she planned to be certain she sat between two of the sisters, to play it safe. If she sat next to Spencer and he accidentally brushed his hand against hers, she'd probably spill her drink or break something. She still hadn't gotten used to that tingly thing that happened when he touched her.

She paused before she knocked on the door. Maybe she should check the dessert one more time. She lifted the lid, and the sweet scent of chocolate assaulted her nose. Assured her treats were intact, she closed the lid tight again and steeled her nerves. She raised her fist to knock when the door flew open and a slim arm snaked out.

"Here she is!" Claire grabbed her hand, pulling her inside, her brown bob bouncing as she led her into the dining room.

"Hi, Emily." Hannah glanced up from setting the table. Her dark red curls were confined to a braid.

"Are these the Hello Dolly Bars?" Olivia took the dessert from her hands, popped the lid open and pinched off a piece of the chocolate dessert to pop in her mouth.

"Olivia." Grace spoke sternly up at her sister, who quailed despite her superior stature. Grace took the plastic container away. "Come meet Momma and Papa."

Emily obediently followed Grace into the kitchen where she spied Spencer busy at the stove. He had on shorts and a t-shirt, and she couldn't help but note his leg muscles again. He really looked good when he was cooking. Wow, she was thinking like a female chauvinist pig. She tore her eyes away to greet his mother, busy washing a pan in the sink.

"Momma, this is Emily... Uhmm what's your last name?"

"Hi, I'm Emily Best. It's nice to meet you, Mrs. Marshall."

"Connie. Call me Connie. And this is Joe."

"Hi, Emily. We're glad to meet you. I'm sorry it's so chaotic around here," said Joe. "But to tell you truth, this is normal."

"Especially on Sunday night when Spencer's here," said Grace.

"Oh no. You're not blaming this noisy mess on me; I'm just the cook," said Spencer.

"Table's set," announced Hannah. "Everybody get your own drink."

"Except you," Claire told Emily. "I'll get yours. Is ice water okay? Or we've got milk or juice?"

"Ice water," agreed Emily.

In a seeming frenzy, the family scurried around getting glasses and ice and drinks and moving the food to the table. Emily found herself sitting at the table between Spencer and Grace. Hannah, Olivia, and Claire sat across, with Joe and Connie at the ends. Her heart raced. What if they touched? Would the sisters notice her reaction? She practiced the breathing exercises she used to calm herself before a test or a dance recital. In-two-three-hold... Out-two-three-hold...

Joe said a blessing before the group dove into the food.

"Shrimp scampi—woo hoo!" said Claire.

"Pass the rice, please," said Olivia.

Emily and Spencer reached for the bowl of rice simultaneously. Their fingers touched, and Emily felt a tingle. She twitched at the sensation, but she didn't pull her hand away.

"Sorry," mumbled Spencer, as he allowed Emily to pass the bowl across the table.

"Son, dinner's delicious, as always." Joe smiled at Emily. "We all got used to his cooking—took it for granted all those years. Now he's moved away from home, we only get to enjoy it on Sundays."

Connie said, "The rest of the week, they have to suffer with my cooking."

The whole family laughed, but Grace explained to Emily, "She's only joking. Momma hates cooking. When it's not Spencer, it's me or Papa."

"Sometimes I cook," declared Hannah.

"Hannah does brinner," said Olivia. "You know, breakfast for dinner? Eggs, toast, pancakes, bacon—she loves cooking breakfast food."

"I bake," said Claire. "And I want your recipe, Emily."

"Shouldn't you try them first? You might not want the recipe." Emily chuckled.

"So... Emily," Grace spoke in an intentionally casual tone. "Who are your parents?"

"Grace," Spencer warned. "That's none of your business."

"Why? She met my parents. Surely she's not ashamed of her parents."

"Grace." Spencer said the name between clenched teeth.

Connie said, "Grace, if Emily doesn't want to talk about—"

"It's okay. Really, it's okay. It's no big deal, really." Emily steeled herself against the embarrassing reaction people always gave when she revealed who her stepfather was.

"Aunt May lets her parents sit in the back room, so I know they're famous or important or something." Grace waited with rapt attention.

Spencer studied his plate while the rest of the family gazed expectantly at Emily.

"Uhmm, my mom's name is Anne, and she's been a widow for fifteen years. My dad died in a car wreck, along with two of my grandparents."

Connie gasped. "I'm so sorry."

"I'm really okay. It's been fifteen years, so it doesn't really hurt any more—not much."

"So is your mom rich or famous or something?" asked Grace. "What's her last name?"

"Her mom is married to my boss," said Spencer. "Okay? Now you know."

"Your boss, as in, your immediate boss? Or the one who owns the company?" asked Joe.

"Steven Gherring," said Emily. "She's married to Steven Gherring."

"Wow," Claire spoke into the ensuing silence. "You're rich, huh?"

"Claire!" scolded Connie.

"I don't live with them, so it's not my money." Emily knew her face was glowing red.

"I'm sorry," said Spencer miserably. "This whole thing was a bad idea. I shouldn't have let you come."

"Nonsense," said Connie. "Now we've gotten over the shock of the idea, we won't embarrass you again, Emily. I imagine you were a little shocked yourself when it first happened."

Emily let out a breath, and smiled gratefully at Connie. "Actually, my sister and I were both a bit shocked at the whole thing. That's a long story. But Steven's a really great guy, and he's nothing like they say in the tabloids. He's super nice, and he really, really loves my mom."

"I told you guys when I met him six months ago he was nice and down-to-earth. I told you he didn't act like a billionaire," said Spencer.

63

"Yes," said Olivia. "But you didn't tell us you were dating his daughter."

"We're not dating," he corrected before Emily had a chance to respond. "We're friends. Right, Emily? At least I hope we're still friends, after this."

"We're still friends." Her heart broke a little at his apologetic smile. He was trying so hard to protect her. Not that she would ever need protecting by a man. She was self-sufficient.

*****

Anne opened her eyes again. She was shivering. There was a metal rail on her bed. Hospital. She must be getting her IV. How did she get here?

"Are you cold?" Steven said, adding a white blanket to her covers. "You've got like four blankets on."

"Did I get my IV?" she croaked. "Can I go home now?"

"Well, we need to talk about that," he said, coming to sit beside her and hold her hand. "The doctor met us here. It turns out she was angry we didn't call her earlier. We discovered you don't have morning sickness. She said you have something called hyperemesis gravidarum. It can be really dangerous—to you and the baby. Since you didn't respond to the Vitamin B6 and anti-nausea meds, you're probably going to need to stay in the hospital."

"But I feel better now. I don't even feel nauseated."

"That's because they gave you medicine in your IV. You were throwing up your oral meds before they even got into your system. You need the IV."

Now fully hydrated, her eyes were swimming in tears that pooled and flowed down her face in rivers. "Please, can I go home? I don't want to stay here."

He squeezed her hand. "First, we're gonna talk about something else. I have to call Emily and Charlie. They have to know you're in the hospital. They'll have to deal with keeping your secret."

She nodded. He was right, of course. She couldn't put it off any longer.

"Okay. Just get Emily here. I'll tell her in person. But don't scare her, okay?"

Steven rolled his eyes. "Dealing with you Best women can be so difficult."

*****

The food disappeared quickly. With so much laughing and teasing and conversing, Emily was surprised anyone managed to eat at all.

"Time for dessert." Olivia emerged from the kitchen with the Emily's container in hand.

She set the Tupperware in the middle of the table after snatching a bar for herself and taking a bite.

"Yum!" said Claire, her expression ecstatic as she relished the chocolaty dessert.

"These are really good," Spencer confirmed.

Emily watched the Marshall family devouring the sweet bars. "I'm so full from dinner. I can't even imagine eating dessert."

"That's why you should always eat dessert first," Olivia declared.

Grace had been quiet during the last part of dinner. "Are you mad at me for being nosey about your parents?"

"Of course not. I had fun tonight."

"But I'm still mad at you." Spencer crossed his arms. "I told you not to be so nosey, and you wouldn't listen."

"Let's change the subject," suggested Grace. "Momma, how's the job hunt going?"

"Nothing so far—at least nothing that doesn't involve working the midnight shift."

"Momma's been an LVN for years, but she went back to school and graduated with her RN two weeks ago," Grace boasted.

"Congratulations," said Emily. "Oh! My phone's vibrating." When she saw Steven's name, she felt the blood drain from her face.

"It's Steven," she whispered to Spencer as she ran quickly to the den.

"Hello? Steven? Is something wrong with Mom?"

"She's okay. But they're keeping her in the hospital tonight. She... she got dehydrated again. Can you come and see her tonight?"

"I'm coming right now. What's the name of the hospital?"

She heard Spencer's voice behind her. "I know where it is. I'll get you there."

Steven said, "Is that Spencer?"

"Yes, he said he'd bring me."

"It'll take fifteen minutes if we leave right now," said Spencer.

"Don't panic getting here. It's not an emergency—she just wants to see you. Okay?"

But Emily couldn't stop crying. Spencer took the phone from her trembling hand. "I'll take care of her, Mr. Gherring. We'll see you in a few minutes."

He ended the call and opened his arms, and she fell against him, sobbing. He held her until she quieted.

She sniffed. "I... I'm s-sorry. I d-don't know why I'm cr-crying."

"What happened? What did he say?"

"J-just that sh-she's in the h-hospital."

"Okay. Did he say it's bad? Did he tell you what's really wrong?"

"N-no. He didn't say."

"Well, let's go. Let's get there and see what's going on. She's going to be fine."

Emily was suddenly conscious Spencer had his arms around her. And she had her arms around him. She stiffened and pulled away, but immediately felt the loss. Vaguely, she worried she'd sought and found comfort so easily from Spencer. But that's what friends were for, right?

She saw Grace watching from the doorway of the den. Spencer followed Emily's eyes to his sister. "Her mom's sick, so I'm taking Emily to the hospital. This information doesn't leave this house. Understand?"

Emily moved woodenly as he led her out the door. She attempted to reinstate the brave, fearless front behind which she'd hidden so successfully for years. She detested herself for her lack of control, and determined not to show weakness again. She had to be strong.

*****

Anne tried desperately to stay awake, but failed. She didn't see Emily when she entered the room. She didn't get to give her an assuring smile, and she didn't get to prime herself to look strong and healthy. Instead, she woke up to her daughter's tear streaked face.

"Baby, I'm okay. Don't cry." She held up her arms to invite a hug. "I'm just worn out. But I feel better already."

"You don't have an ulcer, do you?"

"No, I don't have an ulcer." She looked at Steven.

"I'm already dialing her number." He held up his hand. "Just a minute. Hey... Hi, Charlie. Yes, I'm calling about your mom. Yes she's okay, but she's in the hospital. Wait... I'm putting you on speaker. Your mom wants to talk to both of you. Yes, Emily's here. Okay, there. Speaker's on. Can you hear?"

"Yes," said Charlie, sniffing already. "Mom? What is it? What's wrong?"

"Nothing... Well, nothing bad. I mean it's mostly good. We have to do the right thing and be careful."

"What, Mom?" Emily asked in a quaking voice. "Do you have cancer?"

"Cancer? No, of course not. No, I'm not going to die. I only feel like I'm going to die." She chuckled.

"Mom," said Charlie. "It's not funny. What's wrong with you?"

"I'm... uh... I'm..." Her cheeks burned and her eyes darted to Steven. "You say it."

He smiled and leaned over to kiss her cheek. "We're pregnant!" His lips split into a broad smile, and his dimples poked in a mile on each side.

After a few moments of silence, Charlie's voice rang out over the speakerphone. "Did you say pregnant?"

"That's right," said Steven.

Emily's eyebrows furrowed skeptically. "And that's why you've lost so much weight you look like a scarecrow?"

"She's got something called hyperemesis gravidarum. Essentially, she throws up everything. So she gets dehydrated, and her meds weren't working because they didn't stay in her long enough to do anything. The doctor thinks she'll be fine if we keep her on an IV. Sometimes it's better after the first trimester."

"Wait, wait, wait! Mom's pregnant? We're going to have a baby brother or sister?" Charlie's voice went up an octave.

Emily's nostrils flared. "Why didn't you tell us? Why did you lie? I was so worried."

She felt the tears starting. "Because there's a pretty good chance I'll lose the baby, and I didn't want everyone to know. I didn't want the press to find out. And I didn't want you to have to lie."

Now Emily was crying again and hugging her, and Charlie could be heard sobbing on the phone.

"I don't want her upset. She's supposed to stay calm." Steven ran his fingers through his salt-and-pepper hair.

"Will you have to stay in the hospital until you have the baby?" asked Charlie.

"I hope not—I want to go home now."

Steven shook his head. "You need to be on an IV for now. Hopefully that will be enough. If it gets really bad, they have something called TPN where you don't eat anything and they give you all the nutrients in a central line."

"Can't I just come every day and get an IV?"

"I don't know, but I don't think so. You got pretty bad today, and it had only been twenty four hours since your last IV."

"Maybe Spencer's mom would take care of you at the apartment. She's an RN, but she hasn't gotten a job yet." Emily pulled her bottom lip in to chew on it.

"Really?" Her suggestion seemed heaven-sent.

"We'll see what the doctor says tomorrow morning. It'd be better if you weren't stuck in a bed all day. But we can't take any chances here. I could have lost you today." For the first time, Steven's strong demeanor cracked, and he blinked at the tears.

Suddenly Emily got a strange look on her face. "Ohmygosh! You're pregnant. My mom's going to have a baby. Who can I tell?"

"Your mom wants to keep this whole thing out of the press for as long as possible. So we really need to keep a lid on it. I'll tell Gram and Gus. But we're not telling anyone at Gherring Inc."

"What about Spencer? He's sitting out in the waiting room. He brought me here, and he knows something's wrong. I've got to tell him something," said Emily.

"I think we can trust Spencer. And hopefully we'll be talking to his mother." Anne watched as conflicting emotions passed across Emily's face. "You can go talk to him."

Suddenly Charlie's voice rang out from the cell phone. "No fair! I don't get to tell anybody."

"You can tell Grandpa, if you want to. I sure don't want to tell him. It's embarrassing." Her face felt warm, even in the frigid temperature of the hospital room.

"Why is it embarrassing?" Steven asked with a frown-creased forehead.

"Because... Well... It's like telling my dad I had sex."

Steven laughed. "I think it's high time your dad found out the truth."

Chapter Five

SPENCER COULDN'T get his mind off Emily. When she fell crying into his arms, it was as if she left a permanent indentation. It felt like she belonged there, and he felt empty without her. It felt like she needed him, and he liked it. And when she told him about her mom's pregnancy at the hospital, he felt important, maybe even honored. They weren't telling anyone outside the family, but they told him. And he'd make sure he was worthy of the honor. He'd never tell anyone, not even his family, about what was really going on with Mrs. Gherring. He wouldn't risk being responsible for a leak that made it to the tabloids. He'd never do anything to hurt Emily or her family.

Somewhere in the back of his mind, he knew he needed to get a handle on his feelings for Emily. She'd made it clear they would never be more than friends. But the more time he spent with her, the closer he got to her, and the more he wanted to spend time with her. It was a terrible spiral that could only lead to heartache. For the first time, he understood why some of those girls would come crying about wanting more from him. He'd always been baffled by their emotional outbreaks. He'd been consistently clear about only wanting friendship. Had he led those girls on? He'd thought as long as he didn't get physical with them, they wouldn't really develop feelings for him. But look what was happening to him now. If his current feelings were any indication, his so-called harmless flirtations had been quite hurtful.

He strolled casually past Emily's desk, where she was hard at work and concentrating as usual. He could probably dance around naked beside her desk without her noticing. He grinned at the thought. That could be fun... Abruptly the vibration of his cell phone interrupted his thoughts. It was a number he didn't recognize.

"Hello?"

"Hi Spencer. It's Candace."

"Hi... uhmm... Why are you calling?"

"It's nothing really. I just... I was like, kind of worried about Mrs. Gherring. You know, like, she didn't look so good after the hike. And I was like, I wonder if she's okay. You know?"

"Well, it's none of my business or yours, really. As far as I know, she's perfectly fine."

"Okay. Well good. I wanted to make sure she isn't dying or anything."

"Why would you think she was dying? What are you talking about?"

"Nothing. I was like... You know... There was a picture in the paper this morning..."

"What paper? What picture?"

"The NYC Word. It's a picture of her and... Well it's a bit blurry, but it looks like Mr. Gherring carrying Mrs. Gherring into the emergency room. And you know, the story said she might be, like, dying. So, I wondered..."

"That paper is trash, and you shouldn't be reading it. And she's not dying. I'm working, and I've got to go."

Spencer glanced back toward Emily's desk to make sure she hadn't heard anything. She was still bent over her computer. Should he tell her about the paper? Should he tell Mr. Gherring? Yes, Gherring would want to know, but he shouldn't tell Emily. She'd only be upset.

He sent a text to Gherring's cell phone, apprising him of the tabloid picture. Hopefully, with a really blurry photo, no one would take any stock in the story.

Back at the break room, he poured himself a cup of coffee. Then he got a great idea... He could make Emily a cup of tea—she'd have to notice him if he brought tea to her. He carried both cups over to her desk, and stood waiting patiently, but she never looked up from her work. Finally, he bent over to put the tea on her desk.

"I brought you—"

"Oh!" She jerked spasmodically at the sound of his voice, flinging her arm and knocking the tea out of his grasp. He jumped back, but not before the hot liquid flew through the air and landed on his pant

71

leg. His sudden movement jostled the coffee in his left hand, sloshing it onto his shirtsleeve.

"Oh... I'm sorry. You startled me."

He stood dripping before her, surveying his drenched clothes. Oh well, at least she was paying attention to him. When she gave him an embarrassed smile, he decided it was probably worth it. When she asked, "Was that tea? For me? How sweet!" he decided it was definitely worth it.

She ran to the bathroom and returned with a handful of paper towels with which he mopped vainly at his sodden clothes.

"Uhmm, I was wondering if you wanted to go climbing Tuesday night. And I thought maybe we could get some pizza."

"Well, I've already got plans. I'm—"

"That's okay. Maybe another time." Of course she'd have plans. What was he thinking?

"Wait. I'm going with your sister."

"My sister?"

"Grace. I'm going with Grace to an art class."

At least it wasn't another guy, but he disliked this development on so many levels. His sister was way too nosey. She'd be trying to meddle in their *friendship*. And now, he'd have to compete with Grace for Emily's time. It wasn't fair. He was trying to be so careful and not make any big mistakes. Grace would be able to plunder in and become best friends with her. And Grace would be able to get reports from Emily about what Spencer had been doing. It would be even harder to hide his growing feelings for Emily from Grace.

"Oh. Okay."

"We could maybe go on Wednesday. If you wanted."

Spencer cursed under his breath. "I promised to help Papa with a project on Wednesday night. Maybe Thursday?"

"There's this jazzercise class I was planning to go to. Pizza after?"

"Absolutely." This wasn't going to be easy. Especially when he was trying desperately to appear so casual about the whole friend thing.

He started to walk away, still holding the damp paper towels.

"Oh, and Spencer?" He turned back to see her cast him a crooked smile. "Thanks for the tea." He swallowed a lump in his throat. He was in trouble.

*****

    Anne hated the hospital. It was cold and hard and scary and full of germs. Really sick people came to the hospital and left their microbes behind. She wasn't usually a germaphobe, but hospitals were different. Everyone had on gloves and a mask when they entered her room—everyone but her. Where was her protection? Was she supposed to be protected by that squirt of antiseptic lotion from the container hanging on the wall in the hallway? Even though no less than five million germy hands had touched the dispenser? She imagined the tiny bugs suspended in the air, riding on invisible air conditioning currents and floating in through her nostrils. Did they collect on her nose hairs? If she blew her nose a hundred times a day could she blow them all out before they wormed their way into her interior?

    She hadn't been in the hospital very many times—once for each birth, and once for a broken ankle. The one thing she remembered from previous experience was still true... No one would let her sleep. The nurses made a habit of coming into her room multiple times during the middle of the night, flipping on the lights and taking her vitals. What are vitals anyway? It must have something to do with vitality, because after a night of having her vitals taken, she never had any vitality left. And why did the guy with the little bucket of vials and needles feel the best time to draw blood from her arm was at three a.m.?

    Steven had slept in her room on a hard little couch that made into a hard little bed—little being the operative word. His feet were hanging off the end, and his arms were dragging on the floor—the germy floor. She'd tried to make him go home to sleep, but he silenced her with his piercing blue eyes beneath a no-nonsense scowl. He was looking for a fight, and she didn't have the strength to engage. But by morning, he was firmly on her side when she begged to go home. Though it hardly seemed possible, he looked more exhausted than she did.

    Being a man who was used to getting his way, he set about to make things happen. Money was never an issue, except for its utility to get what he wanted. When the doctor came by to talk about Anne's treatment plan, Steven had already arranged for Spencer's mother to be her full-time nurse at the apartment. Although the doctor looked as if she might object, she quickly recognized Steven was unstoppable when he was on a mission.

"Okay, so the nurse? What did you say her name was?"

"Connie Marshall."

"She'll need to administer according to this IV prescription. And she'll need to keep exact records and report vitals. I'm going to need lab work at regular intervals. We'll have to make adjustments each day based on her lab results. We can't know yet whether she'll need TPN in the future."

He was nodding his head. "Yes, yes. I understand. We'll do everything by the book and communicate with your office."

"And if her vitals start dropping, you'll have to come back to the hospital."

"Yes, of course," he said impatiently. "Now if you'll please sign the release form."

He checked a text message that buzzed on his cell phone and his lips formed an expletive.

"What's wrong?" Anne asked.

"It's nothing. Just something else I need to take care of."

"Everything's backing up at work, and I'm no help at all. Could you let me work a little bit from home? I'd feel so much better. Like I'm contributing something. Right now I feel like a leech."

He smiled at her. "But you're such a cute little leech."

"Steven, I'm serious."

"No, you can't work from home. Perhaps after we're certain you're not going to pass out at a moment's notice."

"What about the Switzerland trip in two weeks? Will I get to go?"

"No," replied the doctor, not even bothering to look up from her paperwork.

"But what if I'm better by then?"

The doctor ignored her question. "Mr. Gherring," she said as she handed him the release form. "I hope you're making the right decision. I can't be responsible for—"

"I'm well aware of the liability issues here. I know we're responsible for whatever happens outside of this hospital."

"As long as you know." The doctor slipped out the door.

"I'm going home now?"

"Yes, but... I need to take some precautions."

"What type of precautions?"

"Just relax for a bit." He disappeared from the room and came back twenty minutes later with a surgical gown, hat and mask, a baseball cap, and a huge teddy bear.

"Put your hair up in this cap and sit in the wheelchair with the teddy bear," he ordered while donning the surgical gear. "We're not going out the front door; we're going out the side. And I called a taxi—we can't walk outside and climb into a limousine. I think they may have spotted us coming in, so we need to avoid them going out."

"Who's *they*? The press?"

"No. You know... It was just people. I overheard someone saying something about us coming in a limo, and they were wondering who we were. So I want to be more careful this time."

"Okay."

"Ready to go?"

"Yes, but..." She looked at him and started giggling.

"What? What's so funny?"

"Could you keep that stuff at home for later on? I've always had this fantasy about doing it with a doctor."

*****

Emily knocked on the penthouse door. She was so relieved when Steven called her after work to say her mom was out of the hospital. But she was nervous they'd taken her advice and hired Spencer's mother to be their nurse. What if they didn't like her? What if they fired her for some reason? She'd be mortified to face any of the Marshalls again. Steven yelled for her to come in. She opened the door to discover her mom sitting on the couch, attached to an IV bag hanging from a mobile pole.

"Hey, Mom. You look better. How do you feel?"

"Better now I'm away from that awful place. How does anyone get better in a hospital?"

"And you're eating?"

"Yes, and we're figuring out what my triggers are. I can't stand food with strong smells. Everything has to be really bland. And I can't eat and drink at the same time. But I've eaten three crackers since two o'clock and they didn't come back up." She seemed quite proud of this accomplishment.

Emily was thinking this was too much information, so she changed the subject. "Where's Connie?"

"She's gone home for the night," said Steven. "She's only going to be here while I'm at work, and she's on call if we have a question or an emergency."

"Do you like her?"

"She's really sweet," said Anne. "I like her a lot."

"She's keeping the location of her job confidential with her daughters," said Steven. "Her story is she got a private nursing job, which is true. And I'll make sure she gets a great reference for her next job."

"But Spencer knows?" Emily asked.

"Spencer's in the loop. He helped us get everything set up with his mother. And he's the one who warned me about..." His words stopped abruptly.

"Warned you about what?" asked Anne.

"Uhmm... about... his family... being so close and all. That it might be good to keep his sisters in the dark."

"I thought that was Connie's idea," said Anne.

"Uhmm, yes, they were thinking along the same lines."

"So what's for dinner?"

"I ordered food to be delivered, so your mom doesn't have to smell it cooking. Some pastas and salad." He turned to Anne. "I'm hoping you might be able to stomach some pasta with or without sauce."

"Maybe." She scrunched up her nose.

"So Mom, I'm going to an art class tomorrow night."

"Really? That sounds fun. How did you hear about it?"

"I'm going with Grace. That's Spencer's oldest sister."

"So, does this mean you're getting closer to Spencer?"

"Lay off, Mom. He's really nice and all, but he's a player. You told me so yourself."

"I said that? I think what I said was there are always girls hanging around him." She cocked her head to the side. "So what do these sisters look like?"

"Well three of them are tall—taller than me. And Grace, the oldest one is short. She only comes up to here." She held her hand up to her chin.

"You know, it's possible some of the girls I saw hanging around were his sisters."

"Oh... Well Grace made a comment about him having a lot of female friends. I guess she could have been teasing, but he didn't deny it." She paused, pursing her lips. "Maybe I'll find out the real truth from Grace."

"That's a good idea—he's been so sweet."

"Yes, but we're only friends, Mom. Don't push."

"I'm not," Anne said innocently. "But I'm trying to find a match for him. Remember? One of my nurses was about the right age. Tall and thin. Pretty. Maybe she'd be a good match."

She felt a small knot in her stomach. "I don't think he'd like to date a nurse. They wouldn't have anything in common."

"She said she liked doing outdoors stuff. They might have that in common."

"Oh." Emily was irritated. And her irritation irritated her even more. "Well, I still think he's not interested right now."

"We'll see... I'm sure Connie will be helpful. And we'll be together eight hours a day. I don't know why you're doubting my abilities. I have a pretty good track record."

Steven grinned. "Let's see... How many different women did you consider as my possible mate?"

"Okay, I didn't do so well with you. But that's because you kept messing with my mind."

"That's because I wanted to mess with more than your mind."

Emily spoke in a pleading voice. "Could you two please remember there are innocent ears in the room?"

"You mean you don't want to hear how I fantasized about your mom—"

"Na-na-na-na. I'm not listening. Na-na-na-na." Emily put her fingers in her ears.

Anne giggled. "Oh. I haven't really felt good enough to laugh in a while. But it makes me dizzy."

With a knock at the door, their food was delivered. Steven and Emily ate at the table to keep any strong food aroma away from Anne, who managed to swallow a few bites of pasta while sitting on the couch.

"I'm going to be so out of shape by the time this is over," complained Anne. "The doctor said I shouldn't stress my body with exercise. When I was pregnant with y'all, I was doing all my normal exercise the whole time. I hardly slowed down at all."

"Well, I think I shouldn't try to do an Iron Man competition this summer. I'm already getting behind on my training."

"But, I hate for you to miss it. If we have a baby—"

"*When* we have the baby," he said. "*When* we have the baby, I can still do a competition next year. I'm not planning to drop the training altogether. I don't have to do it every year, as long as I don't slack off too much."

"Maybe next year, Spencer could do an Iron Man competition. Y'all could maybe train together," said Emily. She noticed her mom's smug smile. "And my suggestion doesn't mean anything. He's only a friend. And you have to promise you won't talk about me to Connie."

"Well, of course I'm going to talk about my children to Connie. And she'll talk about hers as well. That's what moms do."

"You know what I mean."

"Yes, I do."

"So, you promise?"

"I promise."

At her easy capitulation, she was suspicious. "What exactly are you promising?"

"I promise I know what you mean." Her mom's smile was way too devious.

*****

Tuesday morning, Grace called Spencer at work, and alarms went off in his head. They communicated every day, but usually with a text or two. And she'd never called him at work before. His mind was quickly filled with images of accidents and emergencies, as he hurried to answer.

"Grace? What's wrong?"

"Why do you think something's wrong? Can't a girl call her brother unless there's a problem?"

"Not you. What's wrong?"

"It's just... I didn't know if I should even bother you. But I saw these pictures of Mr. and Mrs. Gherring in the paper."

"Oh, yeah, I heard about that yesterday. But it's a pretty blurry picture, right? I mean, you can't really tell for sure who they are?"

"Well, yesterday's was like that, but today's picture is really clear. I don't know what she looks like, but it's definitely Steven Gherring."

"Today's picture?"

"Yes, today's picture shows them walking together. And she looks really sick, and she's hanging onto his arm." She paused and cleared her throat. "It looks like they're coming off a hiking trail."

Spencer's stomach was instantly in knots. "Did she have on a pink tank top? And was his shirt white?"

"Yep."

"And what does the story say?"

"It's something awful about her having some mystery ailment the doctors can't cure. They talk about her body wasting away and so forth. It even says something about Gherring getting back on the Most Eligible Bachelors list."

Before he could stop himself, a curse slipped from his mouth.

"Spencer! Watch your mouth. Anyway, it's only a tabloid story."

"You don't understand how Mrs. Gherring is about this stuff. She gets mortified. Mr. Gherring's going to be furious. Does it look like they're walking toward the parking area?"

"Yes, definitely. You can even see the hood of a car. Why?"

"The four of us were the only ones in the parking area when we were waiting for the Gherrings to come off the trail. It had to be one of the girls."

"Your friends you brought along from the hiking club? One of them took the picture?" asked Grace. "Oh, shoot!"

"I know."

Spencer stared at the picture on the front page of NYC Word. It was clearly the Gherrings, and Mrs. Gherring looked as sick as his sister had described her. The story was worse than he'd imagined—supposed reports of eyewitnesses who'd seen her pass out, a quote from a doctor who proposed likely diagnoses. He berated himself for agreeing to take Becca and Candace on the hike. Now, he was responsible for this fiasco. He could lose his job. But more importantly, he could lose Emily. He was hoping to someday be more than friends, but now he might even lose her friendship.

He had to find out who'd taken the picture. It must have been Candace. She'd seemed all too interested in Mrs. Gherring's health, and she'd told him about the other picture and story in the NYC Word. Sigh. He'd call Becca first.

"Hi Spencer. What's up? Are you going on the overnight hike this weekend?"

"No, I can't. But that's not why I called."

"Why did you call?"

"There was a picture in a tabloid today. A picture of the Gherring's coming off the hiking trail. Does that sound familiar?"

"No. What are you saying?"

"I'm saying either you or Candace took that picture and gave it to the tabloid."

"I didn't do it!" Her voice was indignant. "I would never do something like that. I don't think Candace would either. How do you know someone else didn't take the picture?"

"There was no one else in the parking lot, and the picture was taken from right behind where I was standing. I'm pretty sure it was Candace, but I thought I'd call you first. This is really bad. It was an awful thing to do to them, and I could lose my job over it."

"Oh... I just can't believe Candace would do something like that. I thought I knew her pretty well. I'm really sorry, Spencer. I hope it won't affect things between us. If I find out she really did it, I won't be her friend any more."

He cringed. Did she really think there was something between them? "It's okay, Becca. The damage has been done now."

"S-sorry. D-do you want me to talk to her?" Great—now she was crying. He was going to swear off women altogether.

"No. I'm calling her right now."

"You have her phone number? I didn't know you were friends."

"She called me yesterday, so I have it. We're not friends, especially not now. Becca, I need to go."

"Okay. Bye Spencer. Will I see you this weekend?"

"I really don't know, Becca." He disconnected the call. Was this his fault, too? Had he done something to make her believe they had a real relationship beyond friendship?

He called Candace's number. No answer. He tried again, and left a message.

"Candace, this is Spencer. We need to talk. Please call me." Then he sent her a text asking her to call him ASAP.

He checked the time. He'd used up his entire lunch break. Not that he was hungry anyway—his stomach was lurching. He knew what he had to do. He had to be the bearer of bad news to Steven Gherring. He folded the newspaper to hide the picture and walked back to the office building. To the elevator. To Gherring's office. Blood was pounding in his head, and his vision was blurry. He felt very much as though he were walking the plank. He raised his fist and knocked on the imposing carved wooden door.

Chapter Six

SPENCER THOUGHT HE HEARD a voice inviting him to enter, but his blood was pounding inside his ears so loudly, he couldn't be certain. Tentatively, he opened the door and peered inside. Steven Gherring was sitting at his desk, simultaneously eating his lunch and reading something on his computer. He glanced up as Spencer entered.

"Hi, Spencer. What brings you here? By the way, thanks again for helping us get set up at home with your mother. Anne would've gone crazy if she'd had to stay in the hospital another day. What am I saying? I would've gone crazy."

He fought the sudden desire to retreat back out the door. How was he going to break the news? What would Gherring say? What would he do? Would he realize Spencer had no prior knowledge of the picture? Surely he wouldn't think Spencer was implicit. It didn't matter. It was still his fault. He was the one who'd brought Candace on the hike. Ultimately, it was his responsibility.

"Spencer? Is something wrong?"

"I... Yes..." He moved stiffly to Gherring's desk and placed the offensive paper in front of him. "I'm so sorry... I promise I had no idea."

Gherring stared at the tabloid picture, his jaw flexing. His hands clenched into fists. He grabbed the paper and read the article, cursing under his breath. He wadded up the paper and threw it across the room and let his face fall into his hands, supporting his head with his elbows on the desk.

"It's my fault. I should never have let them come with us. I take total responsibility—"

"Who was it? Becca or Candace?" He spoke between his fingers.

"Candace. I'm almost positive. I tried to call her, but—"

"Does Emily know?" Gherring looked up.

"I don't think so."

"It'll make the six o'clock local news."

"Surely not. It's only a tabloid." Spencer's words were raspy, his throat dry.

"A television reporter called me and asked for a statement. I refused, because I thought it was based on the first picture. But now..."

"What can you do? Can you sue them?"

"I'm a public figure. I can't sue them. Medical professionals are bound by HIPA. But I can't sue somebody for taking a picture of me in public, even though I was generous enough to drive her to and from the hike in my vehicle. And even if I could sue Candace, what would I get from that? And the tabloids know what they can say and get away with it."

"I'm so sorry."

Gherring shook his head. "We were the ones who decided to go on a hike. I never really thought it was a good idea, but Anne can talk me into almost anything. I just wish we'd never gone. Don't torture yourself. It wasn't your fault. But I swear if I ever see Candace again, I might break her neck."

He shivered at the fierce expression on Gherring's face. "What are you going to do?"

"I've got to talk to Anne, and then I've got to do some damage control."

When he left Gherring alone in his office, he heard loud cursing and banging through the heavy wooden doors. He was lucky not to be on the receiving end of Gherring's anger.

*****

Anne was feeling pretty chipper for someone attached to an IV pole. She'd only thrown up once, and she'd managed to keep down an entire piece of toast. She was due to go back to the doctor tomorrow, and she hoped her lab report would be good. At least with the IV, she was well hydrated and her dizziness had eased.

She'd asked Connie all about her family, and was entertained all morning with tales of raising five children in a small New York City apartment. Connie's husband, Joe, was a high school math teacher. They'd met in junior high and fallen in love. But their teen relationship had been stormy, with lots of breakups and fighting and jealousy. They'd broken up for good by their senior year. Then shortly after Connie had been licensed as an LVN and started work at a hospital, Joe broke his leg. He spotted Connie in the hospital hallway and chased her down in a wheelchair to ask her out. They got married a year later and had just celebrated their twenty-eighth anniversary.

"We enjoyed meeting Emily at dinner Sunday night. She must be very bright to already have her CPA license at such a young age.

"She's smart, but she's not great with relationships."

"Because she's shy?"

"Yes, she's shy and cautious... afraid to lose control. I think it all goes back to losing her dad when she was eight. She was the big sister, you know. She tried to be strong for Charlotte. It broke my heart to see that little girl trying to be so grown up."

"She told us she lost her grandparents, too."

"Interesting. She doesn't usually talk about it. She must feel really comfortable with your family."

"She does seem a little timid."

"Yes, we had a really rough few years after that. But Emily changed. She'd always been a good kid. But after the accident, she was—I don't know—driven. Driven to be perfect. She studied. She obeyed. She danced ballet. She made good grades. She excelled. But she never played or relaxed."

"She didn't do anything for fun?"

"Well, I think her only escape was reading. Even ballet was something to be conquered with discipline. But she loved reading. That and painting. But she always painted for herself, not for competition or to show anyone." Anne pursed her lips. "That's why I was really surprised she agreed to go to an art class with Grace."

Connie chuckled. "Grace is a force to be reckoned with. She could probably talk an ostrich into flying. Everyone seems to do exactly what she wants."

"Well in that case, I'm glad they met. Emily's the type who'd work and read and never get out and do anything. I think this class could be really good for her."

Her cell phone rang, and Connie left the room to give her privacy.

"Hi, Sweetie. I'm feeling better. I bet I've gained a pound."

"Really? What have you eaten? I mean, what stayed eaten?"

"A piece of toast."

"Well if you gained a pound from that, it must have been some really heavy bread."

"Okay, maybe I haven't gained a pound yet, but I feel like I'll be able to."

"I'm glad you're better." His voice became serious. "I need to talk to you about something. Okay?"

Her heart began to beat rapidly. She could tell from his tone something was wrong. "What is it? Is Emily okay? Did something happen? Is it work?"

"Calm down—Emily's fine. There's no emergency. But there's been a development, a kink in our plans to hide the pregnancy. I think we may have to go public sooner than we thought. I don't think we can wait until you're showing."

"Why? Did someone slip and say something?"

"No... I'm so sorry, Anne. You know you're more important to me than anything. Right? I'd give up all my money, Gherring Inc., everything for you. In a heartbeat."

"What are you saying?"

"I'm so angry I couldn't protect you—that my money and my position put you in the public eye. And I'm so frustrated I don't have the power to shield you."

"Shield me from what?"

"From people. From the press." He groaned. "Someone took a picture of us, and it's obvious you aren't well in the photo. And the story is speculative and nasty."

"It's... It's in the paper?" She couldn't help the tears that came to her eyes.

"Yes, only a tabloid. But... But someone called me about it, asking questions. A television reporter."

She tried to respond, but she couldn't think of anything to say. She let the tears roll down her face.

"Anne? Are you there?"

"Y-yes. I'm h-here."

"Sweetheart, I'm so sorry. If you want, we'll fly to South America and hide out until the baby comes."

She didn't say anything. They both knew that scenario couldn't happen.

"Y-you tell them th-the truth. T-tell them the whole st-story. You make something g-good come out of th-this."

"What do you mean? What good can possibly come out of this?"

"My problem. M-my condition is r-rare. But I'm not the only one. And th-the other women. People don't underst-stand it. Th-they think it's only morning sickness. A-and those other women don't have the m-money for a private nurse."

"So what do you want me to do? Pay for private nurses for all those other women?"

"No. If I'm going to have my p-picture plastered all over, I might as w-well be a poster child for this thing."

She took a deep shuddery breath. "There's probably a foundation or a society or something. We can raise awareness and help people understand and raise money for research."

Anne felt humiliated, but she also felt militant. She hated losing. Ever! This seemed like the only way to win.

"Wow. Okay. That's not the response I expected. But then again, I never seem to be able to predict anything you're going to do."

"So, will you do it?"

"I'll do anything you want. But you'd better be sure. There's no going back with something this big. We're talking television interviews, magazine interviews, public speaking. Do you really want to do that?"

No. She didn't want to do any of those things. None. Not a single one. She wanted to be anonymous. Her tears began to flow again.

"Yes. Just do it."

*****

Emily wondered why Steven had called her into his office. When she arrived, his office looked as if a bomb had gone off. He must have thrown an awful tantrum.

"What happened in here?"

He looked around as if noticing for the first time the books and papers he'd flung across the room. "Oh. I must have lost my temper. I'm okay now."

He strode quickly across the room to grasp her shoulders. "I need to warn you about something."

"What?" Emily couldn't even imagine a scenario that would cause Steven to lose his temper and then require her to be warned.

He started pacing as he pushed his hand through his hair repeatedly. "It's a long story. But, basically, the press has gotten wind your mother is sick. Actually, they've got two pictures and a lot of speculation."

He stopped in front of her, his hair askew. "And we're going on television tonight to explain everything."

"What? Mom agreed to this?"

He shook his head. "I know. I can't believe it either. It was her idea. Her way of making lemonade out of lemons."

"Tonight? But Mom looks terrible."

"Personally, I think she looks beautiful, but she agrees with you. The news crew is sending over a makeup artist right now. I'm mostly worried the stress will be bad for her. Our doctor's agreed to be interviewed as well."

"Why are you doing this? Isn't this going to make everything worse? I thought Mom hated being in the papers, much less on TV."

"I know. Believe me, I know. I hope she doesn't regret it. She's planning to raise awareness for women suffering from hyperemesis gravidarum. She says it's the only way something good can come out of this."

"Okay, thanks for the warning."

He rubbed his forehead with his fingers, squeezing his eyes shut. "This isn't how I wanted to tell people about the baby. I wanted to announce it some fun way and hand out cigars."

"Well, it's not too late."

"For what?"

"It's not too late to announce it and hand out cigars. You've got an hour and a half before five o'clock. I'll go buy cigars or candy or whatever you want. You call a meeting for the whole company."

His face brightened. "You really think I should? It could be fun, I guess."

"Let's do it!"

*****

Spencer was nervous when he got the notice about the company-wide emergency meeting at four thirty, with only an hour's notice. Did this have something to do with the newspaper story? He was relieved Gherring hadn't blamed him, but he still felt responsible. Gherring had been angry, as expected. What he hadn't expected was how frustrated Gherring was. He thought someone as rich and powerful as Steven Gherring would've been able to fight the paparazzi and send some heads flying. But evidently that wasn't the case.

Sam found Spencer, and she pulled him to the side. "This is really weird. We've never been called together for a last minute meeting before. Maybe he's going to close down a branch and lay some people off."

"Why would he do that? Is the stock doing badly?" He wondered if the tabloid speculation could actually hurt Gherring Inc. financially.

"No. No the stock's up, actually. I don't know—I'm worried because this isn't normal."

The noisy group fell completely silent as Gherring entered. His face was stern as he looked over the large group, standing awkwardly and craning to see. He motioned to the side. Emily and Gherring's secretary approached him, carrying two large boxes. Gherring stood up on a chair.

"I'm sorry we don't have a conference room large enough to accommodate all of you. I have a very important announcement to make." He paused, and the audience waited in uneasy silence.

"The timing on this is a bit awkward. We didn't really want to make this announcement until we were closer to the actual time, so we'd be sure it would actually happen." He paused again, and the group began to murmur. Suddenly Gherring's face changed. His dimples flashed, and mouth stretched in a huge grin.

"I'm going to be a dad!"

There was a moment of shocked silence, and then the whole group started cheering and clapping, sending out shouts of congratulations. Spencer could tell the employees really liked Gherring and were genuinely happy for him.

"And!" Gherring shouted over the crowd noise, "I've got cigars and candy for everyone so we can celebrate. But please, remember no smoking at the office." He chuckled with the employees.

"But... there is more," he added, with a more somber expression. "Anne's having some serious complications, and the media got possession of some pictures... To make a long story short, we've got a television interview about it tonight. But we didn't want you to be the last to know."

Sam whispered, "I thought she didn't look well this week. And she's so thin—that can't be good."

"She's already considered a high-risk pregnancy," Gherring continued, his face lined with worry. "And she has a condition called hyperemesis gravidarum. Anne and I would both really appreciate your prayers."

He reached out to Emily and caught her hand, giving it a squeeze.

"But we're not going to let that stuff take away from how excited we are." He grinned sheepishly. "We're pregnant!"

*****

"I saw your mom and dad on the news tonight," said Grace as she and Emily made their way toward the art class. "It sounds really scary. Are you worried about her? I thought she was really brave to go on television like that, but she looked really thin. Has she gained any weight at all?"

Emily giggled as Grace prattled on. How on earth would she ever answer a question? Grace never stopped talking long enough for her to say anything. But she enjoyed her new friend's enthusiastic chatter.

"I'm so excited you're going to this class with me. Just wait until you see the art teacher. He's so hot! And he's mysterious and sort of, I don't know, sultry." Grace gave a little shiver to emphasize her words. "But he's got this strict policy of not dating students. Which is too bad, because I'd love to lock lips with the guy. His voice is even romantic, and he talks so... You'll have to meet him to understand."

"How old is he? I pictured the art teacher as being about fifty for some reason."

"Oh, he's older, but not that old. He's like thirty-two I think. And the whole class is girls. I think there's maybe one guy out of twenty.

And the girls all flirt with him and try to get his attention, even though he says he won't date a student."

"Well I won't flirt with him—I'm going to this class to improve my technique."

"Me, too. But I'd like a chance to improve my technique with him in other areas in addition to art."

"My, oh my! What would your brother say if he heard you talking like that?"

"Spencer? He's already got his technique down pat. He can't fault me for getting in a little practice."

For some reason the topic of Spencer's love life irritated her. How many other girls had there been? She decided to change the subject.

"Are you sure I can join the class now? Isn't it the middle of the course?"

Grace shrugged. "It doesn't matter because it's not for credit or anything—they'll prorate your fee. He's the most popular teacher at the Art Academy. You'll understand why when you meet him."

Emily decided she wouldn't mind a little eye candy. But she wasn't going to be swept off her feet by any guy, no matter how suave and debonair. At least that's what she told herself before she actually met Asher Denning.

He greeted each student by name as they entered the classroom. His blond hair was a bit too long, but it suited his face, which could only be described as beautiful. His eyes were a brilliant blue and his jaw was strong. Emily couldn't stand a guy with a weak jaw. His face had a few days of stubble on it, giving him a laissez faire appearance. He was about six feet tall and tanned, with the broad shoulders and chest that came only from hours of lifting weights. His athletic build was at odds with his artistic bent and smooth mannerisms. He looked good, and he knew it. No wonder he didn't date any girls in the class, he was probably in love with himself. Then he spoke to her and she was lost. He had an English accent—he was her dream guy.

"Hello. Who have we here? I know we haven't met, for I could never forget such a lovely visage."

She felt her face heat up. "I'm Emily Best. This is my first night, but I've painted before." That sounded so stupid. Why hadn't she thought of something clever to say?

"Well, Emily Best, I can't wait to see the results of your efforts tonight." He raised her hand and turned it over to examine her long slender fingers. "Such beautiful hands must do beautiful things." He pressed his lips to her hand before releasing it, and Emily giggled nervously. What was wrong with her? He was way too old for her, and she didn't trust him. But as he gazed at her through half-lowered lids, she felt a little thrill. Maybe it wouldn't hurt to enjoy a little flirtation. After all, he didn't date his students anyway.

Grace elbowed her. "Told ya."

As the two-hour class progressed, she was engrossed in her work. There was a lamp burning on a table in the center of the room. Each student was painting the lamp, with particular attention to recreating the glow emanating from the bulb behind the silk shade. Emily jumped as she felt someone touch her elbow.

"That's absolutely smashing." Asher breathed the words into her ear. "You've not only captured the glow, but you've revealed how the light illuminates the objects nearby."

Emily couldn't help but preen at his praise. "I've been painting for a long time."

"It's obvious. This class may be a waste of your time. I do provide private lessons as well." Then he leaned to whisper in her ear, "Perhaps we could meet for coffee and discuss the possibilities."

"But, I thought you didn't date your students." She spoke in a low voice, glancing to see if anyone could hear their conversation.

He raised his eyebrows in feigned innocence. "I only want to discuss your future educational opportunities, but I'll let you in on a little secret."

He moved closer to her ear. She could feel his warm breath on her neck. "I only say that so I don't hurt anyone's feelings. There's no policy here against socializing with students. I've simply not met a student who captured my interest before."

Emily blushed as her heart sped up. Asher Denning had turned down every other girl, but he was interested in her. She couldn't help but thrill at his attention.

"What do you say? Thursday night?"

"I don't know…"

"I promise I'm not a dodgy chap—totally above board. We'll just have a friendly chat."

Thursday night. She was supposed to go to a jazzercise class with Becca. And she'd told Spencer she'd get pizza afterward. She could go with Becca the next Thursday and make up some excuse for Spencer. She felt a little pang of guilt. It's not like she was doing something wrong. She and Spencer were only friends—they weren't dating. But she couldn't tell him about going out with Asher, since she'd declared she wasn't interested in dating anyone. She'd better not tell Grace either. Anyway, it was merely a chance to discuss her artwork. Ha—it was a chance to ogle Asher Denning and let him stroke her ego a little. She knew she was playing with fire, but she could handle it.

"Okay. But only coffee, right?"

"Yes, well it's a little place that has coffee and other beverages as well. There's a great new jazz trio playing on Thursday. I think you'll love it." He spoke a little louder. "Yes, that's great work with the light, Emily. Outstanding!"

"So what was Asher Denning saying to you during class tonight? I saw you turn red." Grace questioned Emily as they walked together toward the subway station. Her voice was teasing, but insistent.

She was grateful the darkness hid her fresh blush. "He was complimenting me on the way I used light. That's all." She felt a little bit guilty over the partial lie. It was true he'd been complimenting her technique. Grace didn't need to know he'd flirted with her and asked her out as well. Anyway, it was nothing. Just coffee. She wasn't really hiding anything, was she?

"I have to admit you're really good. Have you had a lot of lessons?"

She laughed. "No, not at all. But I read a lot of books about it and practiced religiously. I had a lot of finished watercolor paintings that looked like mud, but I kept plugging away. It's an escape for me."

"Wish I'd known about that when I was younger. With a bossy big brother and three whiney little sisters, I could have used an escape."

"But I think you're pretty good. Haven't you been painting for a while?"

"Only since last spring, when I took my first class with Denning. But I've been practicing a lot, just so he'll come by and exclaim about how expressive my paintings are." She chuckled. "I think expressive is code for tries hard but not very talented."

"Don't sell yourself short. I think you've got talent."

"Well, I'm not as good as you. You're amazing! Have you ever tried to sell anything?"

"No way. I'm not that good. And really, I only paint for myself."

"You must be pretty awesome to get Denning's attention your first night. Several girls were giving you dirty looks. Better watch out they don't slip some poison in your water bottle. Especially the way he was cozying up to you, like he wanted to see more than artwork."

Emily's cheeks burned furiously. "Grace, he wasn't—"

"Settle down—I'm kidding. I forget you don't know me that well yet. Our family teases all the time. But just for curiosity's sake... Are you and Spencer really friends?"

"Is this question an example of you teasing me again?"

"Oh, no. I really want to know the answer because I'm nosey. So, are you friends? Really?"

"Of course we're friends."

"No, I mean are you only friends?"

"We're only friends. Neither one of us wants to date anyone right now." That was true, wasn't it?

"Really? Spencer said he didn't want to date anyone?"

"That's what he told me. Why? Is he dating someone else?"

"That's just it—I can't figure him out. He's with girls all the time. But when he's around the family, he never lets us in on who he's actually dating. I'm itching to know what he's really up to. You two seem pretty close, so I thought you might be secretly dating."

She opened her mouth to deny the statement, but Grace cut her off before she could protest.

"No, it's okay. I believe you. But you still might be an inside source. I was hoping you could find out who he's dating. I'm pretty sure one girl's really after him, but I don't know if the feeling's mutual."

"Really? How do you know?"

Grace looked around as if someone walking beside them might be listening. "He forgot his cell phone at the house last night. And during the two hours before he came back for it, he got about ten phone calls from some girl named Becca." She smiled smugly.

She tried to keep her face neutral. Becca? Why was she surprised? She'd seen how aggressively Becca had pursued Spencer on the hike. He'd said they weren't dating, and claimed they were only friends from the hiking club. And Becca had been so friendly to her, even calling her Saturday night to ask her to go to Jazzercise this Thursday. Could she have an ulterior motive? Now she thought about it, she remembered Becca asking a lot of questions about how she knew Spencer. Maybe it was a good thing she was cancelling the jazzercise with Becca.

"I know Becca," she said carefully. "But I didn't realize they were dating."

"Honestly, I don't know for sure, but he's acting different. He usually talks about a ton of different girls, claiming all of them are friends. But recently, he quit talking about any girls at all." She arched her eyebrows. "That's why I know he's hiding something."

"Or maybe he isn't hiding anything. Maybe he got really busy—he told me he didn't have time to date anyone right now."

"Yeah, right," Grace scoffed. "Spencer claiming he doesn't have time to date? He always has time for girls. I don't know why he said that to you, but he knows better than to say something like that to me. I'd call him out in a second." She looked more determined than ever. "I'm gonna figure this out if it kills me."

"Well, let me know what you find out. I'm curious, too."

"Truthfully, I was hoping it was you. Why don't you want to date anyone right now, anyway? You're finished with school. You should have plenty of time to date."

"It's just... I don't really like to talk about it."

"Oh, well sorry to pry." Grace was quiet for a moment before busting out laughing. "No, that's not true. I love to pry. What happened? You'll feel better if you tell me. And I won't tell anyone—I'm great at keeping secrets."

"No really. It's embarrassing. I can't tell you."

"Okay, I'll tell you something embarrassing, and then you won't mind telling me your thing. Let me see... There are so many things to choose from..."

Emily chuckled. "No, you don't have to—"

"I know a good one. And it's about a guy, too. There was this really cute guy in my Geology class named Jake, and I was dying for him to ask me out. Then one day I got a text that said, *Hey this is Jake. Do you want to catch a movie on Friday?* So of course I text back *Yes*. And the next day I went up to him in class and asked him about it. And he was all confused and asked what I was talking about. It turns out the message was from a different Jake. It was sooooo awkward!" Grace laughed out loud.

"That really happened? That's awful. How can you laugh about it?"

"Stuff like that happens to me all the time. I'm an awkward disaster magnet. I guess I'm used to it. I drop stuff, trip and fall, say stupid things. I'm like a walking comedy skit. Okay, so give it up. What happened to you?"

Grace was certainly persistent. Maybe it would feel good to tell someone. She hadn't even told Charlie. "Okay. You promise not to tell anyone? Not your sisters? And especially not your brother?"

"I promise. Really. I mean it."

She sighed. "So there was this drop-dead gorgeous guy at my firm in Fort Worth. His name was Tristan. We went out four times. He was always making suggestions, you know, sexual suggestions. But I thought he was just flirting. On the fourth date, he declared if I really liked him I would prove it by sleeping with him, although his exact words weren't even that nice. And when I turned him down, he took me straight home without speaking to me. Two days later he was in a relationship with another girl in the office. After that, I swore off dating."

"Okay, he was a jerk, but that's just one guy. You shouldn't give up because of him."

"He was only the straw that broke the proverbial camel's back. Every other good-looking guy I've known has turned out to be a jerk or conceited or a player or something. I'm never attracted to the nice ones."

"So you don't want to date? Or you don't want to date Spencer? Do you think he's a player?"

"Isn't he?"

"To tell you the truth, I don't know. I know he's had a lot of different female friends. He's always claiming they're only friends and nothing more, just like with you. So maybe it's true. I only know one thing for sure. He's a crabby, bossy big brother, but he's really a sweet guy. He's not a jerk like most guys who're that good-looking. That may sound weird coming from a sister."

"I think he's lucky to have a loyal sister like you. And I don't think he's a jerk either. He's been really nice to me. But I can't take a chance on getting hurt again. I'm thinking maybe the guys I've dated are too young. Maybe an older guy, someone who's more mature. Maybe someone like that would've outgrown the tendency to play games."

"Maybe... But I think you should give Spencer a chance."

"But he doesn't want a chance, remember? He told me he didn't want to date right now."

"Yeah, whatever." Grace rolled her eyes. "He may be selling, but I'm not buying."

Chapter Seven

Wednesday morning dawned, and Spencer was still angry and frustrated.

"Candace... This is Spencer calling. Again! Please call me back!" Spencer ended the call and resisted the urge to throw his phone across the room. He'd called and texted five times on Tuesday and called three times already on Wednesday. Candace hadn't returned a single phone call or text. He was more convinced than ever she was responsible for the Gherring's picture being given to the NYC Word. She was obviously avoiding him. He didn't even know what he was going to say when he finally talked to her, but he needed to give her a piece of his mind.

His cell rang, the caller ID showing Becca's name. She'd been calling him nonstop since the hike on Saturday, seemingly undiscouraged by his accusations on Monday. He let the call go to voice mail, but his phone slipped out of his hand and fell to the floor, bouncing under his desk. He rolled his chair back and leaned under the desk to reach the phone.

"Hey, Spencer. What're you doing?"

He jumped at the sound of Emily's voice, banging his head on the desk.

"Ow!" He sat up slowly, rubbing his head.

"Sorry. Are you okay?"

"No. I mean, yes. I guess I bumped my head. I was trying to pick up my phone." He held up the retrieved object.

"Sorry I startled you. Uhmm, I needed to talk to you."

"Sure, what's up?" He tried not to sound too eager. This was the first time she'd come by his desk—maybe it was a good sign. "How was art class with Grace? I'd love to see what you worked on."

"Uhmm, great. It was great." Her cheeks reddened.

"That is, if you want to show me. You don't have to."

"No, I don't mind. But, uhmm... about Thursday... I'm going to have to cancel pizza. I'm having dinner with Mom and Steven, so uhmm... I mean, I'm not going to jazzercise either."

He felt a knot in his stomach. She was ditching him, and she wasn't making eye contact. "It's okay. Your mom's more important. How's she feeling? Must be better if they're planning dinner."

"Yeah. Well, Steven and I will probably eat a real dinner, and she'll probably eat toast or something like that." She twisted her braid with one hand. "We could do it another time. Maybe this weekend?"

"Sure. Well, I'm supposed to go on an overnight hike this weekend."

"Oh. With Becca?"

"I don't think so. I think it's mostly guys from the hiking group, maybe one or two girls." He cocked his head to the side as an idea had popped into his head. "You could come if you want to."

Emily's face paled, and her eyes widened. "Oh, uhmm, I don't have the camping stuff."

"You could borrow some if you want to go. But, no pressure."

"Well, thanks for asking. And... and thanks for being so sweet about my mom and taking me to the hospital and getting your mother to be her nurse and all that."

"You don't need to thank me. I really like your mom and Mr. Gherring. And my mom's glad to have a good job."

"Okay. I'll see you later."

"Yeah, later." Watching her walk away, he felt like his chances of being more than friends were dwindling with every step.

His phone rang—Becca again. He declined the call and turned his phone off, running frustrated fingers through his hair until it looked as crazy as he felt. He must have done something to make God mad at him.

*****

Emily felt relieved she'd finished that detestable chore. She hated lying to Spencer, but she didn't want to hurt his feelings. Now she needed to cancel with Becca.

Becca answered the phone call quickly. "Hi, Emily. I'm glad you called. I was about to call you. I've been trying to reach Spencer. Don't you work in the same office? Is he there today?"

"Uhmm. . . Yes, I think he's here. But he probably doesn't answer his phone during work hours. You know how it is." She felt a surge of guilt at how easily the lie came to her lips. "I called you because I have to cancel for jazzercise tomorrow night."

"Oh."

"I'm sorry. I really want to go. Maybe next week?"

"Sure, that's fine," she said with a heavy sigh into the phone. "It's just that, uhmm... Well, I really wanted to talk to you. I mean, you're probably too busy to talk now, but..."

"No, I've got a few minutes to talk. What is it?"

"Well, it's about Spencer. You see, I thought we had a good thing between us, but lately he's been distant. And so I wondered if you two were... You know. Do you like Spencer? Is there something going on between you?" Emily could hear her sniffling. "Is that what you're doing Thursday night? Are you going out with Spencer? Because he isn't returning my phone calls."

"No, we're only friends, Becca. We're not dating."

"Are you sure? Because I wouldn't want to come between you or anything. You're not going out with him Thursday night?"

"No, I'm not. Actually Becca, if you can keep a secret..."

"What? I won't tell. What is it?"

"Well, I'm sort of going out on a date with my art teacher Thursday night. Although it's not really a date—it's only coffee."

"Really?" Her voice sounded hopeful. "So you don't mind if Spencer and I date?"

Emily felt her stomach churn. She didn't really like to think about Spencer dating Becca. But she couldn't really be upset about it if she was going out with Asher.

"No, of course I don't mind. Spencer and I are good friends. But he told me he wasn't really interested in dating right now. Maybe that's why he's been a little standoffish."

"Maybe so. I thought it might have been because of the picture. You know, the one in the tabloid."

"What picture? What are you talking about?"

Now Becca began to cry again. "He called me yesterday and accused me of taking a picture of your mom and sending it to the NYC Word. It must have been Candace. But he was pretty mad. And he hasn't answered my phone calls since then."

"What picture are you talking about? I didn't know about a picture."

"It was a picture of your mom when she came off the hiking trail. I guess Candace took the picture. But Spencer accused me. Isn't that why your mom went on TV last night?"

She tried to remember what Steven had told her. Something vague about the press having a couple of pictures.

"Candace had better steer clear of me for the rest of her life. I don't know what I might do or say if I see her again. And I can't believe Spencer didn't tell me about it yesterday."

"Oh, I hope you won't be too mad at him. I probably shouldn't have mentioned it. I think he told me he was going to keep you from finding out. He probably didn't want you to know."

"He has no right to keep something like that from me."

"That's how Spencer is. He does stuff like that all the time. I don't mind though—I think it's cute."

"Well I don't think it's cute at all."

"I'm sorry. I didn't mean to start a fight between you. Please don't tell him I told you. Then he'll be even madder at me. Please! I shouldn't have said anything."

"I won't tell him. But if you didn't take the picture, he shouldn't be mad at you anyway."

"I know." She sniffed again. "It's so awful. I like him so much, but he gets angry for no reason. But I always forgive him... I can't help myself."

This was a side of Spencer she'd never seen—controlling, angry, accusing, unforgiving. She felt a little better about her date with Asher, and a little less guilty for lying to Spencer about it.

"So where are you going on your date Thursday night?" Becca asked.

"We're supposed to meet at some place called Green Scene. It's not really a date, though. We're only going for coffee, and I'm paying for my own."

"I've been there. It's a cool jazz bar. What time are you going?" she asked casually.

"We're meeting at eight thirty. So jazzercise is definitely out."

"What are you wearing?"

"I don't know. I figured jeans."

"Oh, no. You need to dress up for that place. I think you should wear a dress or a skirt."

"Really, I thought it was a casual place."

"I'm sure you'll feel underdressed if you wear jeans. Is your art teacher cute?"

"Actually, he's pretty hot, but we're just going to talk about art class."

"Sure you are. Anyway, thanks for talking to me. I feel better."

"No problem. Maybe we'll do jazzercise next week."

"Sounds great."

Why would Spencer hide his relationship with Becca? Grace had mentioned how many times Becca had called his cell on Monday night, although he'd denied dating her. Maybe he preferred his girlfriends to be well endowed. Since he'd apparently lied to her about Becca, she wouldn't feel guilty for her little white lie concerning Asher.

*****

"Are you sure you feel up to it? I think it's a bad idea." Steven asked for what seemed like the umpteenth time.

"Steven. I'm much better. I've gained back two pounds."

"But the doctor said it's only water weight."

Anne put on her most sad puppy face. "Please, Steven. I haven't seen Gram and Gus in weeks."

"But you're not supposed to over-exert."

"I only have to walk to and from the car. I should be fine without the IV for three hours. And we can take it along just in case."

"But Gram will be upset when you don't eat anything."

"She's already upset. She'll be less upset when she sees I'm feeling fine and I can walk around. And I'll eat a bit. I'm doing pretty well with bread. Please, please, please! I'm going stir-crazy in this apartment all day."

"But it's only Wednesday night. You've only spent two days in the apartment, and you have Connie to keep you company."

"Yes, Connie's great, but I miss seeing people and doing things. You know how I am. One short evening out at Gram's house can't hurt anything."

"Fine. We'll go. But only if you have a really good day tomorrow." He seemed irritated. "I can't believe I let you talk me into these things. If something happens—"

"Nothing's going to happen."

"That's what you said when we went on the hike. Remember?"

"That marriage book said you couldn't bring up the past when you're having an argument. So you can't bring up Saturday."

"This is not an argument. This is you getting your way again, like you always do."

"Oh, and another rule was you're not supposed to say things like *you always* and *you never*."

"How about this... I seldom get my way because you *constantly* get your way because I'm a big *pushover* where you're concerned."

"Oh you're definitely not a pushover. I have to work hard to win every single battle." Steven started to tickle her, but she cried out, "Ouch, ouch!"

"What? Did I hurt you? Is it the IV needle?"

She laughed. "No, I was kidding."

"You're going to cry wolf one too many times."

With one hand, he pinned both of hers, and reached to tickle her side. She squirmed and cried out, laughing. He stopped when her cell phone rang.

"Saved by the bell, but only temporarily."

She answered the call, winking at him. "Emily, I'm glad you called. Really glad."

"Only a temporary reprieve," he whispered in her ear.

"Hey, Mom. I thought I'd invite myself up there for an early dinner on Thursday."

"You're in luck. We're going to Gram's on Thursday night for dinner. You can come with us. She'd love to see you, I'm sure."

"Oh... well I have plans for later in the evening on Thursday."

"Okay. We haven't eaten tonight. Why don't you come up? I really miss seeing people. Especially you."

"I can come tonight, but it doesn't really solve my problem."

"What's your problem?"

"I've sort of told a white lie, and I was trying to make it mostly true."

"How on earth did you get yourself in this sort of a pickle? Who did you lie to?"

"If I tell you, Mom, you can't tell anyone. Not even Steven."

"I won't tell Steven." At her declaration, he opened his eyes wide. "What happened?"

"I'm going to meet my art teacher for coffee Thursday night, so I canceled pizza with Spencer. And I told him I was having dinner with you so I wouldn't hurt his feelings."

"Honey, I can't give you any advice on telling lies. They always backfire on me. My recommendation is not to do it."

"But it's too late. I've already told it."

"Why would you lie to have coffee with this art teacher? Why didn't you meet at another time instead of canceling your date with Spencer?"

"It wasn't going to be a *date* with Spencer. I planned to buy my own pizza."

"Still, you made plans with him first."

"I know, and I feel bad. But not too bad, since Becca told me today they'd had a relationship. He evidently lied to me about her."

"I don't think I'd trust everything Becca says if I were you. I'd trust Spencer over Becca any day. And you haven't told me about this art teacher yet."

"He's... He was really impressed with my work. And he said we should have coffee and talk. He gives private lessons. And... Well, he's really good-looking."

"Better looking than Spencer?"

"No, just different. Older. More sophisticated. More mature. I don't know. Maybe I need someone older who wouldn't do immature things, like lying about a relationship with another girl."

"Sweetie, I can tell you from experience age doesn't equal maturity. And it seems odd you're criticizing him for a possible lie,

103

when you've told one yourself. But you're a smart girl—I trust your judgment. On the other hand, let me give you one little guideline."

"What is it? I really don't want a lecture, you know."

"If you find yourself changing or doing things you wouldn't normally do to please a guy, take a step back and analyze the situation. Ask yourself this... Is he helping you grow and be a better person, or are you changing in a bad way?"

"I can't blame Asher for my decision to tell a lie. I did that on my own."

"I trust you, Sweetie. I'm honored you talked to me instead of Charlie. I assume you haven't told her about this."

"No. I don't think she'd understand."

"You don't think she'd understand? Or you don't think she'd agree?"

"Same difference." Emily's voice was pouty. "Mom, he's got an English accent."

"Ah! Now I understand. We Best girls have a weakness for men with accents, I think." Steven's eyebrows knit dangerously, but she waved him off with a grin. "Be careful, Sweetie. I know you'll do the right thing. Are you coming up for dinner?"

"Do you promise we won't talk about this?"

"Hmmm? Talk about what? I don't even remember what we were discussing."

Emily chuckled. "Okay, I'll come."

"What was that about?" Steven asked as she disconnected.

"I can't tell you. I promised not to."

"But I overheard your side of the conversation."

"Yes, I didn't promise you weren't listening, and she didn't ask."

"You are getting more devious by the day."

"I'm learning from you, I think."

"I gather she cancelled with Spencer to go out with her art teacher who has an accent. And she lied about it to Spencer. And she believes something Becca told her about Spencer. Does that about cover it?"

"I couldn't really say."

"I have to admit, I don't much care for Becca after spending several hours with her. Her chatter was pretty inane. And I agree with what you told Emily about trusting Spencer. I have a lot of respect for him."

"Well, Emily's coming up for dinner, and you've got to pretend not to know anything."

"Got it," Steven agreed. "Now where were we?" He bent over to snatch her hands, pinning them together again, and reaching out to tickle her side as she squealed. "And this is for that remark you made about liking men with accents."

"Steven! You're making me scream. The neighbors will hear and think you're murdering me."

A wicked grin slid onto his face. "Penthouse, remember? No neighbors up here..."

*****

"Hi, Becca." Spencer finally surrendered and answered Becca's call while walking toward his parent's home.

"What's wrong? Why haven't you answered my calls? Are you mad at me?"

"No, Becca, I'm busy. I work—I don't have time to chat during the day. What did you need?"

"I wanted to make sure you weren't mad at me about the picture thing. You believe me don't you? About not giving the picture to NYC Word?"

"Sure, I guess I believe you, but I haven't talked to Candace yet. She won't return my phone calls. Have you talked to her?"

She hesitated. "Uhmm, no."

"Okay, Becca. If that's all, I've got a lot to do tonight."

"Well there's one other thing. There's a bunch of us going to the Green Scene Thursday night at eight thirty to listen to jazz. I thought you might want to come. Maybe Candace will be there, and you could ask her about the picture."

Spencer considered her offer. He really didn't want to spend any more time with Becca, especially if it might make her think they had a real relationship. On the other hand, he didn't want to sit at home and think about getting ditched by Emily.

"A bunch of people? Who's going?"

"I'm not sure. People from the hiking club."

"Landon usually texts me when the group is doing something."

"Well... it's not official, I think... Maybe Landon isn't going. We could go together if you want."

"No, I'd rather just meet everyone there."

"So, you'll come for sure?"

"I'm not positive. But, I'll probably come. I'd really like to talk to Candace."

"Do you want me to meet you outside?"

"No. Look, Becca... This is not a date. Okay? I don't want you to think I'm sending you any signals. I'm not interested in a relationship."

"I know. I don't expect anything from you, but I like spending time together. You know, with the whole group."

"Right. Okay. See ya later."

"See you tomorrow night. Eight thirty. Don't forget."

Spencer paused on the steps outside his family's home. He was helping his dad with a tiling project. He actually looked forward to some hard labor to work out his frustrations. When he opened the front door, he was immediately assaulted with the familiar noises of his sisters' gaiety. Laughter and squeals emanated from the kitchen, along with a cloud of something white. Smoke? Was the kitchen on fire? He ran into the kitchen, flinching as something hit his head.

"Oops! Sorry, Spencer! That was meant for Claire," yelled Olivia. Flour. They were fighting with flour.

"Are you crazy?" Spencer roared out. "Momma's going to flip when she sees this mess."

Claire giggled. "We'll clean it up before she comes home from hot yoga."

"Momma's doing hot yoga?"

"Yeah. She's decided she's fat, and she's planning to melt away her excess weight," explained Hannah as she ducked behind the table.

"She's not fat. And stop making any more mess—this flour will be impossible to clean up." He went to the sink to wet a towel and wipe his head.

"You're getting crabby," said Grace as she entered the kitchen. "I think you need a woman."

He pressed his lips together, refusing to take Grace's bait.

"Really, Spencer. What's wrong with you lately? Girl troubles?"

Ignoring her, he concentrated on wiping his shirt.

"Are you having problems with Becca?"

"Becca?" He was startled out of his silence. "Who said anything about Becca? Did Emily say something last night?"

"Ah ha! I knew it! I saw Becca's been calling you. Does Emily know something about Becca?"

He frowned. "No. She doesn't know... I mean, there isn't anything to know about Becca except she's a pain in the butt. But I don't want you talking to Emily about me."

"Hmmm... Maybe we could work out some sort of deal." Grace crossed her arms, drumming her fingers on her elbow.

"No way. I'm not working a deal with you. It couldn't possibly be fair."

"Fine. That's fine. If you don't want to know what Emily and I talked about..."

"Why did God give me sisters? If I had brothers, I could just beat you up until you gave in. Four chances to get a brother, and what did I get? Four sisters. Four sneaky, conniving, manipulative sisters."

"Come on, Spencer. You know you love me. I'm just asking for a little something in return for my knowledge."

"Fine. What type of a deal?"

Grace's face split in a triumphant grin.

"I don't even think I need to make a deal now. Knowing you're willing to consider this deal tells me what I need to know."

"No, it doesn't tell you anything." He stepped forward to glower down at his petite sister, forcing her to crane her neck to look up at him. "Whatever you think you know, you're wrong."

"I know you care what I talk about to Emily."

"What did you say to her? Are you the reason she— Never mind. Forget it." He spun his back to her, using a rag to make angry swipes at the messy kitchen. It was suddenly quiet behind him. When he turned around, he found himself alone with a contrite-looking Grace sitting at the table.

"I'm sorry... I didn't know."

"Didn't know what?" he asked, still frowning.

"I didn't know Emily was different. I didn't know you really liked her."

"I don't—"

"Good grief! Don't try to deny it. I'm your sister—I can tell. But maybe you're lying to yourself."

"I... I'm not... She doesn't like me. Not like that." He slumped in a chair across from Grace.

"Spencer, I didn't know." She put her hand on his. "I... I may have said something I shouldn't have."

"What? What did you say?"

"I told her about you getting all those phone calls from Becca."

He groaned. "Becca! I'm beginning to wish I'd never met her. Why would you tell Emily about that? How did you even know?"

"She called about eleven hundred times when you left your phone here Monday night. She's got a serious crush on you, for sure. Did you break up with her or something?"

"No! We've never even been on a date." He let his face fall into his hands. "I can't believe you told Emily about her calling. She probably thinks I've been lying to her."

"Well... I think she thinks you're a player."

"Why do you think that?"

"It's kind of what she said."

"So did you tell her it isn't true? Did you tell her I'm not a player?"

"Well, no... I mean, I thought you were a player, too. Why are you getting mad? It's true, isn't it? You've never denied it before. You're always with a different girl. You never seem to stay with one girl long enough for us to even meet her. It seems like you go from one girl to another or even more than one at the same time."

He stared at her in disbelief. "Really? That's what my own sister thinks about me? That's what you told Emily?" His face dropped back into his hands. "Great. That's just great."

"So what are you saying? All these girls are okay with it? Or they're all doing the same thing?"

His frustration reached a boiling point. "All these girls! What girls? Can you name one? Huh? Can you? No! You can't, can you? Because I've never actually even dated one. Not! One! Single! Girl! There—are you happy? Now you know."

Grace sat dumbfounded for a moment. "But... I've seen you with lots of girls. All the time. They were hanging all over you. They were practically drooling on you."

"So? Did you ever see me with one girl? Did I ever tell you I had a girlfriend?"

"Are you saying you were only with all those girls physically? That none of them meant anything?"

"My god, Grace! Don't you have any respect for me? I'd never do that. I wasn't with any girl physically—I've never even kissed a girl before."

"Oh," she said. "Oh!" she repeated, grinning. "Now there's something I never would have guessed. Why didn't you deny it before now? We've teased you about it for years?"

"Oh yeah. That's a great idea. I could go from being teased about having too many girlfriends to being tormented about not having any. And now I'll never hear the end of it."

Grace was quiet. "I'm sorry. I really am. I'm not mean, you know. I care about you—you're my brother. I'm actually on your side. We... We won't tease you."

"I don't care. Go ahead. It doesn't matter any more."

"So, uhmm... Do you like girls? I mean, it's okay. I love you no matter what. If you—"

"No. I don't like girls. Not girls, plural. I like Emily. Okay? Only Emily. But I guess it doesn't matter now." He buried his head in his arms on the table.

"It can't be too late. I'll tell her you're not a player."

"And tell her what?" He spoke into his arms. "That you were mistaken? That I've actually never had a girlfriend?"

"Uhmm. No. Maybe not that." She screwed up her face. "But I'll think of something."

He pushed back from the table and attacked the floury mess with a vengeance.

"No, I think you've done enough damage. I'm telling you, it's too late. Today, she acted really strange, and she blew me off for a date we'd planned tomorrow night. Not that she would do anything with me that qualified as an actual date, anyway."

"That doesn't necessarily mean anything."

"Sure. Whatever. Look, I need to go upstairs and help Papa with the tiling. Can you get them to clean up this kitchen before Momma sees it?"

109

"Don't worry about the kitchen. We'll take care of it." Grace followed him as he headed to the kitchen door and caught his arm. "Wait. I'm really sorry, Spencer. I never meant to hurt you."

He turned around to see her eyes welling with tears. "Don't cry, Gracie." He reached out and pulled her into a hug. "It'll be fine. It probably wasn't meant to be. And you were right... I never worried about my reputation before. So, it wasn't really your fault."

Truthfully, he'd always rather enjoyed having a status as a player. His guy friends had treated him with a sort of awe and reverence. And the constant flirting of the girls had been enjoyable as well. His reputation had never mattered until he met Emily. He rubbed his temples—his head was hurting. This had been a terrible day, but he felt almost relieved his sister knew the truth.

He brightened a bit. "You can make it up to me."

"How?" She narrowed her eyes.

"There are some people going to the Green Scene tomorrow night, and I think the girl who took that tabloid picture might be there. I want to go so I can confront her. But Becca's going to be there, and I don't want to do anything to encourage her."

"So you want me to go with you and run interference?"

"Would you do that?"

"Absolutely, big brother. It would be my pleasure."

"I thought that sounded like the sort of devious thing you'd like. And one more thing..."

"What?"

Spencer took three quick steps to grab the kitchen door and pull it open. Three sisters tumbled into the room on top of each other.

He speared them with a stern look until they all stopped giggling. "All of you will keep this information to yourselves. Or else!"

"Don't worry. I'll make sure they keep their mouths zipped. Really. I mean it. You'll see."

"I'm not holding my breath." He headed up the stairs to work with his father.

Chapter Eight

"So, I went to a hot yoga class last night," Connie confessed to Anne as she set up a fresh IV.

"I've heard of that. What is it, exactly? Was it fun?"

"Well, let's see. How can I describe it? They put you in what you think is an exercise room, but actually turns out to be an oven. Then they turn the temperature up to about two hundred degrees. I know it was below boiling, because all the sweat that ran off of me soaked into my clothes and then started falling into puddles on the floor mat. Only a little hotter and it would have turned into steam."

Anne started giggling. "So you just stood in a room and roasted?"

"Oh no. Then they make you get into strange and contorted positions, so you can lose your balance and fall into the sweat puddles and splash your neighbors."

Anne was laughing harder. "Ow! You're making my stomach hurt."

"I should have suspected something when I first went in the room because it smelled so bad. But you can't imagine the aroma of all those people sweltering and sweating together for an hour. I don't know if my eyes were watering from the fumes or from the sweat running into my eyes."

"Stop! Please!" Anne laughed. "I can't believe you stayed in there for an hour."

"I tried to get out," Connie declared with a straight face. "The door was locked. I banged on the glass door and screamed for help, but the people on the outside of the glass simply laughed and turned up the thermostat."

"Ohmygosh—you're killing me!"

"I passed out and almost drowned in my personal pool of sweat. But just in time the class ended. When I stepped out into the air conditioning, my sweaty clothes froze stiff. So I had to pry them off in the locker room, and I threw them away, rather than touch them again."

"So, I guess that's the end of hot yoga for you?" Anne wiped at tears of laughter.

"Oh no. I sweated away five pounds in an hour—it was worth it." Connie laughed. "I've known I needed to lose a few pounds for a while, but being around you has made me feel like an elephant."

"Right now, I'd make a stork feel like an elephant. Please don't use me as your measure."

"No, I'm kidding. My nursing training has motivated me to try to be healthier. I'm trying to exercise and eat better, too. And I'm determined to fatten you up a bit as soon as we can."

Would she ever really be able to gain weight? Every bite of food was still a challenge. Her nausea was barely in control, and strong smells still made her sick. But she couldn't let people know, especially Steven. She had to be strong for him—he already worried too much. She plastered on a happy face.

"Thanks, Connie. I'm sure I'll be able to eat more and more each day. You've been a life-saver for me."

Connie gave her shoulder a little pat. "You hang in there, honey. We'll get it figured out."

"How's Spencer?" Anne asked, trying to sound casual.

"He was over at the house last night, working with Joe. I only saw him for a bit after I came home from hot yoga. He seemed more quiet than usual, but he was probably tired." She smiled proudly. "He always makes time to come and help his father."

"He seems like a great guy. I can't imagine raising five kids. Are your girls as mature as Spencer?"

Connie shook her head. "Uhmm, no. Not quite. But they're getting there."

"I'd love to meet them. Emily really likes your family. Maybe we could get together when Charlie comes to visit."

"Now, Charlie is...?"

"Charlotte, actually. She goes by Charlie. She's my younger daughter."

"That could be really fun, although it might be a little loud, with six girls together. How old is Charlie?"

"She's about to be twenty-three."

"And is she a CPA like Emily?"

"Oh no. Charlie is more of a... free spirit." Anne chuckled. "She started college, but she had no idea what she wanted to do. So—at least for now—she lives in Colorado and leads rafting trips in the summer and teaches skiing in the winter. She's my adventurous, outdoorsy girl." Anne cocked her eyebrow at Connie. "To tell you the truth, when they all met last fall, I thought she and Spencer might hit it off."

Connie's eyes sparkled. "But it seems like Emily and Spencer have hit if off instead, doesn't it?"

"Well, not that I want to be an interfering mother—" Anne paused and then smirked. "Who am I kidding? I love being an interfering mother. I wonder if there's anything we could do to spur the relationship along?"

"What about Emily? Do you think she likes Spencer?"

"I think she's afraid of liking him. I think she's afraid of liking anyone."

"Why's that?"

"She wants everything planned out, and she likes to control things. And I think she's afraid to trust a guy. I'm really afraid Spencer will give up before she lets her defenses down."

"He doesn't really talk to me. Maybe the girls—I don't know for sure. I might ask Grace what she thinks. Surely we'll think of something."

"Yes, we'll have to think of something."

Anne's cell phone rang. "Hi, Steven."

"Hey, Sweetheart. I've got news for you."

"What's that?"

"Your first fan mail has started arriving. At least I assume that's what it is. We have a stack of letters addressed to Mrs. Anne Gherring, care of Gherring Inc."

"Seriously? Fan letters? What if it's hate mail instead?"

"It's possible, but not likely. Or it could even be people asking for money. But the HER Foundation told me they thought your interview would raise awareness. They expected some women to contact you.

You can even refer them all to the foundation if you want. I want to screen them for you, though, just in case there are any nutcase letters."

"Have there been any more articles in the tabloids?"

"No. Evidently, NYC Word doesn't consider you newsworthy since you went mainstream."

"I'm really glad it's over," said Anne.

"Yes, well... You know it's not exactly over. The HER Foundation mentioned having you as a keynote speaker for a fundraiser."

She felt the blood drain from her face. "I'm actually hoping my appeal will wear off before I have to do something like that."

"We'll see. But don't count on it. You could work on writing a speech in all your spare time at home," he teased.

"I'd like to do some real work. Surely there's something I could do from home. I'm hoping I can go back to work in a week or two."

"Hmmm."

"Hmmm? What does that mean?"

"Nothing. Just hmmm."

"I think that's short for I'm avoiding this subject. Don't you need me at work?"

"Nope, not at all. Things are so much better without you here."

"Steven!"

"What do you want me to say? Of course I miss you. We all do. But right now your health and the baby's health are the priority."

Anne let out a huge sigh. "I know, but I don't feel useful."

He chuckled. "When I come home tonight, I'll feel you and see if you feel useful."

"No thanks. I don't need any help to know how I feel."

"But I want to help." She could hear the smile in his voice.

"Steven, you're incorrigible."

"Oh yes, I'm definitely encouragable."

*****

Spencer's heart was beating fast. He was simply planning to drop by Emily's desk and have a casual conversation. But then he'd seen her. She'd worn her hair down today, and she was even more beautiful than before. He steeled his nerves and stopped beside her cubicle.

"Hey, Emily. Your hair looks nice. What's the occasion? I've never seen you wear it down before."

Two rosy patches appeared on her cheeks. "Uhmm, I don't know. I just thought I'd try something different."

"I didn't even know you had curls. Or do you curl it? I never understand my sisters. They use curling irons and straightening irons. Sometimes they use both of them at the same time. Sometimes they use the straightening iron to curl their hair. It doesn't make any sense to me."

"I'm too lazy to do all that. Mine's always curly, so I put it in a braid most of the time. It's easier to control."

"Oh..." He suddenly felt tongue-tied. "Uhmm... I talked to my mom last night. She said your mother's doing really well. I'm glad she's better."

"Yeah, me too."

"Uhmm, so... Are you going to be with your parents all night? I mean, if you finish early, you should call. I'm probably going to listen to some jazz tonight." When she looked hesitant, he quickly added, "And Grace is going to come."

Emily's entire face turned red. "I'll... I'll probably be there all night."

"Oh, okay. Sure. I understand." Was she really going to be there all night? Or was she merely making up an excuse to avoid being with him. He was probably being too pushy again. "I just thought I'd let you know. I thought Grace would like it if you came."

"But next time I'll go." She was tapping her fingers nervously on her desk. "I mean... I like jazz. So, you know..."

"Yeah. Okay. Next time."

"Or who knows? Maybe I'll get a wild hair and go on the hike." She kept her gaze fastened to her hands.

"The long hike this weekend? The one with the overnight camping trip?"

"Oh yeah. I forgot about the camping thing. Maybe next time." She glanced up with a shaky smile.

"Sure. Next time. See ya later."

He pondered Emily as he returned to his desk. She was definitely acting awkward. Was it because of what Grace had told her about Becca's phone calls? He tried to think of some casual way to let her know the truth. Well, the truth about Becca. He didn't want her to know he'd never actually dated any girls before—she'd think he was a geek.

His phone vibrated with another message from Becca. She'd already sent three texts that day. What this time?

Found a new drink to try tonight. Slippery Nipple. LOL!

Why would she send him a text like that? The girl was certifiable. He turned his phone off and tried to concentrate on work and ignore his headache. And his heartache.

*****

Emily couldn't decide what to wear to her date—no, her *meeting*—with Asher Denning. It wasn't a date according to strict interpretation of the Best Dating Rules. She'd planned to dress casually until Becca suggested wearing a dress.

She'd avoided talking to Charlie about it, suspecting her sister might disapprove. But after pulling almost everything she owned out of the closet, she gave up and called her.

"Hey, Sister," Charlie answered. "It's about time you called. I've called twice this week, and you didn't call back."

"I know, I know. I've been... busy. But, I need clothes advice for tonight. Can you Skype with me?"

"Sure. Give me a few seconds."

They connected on Skype, and Charlie appeared on the screen, her curly hair tucked up in its usual baseball cap. "You must be desperate to be asking me for advice on what to wear." Charlie chuckled. "You usually scoff at my wardrobe."

"That's not true. You have great taste in clothes, but you usually choose not to wear your cute things and dress like a guy instead."

"Yes. That's because I like to shock people when I actually dress up. So what's the deal tonight?"

"I'm going to get coffee with my new art teacher. We're gonna talk about my options. He thinks this class may be too elementary for me."

"And you couldn't have talked about this after class? And you're worried about what to wear. Let me guess. This isn't a fifty-year-old, fat, bald guy. Is it?"

"No. He's thirty two and really good-looking. Blond. Weight lifter. English accent. But it's not a date. We're meeting at the coffee place, and I'm planning to buy my own drink."

"So, you've decided to start dating, and you're not giving Spencer the first shot?"

She'd known Charlie would react like this. "It's not a date. I told you—"

"I know what you said. But, you're wearing your hair down, and that look on your face tells me you might let him kiss you if he tried."

She felt heat rising in her face. "I would not!"

Charlie raised an eyebrow. "Okay. Whatever you say. Tell me about the place you're going. And what are my clothing options?"

Emily picked up the computer and pointed it toward the bed littered with clothes.

"Ohmygosh! That's everything you own." She sighed. "Pants, shorts, dress?"

"Well, Becca said I should wear a dress to this place."

"Becca?"

"Yes. That's one of the girls from the hiking trip. You know—Betty Boobs?"

"And you're taking advice from her?"

"No, I'm asking for your advice."

"Okay. I wouldn't go really dressy. Why don't you wear a skirt and a blouse?"

"This one?" Emily held up one of her black linen work skirts.

"No. Wear something short. You might as well show off your legs. Yeah, that one."

"I have to be careful how I sit in this one. It's really short."

"But it's tight. If they're short and loose, you have to worry about the wind catching them."

"Okay. And the blouse?"

"Wear that black one with the ruffles."

"You don't think it's too low cut?"

"No, it's not even as low cut as what most people wear to work. It's seems low cut to you because you're not used to it. And wear a necklace, you know, the black one with the dangly chains. It's not too flashy."

"Heels or flats?"

"Is he tall?"

"Probably six feet tall."

"Are you walking from the subway?"

"I'm taking a taxi."

"Definitely heels," she said. "But Emily—one more thing."

"What?"

"Don't let this guy hurt you. Okay?"

"I told you—"

"I know what you said, but I can tell you're hot for him."

"Even if I did decide to date him, I don't think he'd hurt me. He's older, more mature. I don't think he'd be into playing games like that."

"Sister, trust me. I know from experience older guys can play games right along with the rest of them. They have more years of practice at doing it."

"What do you mean? Is there something you haven't told me?"

Instantly she masked the emotion on her face. "Nope. I'm simply giving you some sisterly advice."

"Okay, thanks for the help." Emily smiled. "Love you, Sister."

"You, too."

Emily arrived ten minutes early to the Green Scene. She was surprised to find it looked much more like a club than a coffee bar. She found a small table on the far side and sat in a chair where she could watch the door. There was a jazz band setting up to play, so she tried not to sit too close to the stage. She wanted to be able to talk to Asher without yelling. She ordered a café mocha from the waitress, feeling relieved she'd be able to pay for her own drink as she planned. She drummed her fingers nervously on the table while she waited for Asher Denning to make his appearance.

"Hey, Emily. What are you doing here?" Emily looked up in surprise to see Grace standing beside her table, looking anxiously over her shoulder.

"Hi Grace. I, uhmm... What are you doing here?"

"Spencer told me you were having dinner with your mom and stepdad tonight. What happened? Why are you here?"

"Spencer? Uhmm... I had a change of plans. But don't tell—"

"Hullo, Emily. You look smashing!" Asher Denning slipped into the chair beside her. He had on a tight black t-shirt that accentuated the bulge of his muscles and contrasted with his blond hair. "Have you been here long?" He glanced up, recognizing Grace, who was staring at him with wide eyes. "Oh, hullo! Grace, my love, you won't let on to the rest of the class we were here together. Will you, love? Why don't you sit down and join us? We're just having a little chin wag."

Emily's cheeks were burning, and she could hear the blood pounding in her ears. She turned pleading eyes to Grace, whose face was blanched. "Grace, I can explain. But don't tell Spencer." She tried to keep her voice low enough Asher couldn't hear as he waved down a waitress.

"Spencer's here," whispered Grace, throwing frantic glances behind her.

"He's here?" Emily slunk down. "Where?"

"Hey, Grace," she heard Spencer's voice. "We've got a table over here. Who're you talking to?"

Spencer's smiling face appeared over Grace's shoulder as she spun around quickly and tried to herd him back toward their table. But Spencer stopped in his tracks when his eyes fell on Emily. At first he brightened with a smile and opened his mouth to speak to her. But then his face fell as he glanced from her to Asher Denning and back again. She cringed while he took in the low cut of her blouse and the lip-gloss she'd added at the last minute. He nodded his head in her direction.

"Hi, Emily." His lips pressed firmly together. He turned and began making his way toward the door.

"Wait, Spencer," called Grace as she tried to catch her brother.

Emily sat in stunned silence. She didn't get up and chase him out the door. There was no point. What could she say? She really had no defense. She was a worm—lower than a worm—worm excrement. She'd seen the hurt in his eyes, and she knew she was solely responsible for that pain. She'd made up excuses to justify her behavior, but none of it changed the lie she'd told to Spencer.

"Hullo, love. Did Grace leave?"

She swallowed, but couldn't manage to speak. She struggled to hold back tears as she nodded at Asher.

He flashed her his million dollar smile and leaned forward to put his elbows on the table, his biceps flexing as he moved. "Did I tell you how smashing you look?" he asked with hooded eyes. "What type of bevvy did you get?"

"It's a mocha." Emily managed to spit the words out.

"Coffee? Oh yes, I did ask you out for coffee, didn't I? I hope you don't mind I got a pint of lager, instead." The band started playing, and Asher slid his chair closer to Emily's, turning it to face the band.

The waitress returned with his beer and managed to rub most of her upper body against him while placing it on the table. He rewarded her efforts with a wink, smiling at the astonished expression on Emily's face. "She's a friendly sort, that one."

Emily stiffened when he placed his arm around the back of her chair. But he didn't actually touch her, so she relaxed and tried to concentrate on the music, asking herself why on earth she'd agreed to come.

As if sensing her uneasiness, he leaned his head in close and said, "You know, you really do have an amazing talent with watercolor. That truly is why I asked you to come."

She warmed at his praise, but only managed to murmur, "Thanks."

"I speak truly. I'm well chuffed with your work. Quite extraordinary for your age. How old are you?"

"Twenty four."

"Blinding!" he said with a warm smile. "I've found there are plenty of fit girls in New York. But talent—real talent—that's hard to come by. Finding them together is extraordinary." He gave her shoulder a casual squeeze and left his hand there.

The hand remained unmoving on her shoulder until the next song was finished and he pulled it down to clap for the band. "Are you enjoying the music? This group has talent and a quarter. Can I buy you another beverage?" he asked as he flagged down the waitress. "How about a glass of wine? You seem like a red wine girl to me."

"I am," she admitted. "Sometimes, but not tonight. I'll stick with coffee."

Undeterred, he ordered another beer for himself and a glass of wine for her. "You seem a bit stressed. You need a glass of wine, not more coffee. Relax! You'll suppress your talent if you stay uptight."

He put his arm back around her but his hand never strayed past her shoulder.

When another couple strolled past he haled them to the table. "This is Rachel and Travis, friends of mine, newlyweds actually. They're both teachers. And this is Emily Best, my most promising student." He had the grace to add, "I'm afraid I'm not responsible for her talent as she's only attended a solitary class." Emily smiled at the friendly-looking couple, but inside she was still tormented over the memory of Spencer's hurt expression.

"So you're an artist?" asked Rachel, her bright eyes framed with spirally curls and a genuine smile.

Emily endeavored to control her growing despondency; she couldn't be rude to such a sweet girl. "No, I'm an accountant, really. Art is a hobby."

"But she has amazing talent. You should see the things these hands can do." Asher reached across the table. She watched dispassionately as he lifted her hand to press his lips against it. She realized with shock she felt no tingle whatsoever from his touch, nothing like the sensations she fought against when Spencer touched her.

"How long have you been dating?" Rachel asked.

"Oh, we're not dating," Emily protested.

"This is our first date," Asher corrected, "but hopefully not the last."

"Well, I hope you'll be as lucky as we are," declared Rachel, as she glanced adoringly at her handsome husband who returned the look."

Watching the happy couple interact only plunged Emily further into dejection. The glass of wine beckoned and she gave in to the temptation to take a few sips. A few sips gradually morphed into an entire glass. The resulting numbing effect allowed her to focus on the music and conversation rather than thinking about her earlier confrontation with Spencer. Then his face flashed into her mind and she plunged back into her depressed state. In desperation, she stepped into the ladies room to call Charlie, but her sister didn't answer the phone. She left a pitiful message, begging her to call back.

When she returned to the table, she found herself once again alone with Asher and a new glass of wine on the table. She considered calling it an evening, but Asher pleaded, "Let's stay until the band breaks, and then we'll take a stroll. It's still early."

Sinking back into her chair, she sipped her wine again. She usually didn't have more than one glass of wine, so she knew better than to drink the entire glass. But after a few more swallows, she finally began to feel less miserable about the evening. The music was soft and soothing, and she relaxed as Asher rubbed lightly on her arm. Soon she felt herself drifting off, and she laid her head against his shoulder.

She awoke abruptly as a flash went off in her face. Opening her eyes, she blinked to focus on Becca standing in front of her with a victorious expression.

"Thanks for the picture! I don't know whether to send this one to the NYC Word or to just send it to Spencer."

Her heart was pounding, and she tried to stand up. But her legs felt wobbly and the room started spinning.

"Where are you going?" asked Asher as he gently pushed her back in her seat. "A few more songs until the band breaks. I'll make sure you get home."

Tears began to stream gently down Emily's face as she laid her head back on his shoulder. She'd ruined everything. After Spencer saw this picture he'd never forgive her. And for what? Asher might have a cool English accent, but he wasn't any better looking than Spencer. In fact, Spencer had nicer teeth. And he was taller. She liked really tall guys. And Spencer was sweeter. And he didn't talk her into drinking alcohol. She liked Spencer better than Asher. She liked… Spencer. She liked Spencer, and it was too late. She'd ruined everything.

She dozed off again and woke up at Asher's gentle urging. "Wake up, love. Here, finish your drink." She sat up and grabbed the table to stop the room from spinning. Only a glass and a half. She shouldn't be dizzy.

"No. I don't feel good. I don't want any more wine."

"But you haven't even finished a second glass."

"No. I need to go home. I have to work tomorrow."

"Okay, fine." His voice was terse. "Let's go."

She stood up, leaning against him for support as they started for the door. He chuckled. "You don't drink much, do you? Less than two glasses of wine, and you can't even walk by yourself?"

The room tipped at an awkward angle. "I—I think I need to sit down. Can you call me a taxi?"

"Sure. Are you okay?"

"Yes. I'm fine." His eyes appeared in her vision, topped by brows wrinkled with concern. His face flew away as everything went black.

*****

Spencer couldn't believe it. Emily was totally smashed. Passed out, drunk! When Grace had called him to come and help her, he'd almost refused. He wanted to throw up when he first received the offensive picture of Emily cozying up with the blond guy whose muscles were busting out of his shirt. Now he was just angry. Angry with Becca for sending him the photo. Angry with Emily for lying to him. Angry with himself for wasting his time and emotions on her.

She'd evidently passed out at the bar, and the stupid blond guy didn't even know where she lived. What was she doing out with a guy she barely knew? He'd looked in her cell phone and found Grace's number and called her to come fetch Emily. He hadn't even stayed around to make sure she'd come. When Spencer arrived with Grace, the blond guy was long gone. And Emily was drunk. Incoherent. Asleep. He'd had to pick her up and carry her to the taxi, and she hadn't even woken up.

"Should we call her parents?" Grace asked.

"No, we should probably stick her in her room and let her sleep it off."

"Spencer, I know you're hurt. But think for a minute. She's not waking up. I don't think she drinks that much."

"Well, maybe she drinks more when she's out on a hot date."

Grace grabbed his arm. "Or maybe it's something besides alcohol. Maybe you're right—maybe she's just drunk. But if not, if someone gave her something—some type of drug—she could die from it."

She could die? He wanted to yell at her or maybe he never wanted to speak to her again. But he didn't want her to die. "So what do you propose?"

"I say, let's call Mr. Gherring and let them make the decision. It's the right thing to do."

"Okay, but I don't want him to think I got her drunk."

"He won't—I'm your witness."

Gherring answered on the second ring.

"Spencer? What's wrong?"

"Uhmm. Well, this is a little weird. But Grace got a call that Emily was passed out at a bar, and we came to get her. We have her in a taxi, headed for home. But... Well, she isn't waking up. So, do you want us to take her home or to your place or to the—"

Gherring interrupted. "Wait. Just a second." Spencer heard muffled talking in the background and raised voices. "Spencer, thank you. I'm sorry to ask this. But will you please take her to the hospital. I'm on my way." He heard arguing. "No, you're not going. Don't be ridiculous." More muted words. "Okay. Okay. I'll tell the doctor she's never been drunk before. I'll tell them. I'll tell them. They'll test her. They'll do blood tests. They'll figure out what she needs. You don't need to come. Okay. Okay."

Gherring groaned into the phone. "Spencer, we're both coming. Thank you so much."

Spencer told the taxi driver, "Okay. We need to go to the emergency room now."

"Spencer? Is she breathing? I can't tell." Her voice was shrill.

"Quick! Lay her across my lap!" He bent over to feel for her breath and listen and watch to see her chest move.

"Drive faster! Grace, call nine-one-one, and tell them we're coming." His heart was hammering in his chest. Did he remember what to do? He gave her two quick breaths and felt for a pulse. Thready. Only a few beats. He moved awkwardly to crouch on the floorboard and lay her down onto the seat, attempting to do chest compressions. "Oh God! Please, help us! Hurry up! I don't have enough room—I'm too big. I can't remember how many I'm supposed to do." Tears were pouring down his face now. He breathed into her mouth again. "I can't even get her in the right position. I don't know if it's working." He pushed desperately on her chest, trying to keep his balance as the taxi careened around corners and sped along the streets. Again and again he breathed into her still body, praying the air was going into her lungs, praying the taxi would hurry. Over and over he pushed on her chest, begging God to let her live, his tears dripping on her.

Suddenly the door opened and someone tried to take her body away from him. "No! She needs CPR!" He held onto her and tried to drag her back.

"Spencer, let them take her!" Grace cried, pulling his arms away. "They know what to do."

"Oh God, Gracie!" He buried his face in her arms, sobbing. "I've lost her. I didn't do it right—I couldn't save her."

The fierce hug Grace returned did little to calm his sense of desperation as Emily's lifeless body wheeled into the emergency room.

Chapter Nine

ANNE SHUDDERED, tamping down another wave of nausea while sitting in the cold sterile room staring at the machines and tubes that were connected to her daughter. Grace was slumped in sleep in the chair beside her. Spencer sat in the chair next to Emily's hospital bed bent forward and resting his head on the metal railing. Four a.m., almost six hours since Spencer had called to give them the alarming news about Emily passing out at a bar. Arriving at the hospital in fifteen minutes, the scene awaiting them was even worse than they feared.

The emergency room doctor regurgitated mumbo-jumbo about her respiration being severely depressed, causing cardiac arrest... doctor-speak for "she quit breathing and her heart quit beating." Why would a healthy twenty-four-year-old's lungs and heart quit working? Drug overdose. Probably a combination of drugs and alcohol. Doctors restarted her heart and hooked her up to a respirator.

Then came the infuriating questions. Did Emily have a history of drug and alcohol abuse? Did she have problems with depression? Had she ever been hospitalized for drug or alcohol use? How much alcohol did she consume on a weekly basis?

But when the doctor recognized Steven, her words in Emily's defense were suddenly more plausible. Yes, it was possible someone put something in her drink. Blood and urine samples were sent for analysis and the doctors performed gastric lavage, fancy words for pumping out her stomach. Steven insisted they call the police.

Charlie called on Emily's phone, returning Emily's earlier call. "If I had only answered my phone, I would have made her leave that place. I didn't hear it ring, and I didn't realize she'd called me until I got home. I should have talked her out of going in the first place."

Anne felt equally guilty. "It's not your fault, Charlie. She told me about it, too. She wasn't interested in being talked out of it. For some reason she was determined to go out with this guy."

"Mom, she wouldn't have listened to you. But I might have been able to talk her out of it. I figured it was too late, since she didn't call me until right before she left."

Charlie booked a flight to New York in the morning. She insisted on coming, saying Emily would come for her.

Anne was emotionally and physically exhausted, but tried to hide the fatigue and the returning nausea from Steven. He was in power mode, ordering everyone around and using his considerable influence to make things happen. He was like a dictator—a well-meaning dictator, but a dictator nonetheless. If he suspected she wasn't feeling well, he would send her home or simply check her into the hospital. She had no chance of winning an argument with him right now.

Steven marched into the room, surveying the surrounding scene.

Spencer stood, keeping his hand clasped around Emily's limp one. "What happened? What did you find out from the police? Did they talk to Denning?"

Steven's jaw muscles clenched. "Yes, they talked to him. They don't think he did it. It wasn't long from the time Becca sent you the picture until Denning called Grace. In his statement, he claimed she was acting really drunk when they were leaving. He said she complained about feeling bad, sat down, and passed out. They never even left the bar."

"He was still a jerk. He didn't even stay with her until we got there. He left her passed out on that chair." Spencer released Emily's hand, pacing with long strides while he pulled at his hair.. "I should never have left her there. She's too naïve, and I thought he looked like a sleaze. But, I was so mad she lied to me." He paused beside Anne's chair. "That guy didn't even know where she lived—she barely knew him. What was she doing anyway? Why would she go on a date with him?"

"I don't know, Spencer. She's normally mature and sensible. But every once in a while, she gets caught on some tangent. When that happens, she gets really stubborn, and no one seems to be able to talk sense into her." What could she say to soothe his obviously raw feelings. "I hope you'll give her a chance to explain... when she wakes up."

He moved back to Emily's side, gently lifting her hand while turning to face Steven. "If it wasn't Denning, then who was it?"

"Denning swears she had a cup of coffee and a glass and a half of wine. He said she was perfectly fine until after she started drinking the second glass of wine."

Anne said, "I can't even believe she started a second glass. She usually has a strict limit of one, and that's if she drinks anything at all."

"She seems to have broken a number of her normal rules for this guy," Spencer remarked sullenly.

Steven continued. "But the tests showed an extremely high level of this drug in her system. If it was all in the second drink, and she only drank half of it, someone must have spiked it with a huge amount of this Rohypnol. We're lucky she only drank half of it. And the doctor said she probably won't remember much—the drug gives you amnesia."

"Spencer?" Anne pointed her chin at Grace, still sound asleep in her chair, with her head cocked at a strange angle. "Why don't you go home and take Grace? You've done so much."

"Yes, Spencer." Steven moved to grasp his shoulder. "The doctor's tell me you probably saved her life with the CPR in the taxi."

He slumped into the chair beside Emily, shaking his head miserably. "No. I could barely remember what to do. I don't even know if I got any air into her lungs, and I couldn't get enough room to do the chest compressions the way I needed to."

"You did the best you could, and she's probably alive because of you."

"But we won't even know if she's okay until she wakes up." His eyes dropped to his lap. "I was so mad, I wanted to drop her off at her apartment. I thought she was drunk. It was Grace who said it might be something more. It was Grace who made me call you."

Steven glanced at her contorted form. "Then we're thankful to Grace as well. But you really should take her home and get some sleep."

"No, thank you. I want to stay until Emily wakes up. I have to. I can't leave until I see her awake."

Steven opened his mouth to object, but Anne caught his eye and silently bid him to her side. She whispered in his ear, "Let him stay. He needs to stay. Let's send Grace home."

Nodding, he roused Grace and guided her half-sleeping form down the elevator to be driven home. Meanwhile Spencer kept his bedside vigil with his head on the bedrail and his hand firmly clasping Emily's. Steven returned to the room and collapsed into the chair beside Anne. She reached out to grab his hand and squeeze it.

"Thank you. I'm glad I'm not doing this by myself. I'm glad we have you." With a weak smile she added, "Welcome to fatherhood."

He heaved a heavy breath. "I don't much care for this hospital stuff. Between you and Emily, it's becoming way too frequent for my taste."

"Mine, too. When did they say she'd wake up?"

"They can't be sure. It doesn't usually progress all the way to cardiac arrest like hers did, so they have a hard time predicting."

Anne felt fresh tears forming and blinked hard. "But she will wake up, right? And they don't think her brain went without oxygen?" She saw Spencer raise his head, hanging on Steven's reply.

He paused, obviously thinking carefully before he spoke. "The doctors refuse to make promises, but it's very unlikely she'll have any permanent damage from a single incident. On the other hand, she'll likely be very confused, and she'll probably have a really bad headache and nausea. And that can last up to forty-eight hours."

Anne swallowed hard. She wanted assurances not probabilities.

He said, "Look, I know you don't like that answer, but it's the best one I've been able to get. At least she's breathing on her own now. That's a good sign, and she won't be terrified, waking up on a ventilator."

"You're right. I need to be thankful for every positive thing instead of worrying about the things I can't change."

She felt his eyes looking her over. "I know you're exhausted. We all are. You won't be able to stay up here all day tomorrow. Not unless you want to end up in the hospital yourself."

"But I have to be here for her."

"You can stay until she wakes up. But then I'm sending you home so Connie can take care of you." Squinting his eyes, he added, "And don't think I'm unaware you're already feeling sick. I should probably check you into your own room."

As Anne was formulating a counterargument in her head, Spencer stood to lean across the bedrail. "She's moving, and her eyes are blinking. I think she's waking up."

*****

Emily had never felt so sick in her life. Her head pounded, and a blinding light assaulted her eyes. She struggled to open them, but it hurt too much. She could hear voices, vaguely familiar. Someone squeezed her hand. A heavy fog dragged her down. She willed herself to wake up. Her eyes squinted open slightly. Was that Spencer? Where was she? What was wrong with her? Why didn't her body work right?

She blinked her eyes open again. Her mother's face floated into her vision. Why was her mom here? Where was she? Turning her head to the side, millimeter by millimeter, she saw Steven and Spencer. Both wore frowns. Her mother's voice was in her ear.

"—hurt anywhere? How do you feel?"

She drifted into oblivion.

Prying her eyes open, she felt a hand squeezing hers and gazed up into her mother's eyes.

"What happened to me?" her voiced croaked. Her mother held a straw to her lips. Cool water soothed her parched throat. "Thanks. My head hurts."

"You don't remember anything?"

"No… Wait…" Her mind struggled to retrieve the muddled details. "I'm in the hospital. Was Spencer here?" She gazed around the empty room.

"He was here. Yes, he stayed until you woke up."

"What happened to me?"

"You remember going to a bar with Asher Denning?"

The painful details of the evening trickled into her head, driving salty tears to pool and drip down her face. "Oh Mom, Spencer was there. It was awful. I knew I shouldn't have lied to him. I feel terrible."

Anne's face was grim. "I wish now I'd tried to talk you out of it."

"But he was here? Is he mad at me? What am I saying? Of course he's mad." She wiped her damp face with the back of her hand.

"He saved your life."

"What? How did he do that? What happened?"

"Try to remember."

She forced herself to replay the uncomfortable evening in her mind. "He saw me and left at the very beginning. He was with Grace. She tried to warn me, but it was too late."

"Then what happened?"

"I stayed with Asher and met a couple of his friends and listened to music."

"What did you drink?"

"Uhmm, a café mocha. And then Asher bought me a glass of wine. I was so stressed I decided to drink it. But I didn't feel any better."

"When did you call Charlie?"

"Oh yeah. I went to the bathroom and called Charlie, but she didn't answer. How did you know I called her?"

"She called back. She's on her way here."

"She's flying here? And I almost died? Was there a car accident?" She ached all over, but she didn't feel like anything was broken.

"You drank something with drugs in it."

"What? Who put drugs in my drink? Asher?"

"We don't think it was him. What happened after you called Charlie?"

"There was another glass of wine on the table when I came back. I knew I shouldn't drink more than one, but I was feeling so depressed I drank some anyway. And then I remember feeling sleepy. That's it. That's the last thing I remember. What happened?"

"You evidently passed out, and Asher called Grace to come take you home."

"Why didn't Asher take me home?"

"He didn't know where you lived."

"Oh. That's right." She cringed. "And Grace came to get me?"

"Grace and Spencer came to get you. Apparently, Asher was already gone. He left you there, asleep."

"Wow—great guy. I sure can pick 'em."

"You wouldn't wake up, so Spencer called us when they had you in the taxi. They were taking you to the hospital when you quit breathing."

"I quit breathing?"

"And your heart stopped, too." Tears were rolling freely down her mom's face. "And Spencer did CPR in the back seat of the taxi until they got to the emergency room."

Emily suppressed a sob, as she clung to her mom. "I really almost died?"

"Yes, we nearly lost you. But Spencer probably saved your life. And then he sat beside you all night, holding your hand. Waiting for you to wake up."

"I thought I saw him for a minute. I thought I imagined it."

Anne shook her head, sniffing. "No, you probably saw him when you first woke up. But once he knew you were okay, he left. I... I don't think he wants to talk to you. He was pretty hurt."

"That's okay," said Emily. "I don't deserve him anyway." She turned her head away, tears dropping onto her pillow.

"Emily... Do you want to talk about it?"

"No, I don't. I really don't. I really want to go to sleep and wake up and find out this was all a bad dream. Talking about it makes it seem too real. I... I almost wish he hadn't saved me."

"Emily! Don't ever say something like that!" Her mom's voice was angry and frightened.

"I don't mean it that way. I'm not wishing I were dead, but I don't feel like facing my life right now." She turned her tear-streaked face back to her mom and took her hand. "Don't worry, Mom. I'm too much of a chicken to ever actually kill myself."

"The important thing is you're alive. You simply need to make better decisions from here on out. And I won't let you down again."

Emily opened her mouth to protest, but her mom interrupted. "No. I should have spoken up and read you the riot act when you told me about your lie. I didn't say anything, but next time, I'm speaking the truth no matter what."

"I'm a big girl, Mom. I made that choice all on my own. But yes, I hereby give you permission to tell me the next time I'm about to make a huge mistake, even if it makes me angry."

Anne pushed a curl off Emily's face and tucked it behind her ear, just like she used to do when she was a little girl. "How do you feel?"

"Pretty much like I've been run over by a dump truck."

"Okay," said Steven as he swept into the room, "I hate to break up this party, but Emily needs to sleep, and you..." He kissed Anne on the cheek. "You need to go *home* to sleep. Connie's already there waiting for you."

"Connie?" Emily groaned. "Does she know? I guess she does. She probably hates me. I'm sure Grace does. The whole family probably does. That's good. I deserve it. You should hate me, too."

Anne and Steven exchanged a meaningful look. Steven said, "I think hate would be too strong a term. No one hates you. Disappointment would be more accurate. But the main thing everyone felt was fear, and now we feel relief. And we feel those things because we love you."

Emily shook her head, refusing to let herself off that easy. "Have you both been here all night?"

"Yes, you gave us quite a scare." Steven leaned over to kiss her forehead.

"I'm so sorry. I'm sorry about everything. I can't believe I was so stupid. I know not to drink something that's been sitting on the table when I wasn't there. I'm that stupid girl I always despise in the movies—the one who does stupid stuff and gets herself in trouble. I hate that girl."

"Charlie will be here soon," said Steven in an effort to cheer her up.

"Ughh! Charlie will never let me live this down. I was way more irresponsible than she's ever been."

Anne chuckled. "I'm afraid you may be right about that. Once she gets over almost losing you, she'll probably hold this over your head for the rest of your life."

Emily moaned. "And I'm missing work. I never miss work. I had something I really needed to finish today."

"Work will wait. Although I hear your boss is something of a tyrant." Steven winked at her.

"She's usually a lot harder on herself than any boss," Anne remarked.

"Well, do me a favor," said Steven. "Cut yourself some slack here. You've discovered you aren't perfect and you actually make mistakes. I know from experience that's a hard lesson. Forgive yourself. Learn from it and move on. And you'll find yourself much more forgiving when others are less than perfect."

Emily nodded at Steven. But she knew she could never forgive herself. She would do everything possible to make up for her mistakes, but she would never let herself forget. And she would never quit punishing herself. If she did, she might make another mistake, and it might be worse than this one. Look how many people she'd hurt by her reckless actions. She didn't deserve to be happy.

"Thanks, Steven. Thanks, Mom. You guys go home and sleep. I'll be fine. I'm planning to go to sleep, too."

"Are you hungry?" asked Anne.

"No," she said emphatically. "I don't think I'll ever be hungry again."

Anne chuckled. "I know the feeling, Sweetie. We'll see you in a few hours."

"Charlie will see you," corrected Steven. "Your mom won't be back until after five."

"When will I get to leave here?" asked Emily. "I don't want to spend the night."

"I don't know," Steven said. "It's possible you'll get out today or it might be tomorrow. You'll do whatever the doctor says. Right?"

"Yes, I won't cause any more trouble."

*****

Spencer tried to sleep. He was so exhausted he thought he'd sleep all day. But when he closed his eyes, he saw images of Emily in his head. Her surprised face when he saw her sitting with Asher Denning. The picture of her with her eyes closed leaning against him, tucked inside his arm. Her limp body as he tried desperately to give her CPR in the back seat of the taxi. Her helpless form with wires and tubes coming out of her and a machine pushing air into her lungs. Her frightened eyes when she finally woke up with no idea what had happened.

He'd waited all night to see her wake up, but he couldn't bring himself to stay and talk to her. He didn't want to hear her meaningless apology. Oh, he was certain she would apologize. She was certainly sorry this had happened. She hadn't meant for Spencer to see her with Asher Denning. She hadn't meant to swallow a drug-tainted beverage. She hadn't purposely stopped breathing. But she'd made a conscious decision when she went out with Asher. She'd chosen him.

Grace had told him about Denning. He knew he was an art teacher. He knew Emily had only met him once, that she hardly knew him He was older and artistic, blond and handsome. He had an English accent and all the girls in his art class were hot for him. He was smooth and sophisticated. He was obviously a weightlifter. He was the polar opposite to Spencer. So, Emily had made her choice. It hurt, but he'd learn to live with it. If only she'd been honest with him. He was humiliated to find out the way he did.

Spencer gave up on sleeping and went into the office instead.. At least he could keep his mind occupied and not think about how much he was hurting. His phone buzzed again. Becca continued to call and text, over and over. He was sick of her. He wasn't sure, but he suspected she'd known Emily would be at the Green Scene last night. He glanced at his phone, expecting to see Becca's name again. But it was Candace. Finally, she'd gotten the nerve to call him. He answered quickly before she could hang up.

"Candace?"

"Hey, Spencer. I got all of your messages. I'm sorry, but I just got them. I've been in Mexico since Monday night. I guess you're not a Facebook friend, or you would have seen my posts. What's up? What's so important?"

"You went out of town on Monday and just got back today?"

"Yes. Me and Sherry and Brianna. Why?"

"Becca said you might be at the Green Scene last night."

"Really? She must have forgotten I was in Mexico, but she knew I was there. She even posted several comments on my pictures. Why? Was I supposed to be there last night?"

"Do you know anything about a picture that was in the NYC Word on Tuesday?"

"You mean Monday? The one I called you about?"

"No, I mean the one on Tuesday. A different picture."

"No. I admit I usually read it, but I didn't read it this week. What was it?"

"A picture of the Gherrings, taken when she was coming off the hiking trail last Saturday."

"No way! Becca put that in the paper? Did she put any of the others in? She took quite a few. I promise I didn't know she was planning to do that."

"You saw her take the picture?"

"Sure. You mean, when we were standing around waiting for them to come back to the parking lot? She took several pictures."

"That's interesting. She denied it and suggested you must have taken the picture."

"I can't believe it! We're not really close friends, but I thought I knew her better than that. I promise I didn't take it. I don't know how to prove it was her, but I promise it wasn't me. I felt really bad for Mrs. Gherring. So was the paper right? Is she sick?"

He sighed. "Well it's old news now, but she's actually pregnant and having a difficult pregnancy."

"Pregnant—oh, that's crazy. She's kind of old for that, isn't she? I mean, I'm happy for her and all. She was brave to even go on the hike. Listen, Spencer. I didn't take that picture. I hope you believe me."

"Sure, Candace. Thanks for calling me back."

"You're welcome. I really am sorry it happened. And the Gherrings were so nice to give us a ride to the hike. By the way, are you going on the overnight hike this weekend?"

"I'm not sure. I was planning to, but I'm awfully tired."

"Same here. I only got back from Mexico a few minutes ago. Do you know if Landon's going?"

"I don't know, but I think so. Look Candace, I need to get back to work."

"Okay. See ya."

Spencer hung up the phone. He wasn't sure whom to believe. But he was beginning to think it really might be Becca. At this point, it didn't seem to matter. He planned to have nothing to do with Becca anymore. In fact, he could take care of that problem right now. He pulled out his phone and blocked her number. Feeling a sense of relief, he started concentrating on his work. Despite his fatigue, he poured himself into his project, enjoying the respite from his painful memories. Perhaps there was life after Emily Best.

*****

"Hey, Sister." Charlie's gold eyes studied Emily from a close perspective. "I've been waiting hours for you to wake up." She smiled. "Well, maybe only about five minutes. But, you slept right through some really loud humming and several throat clearings. Eh-hem!"

"What time is it?" Emily croaked.

"Almost two o'clock. How do you feel?"

"Better than before. My head feels a little better, and I'm not dizzy. But I still feel nauseated."

"We'll give you something for that," said the nurse who entered the room to take vital signs.

"No, I don't want anything. I really don't like taking any medicines. They mess with my head."

"Okay, but the medication would make you feel less nauseous. And I'm also authorized to give you something for pain."

"I'm not hurting anywhere," Emily lied, anxious to avoid taking pain medication. "And I don't really feel that queasy, either."

The nurse tsked behind her teeth. "Okay. I won't give you any meds. Let me know if you change your mind."

"Can I go home?"

"You want to leave already?" asked the nurse. "You just woke up at five a.m. The doctor hasn't seen you yet, has he?"

"Maybe he came while I was sleeping."

The nurse shook her head as she checked the patient notes. "Nope. He hasn't come. But your vitals are fine. It's possible you could get dismissed today."

"Can you ask the doctor to come? As soon as he can?"

She chuckled. "I'm betting you'll see the doctor pretty quickly. You've been designated a priority one. Everyone likes to keep Steven Gherring happy around here. He was evidently on a rampage last night." Then she leaned in as if to tell a secret. "But I've seen him come up here and visit with the kids on the cancer wing he built. He's really a sweet man even though he sometimes looks really stern."

"Yeah. We've seen that side of him more often than not," agreed Charlie.

"Well, I'll send a message to the doc and see if he'll get up here to see you."

"Thanks. I appreciate your help."

When the nurse left the room, Charlie said, "So... Let me make sure I have the story straight. My smart, sensible, conservative sister decided to go on a date with an older guy she hardly knew. And she ended up drinking something with drugs in it and almost killed herself. Does that about sum it up?"

"Please, Charlie. I was technically dead less than twenty-four hours ago. Can't you cut me some slack?"

"Hmmm." She held her chin, tapping a finger on her lip. "Let me think. What would my dear sister do if the circumstances were reversed? Hmmm... No, I don't think I can cut you any slack."

"I would too cut you slack."

"When I tried that ski jump and broke my wrist, you lectured me on the slope before they even strapped me onto the sled."

"That was one time—"

"When I wrecked the car, you yelled at me before you even asked if I was hurt."

"But you weren't hurt."

"I could've been. You didn't know."

"Fine. You might as well yell at me. I'm so angry with myself I can't stand it. I admit it—I was really stupid."

Charlie leaned over and hugged her fiercely, blinking back tears. "I'm mad, too. And I'm mad at myself I didn't hear your phone call. I could've lost you. What would I do without my sister?"

"I don't know, I think you'd be better off."

"First of all, the drink. Don't you know—"

"Yes, I know. I know I should never drink something that was left on the table. But, Asher was there. I would've thought he'd watch it."

"For all you know, he did it. You don't even know him."

"The police don't think he did it. But you're right—I didn't know him. I was... I don't know... I was flattered, I guess. All the girls liked him, and he picked me. At the time, it seemed really great. I was blinded by his petty star status. I can't believe it, now."

"So, tell me about Spencer. I know he was there. I know he saw you. Steven told me, despite everything, Spencer ended up giving you CPR and saving your life. So, what's the deal? After all that, you don't like him? You still want to be friends—nothing more?"

"No... I... That is, yes. I like him. I really do. But, it's too late. I finally realized it, but it's too late. I was so awful. I lied to him, and I hurt him." She turned her head away. "I don't even think we can be friends, now. And I've probably lost Grace as well."

"You haven't lost me yet," said a voice from the doorway. Grace's face appeared around the door. "I was eavesdropping. I could apologize and say I'm sorry, but it wouldn't be true." One corner of her mouth kicked up in a smile. "You know how nosey I am."

"Hi, I'm Charlie. You must be Grace. Have you come to help me yell at my sister?"

"Absolutely." Grace moved to stare down at Emily with her arms on her hips. "It'll be so much more fun to do it together."

Emily felt tears welling up. "I'm so sorry. You have every right to hate me. I know I do—I hate myself."

"Oh, no," said Grace. "You will not feel sorry for yourself. No one hates you, and you know it. If you'd seen my brother last night, you'd know he doesn't hate you. Crying while he gave you CPR. Sitting by your bed for hours holding your hand. Quite the opposite—I think he's in love with you."

"He can't be," Emily declared. "He's too good for me. Even if he does love me, I don't deserve him—not anymore."

"Last night, I was inclined to agree. But my opinion is subject to change. It all depends on what you do next."

"But, it's too late. I saw his face. I hurt him. He thinks... I mean, he knows he can't trust me. He knows I lied to him. I don't even think he likes me anymore, and I really can't believe he loves me."

"Oh, I think you're partially right," said Grace. "I don't think he likes you right now. But that doesn't mean he doesn't love you." She paused while her words sunk in. "So the question is... What are you going to do about it?"

*****

Spencer came home from work and ate dinner while watching a movie. Then he took two Benadryl and went to bed early. He congratulated himself on finishing his Friday without thinking about Emily. Well, not too much. Maybe he did wonder a bit about how she was doing, but he refused to call her. He wouldn't lower himself. If she needed someone to check on her, she could get Asher Denning to do it.

His phone rang, and he felt a flash of disappointment when he saw Grace's name rather than Emily's on the caller ID. He pushed that emotion down, concentrating on his anger.

"Hey, Gracie. How are you? Did you get some sleep?"

"I did. I slept 'til eleven o'clock. What about you?"

"Nah. I couldn't sleep, so I went to work."

"You haven't slept at all?"

"No, but I'm going to bed now. So, I'll make up for it."

"Now? At seven o'clock?"

"Yeah. I'm already in bed."

"So, uhmm... I went up to the hospital this afternoon."

His heart sped up. How was she? Was she in pain? Was she sorry? Did she even remember what had happened? He spoke slowly, careful to keep the emotion out of his voice. "Oh. That's good, I guess."

"Uhmm... Do you want to ask me anything? Or would you rather not know?"

Of course he wanted to know, but he needed to make a clean break. He couldn't bear being hurt any more. No, it was better if he didn't know anything. The less he knew about Emily, the better.

"No. I don't think I want to know. It's... It's too hard to think about her. I can't handle it—not anymore."

"Okay. I understand. But, Spencer—"

"Look. You can still be friends. I just can't."

"So, it's impossible now? I mean, what would it take for you to give her a second chance?"

"I don't know. I guess..." He laughed harshly, "I guess if she suspended all of her rules and did something dangerous to be with me, like she did for that Asher Denning guy. Maybe that would mean something."

"Spencer. You don't really want her to do something stupid again. You know she's really sorry—"

"I don't want to hear it, Gracie. Look. I love you, but I don't want to talk about her right now. I'm going to sleep, and I'm going on a really long overnight hike tomorrow. When I come back on Sunday, I hope I'll be okay enough to stand seeing her at work on Monday. That's about as good as it's going to get for me."

"Okay. I understand. Will I see you for Sunday night dinner?"

"Sure. I'll be there. I told Momma we'd cook hamburgers on the grill."

"See you, Spencer."

"Bye, Gracie."

*****

Emily couldn't hear what Spencer was saying to Grace, but she got the gist of it. Grace hung up the phone and turned wary eyes to Emily.

"He doesn't want anything to do with me, does he? I told you, Grace. I hurt him too badly."

"Emily, I think he just needs time. He said he's going to bed early, and he's going on an overnight hike. He's a physical guy. He needs to work out his anger. He'll probably be better by Monday."

"Oh right. Earlier, you were telling me I should call and talk to him or go see him. Now you're telling me he might be better by Monday."

"He was angrier than I thought. I think it'd be better if I talk to him at family dinner on Sunday night. I can feel him out and help you plan a strategy for Monday."

"What did he say, Grace?" Charlie asked. "What did he say when you asked him what it'd take to give her a second chance?"

"He was only spouting off."

"It was something impossible, wasn't it?" asked Emily.

"He didn't mean it. He's just mad about Asher. He said something about you breaking rules and doing something dangerous to be with him. But it doesn't make any sense, and he knows it."

"I would do it," declared Emily. "I would do something dangerous for him."

"Maybe we could stage something dangerous. Like, you could jump out and push him out of the way of a bus or something," Charlie said.

"No, I've got a better idea," laughed Grace. "What if we string up a tight rope between two buildings, and you could walk across and bring him some life-saving medicine?"

"I'm glad you two can laugh." Emily pouted.

"Cheer up," said Charlie. "You're alive to fight another day. The Sister I know would never give up."

"We'll figure something out," said Grace. "I'll talk to you tomorrow. I'm beat. Someone kept me up really late last night." She chuckled as she gave Emily a goodbye hug. "Hang in there, okay?"

"I'll walk you out, Grace," said Charlie. "Hopefully, Emily will get to go home tonight. And Steven promised to get us tickets to a play tomorrow night. Maybe you could come."

"Actually, that sounds fun. As long as seeing me won't be a sad reminder for Emily," she teased, glancing her direction.

Emily forced the corners of her lips upward. "No. I'm so relieved you're forgiving me for being stupid, I promise I'll be happy to see you."

"And you'll try not to lose hope about Spencer?"

"I'll try." But in her heart, she was already fighting a sense of despair.

By the time Emily had been released from the hospital and returned to her apartment, she was already formulating a strategy. She couldn't wait until Monday. Spencer would go on that hike and spend two days working her out of his system. She had to do something. He'd said he wanted her to break her rules and do something dangerous to be with him. If she went on that overnight hike, it would prove something. Wouldn't it? He knew she didn't like camping and sleeping on the ground. Hiking and camping weren't really dangerous, but it was definitely way out of her comfort zone. Surely, he'd be at least slightly impressed, especially if she went the day after she got out of the hospital. Maybe he'd at least give her a chance to apologize.

She began to plan the details. She couldn't show up at the beginning of the hike with the whole group. If he saw her, he might simply refuse to go on the hike. He might walk away, never giving her an opportunity to prove herself. She had to find out where they were camping and meet the group there. All she had to do was start an hour behind them. She'd call Becca. Becca would know where they were camping. It was summer, so it wouldn't be very cold. She could get by with a lightweight blanket since she didn't own a sleeping bag.

How to keep her family from worrying? Hmmm. She could convince Charlie to sleep upstairs with their parents, telling her she wanted to sleep as long as possible tomorrow—until noon. She could leave a note, telling them she was going to meet Spencer on the overnight camping trip. They'd be angry, but not too angry. They'd all be glad she was going to be with Spencer. And he'd be out of cell range, so they wouldn't find out she hadn't gone with the whole group. When she met up with Spencer at the top of the mountain, he'd have to listen to her. He'd see she was willing to do risky things for him. She could apologize. And maybe, just maybe he'd forgive her. It was her best chance and one she was willing to take. She picked up her phone and pushed a few buttons.

"Hey, Becca?"

Chapter Ten

"EMILY? WHY ARE YOU calling?" Her voice sounded a little hostile. Emily tried to remember her last conversation with Becca. She'd seemed fine. But she'd forgotten Becca liked Spencer and probably wouldn't want her to go on the camping trip. She fumbled for something to say.

"Uhmm..."

"I'm not apologizing for the picture."

"What picture?" She wracked her brain, trying to remember a picture.

"The one I..." Her voice trailed off. "Wait. You don't remember the photo?"

"Uhmm. You mean the one in the tabloid? The one you told me about? I never actually saw it. But you told me Candace took the picture, so I wouldn't expect you to apologize, anyway."

"Oh. Right." Her voice sounded happier. "Yes. That's the picture I'm talking about. I thought you might be mad about it."

"No, I'm not. But, uhmm, I need your help with something."

"What's that?"

"Well, uhmm. You know the camping trip tomorrow? The overnight trip? Are you going?"

"I am, but I don't think you should go."

"I... Well... I'm sure I wouldn't be able to handle a trip like that."

"No, you wouldn't," Becca agreed.

"But, I wanted to know where y'all were going."

"Why didn't you ask Spencer where we're going?"

"Uhmm, to tell you the truth, Spencer's pretty mad at me."

"He is? Sorry about that." Her voice didn't have the slightest hint of sincerity.

"Yes. He... He found out I lied about last night."

"Oh, that's right. You had a date with your art teacher. How did that go?"

"Not great. I doubt we'll go out again."

"But didn't you say you and Spencer were only friends. Why should he be mad?"

"It's... It's because I lied to him."

"Well, frankly, I think you've been leading him on. I think that's why he always comes back to me, over and over again. Every time we've broken up for some reason, he always comes back to me. I think it's because he knows he can count on me to be honest." At this revelation, Emily fought the urge to abandon her quest. But since she'd finally admitted to herself how much she liked Spencer, she wasn't going to give up without trying.

"I don't think I've been leading him on—at least I didn't mean to. But you still haven't told me where the hike is tomorrow."

"Why do you want to know if you're not planning to go?"

"Uhmm... well... my sister might want to go. She's in town."

"Your sister?"

"She likes outdoor stuff like that. Hiking and such. So, where is the hike? And where are y'all camping Saturday night?"

"We're, uhmm... Let me think. We're hiking a trail called Devil's Path and camping at Devil's Tombstone."

Devil's Tombstone sounded intimidating, but surely it couldn't be too bad. After all, Becca had been more winded than her on the last hike. "Thanks, Becca. I... I hope you have a good time."

"Sure... Whatever. I need to go."

"Okay. Goodbye—" A click sounded in her ear. It seemed Becca was no longer her friend, but then again, their friendship had been on shaky ground from the beginning. She didn't have time to worry about Becca now—she had to concentrate on proving herself to Spencer.

Emily pulled out her laptop and located a website describing the Devil's Tombstone hike. The more she read, the more discouraged she felt. It sounded incredibly complicated and difficult. As weak as she felt, she'd be better off starting an hour or two ahead of the group, instead of an hour behind. She'd probably make slow progress on the hike. If she started an hour late, it might be dark before she got to the campground. Starting ahead of them would be much safer. That way, if she were having trouble, the group would eventually catch up with her. A bus would take her to Tannersville, followed by Smiley's taxi to the trailhead. She needed to leave at the crack of dawn.

She was a great planner, and she'd really thought this through. She started ticking off all the things she needed to pack—food, water, toothbrush, etc.

"Hey!" She jumped at Charlie's voice behind her. When had she come back down from their parents' apartment? "Wanna make popcorn and watch a movie?"

"Sure, but I don't think I'll be able to stay up too late. I was thinking you might sleep upstairs tonight..."

*****

Spencer didn't sleep well, despite taking two Benadryl. He couldn't stop thinking about Emily. For the first time he was learning how much rejection hurt. He had no desire for friendship with her. Friendship was fine when he thought there was a chance for something more. But since he knew the truth, it hurt too much. He needed a clean break. In fact, he might try to end his internship with Gherring Inc. early. Steven Gherring would probably understand and help him find an alternate internship through his business connections. That might be the best alternative.

Spencer forced his mind back to the task at hand—packing all his gear for the hike. He looked forward to the physical exertion. It would be a great way to clear Emily from his mind. Forever.

At the bus station, he hauled his gear to join the hiking group. But he noticed something extremely unpleasant—Becca.

"Hi, Spencer." She tugged his arm as she spoke. "I'm so excited you're coming. Isn't it going to be great? The weather is perfect. I wasn't sure you were coming. You didn't answer my calls."

"Becca. After the little stunt you pulled Thursday night, I really don't want to talk to you any more." He pivoted and jerked his arm away.

"What stunt? I didn't do anything. What do you mean?"

He spun to face her, holding his arms out of her reach. "You tricked me into going to the Green Scene by telling me Candace was going to be there. You knew she was in Mexico."

"I didn't know."

"Becca, I talked to her. I know you knew. And that's not all I found out from Candace. But I won't even go into that discussion. You told me the hiking group was planning to go the Green Scene, and guess what? I found out that was a lie as well." He glared at her. "I really don't like it when people lie to me."

"Well, what about your precious Emily? I guess you found out she lied to you."

He ignored her bait. "And I really didn't appreciate the picture you sent me."

"I thought you needed to see the truth." She pushed her lower lip into a pout and crossed her arms. "Emily's a slut!"

Spencer raised his hand to slap her, stopping himself just in time. Acutely aware of his shaking hands, he clenched them into fists before stomping over to collar Landon in the crowd of interested onlookers.

"Hey Landon, I'm not going. Sorry to back out on you."

"I totally get it, bro. If I were you, I'd make like a banana and split." Landon shot wary eyes toward Becca. "See ya later."

Spencer hailed a taxi and headed to Emily's apartment.

*****

Charlie listened while her mom chatted with excitement, but she was anxious for her sister to wake up and join them.

"So, Steven got all of us tickets to see *Let It Be* tonight. It's all about The Beatles and has Beatles music. It should be so much fun. I'm hoping it'll cheer up Emily."

"It's almost ten-thirty. Don't you think we should wake her up? I'm only here for a few days." Charlie spoke around bites of chocolate covered donut.

"I don't know. She probably needs the sleep. We'll wake her up by noon for sure."

"But you're not much fun, tethered to an IV pole."

A hurt expression came across Anne's face, so Charlie sprang from her seat to give her a chocolate-smudged kiss on the cheek. "I'm sorry, Mom. I didn't mean it. You're always fun, but I wanted to do something with Emily." She chuckled as she licked her fingers. "But we want you to come, too, because you have more money."

"Do you want to go out for lunch?"

"Do you really think you could stomach a restaurant?"

"Probably not. I think I'll just send you and Emily. Y'all can take pictures, and I'll live vicariously through you."

"Poor Mom. I know how much you love to eat. This must be torture for you."

"It is."

They both jumped at a trilling sound from the doorbell.

"It's Emily! Yay!" Charlie ran to the door to fling it open. "Sister! Oh... Spencer. Come in. I thought you might be... uhmm..."

He stepped through the doorway and stood, shuffling his feet. "Hi, Charlie. Mrs. Gherring."

"Hi Spencer. Your mom's already come and gone today. She's coming back for a while this afternoon." Anne's smile was full of sympathy.

"No, I didn't come to see Mom. I came to see Emily. She didn't answer her door, so I thought she might be up here with you. Is she here?"

"She's still sleeping, I guess. Although you'd think she would have heard you knocking." It was all the excuse she needed. Charlie was out the door, headed to rouse her sister from bed. Spencer followed behind with a worried expression.

"I don't want to wake her up. I... uhmm..."

"Well, I want to wake her up. And I happen to know she would like to talk to you." She grabbed Spencer's arm and pulled him onto the elevator.

"No, really, don't wake her up. It can wait."

"Look, Spencer. If she found out you were here and I didn't wake her up, she'd kill me."

"Okay." They stood in awkward silence watching the numbers flash above the elevator door.

"So... Are you going to give her another chance?"

She watched a red color creep up from his neck to envelop his entire face. "I really don't know. I guess I just need to talk to her."

"She likes you."

"Well she has a funny way of showing it."

"She likes to be in control of everything. She couldn't control her feelings around you. It scared her."

"And you know this because...?"

"I'm her sister... I know her. She can be a pain in the butt, but she's worth it. I hope you'll give her a chance."

"Maybe."

"Okay. Here we are. Let me go in first and wake her up. I know my sister, and she's going to want to brush her hair and her teeth before she sees you." Charlie unlocked the door and slipped inside, excited to wake her sister with the news of her early morning visitor. Discovering an empty bed, she hurried to the bathroom. But instead of Emily, she found a note.

*****

Emily arrived at the trailhead at ten thirty, her travels devouring more time than anticipated, but she felt optimistic she was still ahead of the hiking club. Either way, she knew time was of the essence. She pulled out her printed directions and started hiking. The first mile and a half were relatively flat, with the worst encumbrance being the rocky crud she encountered on the footpath. But as promised, when she took a right turn up to Indian Head's summit, the path became steeper. Her back protested the weight of her pack with a steady ache. Carrying a lot of water significantly increased the load, but all her research emphasized the necessity. Nothing to do but plunge ahead.

A few miles in, she encountered her first chute. Astounded, Emily checked her directions again. Surely people didn't actually climb these things? It was nothing but a steep rocky slide. To her dismay, two guys whipped past her, attacking the chute with relish.

"This isn't part of the Devil's Path, is it?" she called out.

"Sure is." One guy stopped, turning back to chuckle at her question. "Awesome views at the top, though. It's worth it."

Emily was thinking she didn't care at all what the view was like. These hiker people were crazy.

"Are you hiking alone?" the other guy asked. "You can hang with us if you want."

"I'm supposed to meet some friends at the Devil's Tombstone."

"That's a long way to hike by yourself."

"I'm pretty slow. I might not be able to keep up with you."

"We're in no hurry." The guy with close-cropped hair and a goatee gave her an encouraging smile. "I'm Brad."

"I'm Josh." The blond guy winked at her. "Don't worry, we'll be glad to slow down and take breaks on this hike. If you're along, we can use you as an excuse."

"I'm grateful," she said.

"Well, come along, Grateful." Josh laughed.

"Emily. I'm Emily." She let out a sigh of relief. Perhaps everything would work out after all.

*****

"I can't believe it!" Spencer repeated the words for probably the tenth time. Emily had gone on the stupid hike with the intention of talking to him, and he wouldn't even be there. And she shouldn't have gone when she'd just gotten out of the hospital. He had a panicky feeling in his chest.

"Read the note to me again," Anne said.

He held it up with shaky hands. "I'm going on the overnight hike so I can talk to Spencer. I left early so I can take my time and meet him at the camping area. I knew he might not go if I showed up at the beginning. I did my research and packed everything I need, so I'll be fine. Don't worry about me. I'll be back Sunday with the group. Sorry to leave you, Charlie, but you know this is the only way. He said he'd give me a second chance if I did something dangerous for him. I thought about it, and this is my best shot. Love you, Emily"

"Can you call someone, Spencer? One of your friends on the hike? So they'll be looking out for her?" asked Anne.

"No, Mom. They usually can't get a cell phone signal out there. They won't even have their phones on." Charlie paced the floor behind the couch.

"I have to go find her," said Spencer. "I'm already packed. I can go now and run most of the way until I catch up with her. I'll bring her back safe tomorrow."

"No," Gherring argued. "We'll need to know you found her. I can tell you right now Anne won't be satisfied until we know she's safe.

We can't wait until tomorrow afternoon." Then he walked over to a utility closet. "But I may have a solution. I've got a sat phone."

"Of course you do. I should've guessed." Charlie chuckled, and Gherring gave her a crooked grin.

"What's a sat phone?" asked Anne.

"A satellite phone," explained Gherring. "I think the best plan is for Spencer and I to go up together. When we find her, we can call you on the sat phone to let you know she's safe. Because just in case she's having ill effects from the drug overdose, it might take both of us to get her down."

"What about me? I'm great at hiking. You can't leave me here." Charlie crossed her arms, twisting her lips sideways.

"Yes, I know you are. But I'm betting you don't have your gear in New York."

"No." She gave a small stomp with her foot.

"Anyway, I don't want to leave your mom alone."

"We should go now," urged Spencer. "It's a long hike."

"Where is it?" asked Steven.

"It's Harriman State Park—the Long Path Loop. Have you been?"

"I've been a few years back. How long is it?"

"It's about eighteen miles. They'll go about ten before they set up camp."

"What if she gets on the wrong trail, hiking by herself?" asked Charlie.

Spencer gritted his teeth. "I'll find her. And when I do, I may tie her to a chair for safekeeping!"

*****

"Now, we get to go down a chute instead of up. You should like that," Josh said to Emily with a smirk. Each time they faced another steep rocky chute, she questioned whether they were truly on the right path. Even with pants on, she had bruises and scratches on her legs from scrambling, climbing and slipping on the loose rock climbs. She hurt in every part of her body, but she refused to complain. She was afraid her companions would lose patience with her and leave her to fend for herself. She looked dubiously at the steep descent as Josh crawled down.

"You go next," said Brad. "Just let him get down a bit so you don't knock rocks on top of him."

Emily wanted to stop and rest, but she kept the thought to herself. She managed to climb down the precipitous drop with only a few additional injuries. At the bottom she stood up and felt herself sway a bit.

Josh frowned at her. "Have you been drinking enough water? You look a little washed out."

She tried to remember. "I'm not sure. Maybe not."

"Sit down and drink something." Obediently, she sat and dug into her pack for a water bottle.

"Why are you out here by yourself, anyway?" he asked. "It's actually dangerous—you should always hike with a buddy. Why are you meeting your friends instead of hiking with them?"

She dropped her face in her hands. "It's a long story."

"It's about a guy, isn't it?" Josh grinned before taking a long drink of water. "Girls do really stupid stuff for guys."

"Hey!" she objected.

"Guys, too." He held up his hand. "Brad once ran naked in the snow to impress a girl."

"And she really was impressed." Brad plopped down beside Emily. "It was worth it."

"So," Josh asked, "are you trying to impress some guy by doing this hike by yourself? Because, he might think it was a dumb thing to do."

"Do you think so?" She hadn't considered her plan might backfire.

"Oh, yeah," said Brad. "He'll think it was a dumb thing to do. You should tell him you planned to hike with us all along. Except, I guess that might make him jealous. Who is this guy, anyway? If you were my girlfriend, I'd be hiking with you. I'd never let you out of my sight."

"I agree," Josh said. "In fact, this guy sounds like a jerk. I'll be glad to take his place."

"He's not a jerk. He doesn't know I'm coming. It's a surprise."

Brad raised his eyebrows. "You're doing this to surprise him?"

"Okay, fine." She covered her face and spoke through her fingers. "I screwed up and hurt his feelings, and I'm trying to impress him so he'll give me another chance."

"Well if it doesn't work, my offer still stands. I don't get my feelings hurt easily. And I've never met a girl who'd hike a trail like this just to impress me." Josh stood and offered her a hand up.

"We should pick up the pace." Brad tightened the strap on his backpack. "We've got another tricky downhill before we start back up. And then it's going to get really steep."

"Steeper than it's already been?" She felt queasy at the thought.

"I'm afraid so," Brad confirmed.

Time blurred in Emily's head. It seemed she'd been climbing forever. Even when the trail took a downturn, she couldn't relax due to the sheer angles and the loose rocks.

"This is the last climb before a fairly flat part with a nice view." Josh patted her arm as she stared at the cliff before her.

"This is not just steep," she declared. "It's straight up."

"You've got to go up, or else go back the way you came. Do you want me to refill some of your water bottles?" He stowed away two water bottles he'd filled from a spring using a filter pump.

"I think I have plenty," she said, checking her pack. "Oh, wow! I only have two left. It still feels so heavy. I thought I had four or five. Yes, Josh, thanks. I guess I need some more."

"No problem."

"Do you want to let me carry your backpack up this last steep part?" Brad offered.

She shook her head. "Y'all have been great, but I'm determined to at least carry my own pack. I need to prove to myself I can do this."

"You're a bit on the stubborn side, aren't you?" Brad flashed a grim smile.

"So I've been told." The climb was even more difficult than it appeared. To her great consternation, she found the backpack pulled her so off balance she couldn't keep her grip. After numerous attempts she found herself at the bottom, bleeding from multiple cuts.

Josh threw a small rope down from the top. "Brad, tie her backpack on."

Her shoulders screamed their relief as Brad pulled the pack off. This time, she offered no resistance.

"Don't feel bad," he said. "You gave it a good try. But it's too heavy, and you're too small to climb something this steep with it on. If it makes you feel any better, I'm planning to send mine up by rope as well. Too bad we don't have the equipment to set up a climb with a belay for you."

She was in so much pain she didn't argue. Not for the first time, she questioned whether this hike was a good idea. But she was way past the point of turning back. She had no choice but to struggle on.

Arriving safely at the top, Brad pulled out a first aid kit. "We should all take a minute to wash out these cuts and doctor them up a bit." Emily noted the guys only had a few small cuts, compared to her multiple gashes. But she accepted the help and the antibiotic ointment with gratitude.

The next part of the trail wasn't flat as promised, but it was broader and not nearly as steep as the previous parts. Comparatively, Emily guessed she could understand why Josh would call it flat.

At the edge of another drop, she looked behind her. "I'm surprised they haven't caught up with us yet. We've been going pretty slowly, haven't we?"

Josh considered her question. "Who is *they*? If it's a large group and there are girls in the group, they may be slower than we were. No offense, but girls do tend to slow things down, especially when they're carrying packs."

"I'm really not sure what the group is like. I only know two people that were going. There's at least one girl—probably more." Her mind wandered. What would happen when Spencer caught up with her. She glanced at her filthy hands and clothes. She must look awful. Maybe she could wash her face and freshen up a little before she saw him. What if he refused to talk to her?

"Are you sure they're camping at the main campground?" asked Brad. "They might go up the trail a bit to a more remote part. Sometimes the campground is crowded."

"Crowded? That many people come up this horrible trail to go camping?"

Brad shook his head, chuckling. "No. But you can access the campground without doing the whole hike."

"Now you tell me," grumbled Emily, as she scrambled downward, leaving her skin on the rocks.

*****

Despite their best efforts to hurry, it was twelve o'clock before Gherring and Spencer parked the car at the trailhead. Quickly shouldering their packs, they started out at a slow trot.

"Don't take any chances," warned Gherring. "We can run when the trail is flat, but not on the climbs and not when we hit the loose rocks. We can't afford for either of us to be injured."

"Agreed." Spencer led the way with Gherring close on his heels.

They made steady progress, speeding along the broad, smooth areas, and making quick work of the climbs. In three hours, they were approaching the area Spencer expected the group to camp.

"We're almost there, I think," said Spencer, breathing heavily. "If she left early this morning, she's probably already with the group. My biggest worry is actually Becca."

"Becca? The Becca that went hiking with us?"

"Yes. She's turned out to be sort of a... a witch."

"A witch? Is that the word you really mean?"

"No sir. It's not the word I really mean."

"What did she do?"

"I can't prove it, but now I think she's the one who took your picture and sent it to the tabloid. And she took a picture of Emily cozied up to that Denning guy and texted it to me. And she and I had words this morning before the hike. She's the reason I didn't go. I... I think she hates Emily."

Gherring's eyebrows furrowed. "Hates her? Why? What did Emily do to her?"

Spencer felt his face heat up. "Becca's jealous of her. She knows I like Emily."

"Ah. Got it. Hell hath no fury and all that."

"Right."

"Well, hopefully we'll get there in time to save Emily from the... uhmm... witch."

"We should. I've never made a pace like this on a hike before. I've sweated all the way through my backpack." Spencer picked up the pace as he spotted the camping area, praying the group had chosen to stop here rather than continue to the next area. Relieved, he spotted a familiar face.

"Landon! Hey!" He ran to his friend, frantically scanning the group looking for Emily's face.

"Spencer? Hey, man. What're you doing here? I thought you weren't coming?"

"I came for Emily." He doubled over, panting for breath. "Oh, man. I'm so tired. Have you seen her?"

"Who?"

"You don't know her, I guess. But she was planning to meet me here, meet us here. Tall, pretty, brunette, with a long braid?"

"Uhmm, no I haven't seen her. But we only got here ten minutes ago. Why don't you ask around?"

Spencer's heart turned over. Gherring was already making the rounds, calling her name. Where could she be?

"Spencer?" He suppressed a shudder as he pivoted. "You came!" Becca smiled as she threw her arms around him. "I'm sorry I made you mad."

"Becca, do you know where Emily is?" He peeled her arms away.

"I have no idea where she is. That's the truth."

"She left a note saying she was going on the hike. But now I think about it, she didn't know where the hike was going to be. Did you tell her?"

"I didn't know she was going on the hike. I promise." She jutted out her chin, and her lower lip quivered. "Why don't you ever believe me?"

"Never mind." He left her to join Gherring in his search.

"No one seems to have seen her. Maybe I should call and see if the girls have heard from her. Maybe she went back home." Gherring dropped to a rock, rifling though his backpack.

"Spencer?" A petite blond girl walked over to join them. "Are you looking for a girl named Emily?"

"Yes! Have you seen her?"

"No, but... Becca was so mad after you left this morning," She glanced over her shoulder at Becca and bit her lip. "She was ranting about a girl named Emily, and she said something about the Devil's Path. I mean, I don't know for sure. But maybe she went there instead."

Spencer's rage was building inside him—he could feel the blood pulsing in his head. He turned toward Becca, but Gherring stood, putting a hand on his shoulder. "No. Let me talk to her. Less emotion."

Spencer followed as Gherring marched to confront Becca. He towered over her, his eyes harsh, his eyebrows furrowed, the muscles in his jaw bulging. "Becca. I'm going to ask you some questions. And you will tell me the truth. Where is my daughter? Did you send her to a different hike?"

She swallowed convulsively, and her pleading gaze darted toward Spencer. But he crossed his arms and glared back without sympathy.

"I... She said she wasn't going on the hike. She said her sister might go. She told me she just wanted to know where the hike was. I swear!"

"And so you told her the hike was on the Devil's Path?"

Her mouth dropped open. "How did you... I mean, I didn't know she'd actually go."

"And you remember clearly? You told her Devil's Path? What else did you tell her?"

"I think I told her we were camping at the Devil's Tombstone. But I didn't think she'd actually go. I mean, after she had that ruffie, you'd think she wouldn't go on a two-day hike."

He pinned her with his eyes. "Who told you that? Who told you she had a ruffie? You were there weren't you? It was you!"

"No... No, I..."

Gherring loomed over her, his entire body shaking. Spencer wondered if he was going to hit her. "I'm going to deal with you after I find my daughter. Attempted murder is a serious charge!"

He turned to Spencer. "How do we get out of here? We need to get to Devil's Tombstone now."

"Don't you have a helicopter or something?"

Gherring laughed bitterly. "No, only a jet. But I might buy a helicopter after this, just in case."

"It'll take us three hours to get back out of here, and over an hour to drive to Tombstone Campground. It'll be dark by then. I hate to say it, but we need to send Charlie. They could drive straight to the public campground and search from there. It'll still take them probably two and a half hours to get there."

"Anne can't go," Gherring stated, "and Charlie shouldn't go by herself."

"Grace. Grace will go with her. Maybe Charlie can borrow some hiking shoes from my other sisters."

With a groan, Spencer dropped onto a nearby rock and buried his face in his hands. "That hike... Do you know that hike, Mr. Gherring?"

Gherring sat beside him, pulling out his sat phone. "I do." He squeezed his lips together, shaking his head. "It's one of the hardest hikes I know. Maybe the toughest."

"Do you really think she could make it on her own? I mean, she could be anywhere on the trail. Or off the trail, for that matter."

"Despite some of her recent decisions, she's usually a smart, resourceful girl. She'll be okay. Her note said she had supplies."

"She just got out of the hospital after almost dying from a drug overdose."

"She'll be okay."

"She'll be okay," Spencer repeated. "And when I see her again, I'm going to kill her."

"Me first," Gherring said with a wry grin.

*****

Emily stood on the trail with Josh and Brad, looking at the fork leading to the Tombstone Campground. It was six o'clock—almost eight hours of hiking. No, not hiking. Crawling, climbing, scrambling, stumbling, falling, with a small amount of walking. She'd never hurt so much in her entire life. And the temperature was beginning to drop. She'd already had to add a layer for warmth. On the last climb, her ankle started aching, so now she was limping.

"I know you're hurt. Will you take a pain pill if I give you one?" asked Josh.

"I don't know." Emily hesitated, but her ankle had settled into a constant throb. "I tend to over-react to drugs. I don't take much medicine."

"Let me see your ankle." He pulled up her pant leg to probe around on the tender area.

"Ouch!"

"You see—you need to take something. Your ankle's already swollen. There's no way you'll be able to hike tomorrow."

"I will, too. I have to. How else will I get home?"

"Fine. Then at least take something for the pain."

"All right. At least my ankle is making me forget about all the other places that hurt."

"Are you allergic to codeine?" he asked.

"No, but it makes me sleepy." She accepted the pill from Josh and downed it quickly with some water.

"Too bad we don't have any anti-inflammatories," Brad commented.

"Yeah," said Josh. "We really need to ice it, too. You should seriously consider abandoning this hike. We could get Smiley's Taxi to pick you up here."

"Please, I can't leave now. I need to talk to him first. Maybe I could leave in the morning."

"I stIll don't get why you're doing this hike," said Brad. "What guy could possibly be worth this? If we hadn't happened along, you might still be out there."

"I know, and I'm grateful. I really am."

"I still say this guy's a jerk," Josh insisted.

"No, he's not. I was the jerk. I went out with this other guy, and he saw me. But now I know it was a mistake. I only want the chance to tell him."

"And you had to do this hike just to talk to him?" asked Josh.

"No. I... Oh, I'm stupid, I guess. I wasn't going to have a chance to talk to him until Monday. And I was afraid if he went on this big weekend hike, he'd hike me right out of his system. And I wanted to prove he was important to me."

"You're not stupid," said Josh. "I think you're really brave. And really cute. And I hope you drop this other jerk and date me instead. You think I'm kidding, but I'm not."

"Josh, you don't even know me. But thanks for the sentiment. That's really sweet."

"Are you sure that's where your friends are going to be?" asked Brad, indicating the trail to the camping area. "It's a public campground, and it's usually full in the summer. The backpackers usually camp up here on the trail."

"I don't know. I thought they'd probably catch up to me on the trail." She blinked back a few tears, angry with herself for losing control.

"Look, Emily," Brad said. "We're going about twenty minutes from here to set up camp. If your friends don't show up, you can camp with us."

Josh and Brad exchanged a look. "I don't think we can leave you here," Josh said. "We'll walk down with you and make sure you find your friends. If they don't come, you'll camp with us. We can set up in the dark. We've done it before."

She nodded mutely, swiping away the tears that streaked through the dirt on her face. Josh led the way down the trail, and Emily limped behind him with Brad taking up the rear. A few minutes onto the trail, Josh turned his head, aiming a comment at Brad.

"Hey, looks like this detour was worth it for the scenery."

Brad craned his head to look around Josh. "How many?"

"Five, I think!"

"Five what?" asked Emily.

"Girls." Josh chuckled.

Emily peered around Josh down the trail. "Charlie?"

"Ohmygosh! Emily? Is that you?"

Josh stepped back as Emily limped down and six girls collided together, hugging and crying.

"What are you doing here?" Emily asked.

"Looking for you!" exclaimed Charlie. "What do you think? This is even stupider than Thursday night. What happened to my sensible sister?"

"I'm meeting the hiking group up here," Emily said. "I would've been fine. You didn't need to come."

"You don't look fine," said Grace. "You look pretty beat up."

"I need to clean up before Spencer comes. But I'm not leaving before he shows up. I didn't suffer for eight hours just to give up and go home. He's got to give me a chance to talk to him."

"Well, he's not here," said Charlie. "So you might as well go back with us."

"He didn't come?" Her chest constricted, and she couldn't breath.

Charlie reached out to steady her. "Woah! Are you dizzy?"

"Emily, this isn't even where the group went hiking," said Grace. "Becca lied to you."

"She lied? He's somewhere else?" Emily bit back bitter tears. "I really did this for nothing, and now I've lost him anyway."

"You haven't lost him," said Grace. "I told you he loved you."

"Yes, I have," said Emily. "He hiked all day and worked me out of his system."

"I'm confused... I thought he didn't go on the hike," Olivia said.

"No, he went on the hike looking for Emily," said Hannah.

"Actually," Charlie told Emily, "Spencer didn't go on the group hike—he came to your apartment to talk to you. Then Steven and Spencer almost killed themselves, running the entire ten-mile hike and back at Harriman trying to find you. And Steven got us tickets to see *Let It Be*, tonight, and we're missing it!"

"Eh-hem." A voice cleared behind them.

Charlie looked up at Emily's companions and grinned. "Sorry. Are we blocking the trail?"

"No," Emily corrected. "These two guys pretty much saved my life today. There seems to be a lot of that going on lately. This is Brad, and this is Josh." She gave each of the guys a hug. "And this is my sister, Charlie, and my friends, Grace and Hannah and Claire and Olivia." She gave the guys a shaky smile. "I know now I'd never have made that hike without y'all. I really owe you."

"I've got a great idea," said Charlie. "Let's bring the guys back with us, and we can take them out for a late dinner to thank them."

Emily examined the two men, noticing for the first time both were extremely attractive, with well-muscled physiques. No wonder Charlie wanted to bring them back to the city. Grace also seemed interested in the idea, or in the guys. She was giggling at something Brad said to her. Well, she'd be glad if something good came out of this awful day. Maybe someone else could find love. As for her, she'd blown it again.

"We appreciate the offer," Brad said. "But, I doubt we could all fit in your vehicle. Or did you come by taxi?"

"Nah," said Charlie, "We're in a limo—plenty of room. Do y'all live in the city? We could drop y'all by your places to clean up, and then meet for dinner."

"A limo? You're kidding, right?" said Josh.

"No," said Claire. "It's a real limousine. You should come—it's fun."

"Why on earth did you come out here in a limousine? Are you rich or something?" asked Josh.

"Heck, no," said Charlie. "But my stepdad is. Are you guys coming? Or are you camping on the cold hard ground and hiking all day tomorrow."

"Well, that was the original plan." Brad said. "But... I'll leave it up to Josh. Whatever, you want. I'm game."

"Why not? We can hike any time." Josh sent a concerned glance in Emily's direction and moved to steady her as she swayed against him.

She was dizzy and bone tired. She was also heartbroken, but she tried not to dampen the spirits of her friends. Josh supported her as she limped along, following the animated group down the long trail to the parking lot where the limousine waited. She climbed in and wedged herself into the corner seat, where she promptly fell sound asleep.

*****

"They found her," Gherring told Spencer. They'd reached their car and were trying to decide whether to drive toward Devil's Tombstone when Charlie called. "They have her in the limo, and they're headed back to town."

Spencer felt his body relax as relief flooded his system. He hadn't realized how tense he'd been. "Is she okay? I can't believe she made that hike on her own."

"She's apparently okay, but a bit torn up. Nothing broken. They're bringing two guys back with them. Evidently, these two met up with Emily on the trail and helped her out." Gherring shook his head. "The girls are planning to take those boys out to a late dinner as a thank-you."

Spencer felt a surge of jealousy. What was wrong with him? He should be grateful she had help. Otherwise, she'd probably be stuck alone on the trail or even lost. But he couldn't help wondering how friendly they'd been.

"We should beat them home by an hour. Do you want to wait with us? Or do you want to go home."

"I'll go home. I really need a shower."

"And then come back over for dinner with the group?" Gherring asked.

Spencer considered his options. He was exhausted, and he really didn't feel like going out for a late dinner. On the other hand, he wanted to see Emily.

"I guess I'll take a quick shower and then wait at your place for Emily to come back."

"So you can kill her before I do?"

"Absolutely." Spencer grinned before heaving an exhausted breath. "I'm so tired. I've hardly slept in two nights. And then today's marathon..."

"I agree, but I'm okay to drive if you want to sleep on the way home."

"Awesome. Thanks."

He fell into a restless sleep, fighting images of Emily careening down a rocky chute.

Chapter Eleven

"That was Charlie. They're on their way up," Anne told Steven as she hung up her cell phone. "All of them."

"All of them?"

"The whole crew. I'm excited to meet Spencer's other sisters." She was munching on a cracker, relishing the sense of relief both of her girls would be home safe again.

"What about the guys? Are they coming up as well?"

"I don't know. She said everyone, but weren't they planning to drop the guys off to take showers?"

"We'll find out," said Steven as he walked to answer the doorbell. Anne was thinking how nice it was to be a part of something fun after being locked away in the apartment all week. Going to the hospital for Emily's emergency didn't count as an outing.

The doors opened and chaos erupted. Charlie came in, laughing, followed by three girls, about her height. All were excited and giggling as they rushed into the penthouse checking out the interior with curious glances. Then came Grace, conversing with a young man with close-cropped hair and a goatee. Next came a tall, broad-shouldered fellow with blond hair, cradling the limp body of Emily in his arms. Spencer, who was obviously fuming, followed right behind him.

Anne struggled to stand up. "What's wrong with Emily?"

"She's okay," said the blond man with a smile. "She's just sleeping."

"Because you drugged her!" accused Spencer.

"I didn't drug her. I gave her some pain medication."

"Like I said, you drugged her. And you should've let me carry her." Anne could almost see steam coming out of Spencer's ears. "What did you give her, anyway?" he demanded.

"I gave her some acetaminophen with hydrocodone. Where should I put her?" he asked Anne.

"Please, lay her here on the couch."

"Okay, but you should know she's pretty dirty." He nodded to Anne. "Hi, I'm Josh."

"He saved Emily's life today," said Charlie. "Him and Brad."

"I saved her first," grumbled Spencer.

"Hi, I'm Brad." The other young man walked over to offer his hand to Anne.

"I'm Anne, Emily and Charlie's mom, and this is their father."

Steven moved through the crowd to offer his hand to the young men. "Hi. I'm Steven."

Brad and Josh stared with wide eyes at Steven.

"Steven Gherring? Are you Steven Gherring?" asked Josh, pumping his hand.

"I'm afraid so." He chuckled.

Brad grabbed his hand and shook it. "Nice to meet you, sir. Charlie didn't tell us who her dad was."

"Technically, I'm their stepdad, but today I think I deserve to be called Dad."

"I agree," said Anne. "You definitely get dad status."

"I'll give you dad status for letting us use the limo," said Charlie, giving Steven a hug and kiss on the cheek.

"Nice to meet you," Josh said to Steven. "And thanks for the ride home."

"Thanks to both of you for taking care of Emily for us and bringing her home," said Steven.

Spencer added sullenly, "And for giving Emily illegal drugs."

"It wasn't illegal," Josh growled.

"Codeine—without a prescription!" He spat back.

Josh's smile didn't reach his eyes. "But you see, I'm a doctor and so is Brad. So it was perfectly legal for us to give her hydrocodone."

Spencer's face deflated and he stomped into the kitchen.

"You're both doctors?" asked Anne.

"Yes, Ma'am," said Brad. "We're third year residents at Mercy General."

"She needs that foot elevated, and she needs to take some anti-inflammatories for the sprain," Josh said. "But, I'm pretty sure nothing's broken. Icing it would also be good—twenty minutes on, twenty minutes off."

"What about dinner?" asked Charlie. "Can you wake her up?"

Anne frowned down at her sleeping daughter. "If you gave her hydrocodone, she'll probably be out cold until tomorrow morning."

Josh chuckled. "Well, she warned me she had a strong reaction to drugs. But I didn't know she was that bad."

"Mom," said Charlie, "I told the guys they could shower off and change here, so we could go eat. Is that okay?"

"Sure," said Anne, glancing at Steven for confirmation.

"No problem," Steven said. "Follow me. We've got a couple of showers available." He led Josh and Brad into the back.

Grace dragged her sisters over to the couch. "Mrs. Gherring, these are my sisters. Olivia, Hannah, and Claire."

"Nice to meet you," said Anne. "They're so tall! What happened to you, Grace?"

"We think her dad was the mailman." Olivia waggled her eyebrows at Grace, who whacked her sister on the back of her head.

"My Grandma was short, too. And she tells me what we lack in height is made up for in beauty."

"I think it's made up for in mouth. Ow!" Olivia giggled as Grace whacked her again.

"Are you in school, Olivia?" asked Anne.

"Yes, ma'am. I'm in nursing school."

"And what about you, Hannah?"

"I just finished my first year of college—majoring in undecided."

"Way to go Hannah. Keep it up and you can come be a ski bum with me." Charlie gave her a high-five.

"Claire? What about you?"

"I'm a junior in high school next year. And I'm going to be an accountant."

"Claire, you can't even keep up with your purse. How will you keep track of people's money?" Olivia stifled a laugh.

"Easy—it's all virtual. I'm great with virtual stuff, like video games."

"What about you, Grace? Are you still in school?"

"No, ma'am. I teach first grade, but I'm off for the summer."

"The bad thing is she's the same size as her students," teased Olivia.

Spencer wandered back into the room and sat down across from the couch, staring at Emily, his mouth downturned.

Anne cleared her throat, catching his attention.

"I'm sorry she's asleep, Spencer. Are you going to dinner? I know you're starving, and she's not likely to wake up tonight."

"You should come to dinner, Spencer. It'll be fun." Charlie walked behind him to nudge his shoulder.

"With the two fabulous doctor heroes?" he asked sarcastically.

"I think you should stay home, you old grump," said Grace. "Why don't you like them? They probably saved Emily's life. You should be grateful."

"Well, I *really* saved her life. And today I hiked twenty miles, running most of the way. It's not my fault she was on a different hike."

"You're right, Spencer." Anne gave him her most reassuring smile. "We haven't forgotten you saved her life. And if you hadn't run twenty miles, we wouldn't have found her. She'd still be out there. And she didn't even have a sleeping bag. I'm sure she wasn't prepared for how cold it is in the mountains at night."

"We would've kept her warm." Josh walked back into the room fresh from his shower, his hair still damp. "I wouldn't have let her get hypothermia."

Spencer huffed something unintelligible, and Anne hurried to change the subject. "Charlie, when is your return ticket? I didn't even ask you."

"I have to go back Tuesday. I'm really bummed Emily made us miss the musical tonight. But Steven still gets credit for getting the tickets. He gets big dad-credit for today."

"Hopefully, when Emily wakes up tomorrow, she'll feel well enough to do something fun," said Anne.

Josh strolled toward the couch. "One thing I'd advise would be to wash off her cuts, although it may be hard to do with her sleeping so soundly. Brad and I washed some of them about five hours into the hike, and applied some antibiotic ointment. But she really has some pretty deep gashes, especially on her legs." He moved toward Emily and started to raise her pant leg.

"Don't touch her," growled Spencer.

Josh pulled his hands back. "Look man, I'm not assaulting your girlfriend. I'm a doctor."

"We've already heard you're a doctor," said Spencer.

Grace said, "Yes. And technically, she's not your girlfriend, either. Right, Spencer? I mean, she'd probably be your girlfriend by now if you hadn't refused to talk to her on Friday."

"Grace!" Spencer said. "That's enough."

"In fact," she continued undeterred, "I think you said you weren't sure you could ever stand to be around her again—"

"Grace!"

"Well, let me just state for the record, if she isn't taken, I'm definitely interested," said Josh.

Spencer stood and faced him with his fists clenched. "She's taken!"

"Fine… at least for now. But I'd take better care of her if she were mine."

"Josh, Spencer! Please sit down." Anne said. "You're upsetting me."

Spencer sat down on the floor next to Emily, and Josh walked around behind the couch.

"Josh, we really appreciate what you did to help Emily," said Anne. "You don't know her well enough to realize this, but no one tells her what to do. It certainly isn't Spencer's fault she got herself into trouble."

"Yes ma'am. I did note she has a mind of her own," Josh admitted.

"That's the truth," Charlie agreed. "She's never been sweet and obedient like me."

Steven returned to the living room. "Oh, were you telling a joke? Was that the punch line?"

"Very funny," said Charlie. "And here I'd been saying earlier what a great dad you were."

"Are you guys ready to go? I'm starving." Brad returned, freshly showered, and took his place beside Grace.

"Come on, Spencer," she urged. "I won't tease you any more. There's nothing you can do here."

Josh moved to Spencer and held out his hand, "I'm sorry, man. I think we both had a pretty tough day. I won't mouth off any more."

Spencer stood up and shook his hand, but his mouth was set in a grim line.

"Come on," said Claire. "We get to ride in the limousine again."

*****

Spencer was still furious. How did this guy dare to insert himself into Emily's life? He'd only known her for half a day. The only thing that made this guy a hero was dumb luck—he happened to be there at the right time. And why did Spencer have all the bad luck? Why did he run and hike all those miles looking for Emily, while this jerk got to just show up and save the day? And after all of his efforts, Spencer didn't even get to carry her up to the apartment. And then the jerk had the audacity to be a doctor. Both of them—doctors. He watched his sister across the table as she laughed with Brad, her head leaning in close to his. Was he looking down the front of her shirt? He needed to have a talk with his sister.

"Spencer, you're awfully quiet," murmured Charlie. "Are you still worried about Emily? I saw her before she fell asleep. She's going to be fine."

"No. I mean... Yes, I'm worried, but that's not it. I don't trust this Josh guy," he answered softly, since the object of his disdain was sitting on the other side of Charlie.

"He's okay. You can't blame him for having a crush on her. It happens all the time, so you better get used to it."

"What do you mean, it happens all the time?"

"Every guy she meets falls for her. She usually doesn't even pay attention. I'd bet a million dollars she didn't even notice Josh is good-looking."

"You think he's good-looking? I think he looks like a jerk."

Charlie chuckled. "He's cute, Spencer. But that doesn't mean Emily thought so. I've known her all my life and I'll tell you she's never done anything like this for a guy before."

"What do you mean? What did she do for him?"

"Not for him, you big dummy—for you. She went on a crazy hard hike and planned to camp out, sleeping on the ground. These things are way out of her comfort zone. And she did it for you, not for Josh."

"She'd never been on that hike. She had no idea what she was getting into."

"But if you know Emily, you know she read all about it before she went. She at least knew it would be really difficult."

"And I'd never have expected her to do that. I was coming to her apartment to talk to her."

"I know, I know. But she didn't know that. And let's face it. You didn't even know you were coming to talk to her until right before you did it."

"If I'd just talked to her on Friday, none of this would have happened. It's my fault she's all bunged up."

"Don't be silly. This is Emily we're talking about. She has a mind of her own, and it works in crazy unpredictable ways."

"So you don't think she's attracted to Josh? The *doctor*?"

"No, I don't. But let me ask you a question. Have you forgiven her for going out with Asher Denning?"

"That seems like it happened months ago. Yes, I've forgiven her. I didn't even think about it after I found out she was in trouble."

"Well, you need to remember she doesn't know that. She thinks you're still angry. And when she wakes up tomorrow, it'll still be on her mind."

"Do you think she likes me?"

"Ohmygosh! Are all men this dense? Yes, she likes you. Of course she does." Charlie shook her head. "Now, can you enjoy dinner?"

"Sure." He felt his spirits lifting… Emily liked him.

An uneasy truce lay between Spencer and Josh for the rest of dinner. Both seemed to acknowledge they didn't like each other, but they didn't have any more arguments. At least not overtly.

"What does Emily do?" Josh asked after everyone else at the table had summarized their present school or work occupations.

"So you don't even know?" He let a little sneer creep into his voice. So great to finally have a one-up on Josh.

"Well, no. While I was attempting to keep her from falling to her death, we didn't discuss mundane things like work or school."

Charlie interrupted. "Really, Josh? Falling to her death?"

"Okay, I might be exaggerating a little. But if she'd gotten off the trail and fallen where no one could find her, it could have happened.

"That's actually true," Spencer conceded.

Brad jumped in. "The hike wasn't so bad and she was great. Carried her own backpack the whole way. Refused help most of the time. That's really why she was so scratched up. She definitely wanted to prove herself."

"You know," said Josh, "she tried to explain it. But I never quite understood why she did that. Maybe you can elucidate, Spencer. Why did she go on that hike today? She said she had to prove you were important."

Spencer felt his face heating up as he struggled to find an answer, but Grace jumped in.

"It was my fault, actually. She wanted to talk to Spencer, and I told her Spencer would be busy on this overnight hike until Monday."

"And then Becca lied to her about where the hike was going to be," Charlie added, "so she ended up at Devil's Path instead of Harriman Loop."

"Becca?" asked Josh. "Who's Becca."

"Becca is this girl who likes Spencer, so she lied to Emily to throw her off," said Grace.

"Oh." Josh gave a knowing nod. "Becca likes Spencer. I get it. Emily did this to attract Spencer's attention away from Becca. He doesn't seem worth the trouble to me. No offense, man."

"No," snarled Spencer. "I've never liked Becca, and Emily didn't need to attract my attention, she already had it."

"Josh, you've got a long way to go before you can understand my sister. Her mind works in complicated ways." Charlie pointed her finger at him.

"I've got nothing but time, and I'm a *patient* man."

"Cute," smirked Charlie, "A doctor—a patient man? That's funny."

It wasn't funny at all.

"Oh, and she's a CPA at Gherring Inc. We never did tell you what she did," Charlie added.

"Ah," said Josh. "A CPA. Hmmm, that could be a great combination."

In his mind, Spencer pictured all the different ways he could kill Josh.

171

*****

"This is fun, Mom. The two of us can sit here together and feel miserable." At seven a.m. on Sunday morning, Emily had already limped down to her apartment to shower off and change clothes. She'd been shocked at how many bruises and cuts were on her body, and her ankle was definitely swollen. But her shower had been a moment of ecstasy as she'd scrubbed the dirt and dust from her body until her skin was pink. Her mother was fighting nausea again since removing her IV due to painful irritation of the skin around the needle. She was braving the mounting queasiness, attempting to postpone calling Connie to insert a new IV needle.

"I'm just so happy to have you here in one piece I don't want to complain. But you may not want to stay up here if I start throwing up again." Her mother's smile was a bit shaky.

"Why don't you let me call Connie?" Steven asked. "You know she won't mind."

"But she's got to have some time off. We can't always expect her to drop everything and come over here," Anne protested.

Steven's answer was cut off by a tentative knock at the door. "I wonder who that could be. I'm betting on Spencer."

"Me, too. He was dying to talk to you last night," Anne told Emily.

"Well, I don't look very good." Emily wished she'd worn long pants to cover her extensive injuries. She couldn't quite see around Steven when he opened the door.

"Oh, I wasn't expecting you."

"Yes, sir. I hope you don't mind. I was hoping to see my patient before I do rounds at the hospital." Josh smiled broadly as he entered the apartment. "Hey, Emily."

She was so confused. "Hi, Josh. What're you doing here?"

"Well, I got called in to work this morning, so I was hoping you'd be awake. I wanted to check on you."

She felt her cheeks burning as he approached her, studying her legs and her foot with a distinct frown. "I'm just fine." She tucked her legs underneath her on the couch.

"Can I check your ankle?"

"Check it? Why? I mean, it's sprained I guess. But I'm sure it will get better."

"I want to make sure we don't need to get it x-rayed."

"Well, if it doesn't get better, I'll go see a doctor."

Anne laughed, "Emily, you don't know? Josh is a doctor. And so is Brad."

"What?" Her face grew even hotter.

"Yes, I forgot you didn't know. We talked about it last night, but you were sleeping." Suddenly a look of consternation passed across his face. "By the way, what were you doing accepting a pill from me yesterday when you didn't know I was a doctor? That was really dangerous. I could have given you something unsafe." His voice was slightly scolding.

Emily bristled at his admonishing tone. "I usually have pretty good judgment about people. I'd been forced to trust you all day, so I saw no reason not to trust you at the end of the day. However, now I'm having second thoughts. You're not my father—"

"Ouch!" Josh held up his hands in mock distress. "Mrs. Gherring, I see what you mean about no one telling her what to do."

The Gherrings smiled at his discomfort. Anne said, "Don't say I didn't warn you."

"I'm sorry, Emily. I only meant to express concern for your well-being. I would never presume to order you around. And I certainly don't aspire to be your father or anything of the sort."

"Okay. Apology accepted. As long as we understand each other."

"I'd like to reach the point where I really understand you, but I think I'm going to need more time. So, seriously... I really do want to check your ankle."

Reluctantly, she unfolded her legs and stuck her right foot out. He pressed around the swollen area experimentally and then moved her foot around to flex the ankle, watching her reaction. She winced, but refused to make a sound at the pain.

"I'm sorry—I know that hurts. I still don't think anything is broken. But it is a serious sprain." He began to inspect the cuts on her legs, which she'd left mostly unbandaged, not having anything large enough to cover them. "Nothing looks too deep. Can I see your arms?"

Sighing, she stuck her arms out at him and he looked until he seemed satisfied. "Don't you have a gash on your back?"

"Yes, but you can't see that one."

He rolled his eyes. "Brad and I cleaned that one off with water yesterday and put gauze on it. Why can't I see it today? It's not in a private place."

"I don't know, but you can't see it." She pressed her lips together in a tight line.

He grinned at her. "Okay. You're the boss. I think you need to be taking anti-inflammatories for your sprained ankle. O.T.C. NSAID's ought to be fine. That's ibuprofen, aspirin, or naproxen sodium. Unless it's hurting badly enough you need more hydrocodone?"

"No, thank you. I'd rather hurt a little than get knocked out again. I've been unconscious a bit too much lately."

"I agree," said Steven. "Let's keep you off the heavy stuff."

Josh frowned at Anne. "Are you all right, Mrs. Gherring? You seem like you're about to pass out."

"Oh, I'm okay. Just a little queasy."

"Actually, you could really help us out. Anne needs a new IV port," said Steven.

"What?" asked Josh, reaching to examine the proffered arm. "Oh, I see. Yes, this area's really inflamed. So you removed an IV port from this spot?"

"Yes, this morning. It was really hurting," Anne explained.

"And why do you need an IV?"

"She's got hyperemesis gravidarum. They have her on IV fluids for nutrition support and antiemetics," said Steven.

"Really? You're pregnant? How far along?"

"We're not sure. Maybe ten weeks," said Anne.

"She was interviewed about it on the news last week," said Emily.

He shook his head. "I never get to watch television. Saturday was the first day I've had off in weeks. I was supposed to be off today, but I got called in."

He turned back to Anne. "Wow, you're really thin. I've studied about this, but I've never seen a real case. It's pretty rare. Well, except some of them go undiagnosed. Do you have a severe case? Have they talked to you about TPN?"

"We're hoping to avoid it—so many complications. But I need to eat so I can gain some weight."

"I'll be glad to put in a new needle for you. Do you want it in the same place on the other arm? Or some place different?" He opened up the sterile IV kit they handed him.

"Yes, please. On the other arm. I really appreciate this, Josh."

"My pleasure," he said, as he quickly inserted the IV needle. "Just a pinch. How's that?" He taped the new port in place and took off his gloves. "I'm hoping to ingratiate myself with your whole family," he said with a conspiratorial grin.

"Thank you, Josh," said Steven. "If there's anything I can ever do to help you, let me know."

"I will. Do you need help starting a new fluid bag?"

"No, we've got it down," said Anne, as she and Steven headed toward the bedroom.

Emily felt her palms sweating when her parents left them alone together. He really made her nervous. Time to give him the boot. "Okay... Thanks for dropping by."

He sat down on the couch next to her. "Can I drop by another time? I'd like to see you again."

Her stomach turned a somersault. "You would?"

"Yes, I would. I don't have a lot of spare time right now because of the residency program, but I'd like to spend it with you."

"Why? I told you I had a boyfriend."

"Well, that's not exactly what you said, but I'll let it pass. Let me explain. When I see something really great, something I want, I'm willing to do whatever it takes to get it. I'm not the type of man who gives up if it's not easy. I'm willing to work at it and wait a long time if I have to. I'm in no hurry. I sense you and Spencer are on unsure footing here. I don't think he's the right man for you. If and when you change your mind, I'll be right here waiting to prove to you I'm the right guy."

The smile never left his face as he stood. After a moment she thought to close her mouth.

"No pressure. Just think about it." He walked to the door to let himself out. "I'll see you later." Before she could protest his promise, he slipped through the door, and clicked it shut behind him.

*****

Spencer checked the time again as he paced in the lobby of the Gherring's apartment building. It wasn't even eight o'clock yet. He didn't want to go upstairs too early, but he didn't think he could wait much longer. He'd hardly slept the night before. He realized Charlie was right. He no longer felt any anger about Asher Denning. He was only aware of the fear and agony he'd felt when he'd almost lost her. Twice. He knew he was in love with her. Both times he would gladly have given his life to save hers. He had to let her know how he felt, but he couldn't say words like "love" too soon. He had to be careful. She liked to be in control, and he didn't want to scare her away.

The elevator doors opened, and he felt instant rage at the sight of the man exiting. "What are you doing here, Josh?" He ground the words out between his teeth.

"Hello, Spencer. How are you?" Josh smiled, his voice filled with unequivocal delight. "I was simply taking care of my patients. I don't usually make house calls. But in special cases I'm willing to make an exception." He waggled his eyebrows. "And this is definitely a special case."

Spencer felt a clear understanding of the term justifiable homicide. "Get out!"

"I'm leaving, but only because I have to go to work. Certainly not because you think you commanded it. Have a good day."

Spencer watched him exit through the lobby door, breathing deeply to calm himself. It was obviously not too early to see the Gherrings. So he punched in the code that allowed him to take the elevator up to the penthouse and knocked on the door, pacing nervously until it opened.

"Hi, Spencer," said Gherring. "This time it really is you. A little earlier—"

"I know," Spencer snapped. "Josh was here. I saw him downstairs."

"Yes, he just knocked on the door. He must have learned the code from Charlie last night. It was a total surprise."

"An unpleasant one as far as I'm concerned. Is Emily available?"

"Sure, she'll be right out." He walked toward the bedrooms, calling, "Emily! Spencer's here to see you."

His heart hammered in his chest. The last time he'd spoken to her, she'd been sitting at a table with Asher Denning. So much had happened since then, but they hadn't communicated. She limped into the room, obviously trying, but failing, to appear uninjured.

"Hi Spencer." Her eyes studied the carpet around his feet.

"I... uhmm... I think I hear Anne calling me." Gherring disappeared into the bedroom.

Spencer couldn't help staring at the bruises and cuts that carpeted her legs. "Hi. How do you feel?"

He stood awkwardly in front of her while she perched on the couch. "I'm okay. I didn't run twenty miles like you did."

"I... uhmm... I came to see you yesterday, but you'd already gone."

"I know. I heard. But it was such a long way to the Devil's Path—I had to leave really early to get there."

"Why did you ask Becca? You should have called me."

"I didn't think you'd answer if I called. Would you have answered?"

"I... I don't know. I'd like to think so."

Tears welled in her eyes. "I was desperate."

"I really hate you went through that. And you have all those cuts all over you."

"I know. They're ugly."

"That's not what I mean. I don't want you to be hurt. Ever."

"I don't know. I felt like I deserved it... after I lied and everything. I was just flattered, you know. Asher didn't mean anything—"

"I know. I know. I didn't... When I thought I'd lost you... When I thought you were... I couldn't handle it."

"I'm sorry. And I know you saved my life. They told me—"

"And then Josh saved your life," he bit out sarcastically.

"Are you mad at me about Josh? I didn't ask for him to come along, you know."

"No, I'm not mad at you, but I can't stand that guy."

"Honestly, I think I'd probably still be out there, lost on that mountain, if Josh and Brad hadn't happened by. I was about to turn off the trail because I couldn't believe my directions were right."

"He's a jerk."

"Funny. He said the same thing about you, and he hadn't even met you."

"Well, he really is a jerk, and he's trying to steal you from me." He gritted his teeth. "It's so unfair. You're not even mine, and he's trying to take you away."

"Well, he doesn't control me. No one controls me."

"What was he doing up here this morning, anyway?"

He watched her cheeks flush. "He came to check out my ankle. And while he was here he put a new IV in Mom's arm. That's all. It was just doctor stuff."

"So he's your doctor now?" She flinched at his sarcasm.

"No. I didn't even know he was a doctor."

"You didn't know when he gave you codeine? When he drugged you?"

"I didn't know until this morning. And don't use that tone with me!"

Spencer beat on his forehead with the palm of his hand, pounding out his frustration. "I can't help it! You almost died! Don't you understand? You don't know what it was like—to see you laying there, not breathing. To think I'd lost you."

He knelt down in front of her, and cupped her face in his hands. "I've dreamed about kissing you, imagined what it would be like. But the first time I put my lips on yours, I was trying to keep you alive. It wasn't supposed to be like that."

He watched her eyes, and she returned his intense gaze. Her tongue darted out to lick her lips, and he suppressed a groan. He hesitated, but when she didn't pull away, he leaned in and touched his mouth to hers. Tentatively, holding back his passion, he explored the softness of her lips with his. His hands moved, caressing her cheeks, marveling at the silky feel of her skin beneath his fingers. His first kiss. No, his second. The first time, she hadn't been breathing. This time, she kissed him back. He tried to control himself, but as he thought about how he'd almost lost her, his kiss became stronger, more desperate.

She pressed her mouth against his, her lips seeking his warmth, eager and terrified at the same time. She could feel his emotion, and she responded with equal fervor. Her hands were on his chest as she leaned forward trying to close the distance between them. The only thing she could hear was the sound of their ardent breathing and the pounding of her heart. She could feel his frantic heartbeat with her fingers. She'd been kissed before, but never like this. He kissed her like a thirsting man who'd crossed a dessert to find water. As if he was drawing his life-blood from her. She was opening herself up—she might be hurt again. Cuts and gashes and sprains were nothing compared to the pain that had been wrenched in her heart in the past. She was a fool to let herself fall for him, but she couldn't stop.

His tongue stroked across her lips, and she parted them to allow him entry. Then her tongue danced with his as his kiss deepened. His hands fisted in her hair, and she was surprised to hear a small moan escape her throat. He responded with a groan she could feel vibrating in his chest. She sensed a tingle radiating down through her body. His right hand dropped down, his fingers trailing down her neck, leaving a fiery brand in their wake.

She was losing herself. She knew at that moment, had they been alone, she would give him everything—her mind, her body, her soul. A burst of panic seized her, and she broke away. She sat back, covering her mouth with her hands, staring at him with stark terror. He'd probably been with dozens of girls. Grace had told her Spencer loved her, but what did that even mean? What did this kiss mean to him? Certainly it wasn't the total loss of self she'd just experienced. He obviously cared for her, and she owed him her life. But she'd sworn to protect herself from this type of assault. She needed to safeguard her heart. Otherwise it would be torn to shreds. And she could tell, simply from that kiss, Spencer could do more damage than she'd ever experienced before.

"What's wrong?" His distress was clearly written on his face. "Did I hurt you? Was it too hard?"

She couldn't formulate the words to express what she felt. How could she explain her fears? How could she describe the precarious state of her heart? He was experienced, where she was naïve. Her own physical response to his kiss shocked her, and she knew she was losing the control she held so dear.

"No... I..." She blinked rapidly at the tears in her eyes. "I can't... I can't do this."

"You can't do what? You can't kiss me? Was it bad?" He moved to sit beside her on the couch, clenching his fists in his lap.

"Bad? Ha! I think you know better than that. But I'm not ready for you. I'm too... You're too... I can't explain it."

"I'm too what? Am I pushing you too fast?"

"Yes. No. You're not pushing me. I... I know you can't understand this, because it's no big deal to you. I'm not... I'm not experienced. And I'm afraid."

He looked frustrated. "I'm not... I won't push you. I'd never do that. I mean, if I understand what we're talking about. Are we talking about physical stuff?"

"Sort of. But I'm afraid of more than that—the emotional part too."

"What if we said we'll take it slow?"

"But slow to you is different than slow to me. I don't know if I can handle another kiss like that."

He squeezed his eyes shut and groaned out loud. "I don't know if I can handle not kissing you again. Not now I know what it's like." He looked at her with pleading eyes, and she felt her resolve melting.

"You see—that's exactly what I'm talking about. You can't look at me like that. It's... it's not fair."

"But it wasn't bad? You liked it, too? The kiss, I mean. Because... I really liked it."

Emily noticed he looked unsure, even vulnerable, as he anticipated her answer. She experienced a little thrill her opinion was so important to him he discounted his own expertise.

She allowed herself a slight smile. "Oh I liked it—a little too much. That's the problem."

Now he was grinning. "I don't see it as a problem. We'll find some way to keep it from being a problem. Just don't think about it so much."

And catching her off guard, he leaned in and brushed his lips lightly across hers, then pulled away with his eyes closed, as if savoring her taste. When he opened his eyes, his pupils dilated in the middle of the pools of deep brown, she thought she might fall into them. She knew she was playing with fire, and her fear of being burned was stronger than ever.

But a seed of a thought formulated in her head. Perhaps there was a way she could be certain she wouldn't get hurt again.

Chapter Twelve

CHARLIE LET HER MOUTH FALL OPEN. "What did you say?" She sat on the couch with her sister, the two having moved back downstairs into Emily's apartment. She'd given Charlie an extremely unemotional account of her morning. It included a surprise visit from Josh who'd asked to date her. After that, she described the awkward talk with Spencer—the first one since the disastrous night with Asher Denning. She gave a very unsatisfactory account of Spencer kissing her for the first time, without any juicy details whatsoever. And then she very matter-of-factly stated she'd decided it wouldn't happen again.

"I said, I don't think we should kiss any more. I think it's not a good idea."

"Why? Was he a bad kisser? Or did you decide you don't like him after all."

"No," she said, looking down as her cheeks flushed. "It was pretty good. Maybe too good. I think that's how I get in trouble. I get way too emotionally involved when things get physical. So, I think we should keep it platonic until it's safer."

"What do you mean? What's safer?"

"I just don't know about Spencer. He's just a little too good at kissing. I guess he's had lots of practice, but I don't want to think about it. I'm not sure I can handle too much of that and still stick to my rules. And then there's the unwritten rule we always told each other... *Guard your heart*. So I think we should just keep it platonic until it's safer."

"So, let me get this straight. Y'all are going to be in an official dating relationship, but you're not going to kiss."

"Yes. That's the plan."

"And Spencer is okay with this?"

"Well, I haven't exactly told him, but I hinted at it."

"So y'all haven't had the define-the-relationship talk?"

"Not yet. Maybe we can talk after dinner tonight. Spencer cooks at his family's house on Sundays. Tonight he's grilling hamburgers. I said we'd both go—I hope that sounds okay to you?"

"Sure... But back to this plan of yours. When will your kissing hiatus be over? When will you trust him or yourself enough to kiss him? When you're engaged? Or not until after you're married?"

Emily's face turned scarlet. "Ohmygosh! I don't know. We're not talking about getting married. He only kissed me this morning. I thought this could kind of be a test. He's been with all these girls, and I don't know how physical those relationships have been. So if that's all he's looking for from me, he'll get tired of me pretty quickly. This will give him a chance to prove he likes me just for me and not for what he can get from me."

"Not for what he can get from you? You mean like, he might date you so he can kiss you?"

"You know what I mean. I'm talking about more than kissing. But that's what kissing leads to."

"Sister... tsk, tsk. What does he have to do to prove himself? Let's see. So far, he's forgiven you for lying to him, saved your life, and then practically killed himself yesterday trying to save you again."

"I know he's done a lot for me and I don't doubt he cares about me. But we still need to be careful about the physical stuff."

"No doubt you need to be careful, but are you sure you don't want to kiss at all?"

"I'm not saying I don't want to—I'm saying it's not a good idea."

"Okay, let's talk about something else. You've been criticizing Spencer all along for being a player. What about you? Are you through dating other guys?"

"There aren't any other guys."

"What about Asher and Josh?"

"Hey! You're supposed to be on my side, Sister! I've already admitted Asher was a big mistake. He turned out to be a jerk—he left me passed out at the bar. And Josh—I never did anything to encourage him. I'm actually worried Spencer might think I'm interested in Josh, because I'm not. To be honest, I barely even noticed him or Brad when we were hiking."

Charlie chuckled. "That doesn't surprise me. You can be so unaware of your surroundings sometimes. You didn't notice he was hot? Or that he had the hots for you? I knew right away, as soon as we met on the trail."

"No, he caught me by surprise this morning when he said he wanted to see me again. But next time, if there is a next time, I'll be ready for him. He obviously likes to be in control, and I don't have the energy to fight for control all the time. Plus, he's a player if I've ever seen one—and really arrogant. I imagine he's used to girls falling all over him, especially being a doctor."

"Sister, I'm still not sold on this no-kissing idea."

"It's not my idea. There's a whole book about it."

"There is? I've never heard about it."

"It's called I Kissed Kissing Goodbye."

Charlie laughed. "No, it's called I Kissed Dating Goodbye, and I assume you haven't even read it."

"No, but I've thought it through, and my mind is made up."

"Poor Spencer."

"You feel sorry for him because he won't get to kiss anyone for a while?"

"No, I feel sorry for him because he's fallen for my sister!"

*****

Spencer was in a good mood, a really good mood. Everyone always talked about love being painful. And it had been painful. But now... Now everything was good. He'd kissed her, and she'd kissed him back. And it was good, really good. Great, in fact. At least he thought it was great, and she seemed to like it. He'd practically floated home from the Gherrings, and he'd been humming all day. And they were officially dating. Weren't they? He replayed the scene in his mind. Hadn't they talked about dating? He hadn't said the big L word, but he'd told her he was crazy about her. Hadn't he?

Suddenly his good mood evaporated. They hadn't talked about their relationship at all. He'd kissed her, but he hadn't even told her he liked her. And she hadn't said anything at all about her feelings, except that she was afraid. Now he thought about it, he didn't feel so great. They needed to talk—really talk.

"Hey, Spencer," said Grace. "The burgers smell good. I've brought you a couple extra to put on the grill. I forgot to tell you I invited some friends yesterday."

"No problem, Gracie," he said, placing the burgers on the grill. "Can you take the first batch into the kitchen?"

"Sure." She took the pan of burgers and started toward the door. Then she stopped, and came back to him, standing on her tiptoes to kiss him on the cheek.

"What's that for?"

"It's for later on when you're mad at me," she said, slipping inside.

Now his mood dipped lower. Grace was up to her tricks again. He repeated the question he asked himself so often. Why did God give him sisters? The door opened again, and he turned, prepared to interrogate his sister, but it was Charlie who slipped outside.

"Hey, Spencer." She waggled her eyebrows, sporting a devilish grin. "I hear you and my sister had an interesting morning."

He felt his face heating up. "What did she say?"

"She didn't give me any particulars, but I know there was kissing involved."

"Oh."

"I'm simply here to do what I feel is my sisterly duty."

"What's that?" At her serious tone, the hair stood up on the back of his neck.

"I've come to ask, what are your intentions with my sister?"

"Oh. Is that your sisterly duty? Does that mean Grace is doing the same thing with Emily?"

She cocked her head and grinned. "I don't know. Maybe. But don't change the subject—you haven't answered my question."

"It's a personal question. Shouldn't it come from Emily?"

Now Charlie's face became truly serious. "Look Spencer. Here's the thing. I like you and I think you're really sweet. But my sister has been hurt by a guy before." She gave him a honeyed smile. "And I'm here to tell you I will beat you to a pulp if you hurt her again."

"Wow! Thanks for the warning," he chuckled. "I'm not planning to hurt her."

"You don't understand. She's not like you. She can't be with one guy and then switch to another one. She's an all or nothing kind of girl. She'll expect commitment. And you'd better not lie to her or cheat on her."

Spencer's jaw dropped. "You obviously have a pretty low opinion of me."

"I don't think you're necessarily a bad guy. I'm not trying to judge you. Lot's of people do the friends with benefits thing. I know you've been a player—"

"I'm not a player! I guess it's true I've had a lot of female friends, but they've only been friends—not friends with benefits. Not even a bit of benefit. No benefit at all. In fact, I had my first benefit of any kind with your sister this morning, and if I have my way, she'll be the only one, ever."

"Oh!" Charlie's eyes grew round as golf balls, and she stared at him.

Embarrassed at his outburst, he turned to the grill and began crossly flipping the burgers, which had managed to get slightly charred on one side. He turned pleading eyes to Charlie. "Don't tell her. Okay? It's so awkward. I can't believe I told you."

"I think it's sweet... And it might help if you told her the truth."

"No way," he said. "Maybe after we've been dating for a while. I can't tell her now. I'll tell her before we make a serious commitment."

"Are you in love with my sister?"

"Yes," he admitted in a low voice, "but I haven't told her that either."

Charlie let out a low whistle. "Well, I can't promise it'll be easy. But you've got my blessing, anyway. And I'll fight for you." She gave him a kiss on the cheek.

"Thanks. That's the second cheek-kiss I've gotten tonight."

She smirked. "You'd better take what you can get."

He felt distinctly uneasy as she slipped inside chuckling to herself.

*****

Charlie joined the boisterous group inside the Marshall apartment. With this new revelation about Spencer, her opinion about their relationship solidified. She'd thought he'd be a good match for her sister because of how devoted, even self-sacrificing, he'd seemed. But now she'd discovered he wasn't the type of guy who'd flit from one girl to another without regard for their feelings. In fact, he was exactly the opposite. She found herself more worried for Spencer than she was for her sister. Well, she had considerable influence where her sister was concerned, and she was not above resorting to tricks and schemes if necessary. Resolutely, she searched for Emily. She wouldn't break Spencer's confidence, but she'd do everything possible to sway her sister's emotions and encourage her to take a chance on this relationship.

Spencer came in the backdoor with the burgers, and the crowd quieted when his father announced he would say the blessing. They had circled and bowed their heads, when a knock interrupted the proceedings. Grace ran to answer the door and returned with Brad and Josh in tow.

"Come in. We're blessing the food. Then I'll introduce you to my parents."

Charlie stole a glance at her sister, whose face had turned pasty white. She followed her gaze to Spencer, who looked as if his face might burst open. She added a silent prayer for peace to Mr. Marshall's blessing.

"Mom, Dad. This is Brad and this is Josh. They're the guys I told you about—the ones that saved Emily on the hike," Grace said.

Charlie couldn't hear the rest of the exchange, but she whispered in Emily's ear. "Sit next to Spencer, and I'll try to keep Josh away from you."

"Thanks, Spencer doesn't look very happy. I think his reaction is a little extreme, though."

"Well, Sister. They have some history. You just slept through it. Josh pushes his buttons and enjoys doing it."

"Sounds entertaining, though. Sorry I missed it."

"It was amusing, but not so much for Spencer. I think Grace hit it off with Brad, and I can handle Josh—I appreciate the challenge. Watch and learn, Sister. Watch and learn."

The table in the kitchen would only seat eight, so a second table had been set up next to it. Tight seating and bumping elbows allowed eleven people to sit together. Emily sat next to Spencer, and Charlie claimed the other adjacent chair, effectively prohibiting Josh from sitting next to her.

Grace sat between Brad and Josh on the opposite side of the table, so Josh was directly opposite Charlie. He immediately turned his attention to Emily.

"How are you feeling? Have you been taking your anti-inflammatories?"

Emily opened her mouth to answer, but Charlie interrupted. "Josh, I hope you're not going to spoil our meal by turning this into a medical exam. Emily's quite capable of taking her required doses of medication without having someone check up on her. She's the most organized and competent person I know."

"It's true," said Grace. "You should see her closet. It's immaculate and everything's arranged by color and season."

"I'm sure Spencer can attest to how orderly her kitchen is. You've cooked dinner for her, haven't you, Spencer? Emily told me all about it. She says you're a really good cook." Charlie cut her eyes to Josh. He regarded her with narrowed eyes, but the smile never left his face.

"Emily's a great cook, too," Spencer added.

The conversation shifted to food and excitement over whatever surprise dessert Emily had prepared for the evening.

Josh was quiet for a while, listening to the various chats, obviously waiting for his next opportunity. But Charlie was waiting, too.

"So, Emily," he said. "That's an amazing apartment your parents have. I bet you could get used to that type of luxury pretty quickly. Tooling around in a limo all the time. I know I can't wait to get a cool place like that when my residency is over."

Charlie almost laughed out loud. He'd really missed the mark on this one. She sat back and smirked at Josh, allowing Emily to cut him to pieces on her own.

"It's all a bit ostentatious to me," said Emily. "I was raised to believe money wasn't all that important. As long as I have what I need, I'll be content. In fact, the best thing about Steven Gherring's money is how generous he is with it."

Charlie flashed an amused grin at Josh. He winked and went back to his waiting game. When the conversation turned to work and school, he tried again. "Emily, it's amazing you're a CPA at what, twenty-four? You must be really smart."

"She is," declared Charlie. "And she loves numbers. You can make them all neat and organized. I guess that's why she and Spencer are so compatible. They both work in accounting at Gherring Inc."

"What about you?" said Josh. "What do you do?"

Charlie was caught off guard by his question. "I... I'm a college dropout," she declared, lifting her chin, daring him to criticize her. She locked gazes with him, but he didn't flinch.

"She had a four point grade average when she dropped out. And now she teaches snow skiing and leads rafting trips. But, eventually she'll give in and go back to finish college." Emily turned to Charlie. "Right, Sister?"

"Maybe. If anything holds my interest long enough," she replied without looking away.

"Maybe you might go into medicine?" Josh folded his arms and leaned back in his chair, still holding his own in their stare down.

"Nah," said Charlie. "Blood is gross. I'm thinking law school. But I might be interested in personal injury law. Then I could sue all those incompetent doctors."

He laughed, but his eyes never left hers.

Brad brought up the high cost of education, and Charlie breathed a sigh of relief, shifting her eyes his direction. Emily and Spencer appeared to be holding hands under the table, and so far there hadn't been any out-and-out fights between Josh and Spencer.

She watched Josh from the corner of her eye, realizing his gaze was still focused on her. She looked back at him, pursing her lips and furrowing her brows, a silent message to knock it off. He couldn't seem to take a hint. He raised an eyebrow, and without breaking eye contact with Charlie, he said, "So Spencer? Have you heard from Becca?"

An awkward silence descended on the table, and Spencer spoke through clenched teeth. "Josh. What's your problem?"

He laughed. "I'm kidding you. Don't be so uptight."

"Josh—" Emily's tone was plaintive, but Charlie held up her hand.

"Josh!" Charlie's chair screeched against the floor as she pushed it back to stand, speaking in the stern mother's voice she usually reserved for her young ski students. "I'd like to speak to you in the other room for a moment, please."

"Yes, ma'am," he said, rising and dabbing his mouth with his napkin. "I'm coming."

Charlie marched into the living room and spun around to face Josh. He entered, closing the door behind him.

"Why are you trying to ruin things between Spencer and my sister?" She reveled in righteous indignation.

"I have no idea what you're talking about." He smiled benignly.

"Yes, you do. Don't play dumb with me."

"I'd rather play something else with you," he said, taking a step closer to her.

"You don't intimidate me," she snapped, backing away. "I've dealt with arrogant guys like you before. You think you're God's gift to women, and you're not."

"I'm not?" He grinned. "So I should start charging them?" He moved closer again, and she went back another step, feeling her face flush.

"Leave my sister alone. Spencer loves her, and he's not a player like you!"

"I'm not a player. I used to be, but I'm not any more." He continued to move toward her, forcing her to lift her chin to talk to him. She backed up until she was against the front door. Her heart raced. When had she lost control of this situation?

"Oh really?" She laid on the sarcasm. "You'll forgive me if I don't believe you."

"No it's true. Although it hasn't been true for very long." He was so close she could feel the heat from his body.

"When did you repent and turn from your evil ways?"

"About ten minutes ago," he murmured as he bent his head down and captured her mouth in a kiss. Charlie's mind felt muddled and confused. His hands were behind her neck, allowing her no escape. She squirmed and protested futilely, but he continued his assault unfazed. Then his tongue swept across her lips, and she felt her knees go weak and her arms go around his neck. Her body moved against him of its own accord, while one of his hands slid down her back and pressed them tightly together. When his tongue slipped between her lips, she whimpered. She could feel his heart pounding against her chest. Or was that her heart pounding? He groaned when her tongue touched his. Suddenly, her mind was clear. What was she doing?

She pulled away abruptly and slapped him across the cheek.

He rubbed his face gingerly. "Ow—that hurt." And to her great consternation, he grinned. "But it was worth it." She stared at him in shocked silence as he vanished silently through the kitchen door.

*****

Emily's eyes shifted back toward the door. When Charlie and Josh left the room, the table had fallen silent, with all ears straining to hear the supposed tongue-lashing Charlie was dishing out. Connie had prevented her girls from following to the door and eavesdropping on the battle. As a consequence, they could only hear the sharp tone of Charlie's voice, followed by Josh's mellow one.

"What are they saying?" whispered Grace. "Can you hear anything?"

Brad chuckled. "I don't know. But I think Josh may've finally met his match. Did you see her face? She was steaming."

The living room had fallen quiet, and the entire group held their breaths. Then they heard a popping sound and Josh's voice. As they trained their eyes and ears intently toward the living room, the door suddenly burst open. Josh entered, his face reddened from his neck to the tips of his ears. He looked around the table from one frozen spectator to another and his lips curved into an impish grin. He walked briskly to Spencer and clapped him on the back. "Sorry, buddy. I wish you two the best." Then he caught Emily's eye and winked, before continuing on around to take his seat next to Grace, attacking his food with renewed relish.

Eating continued accompanied by soft murmurs and frequent glances toward the door. The red faded from Josh's face, except for the clear imprint of a hand on his cheek. He glanced repeatedly toward the door, and actually began to appear anxious before Charlie finally emerged, carrying her cell phone and her purse.

"I had to make a quick call." Charlie opened her purse and making a show of stowing the phone away. "Sorry to keep y'all waiting. Is it time for dessert?"

Emily studied her sister, who sat down, appearing unperturbed to the casual observer. Only one who'd known her for twenty-three years would notice the slight tremor in her fingers as she carefully folded her napkin in her lap. She watched her pick at the food on her plate and pretend to laugh at the anecdotes and comments that crossed the table. But Emily could tell her mind was otherwise occupied.

And her sister no longer made eye contact with Josh, while he couldn't seem to keep his eyes away. She saw it happening. He was getting more and more annoyed he couldn't catch her glance. The more determined she was in avoiding his gaze, the more intent he was to gain it.

"Charlie," he said. "Where do you teach skiing? Maybe I've been there before."

"I teach at Breckenridge." Charlie directed her answer to Brad. She continued to expound for several minutes about the quality of the snow and the length of the season and the number and type of lifts and the best places to ski the moguls. But none of her extensive discourse required her to look at Josh, and she steadfastly refused to do so.

"What do you like to do when you visit New York, Charlie?" He tried again.

"Emily and I like to go see musicals. Don't we Emily? And last fall we took a great tour from a harbor boat with Spencer and his friend, Mark." This time Charlie spoke her answer to Spencer. "Speaking of Mark. I'd like to see him. We should get together, the four of us, and go climbing again at the gym. Maybe tomorrow night, since I have to go home on Tuesday."

"Sure," Spencer replied, although his tone of voice was uncertain. "If Emily wants to go, I'm up for it."

Now Josh was frowning, tapping the end of his fork on the table. Still Charlie refused to look his direction.

Emily bit her lips and lifted her napkin to her mouth to hide a chuckle. "That sounds great. I know we all had a lot of fun together last time. I may not be able to climb with my sore ankle, but I love watching you climb."

Josh cleared his throat noisily. "Eh-hem! Girls aren't any good at climbing." He sat back expectantly, waiting for the fireworks. This time he wasn't disappointed.

"You're an idiot, if you believe that," Charlie snarled, her eyes flashing. "I could beat you with my hands tied behind my back. Especially on a real climb, and not in some silly gym."

He grinned triumphantly. "Prove it. Put your money where your mouth is. Or actually, I could think of something else I'd like to—"

"Shut up, you arrogant son of a... a biscuit!"

"Now, now. No need for a foul mouth. You can prove your superiority to me tomorrow night. It just so happens I'm off."

"You're not invited," snapped Charlie.

"What gym do you climb at?" he asked Spencer.

"Uhmm..." He looked uncertainly at Charlie.

"Or if you want, you could concede now," said Josh. "You could admit I won—that I got the better of you. It's okay. There's really no shame in being a member of the weaker sex."

Charlie's lips pressed into an angry line. "Tell him where we're climbing, Spencer."

"Are you and Grace coming?" Josh asked, interrupting Brad's laughter.

"I wouldn't miss it for anything."

*****

"What the heck was that? What happened with Josh and Charlie?" asked Spencer. He'd finally managed to get a moment alone with Emily. Brad and Josh had departed together, and Charlie was helping his sisters wash dishes. Spencer and Emily were going for a walk down the street to fetch milk for his mother.

Emily chuckled. "I think Josh decided it's more fun to chase Charlie than to chase me."

"Does that mean the doctor won't be making any more early morning house calls?"

"I'm fairly certain. I think he just likes a challenge, and Charlie puts up a great fight. I feel sorry for Charlie, though. She was only protecting me when everything got turned around on her."

"I should have just punched him out this morning when I saw him in the lobby."

"There's no need to be jealous of Josh. I don't even like him."

"Is there someone I should be jealous of? If not Asher Denning, someone else? What I really want to know is... Are we dating exclusively?"

"That's the only way I'd ever date you. I don't date around."

"Good." Relief flooded him. "I realized we hadn't actually specified. I... You need to know... I really like you. A lot. More than I've ever liked another girl." He hoped that was saying enough, but not too much. If he professed love, she'd probably literally run away, despite her sprained ankle.

"I like you, too."

Warmth flooded him from his head to his toes. He stopped and turned to face her, pulling her into a hug.

"Spencer, we're in public."

"There's no one anywhere near us, and no one is watching." He squeezed her tightly, his hands on the small of her back, while he nuzzled her hair. He loved the way she smelled—her hair, her skin, everything. His hands slid up to cup her face, and he lifted her chin, lowering his mouth to hers. But as his lips feathered lightly against hers, she drew back.

"I... I can't."

"Seriously, Emily. No one is watching." He tried to renew their kiss.

"It's not that. I just don't think we need to be kissing right now."

"Why not?"

"Well, kissing leads to other things—more physical things. And I think we need to be ready for more commitment before we do that."

"No more kissing?"

"At least for a while, until we're, you know... more committed."

"Okay." He agreed with his mouth, but not his head. His mind was replaying their first kiss. How soft her lips felt. The caress of her tongue against his. How responsive she was. His heart sped up at the mere thought of kissing Emily. He'd have to find a way around this new rule. He took her hand in his. "Let's go get the milk."

He didn't broach the subject during the entire expedition. Upon their return to the concrete steps outside their apartment he sat down, patting the space beside him.

"I'm not quite ready to face the crowd." She sat beside him, and he picked up her hand, caressing her fingers. "Your hands are so elegant. They seem like an artist's hands." He lifted her hand to his lips and lightly kissed each digit, nibbling softly with his lips. Her eyelids fluttered closed. He leaned against the side rail and put his left arm around her, pulling her against him, cradling her head against his shoulder. His right hand came up and caressed the line of her jaw. "Your skin is so soft and beautiful, and I love that you don't wear any makeup."

He leaned over and pressed his lips to her forehead and breathed in deeply, enjoying her scent. His hand skimmed lightly under her chin. Her breathing quickened and his fingers lifted her face toward his. He kissed her cheek and slid his lips down to her jaw. She raised her chin and exposed her neck, moaning softly. He gently kissed the tender skin on her neck where her blood pulsed madly. He moved back up to her face and feathered gentle kisses on her jaw and around her parted lips, never quite touching them with his.

He pulled away, breathing shallow breaths and concentrating to hold himself back. Emily's eyes fluttered open, her eyes on his lips, moistening her own with her tongue. Abruptly, she leaned toward him and offered her mouth to him, her soft lips pressed to his, her tongue darting out, enticing him. With a groan he answered her invitation. His mouth slanted against hers. Their lips crushed together in passion.

His world shrank. He was aware of nothing but Emily. Nothing but her face, her mouth, her lips, her tongue, her neck. Nothing but the sensations that spread throughout his system. He pulled back and gasped for air, stopping himself just before his hand dropped down from her neck to forbidden parts. She sat up stiffly, pulling away, smoothing her mussed hair, staring at Spencer in alarm.

"That... that didn't count. That was a farewell-to-kissing kiss." He forced a smile, still trying to catch his breath.

"It has to be the last one," she rasped. "We almost... You see what I mean—kissing is dangerous."

"Nothing happened."

"It almost did."

"It did?" He couldn't stop the chuckle that escaped.

"Spencer, this is serious."

"Sorry, sorry. It won't happen again." He made a vain attempt to sound contrite.

"Okay. That was the last time. Right?"

"Right," he answered, hoping she couldn't detect his insincerity. "Ready to take the milk inside?"

They climbed the steps side by side and entered the door without speaking. He was lost in thought. He'd waited a long time to find a girl he wanted to kiss, and it was even better than he thought it'd be. There was no way he wanted to give that up. There had to be another way.

Chapter Thirteen

"Mom gained two pounds," Charlie told Emily as they rode toward the climbing gym in Steven's limo. "The doctor says the antihistamines may be helping. She's actually starting to eat something other than crackers."

Emily tried to picture how her skinny mom would look with a full term pregnancy. "She's got a long way to go before she even starts looking pregnant. I still can't believe it. I think I'm going to feel more like an aunt than a sister to this kid."

"Me, too. But I think it could be fun. I'm really happy for Steven."

"I agree. I know he's putting on a really brave front for Mom, but I can tell he's worried she won't make it all the way."

"Don't their chances of making it go up if she gets through the first trimester?"

"I think so, but he's still too nervous to leave her at home alone. It's too bad, though. It would've been fun to see Josh's face when Steven showed him up on the climbing wall."

"Yeah..." Charlie muttered darkly. "I can't believe I let him bait me into this. I'm sunk if he's had experience, and I think he has."

"But you're really good, and you've had a lot of experience. Don't you think you can beat him?"

"No. I don't have the upper body strength to do the really hard climbs—the ones with overhangs, like Steven did last fall."

"Maybe he's out of shape," Emily argued. "He's been really busy with med school and now with the residency."

"Are you blind Emily? You hiked with him for an entire day, and you didn't notice his muscles?"

Emily tried to picture Josh on the trail at Devil's Path. "No, not really. I think they were mostly covered up."

"No, Sister. Believe me, they were quite visible."

"Well then why did you agree to a climbing contest?"

"I don't know... He's so egotistical, and he made me so mad."

"And what exactly did he do to make you so mad? What happened when y'all went in the living room?"

Charlie's face turned pink. "Nothing happened. I yelled at him and told him to leave you and Spencer alone."

Emily regarded her sister dubiously. "Well, I guess it worked. He left me alone and turned all his attention on you. Is that what you wanted?"

"No!" Her blush spread down her neck.

"Are you sure nothing else happened in the living room? Y'all were in there a while."

"Well, I had a lot to say," Charlie declared.

"So, is it possible you like him a little? I mean, I guess he's cute. You said yourself he had muscles. And he's a doc—"

"No! I don't like him. Not even a little. He's arrogant, egotistical, and controlling."

"Okay. Don't bite my head off. So what are you planning to do if he beats you tonight?"

"I've been thinking about it. As long as he beats me fair and square, I can handle it and a bit of teasing, too. He can brag about it, but there'll be other guys there who are better than him. Whereas, I'll probably be the best girl in the joint tonight. He'll be impressed. Even if he doesn't want to admit it, he'll be impressed. And both of us will know it." Charlie smirked a little. Emily wondered why her sister cared about impressing Josh. Usually, Charlie couldn't care less whether a guy was impressed. She was self-confident to a fault, typically disregarding others' opinions as unimportant. But something about Josh got under her skin and irritated her enough she couldn't ignore him.

"I'm rooting for you, Sister." She'd keep her speculations to herself.

Charlie fumed even while she was putting on her climbing harness. Josh was already geared up. He had a great build, and he knew it. He was probably almost six feet two. She noted with satisfaction Spencer was a little taller. Right now she was happy if anyone could best him in any way. He really needed to be cut down to size. He'd obviously climbed before, at least in a gym, and she knew she had little chance of beating him here. But with her extensive outdoor climbing experience, she'd probably leave him in the dust on an outdoor climb. Still, she wasn't the type to make excuses when she was competing. She'd simply have to do her best.

For liability reasons, the gym didn't allow anyone to belay unless they'd taken their class and passed a test. She was glad Josh couldn't offer to belay her because he made her nervous for some reason. She tried not to think about what had happened with Josh in the Marshall's living room. That kiss. She was furious with herself for kissing him back. Why had she done that? She should've slapped him before he kissed her, not after. He'd simply caught her off guard. But never again—she was prepared for him. She had her shields up and on high alert.

"Hey." Charlie jumped at Josh's voice in her ear. He'd come up behind her while she was concentrating on her gear. He grinned at her reaction. "So, what's the bet going to be? What do I have to do to beat you, and what do I win?"

"Highest point reached on two out of three climbs, or best time if we both make it to the top." She stated the conditions matter-of-factly, carefully hiding any emotions.

"And what do I win?"

"I'll win the satisfaction of putting you in your place."

"I think satisfaction would be a great prize when I win, but I'd rather achieve it some other way." He leaned in close and whispered, "How about another kiss, without the punishing slap afterward?"

Charlie felt her face heat up, but she kept her voice cool and even. "That will never happen again."

"Why not? Are you saying you didn't enjoy it?"

"Yes. That's exactly what I'm saying."

"That's what your lips are saying now, but it's not what your body was saying last night."

"Stop it. Shut up before someone hears you. Spencer's coming." She glared at him while she spoke between her clenched teeth.

He let out a belly laugh. "I'm not giving up just because someone might overhear me. I'll be a little more discreet." His eyes twinkled. "But only a little."

Charlie sent him a glower that could have melted steel as Spencer joined them, seemingly unaware of their friction. "Who's going first?"

"Josh is going first," declared Charlie. "Go ahead. Pick your climb."

He chose a vertical climb with a medium level difficulty. He climbed steadily, easily reaching the top, and Spencer declared the time. "Four minutes, twenty-two seconds."

Josh rappelled down with a satisfied smile. Two blond girls approached him, and he seemed to be busy flirting while Charlie threaded the rope through her harness. She cast him a disparaging glance and started her climb. With experienced efficiency, she fairly flew up the climb.

"Three minutes, forty-four seconds. Charlie wins round one." Spencer shouted her time and her sister cheered, along with Brad and Grace.

Josh whipped around to watch her descend. "Wait, I missed it." He approached her as she touched the floor. "So it looks like I might have to try a little harder to beat you."

Emily sat on the bench with Grace and Brad, watching the show. Brad laughed heartily when Charlie won the first round. "This is the most fun I've had in a long time."

"Do you think he'll beat her on the next two?" asked Emily.

"I don't know how he's going to play this one," admitted Brad. "He's good. He climbs all the time. He did a five-thirteen last week."

"Is that hard?" asked Grace.

"Yeah, pretty tough. It had a rough overhang."

"So what do you mean, you don't know how he'll play it?" asked Emily.

Brad shrugged. "He might try his best, to impress her. Or he might let her win. You know, just barely. But he might let her win if he thinks it'll be to his advantage."

"Hmmm. He doesn't know my sister. She'd know if he did that. It'd be a bad idea."

"But isn't she super competitive? Doesn't she like to win?"

"Oh, she likes to win, all right. But she doesn't take condescension from anyone. On the other hand, if he shows off... Well, she already thinks he's egotistical."

"So, he's in trouble if he beats her or if he lets her win?"

"Pretty much."

"So how's he going to get her to like him?"

"I don't know if it can be done. Many have tried—all have failed and fallen into the abyss." Emily laughed.

Grace asked Brad, "Are you planning to climb tonight?"

"Sure. I'll go after the contest is over. Right now, I'm enjoying the company." He put his arm around her shoulder. "And it's truly entertaining to see Josh fumbling a bit. He's not used to failure of any kind."

Charlie chose the next climb. She picked one with a section at the top that was slightly beyond vertical in pitch. Josh had ditched the girls who'd distracted him earlier and was standing inside her comfort zone as Charlie threaded the rope through her harness.

"Why don't you go back to your fan club? I don't need your help."

"I like to throw them a few crumbs, but leave them hungry."

"They looked like they wanted to eat you up. I'm surprised you didn't let them."

"Jealous?"

"No. I was relieved. Glad to have you otherwise occupied and out of my hair."

"Why?" He reached out to tighten one of her shoulder straps. "Do I make you nervous?"

"No!" She jerked away from his grasp. "Not nervous—more like nauseous."

"Well, that's close." Josh laughed.

Charlie turned to Spencer, who was observing the interchange with wide eyes. "Get ready to start the timer."

This climb was more challenging from the start, even before reaching the over-steep portion, because all the holds were spaced farther apart. Charlie's arms and legs were shaking from the effort. She was forced to stop and rest before beginning the last section. She glanced down and, seeing Josh's amused expression, felt a surge of irritation along with a rush of adrenaline. She took advantage of the new energy and attacked the incline. Sixty seconds into it, her arms were crying out in pain. She lunged for the top and called out, immediately falling back on the belay rope. Her muscles were still trembling when she made it to the bottom.

"Six fifty," announced Spencer.

"Okay," said Josh, "I'm actually impressed. Pretty amazing for a girl."

Spencer frowned. "Are you kidding? It's pretty amazing for anybody."

"Maybe. But you haven't seen the master tackle it." Josh set up and began the climb. Charlie watched with begrudging admiration. He didn't even pause before the last section.

As his hand touched the top, Spencer called out, "Five minutes, forty-five seconds. Sorry, Charlie."

But at his return to the floor, she noted with satisfaction Josh's muscles were also shaking from the exertion, despite his efforts to appear unfazed by the tough climb.

"Spencer, why don't you climb now so Charlie has a little more time to recover?"

"Pretty cheap to use Charlie as an excuse to give yourself a break. We can all see you've got the shakes." Spencer shook his head.

Josh laughed. "It was worth a try. I admit it—I need a break, too."

Spencer set up to do his climb, while Josh and Charlie sat down on the bench to rest. Charlie wedged herself between Emily and Grace, so Josh was forced to sit on the end next to Brad.

"So who's climbing first and who chooses the climb?" Brad asked.

"We're doing that ledge," said Charlie. "Josh can go second."

"That's like committing suicide," said Josh. "You should pick something easy and go for speed."

"No way," scoffed Charlie. "I'm here for the challenge."

"Okay, but I'll beat you." Josh's expression lost its casual grin.

"The straight walls are easy and boring. I don't do boring."

"I understand. You want me to win, right? Are we in agreement about the prize?"

Charlie leaned forward and bored holes in him with her eyes. "No we're not in agreement." Brad stifled a laugh behind his hand.

"What are the options?" Grace asked. "I'll be the fair and impartial judge."

"Well," Josh smirked. "I want—"

"Josh wants a kick where it hurts," Charlie interjected. "And I'm going to give it to him."

Brad snorted. "Good job, Josh. You've got her eating out of your hand, just like you said you would."

Josh elbowed Brad, which only resulted in louder laughter. Charlie crimped her eyebrows down. "Is that what he said? He'd have me eating out of his hand?"

"I didn't say that." Josh planted another vicious elbow in Brad's side when he laughed again.

"Whoever loses should have to pay for the other's climbing tonight," Grace suggested.

"I think that's fair," said Josh.

"But exception to the family rule. If he loses and pays my way, it's not a date," said Charlie.

Emily winked at Charlie. "Hmmm, technically it'd be a date if either one of you pays for the other."

"Nope. Not doing it. Think of something else."

"Family rule?" Josh asked.

"Yes," Emily explained. "Our rule is if he pays for something or— Ow, Charlie! Why'd you kick me!"

"What's the rule?" Josh urged.

"It's none of your business," said Charlie. "It's a family thing. And you're not family."

"What's a family thing?" said Spencer, returning from his successful climb.

"Our family dating rule," Emily said.

"Oh, the one where it's a date if the guy buys you something or kisses you?" Spencer asked.

"Yes. I was saying technically it would be a date even if the girl paid. Charlie doesn't want to have that as a prize for their contest because she doesn't want us to be able to claim she had a date with Josh."

"But, we've already had a date," said Josh. Everyone turned to stare at him, while Charlie felt her face burning. "Yes, indeed," Josh winked at Charlie. "Saturday night, Charlie paid for our dinner."

203

She glared daggers at him. He grinned, shrugging his shoulders.

"No," Grace said. "That doesn't count. She used Gherring's credit card. So technically, you had a date with Steven Gherring."

Josh waggled his eyebrows at Charlie. She closed her eyes and imagined them being on an actual mountain so she could push him off the cliff.

She fled the embarrassing scene, rushing to set up for the difficult climb. Josh came up behind her as she threaded the rope. "Stay back," she growled.

"But we still haven't agreed on a prize."

"How about if I restrain myself from kicking you?"

He winced. "I'd truly appreciate that, but I had something else in mind."

"What this time?"

"What if I promise not to tell everyone about that little kiss we shared last night if you promise to give a repeat performance tonight?"

"That sounds like blackmail to me."

"Desperate times call for desperate measures."

"Look Josh, those two girls that were talking to you earlier? Both of them looked like they were willing to not only kiss you, but probably jump your bones as well. You could probably go to the bar next door and find at least ten other girls to chose from. Why don't you kiss someone who wants to kiss you?"

"Maybe I'm not attracted to those other girls."

"Or maybe it's because I turned you down. You just like the challenge. If I'd fallen all over you and kissed you willingly, you wouldn't even be interested. And you're only interested now until you can make the conquest, put another notch in your belt. Well, I got news—it ain't happenin'! I'm not interested in being a mark on your wall, a notch on your belt, or a name in your black book." She lowered her voice to a whisper as Spencer came to join them. "I'm not interested."

For once, Josh appeared to be speechless. He nodded, set his lips in a grim line, and walked back to join the group on the bench. He sat down next to Emily and watched silently as Charlie started to climb.

"What do I do?" Josh asked Emily in quiet voice. "I've never not known what to do with a girl before."

Emily studied him for a moment. Was he sincere? Did she really even want to help him? "First you have to decide if you're interested in Charlie or if you just don't like to lose."

His sigh was audible. "Both. I don't like losing. But there's something about Charlie—I don't know what it is."

"Well, there you go," said Emily. "When you figure out what it is, you tell her. When you can convince her you're interested in her for who she is, you might have a chance. And frankly, I don't think you know her well enough."

"She's leaving tomorrow. If I can't get her to be at least slightly cooperative, I'll never see her again."

"True."

"Should I let her win? To make her happy and put her in a good mood? I know she likes to win as much as I do. I could sacrifice myself and let her win."

She pondered the question. How she could best be a loyal sister? "I think you should figure that out yourself."

He watched Charlie struggle as she reached the under-hang. Her muscles were straining as she braced her legs, trying to reach as far as possible before she had to climb using only her arm strength.

"Look at her. If she were a guy, I wouldn't stand a chance." Then he shook his head. "Of course, if she were a guy I wouldn't be in this mess." He blew out a breath through his lips. "I'm afraid I can't win this one. Can I?"

Emily shrugged and gave him a sad smile. "Doubtful. Whoever wins my sister is going to have to work a lot longer than one or two days. You really never stood much of a chance. Don't take it personally."

Charlie was hanging by her hands. Shaking, she pulled herself upward with both hands before letting go with one hand and lunging for the next hold. When she missed it, she fell back onto the belay and signaled to descend.

Josh approached as she unwound the rope from her harness. "You almost had it. Are you too tired to try again?"

She held up a trembling arm in answer. "No. Your turn. Let's see what you can do." She watched as he prepared for the climb, eyeing the route from below.

"Got any advice?" he asked.

Surprised, she regarded him from the corner of her eye, trying to decide if he was sincere. "Go up on the left and then move to the right side before you start under the ledge. I watched Steven do this one. You have to reach out and hang from those two mini-jugs. And then the red one looks good from there, but it's a sloper. See it? So you need to grab that yellow one instead. It's a crimper. From there you've got to use your arms to pull up and get your foot on the nib on the edge."

"Good luck, Josh!" said a feminine voice behind her. Charlie looked over her shoulder at the two blonds who had come back to watch him climb. Charlie bit back a chuckle when Josh's expression turned to annoyance. He ignored the girls, and attacked the climb. She was pleased when he followed her advice to a T. Soon he reached the point where Charlie had fallen. He hesitated, and for a moment she thought he was going to let go. She eyed him suspiciously. His muscles weren't even shaking yet. Then he adopted a determined expression, and pulled himself up before reaching to grab the yellow crimper. For a moment he had to hang from two fingers as he grabbed the next hold. He'd passed her up, but she didn't care. She couldn't help rooting for him—that's what climbers did.

Charlie took a moment to admire the muscles flexing on his arms and back as he climbed. His foot found the hold on the corner, and he was effectively past the under-hang. Now his muscles were fatigued, and his whole body trembled as he continued the climb. He lunged for the top and fell back in relief. He rappelled down, while the blond girls clapped and cheered for him. Charlie moved back to join the others on the bench, leaving Josh to his fans. She almost laughed when he sought her out over the heads of the two girls who were giving animated praise to their hero.

"You lost," said Emily. "What do you owe him?"

"I'm paying for his climbing. I'll live with the ribbing—you can call it a date."

"Okay, but you know I won't let you live it down, right?"

"I can handle it. I'm going to pay, and then I'm ready to go."

"Really? It's early and it's your last night in New York."

Charlie looked over to where Josh was still attempting to extricate himself from the girls. "You can stay with Spencer, and I'll go back and visit with Mom and Steven. When you come home, we'll have hot chocolate chip cookies and milk."

She stood up and dug in her purse for some money, which she handed to her sister. "Would you mind paying for me so I can slip out now?"

Emily screwed her lips sideways. "If that's what you want, Sister."

Josh watched Charlie as the two girls continued to ply him with questions. "Yeah, sure," he answered absently.

"Cool. We'll wait while you change clothes," said the taller girl.

"Uhmm, what? What are you waiting for?"

"For you to change so we can go to the Lookout Club," she answered, obviously frustrated at repeating herself.

"Oh. No. Sorry, I can't. Excuse me." He pushed past the girls, rushing to the bench.

"Where's Charlie?"

"She left this to pay for your climbing and took off." Emily held up a handful of money and pointed toward the exit with her eyes.

Josh saw Charlie disappearing through the door without a backward glance. He couldn't believe it—she wasn't even going to wait around to say goodbye. He couldn't understand why it bothered him so much, but it did. It made him furious.

He ran toward the door and burst outside, spying Charlie as she moved to the limousine. She slid inside, but he caught the door before she could close it. Without a thought, he climbed into the back and sat beside her.

Her eyes were wide. Was that guilt? Remorse for running out on him?

"What are you doing?" she asked.

"I've come to collect. I won, fair and square."

"I paid for your climbing. I left the money with Emily. And I'm not kissing you again."

"You didn't even stay to congratulate me," he muttered.

"You were busy," she pointed out. "I didn't want to intrude on the fan club meeting. But, it was a nice climb. Well done."

He searched her face, but she betrayed no emotion. What was she thinking? It was so frustrating. He absolutely couldn't predict her thoughts or her actions.

"So you were just going to leave? Without even telling me?"

She groaned. "Josh. I'm not sure what you expect from me. We barely know each other. I'm leaving tomorrow for Colorado. And we obviously don't think the same way about relationships."

"How do you know that?"

"Really? I've seen you in action. You pick up girls all the time. You were going after my sister yesterday, until you switched gears and went after me. You picked up two extra tonight. And I don't date at all. I think guys are great for carrying heavy gear and belaying me on my climbs. Otherwise, I don't have much use for you."

Josh stared at her, speechless. He'd never met a girl who aggravated him as much as this one. His life would be easier if he forgot all about her. And duller. Boring. What was it Charlie had said? *Straight walls are easy and boring. I don't do boring.*

She cleared her throat, the noise snapping him back to the present. "If you don't mind, get out of the car, so I can go home."

"I can be useful."

"What?"

"I can be useful for more than just carrying heavy gear and belaying your climbs, if you give me a chance."

"Josh, you're only interested in me for the fight, for the challenge. If I didn't fight with you, you'd lose interest and move on to the next girl. You proved it when you switched your focus from my sister to me."

He shook his head. "I know you don't believe me, but that's not true. I admit I was playing a game when I pursued your sister. But you're different." He watched her shaking her head. He was losing her.

"Please!" he said desperately. "I said I wanted to kiss you again, and I do. But what I want even more is for you to stay with me. Don't go home yet. Come and hang out with me. Let me buy you dinner. We'll all hang out together. Totally safe."

"I don't think that's a good idea—"

"It's a date already. You paid for my climbing. It won't hurt you. Just try it. If you don't, we'll never know. But what if you're wrong?

What if I could be good for you, and you gave up without even trying?"

He could see she was wavering. She pursed her lips, and he resisted the urge to lean over and kiss them. How strange. He'd never resisted an urge with a girl before. It felt awkward and uncomfortable. Maybe he should kiss her like he had the night before. But something told him if he did, she'd be gone from his life forever. It felt like that would leave an awful hole. How could it hurt to lose someone you never had? Someone you just met? She was still considering. Should he say something else? Try a different tack?

He felt her piercing stare cutting into his eyes. She crossed her arms. "Just hanging out? Not sex? Not making out? Not even kissing?"

"Hanging out together—that's all I'm asking for." He felt a rock lift from the pit of his stomach. She was going to stay. He had her for a few more hours. He'd never felt so happy about being physically rejected before. He wasn't sure he'd ever actually been rejected before. Hmmm. Not since high school, anyway.

"Okay, but you can't tell anyone we kissed last night, either."

"Can I just tell Brad? You know, it's a guy thing. I like to brag."

"You can brag about the last climb. Leave me out of it."

"All right," he teased. "But can you and I talk about it? Just between the two of us? 'Cause it was a pretty nice kiss."

"Josh!"

"Okay, okay." He climbed out of the car with what must be a silly grin on his face and held out his hand. "Shall we go?"

Spencer was accepting congratulations on successfully completing the climb with the overhang, when Brad let out a surprised, "I can't believe it!"

Emily turned to see what had caught his eye, and found Josh with an absolutely triumphant smile, leading an obviously reluctant Charlie by the hand to join them. He refused to relinquish her hand when they arrived at the bench.

Emily grinned. "Hello again, Sister. Had a change of heart?" She noted Charlie's flushed face. Was that excitement or embarrassment?

"I'm claiming temporary insanity," she answered, still trying to extricate her hand from his grasp.

"Well, Josh. While you were outside somehow coercing my sister to stay, Spencer beat your time on the last climb." Spencer looked absurdly pleased at her praise.

"I've never quite made it before, but I copied Josh's route," he said graciously.

"And I was following Charlie's advice," Josh admitted.

"It's so unfair!" Charlie stomped her foot. "I can do everything perfectly, but I don't have enough strength to make the climb. Sometimes it really sucks to be a girl."

Josh gave her a goofy smile. "I'm glad you're a girl."

Emily saw Brad attempting to contain his laughter at his friend's atypical behavior. He whispered something to Grace, and they laughed together.

Charlie sat beside Josh, her only possible option since he continued to hang onto her hand. They watched as Brad and Spencer made their climbs.

Grace scooted next to her on the bench. "I'm having a hard time keeping my tongue in my mouth. Brad's got the best body I've ever seen. Don't you think?"

Charlie appraised his nicely proportioned build. *But I think Josh's muscles are even nicer. Yikes! What am I doing?*

"So, it seems like you two have hit it off."

"Yeah, I like him a lot. He's so fun. And I just broke up with my last boyfriend—he was getting too clingy."

Charlie noticed her fingers throbbing.

"Josh, I promise I won't run away. But you're cutting off the circulation in my hand."

He blinked, gazing at their joined hands as if he hadn't realized he was holding hands with her. He tilted his head. "Sorry. I just… I'm not sure… I think maybe I've never held hands before. It was nice."

He let go, and she messaged her hand. "Seriously? There's actually something you haven't done before?"

"Not much, but there are a few things." His smile disappeared, and he swallowed. "I know I've never been in love."

"Yeah? Well, you can write and let me know when that happens."

The climbers changed clothes at the gym before the group went out to eat.

Emily was acutely aware of Spencer's presence as they sat at the table. His arm was around the back of her chair while his hand rubbed her shoulder, sending tingles down her spine. And she couldn't help thinking about after dinner. Would he try to kiss her again? Ever since she'd laid down the law about not kissing, she could hardly think of anything else. That was the whole reason she shouldn't kiss him again. She was becoming obsessed with him and losing her perspective. And she really didn't know if she could control herself with him. Kissing other guys had never affected her like kissing Spencer.

She watched him talking, unaware of her perusal. He was so handsome. He wasn't nearly as cocky as he'd seemed at first. Now she knew him, she found he had a vulnerable side. Sometimes he was almost shy. He turned to her and caught her gaze. When he smiled at her, his eyelids lowered slightly, causing her to remember his expression when he kissed her the night before. His hand moved to trace a line from her shoulder up the angle of her neck to her jaw. Her eyes closed involuntarily, and she could have sworn tiny sparks flew from his fingertips.

How did he know exactly what to do? He could control her reaction with the slightest touch. It felt so good, but she wasn't sure she liked the idea of him controlling her. When the waitress came with their food, she was relieved as he pulled his hand away to eat.

She turned her attention to her sister who'd been awkwardly quiet since they left for the restaurant. She couldn't imagine what Josh had said to change her mind, but she intended to find out later. She had never managed to deter her stubborn sister once she made a decision. Well, not never. She knew a few little tricks to get her way with Charlie, but those were closely guarded secrets.

"When are you coming back to New York again, Charlie?" Grace asked.

Josh appeared to be almost holding his breath, anticipating her answer. "Uhmm. I don't know." She studied her napkin with sudden interest.

"Don't you have a break between rafting season and ski season?" Emily asked.

"Uhmm, yes. Usually. But I'm thinking about starting school again this fall."

"That's great," said Josh. "You could come to New York and study at NYU."

"But, I actually already got accepted in Colorado."

"Oh, that's good, I guess," Josh's face fell.

"You didn't tell me you'd even applied." Emily pouted at her sister.

"It was supposed to be a surprise," said Charlie. "Don't tell Mom and Steven. I want to tell them myself."

"It really would be fun if you came here to go to school," said Emily.

Charlie's chin jutted out. "I can't afford to pay out-of-state tuition."

Emily nodded. She understood not wanting to take tuition money from Steven, although he'd be glad to pay. She had the same sense of pride, feeling uncomfortable even taking the job he'd offered despite the fact she was well qualified.

Spencer frowned. "Couldn't your—ow!" Emily kicked him under the table.

"Maybe you could get a scholarship," Emily suggested.

"Couldn't your dad pay for it?" Josh asked.

"No," Charlie said firmly. "He married my mom, not me. He shouldn't be saddled with my expensive tuition."

Brad choked on his drink. "Are we actually talking about Steven Gherring, here? He could pay that without blinking an eye."

"It's the principle of the thing," declared Emily. "My mom still shops at the second-hand clothing stores when Steven's not around to protest. We weren't raised to waste money or take handouts."

"Let's change the subject," said Charlie. "I'll have a Fall Break, and I'll come to visit y'all in New York."

"I can't wait until Fall Break to see you," mumbled Josh.

"I don't think this is a good time to have this discussion," said Charlie.

"When else can we discuss it?"

"Fine," said Charlie. "Then let me state for the record I think you'll probably forget about me by tomorrow and most assuredly by the end of the week. Brad, wouldn't you say that's a fairly accurate prediction?"

Josh glowered at Brad, but as usual, he merely laughed at his friend's predicament. "I would say, based on Josh's past behavior, that's an extremely accurate prediction." Before Charlie could gloat or Josh could explode, he held up his hand. "*However*..." He waited until he had the attention of everyone at the table. "*However*, Josh doesn't seem to be following his normal patterns of behavior. Not since after the two of you came out of the living room last night." His lips spread in a teeth-flashing smile, and he winked at Charlie. "I'm just sayin'..."

"I waited six months to see Emily again, except for Skype," said Spencer. "And she pretty much fought me the whole time. And then when she moved here, she still wouldn't date me. But she was worth the wait."

Josh gave him a horrified look. "Is that supposed to be encouraging?"

"Maybe not encouraging, but realistic. And I'm not as stubborn as my sister." Emily pointed with her water glass.

"Ha!" said Charlie. "That's a laugh. You're twice as stubborn as me."

"Maybe you're right, Sister. Maybe you're getting soft. I've never seen you cave as easily as you did with Josh."

Charlie gave Emily a warning glare, but Josh shook his head. "Believe me, it wasn't easy. None of my normal stuff works on Charlie. I'm really starting to feel insecure."

"Really, Josh? I don't think you even understand the concept of insecurity."

"You're right, Charlie." Brad nodded toward Josh. "But if anyone can give him a taste of it, you can."

*****

Spencer was determined to have a few minutes alone with Emily. Climbing had been fun and dinner was great, but he couldn't stop thinking about her. It was exquisite torture to have her so near and barely be able to touch her. In the back of his mind, the entire evening, he thought about what it would feel like to kiss her again. He knew she didn't want to kiss him, and he'd never force her. But so far, he'd had some success persuading her to bend her rule a little. If only he could get her alone...

After dinner, Brad announced he was walking Grace home. Josh pleaded and cajoled with Charlie until she relented and agreed to walk with him to get ice cream before returning to the apartment. When Charlie invited Emily and Spencer to come, the two men exchanged glances, and Spencer knew they were on the same page. Both of them were hoping to have some alone time with their Best girls. Spencer started rubbing his fingers lightly up and down on the inside of Emily's arm, effectively rendering her incapable of speech.

"I think we'll go back to Emily's apartment and wait for you guys there," he said, pulling Emily toward the waiting car. "She shouldn't be walking too much on her sore ankle."

Josh gave him a knowing smile as he tried to wrap his arm around Charlie's shoulder. But she twisted away, and he grasped her hand. Spencer chuckled to himself. Yesterday morning he'd been ready to murder the guy, and now he felt sorry for him.

Spencer wisely decided to hold off his assault while they were in the car, lest she refuse to invite him upstairs. He could see the emotions flitting across her face. She was obviously nervous about being alone with him. He had to distract her.

"So, my mother says your mom's improving a lot. Maybe they won't even need her much longer. I hope she's still looking for a job."

"They haven't discussed it with me, but Steven is so overprotective. I'm sure he'll want to keep Connie employed just in case they need her again. That's his modus operandi, throw money at things and cover all your bases."

"I can see that, especially where your mom's concerned. Actually, he's pretty devoted to you and your sister, too. You should have seen him when you were in the hospital and then when you went missing."

"I know. I feel so bad about that. I can't understand myself, doing stupid stuff like that."

"Hey, I wasn't bringing it up to make you feel bad. I just wanted you to know that... that I think he really loves you—you and Charlie, both. I think he loves you as if you really were his daughters."

"I know. He really is great."

"You know, if he really were your dad, you wouldn't feel bad when he wanted to do things for you. Like paying for Charlie's college tuition."

"But he isn't really our dad."

"I'm just saying, you should look at it from his perspective. He has money and he likes to spend it on the people he loves. Maybe sometimes you and Charlie might hurt his feelings when you don't accept what he wants to give you."

"Maybe." The closer the car got to the apartment, the more she fidgeted. "Spencer, I'm not sure it's a good idea for you to come upstairs."

"I'd really like a cup of tea. Surely there's no harm in that?"

"Okay, but you have to promise not to kiss me."

"Okay, I promise." But he wasn't promising not to kiss her back if she started it.

Emily sat on the couch beside Spencer, drinking tea. They both had on shorts, and she was incredibly cognizant of where his muscled masculine leg pressed against her smooth skin. It was as if every nerve fiber was hypersensitive, firing rapid impulses to scramble her brain. He sat on her right side, holding his tea mug casually in his right hand, with his left arm around the back of the couch. She waited tensely for his hand to slip onto her shoulder, but he kept it on the couch. She didn't know whether to be grateful or irritated. He was being good. He wasn't trying to kiss her.

Spencer finished his tea and set it on the table next to him. Then he sat back and his hand rested on her leg. And oh-so-casually his fingers moved, gently caressing her skin. And all of her hypersensitive nerve endings started shooting off like fireworks. She put her hand on top of his to stop its movement. He smiled and interlaced their fingers.

"You know," he said, "I could do this for hours."

"Do what?"

"This. Just sitting together. Close. Enjoying your company." He pulled her hand into his lap and turned her arm over, exposing her wrist. He toyed with the soft smooth skin, sliding his fingers up to the inside of her elbow. She felt her heart pounding inside her chest. He was doing it again, making her lose control. She stiffened, prepared to pull her hand away, when he released it and stood up.

"I'm going to get a refill. Would you like one?"

She stared at him, dazed and confused. He wasn't trying to get past her defenses after all. "Uhmm, no thanks."

He was gone for sixty seconds, pouring fresh hot water over the tea leaves. He returned and set his cup down. "I'll let it steep."

He rested his hand lightly on her leg, and she waited for his fingers to move. But his hand remained still. "This is nice," he said, with a gentle smile. She waited for the light tickling motion to assault her senses, but his fingers didn't budge. At last, she offered him her upturned wrist.

He grinned at her. "Do you like this?" Once again he began to delicately stroke the soft skin.

She let her head fall back against the couch and reveled in the tingling sensation that started on her arm and spread throughout her body. It was so nice. And she could stop him any time she wanted to. She was totally in control.

His fingers traveled up her bare arm and across her shoulder to her exposed neck, feathering the skin lightly with his fingertips.

"Mmmmm," she moaned. "You... you won't kiss me, right?"

He leaned over to whisper in her ear, "No... No, I won't kiss you." He nibbled her earlobe with his lips, and she squirmed in response. "But if you kiss me, I won't stop you." His soft breath in her ear sent shivers through her body. His lips skimmed from her ear down her neck.

His mouth felt so good. It would feel so good on her lips. And his mouth was so close. She turned her head toward him. Her mouth searched desperately for his, and his lips willingly accepted hers. His mouth tickled and teased, plying her lips with soft, gentle kisses. He pulled her shoulders, gradually moving backward until he was reclined against the couch and she was leaning across his body, greedily seeking his lips with hers. She wrapped her hands around his neck and pressed her mouth against his. The more frantically she kissed him, the more passionately he responded, deepening their kiss as he enfolded his arms around her back, pressing her against his chest.

A knock sounded at the door, and she jumped back wide-eyed and dismayed, wiping her swollen lips with the back of her hand. "Ohmygosh! Ohmygosh!" she whispered in frenzy.

"It's okay. Calm down." He pulled her hands down and set them in her lap. "Nothing happened, and we didn't do anything wrong. You sit, and I'll get the door."

As he opened the door to let Charlie in, she tried to tell herself she was still in control. But she knew it wasn't true. With every touch and every kiss she gave another piece of her heart. Already she'd be devastated when he moved on to another girl, as she knew he eventually would. Part of her wanted him to declare he would love her forever. Another part of her was absolutely terrified of hearing those words.

Charlie was startled when Spencer answered the door. She whipped around. "Goodnight, Josh. See you later." She slipped in the door and tried to shut it, but it wouldn't close. Josh's foot was in the way.

He grinned. "You see? I told you Spencer would still be here. I get to come inside."

"Spencer was just leaving," said Emily.

"No I wasn't. I was planning to heat some more water for tea. Decaf, anyone?"

"That sounds good," said Josh.

Charlie sighed. She really needed to talk to her sister, without Josh around. He'd messed up her head tonight. He was just so... so something. What was it? He was arrogant and egotistical. But that was nothing new. He was overpowering—he maxed out her senses. And he didn't act threatened by her. She'd always thought that would be a good thing. But now she'd met a guy she didn't intimidate, she wasn't sure she liked it after all.

Spencer had put a kettle on to boil before returning to the couch to talk to Josh. They leaned back and got comfortable, as if they had no intention of leaving any time soon. Emily caught Charlie's eyes and rose from her position between the two men. Charlie knew her intention as soon as she headed her direction. While the guys were deeply engaged, discussing something earth-shatteringly important, like who'd win the World Series, Charlie and Emily slipped out the apartment door.

Giggling softly as they'd done as young girls, they raced for the stairs. "Which way?" said Charlie.

"Up one flight, and then we'll take the elevator."

They hurried, breathless and panting, and then rode the elevator up to the open rooftop terrace.

"What do you think they'll do when they realize we're gone?" asked Charlie.

"I don't know, but I was desperate," Emily confided. "We need to talk."

"Okay, you first. No, maybe I should go first."

"Go ahead," Emily encouraged.

Charlie let out a breath. "He... He gets me to do things I don't want to do. He doesn't back off when I yell at him or say no. He... He confuses me—I can't think straight. And then to top it all off, I'm leaving tomorrow, so I'm probably getting all worked up over nothing."

Emily chewed her lip. "Okay... Advice or sympathy?"

"Advice now. Sympathy later."

"Well... I think you shouldn't close the door on the possibility he's the one. You have so many things working against this relationship, especially with the distance between you. If it lasts, it would have to be amazing. And you have to give amazing a chance."

Charlie thought for a moment. "Okay, and I'm going to confess something, because I don't know what to do about it." She squeezed her eyes shut. "He kissed me in Spencer's living room, and he's been trying to do it again ever since." She opened pleading eyes to her sister. "What should I do?"

Emily laughed. "I thought that might be what happened. But you haven't let him kiss you again?"

"No. But he's very determined to kiss me again before he leaves. Even if we stay out here for three hours, he'll probably still be waiting in the apartment for me."

"Sister, I don't think I can help you. So far, I've kissed Spencer twice since I decided not to kiss him anymore."

Charlie clapped her hands as she laughed. "Good for Spencer."

"You traitor—you're my sister. You know I'll get hurt when he does his thing and takes up with someone new. The more I kiss him, the more it's going to hurt when he leaves me."

"Okay. Advice or sympathy?"

"Advice. You're crummy at giving sympathy. You already laughed at me."

"Okay, here it is. Sister, he's not going to leave you. If anyone ends this relationship, it'll be you."

"But Grace has told me he always goes from one girl to another. I can't get my hopes up he'll stay with me. What if I fall in love, and then he ends it? I have to guard my heart."

Charlie struggled with her secret knowledge. How could she help her sister without betraying Spencer? "I talked to him, and I really believe he's not a player anymore. Look how long he pursued you. A player would've moved on to someone who was less trouble."

"Maybe. I don't know."

"Josh is a way worse player than Spencer, and you told me to give him a chance."

"You're right. He's really bad. Well, if we ever catch either of these boys cheating, I say, No second chances."

"Agreed," said Charlie.

"Let's go back down and kick them out so we can get some sleep."

"Okay, but I'm still going to have to kiss Josh goodbye unless you can think of a way out of it."

"Was it that bad?" teased Emily.

Charlie remembered the assault of his lips and her thudding heart, and she couldn't help smiling. "I don't know—I'm pretty sure I passed out from the shock of it."

As the girls approached the apartment, they found two scowling boys standing outside. "You left us," said Spencer.

"We're sisters," Emily reasoned. "We had to talk."

"And we've decided it's time for y'all to go home," said Charlie. "It's almost midnight, and I've got an early flight and y'all have to work in the morning."

"You're right," said Spencer as he pulled Emily into his arms and held her close, pressing his lips to the top of her head. "I'll see you tomorrow." He held her a moment longer before she pulled out of his arms and slipped inside.

Charlie's heart pounded as she watched Spencer walk toward the elevator, leaving her alone with Josh. She'd put it off all night. She could do this. It was only a kiss. She'd kissed three other guys before. None of them had made her feel dizzy like Josh did, but that was probably a matter of the circumstances. Josh had caught her by surprise, and she'd been angry at the time. Plus, he'd kissed her in Spencer's living room, where anyone might have walked in and caught them. Now, in the apartment hallway so late at night, they weren't likely to be disturbed. She took deep controlled breaths to slow her heart rate.

Josh pulled her against him and wrapped his arms around her. For several long minutes he held her, rubbing her back with his hands. She could feel his heart pounding against hers, even as his movements appeared calm and relaxed.

"You've done something to me—I don't know what. You've cast a spell or something." His voice was gravelly.

"Please, Josh. Don't use your lines on me. They won't work."

His laugh was bitter. "I've never used lines like that—I've never had to. I don't think I've ever even pretended to really like a girl. This is all new territory for me."

"So you've only done the meaningless sex thing?"

"A lot of it," he confessed, "But I'd take it all back if I could. I'm sure a guy like me is pretty offensive to a girl like you. I know I can change."

"We'll see, Josh. Seriously, let's wait and see. Give yourself a week or two, and you'll work me out of your system. I think I'm just an anomaly."

"It feels more like cancer to me. I think you've metastasized, and I'll never be able to get rid of you, even if I wanted to try."

"Okay. Whatever you say. But don't worry—I won't get my feelings hurt when you realize this relationship is way more trouble than its worth."

"You're definitely a lot of trouble." He cupped her cheeks with his hands and tilting her head back. "But like I said before, you're worth it."

He lowered his mouth to hers and touched their lips together, ever so lightly. Then he brushed his lips across hers and planted tiny kisses around her mouth. He continued to tease her lips until she found her own mouth surging toward his, seeking his warmth. But he held her at bay, gently stroking her lips with his own until they parted. He caught her lower lip between his, and she felt tingles radiating from her mouth down her spine.

When his tongue found hers, he groaned and pressed his mouth against hers more forcefully, his hands tangling in her hair. His breathing became ragged as his kiss raged against her senses. She felt the same dizzying sensation she'd felt the night before. Her knees became jelly, and she started to fall away, but one of his arms dropped down on her back and crushed her against him. All the air left the room, and she gasped for breath through her mouth. But he captured her lips again, and played with her sanity until it was gone. Time froze. She had no idea how long he kissed her. It could have been thirty seconds or thirty minutes.

Suddenly his arms gripped her shoulders and pushed her away. She blinked her eyes, waking from a dream, as reality filtered back into her consciousness. Gazing at him through her lashes, she saw his face had a look of alarm, and he was breathing heavily.

"What was that?" he said. "What just happened?"

"I don't know," she mumbled, hurt and confused by his question.

He pulled her back into her arms, squeezing her until she fought to breathe. "I can't believe that was only a kiss," he said. "Just a kiss. I can't feel like that from a *kiss*."

She trembled in his arms, and he soothed her, rubbing her back. "I'm sorry, I scared you. I scared myself, too."

"So I guess... I guess it wasn't good? I don't know. I haven't kissed that many guys."

"I think it was beyond good. Did any of those other guys even survive? I almost went into cardiac arrest." His brows arched together. "You liked it, too, right? I mean, it was totally amazing, right?"

She shrugged, smiling. "It was so-so."

"Maybe I should try again, if that didn't impress you," he threatened, chuckling. "Except I don't think my heart can take any more of that. "

"Okay." She attempted to extricate herself from his arms. "See ya at Fall Break, if you're not busy."

"I really don't want to let you go." He held on as she wriggled in his grasp. "Wait... Just... Can I hold you for a minute? Just a minute more?"

Reluctantly, she nodded and relaxed in his arms. She was uncomfortably aware of the heat of his body against her and embarrassed by the rapid pounding of her heart. But his embrace was gentle, caressing her back, nuzzling his face in her hair, until she was ready to melt right where she stood.

He bent down and gave her a parting peck on the forehead before he released her. He placed his hands on either side of her face and forced her gaze upward. "I'll talk to you tomorrow night."

"Okay," she rasped through her cottony throat. Scrambling inside the apartment, she tried to clear her addled brain. It was a good thing she was leaving tomorrow, and he'd soon forget about her. She surely didn't want to have to deal with Josh again—not after a kiss like that.

Chapter Fourteen

"BUT, I'M READY to go back to work," Anne complained. "I'm going crazy here. And if you say you don't need me, I promise I'll get my feelings hurt."

"But the doctor hasn't cleared you yet," insisted Steven.

"She said I could do whatever I feel up to doing. That should certainly include work." When Steven opened his mouth to argue, Anne jumped in, "Look, I haven't thrown up since a week ago. I can eat more now. And I've gained five pounds." Anne pooched her stomach out attempting to impress him with her weight.

"You're still seven pounds below normal. You're at thirteen weeks and you don't even look pregnant."

"*He's* three inches long and weighs an ounce. I don't need to look pregnant yet."

"*She* needs her mother to be careful. What if the symptoms come back?"

Anne smiled. They had this argument all the time. She wanted to have a boy, and he wanted a girl. They had decided not to find out the sex before the birth, so the argument was going to last a long time. If she didn't miscarry.

"We've got the nausea under control. If the oral meds quit working, I'll go back on an IV. I promise. I'll take good care of him."

"You won't try to hide the symptoms like you did at first?"

"I promise. And I'm second trimester now. We've got a lot better chance of making it."

"*She's* a fighter. I knew she'd make it."

"*He's* a fighter—just like his dad."

Steven chuckled. "Temporary truce. I need to talk to you about something."

Anne's mouth went dry. His face was serious, and she could tell he was attempting to hide his worry. "What? What is it?"

"So, the DA had to drop the charges on Becca. They ran a search warrant based on the information I gave them, but they came up with nothing. I'm convinced she's the one who drugged Emily's wine. But she probably got rid of the evidence after I accused her of attempted murder out there at Harriman." He started pacing. "I should have kept my mouth shut so they could have surprised her, but I was so angry. And I was trying to intimidate her so we could find out what lie she told Emily."

"It's not your fault. Emily's life is all that mattered. Even if you can't make her pay for what she did, you saved Emily."

"Yes, but... We still thought we might have a chance at proving our case. There was one person at the bar who claimed to have seen her at Emily's table. And Denning admitted he left the table for a minute when his friends were leaving the bar. The DA thought he might get her to cave in and confess, but she lawyered up and isn't talking."

"That's okay. Surely this will scare her enough to keep her from ever doing anything like this again."

"That's the thing. The DA said this girl is pretty vindictive. He said he wouldn't be surprised if she didn't try to retaliate somehow."

"But she seemed like a nice enough girl."

"You and your daughters are way too trusting. You always believe the best about people. Usually it's a wonderful thing, but sometimes it can be dangerous. This is one of those times. I think we need to warn Emily. Actually, I should probably warn Spencer instead. Emily's probably already forgiven Becca and invited her over for tea."

"Oh, I don't think she'd invite her for tea—"

"I'm being sarcastic." He pushed both hands through his hair. "I'm only saying she's too trusting and too forgiving."

Anne smiled and wrapped him in her arms. "But she has a great dad to take care of her now."

"That's what I'm trying to do, but I need cooperation."

"Uhmm, hmmm," said Anne, unbuttoning his shirt.

"What are you doing?" he asked with a grin, watching her determined efforts.

She looked up with a sultry smile as she undid the last button. "I'm cooperating."

*****

Spencer felt sorry for himself. It was Friday night, and he was out on a date... with Josh. And Josh didn't look any happier about the situation than Spencer. What a pair they made. But Josh was as good an option as any, since Emily had some pressing engagement with her laundry tonight. Three weeks—three weeks since he'd had a single moment alone with her. She'd always managed to arrange their dates so there were friends along or they were in a crowded public place. And when he took her home, she would insist she needed to go check on her mom. They hadn't been alone together since the night in her apartment after the climbing date. And never alone meant never kissing. Frustrated didn't begin to describe him.

So when Grace had begged him to take Josh somewhere to give her a chance to be alone with Brad, he'd reluctantly agreed. Why not? Josh had evidently sworn off other women since his encounter with Charlie. Consequently, he was moping around with Brad and Grace. Brad complained his once fun-loving friend had turned into a moping grump.

"Can you believe it?" Josh griped. "Brad told me I needed to get laid. Here I am, trying to change, trying to be the sort of man Charlie deserves, and he's fighting against me."

"Does she know you're trying to change? I mean... Is she encouraging you?"

Josh squeezed his eyes shut with a grimace. "She won't talk to me. I call her every day, and I always get her voice mail. Then she texts back about being really busy."

"Sounds like a brush-off to me. Sorry man."

"She'll give in eventually, won't she? I mean, you said it took a while with Emily. Right?"

"Maybe the two of them are plotting together. Emily hasn't ditched me, but she's avoided being alone with me for three weeks."

"That sucks, man."

"Yeah," Spencer agreed glumly. "Want another drink?"

"Good idea. Waitress," called Josh. "Bring me a double."

"Uhmm... A double?" asked the teenaged blond girl.

"Yes. A strawberry-banana-yogurt slush, with a double vitamin shot."

Spencer chuckled. "Are you sure you don't want to go somewhere and get something a little stronger to drown your sorrows?"

"No. I'm on call tonight. Thanks for hanging out, by the way. I guess Brad and Grace are getting tired of me. I never realized how much time I spent chasing women before. I guess I'm going to need a new hobby."

"Emily says Charlie's still convinced you'll forget about her soon."

"She's wrong." His scowl disappeared as his eyes widened. "You could help me—you could call Emily to tell her I've changed. You could tell her I'm not a player anymore."

"I'll do better. I'll call Charlie and tell her. I've been wanting to get her advice anyway." He pulled out his cell phone and dialed Charlie's number.

"She won't answer," said Josh. "She texted me she was going to a movie with friends tonight."

"Hey Spencer," Charlie's voice rang out. "What's up?"

"Uhmm..." Spencer cringed at Josh's angry expression. "I was calling to ask some advice about your sister. She, uhmm, she's making sure we're never alone together."

Her laugh was so loud he pulled the phone back from his ear. "Oh, right. She's enforcing that no kissing thing."

"She told you about that?"

"Yeah, she told me. Sorry. Are you having a tough time?" He was irritated at the lack of sympathy in her voice.

"How do I fix it? I can't go without kissing her. I'm dying here."

Her laughter was musical. "You're not going to die, Spencer. But... she's protecting herself. She's still convinced you're going to drop her for some other girl."

"I'm not." He couldn't hide the hurt in his voice. "I was thinking about... getting a ring."

"Really? That's awesome! I bet she'd quit worrying if y'all were engaged. Oh, and if you want to surprise her, I know what she likes. I mean we've talked about what type of diamonds and settings we like for years."

"But I'll have to save the money. I can't get one that soon. You really think she won't kiss me again until we're engaged." Spencer felt as if he'd been given a death sentence.

"Hopefully, you'll find a way to convince her you're not going to leave her for another girl. But let me warn you. We made a pact—no second chances."

"Meaning what?" Spencer could tell Josh was straining to hear Charlie's words.

"If we catch a guy cheating one time, that's it. No second chances."

Josh waved at Spencer and silently mouthed, "Tell her about me."

"Uhmm, speaking of chances, are you giving Josh a chance? Because I think he's trying really hard."

Charlie groaned. "He thinks he wants me, but he doesn't. For goodness sake, he chased my sister before he went after me. He'll forget about me soon, and he'll be with some other girl. Or maybe he'll be with two or three girls. Who knows?"

Josh was shaking his head angrily and gesturing. Spencer said, "But he... He's changed. He's really trying hard. He's not going out with any other girls. Ask Grace—she knows."

"I just think it's futile."

"No it's not," muttered Josh.

"Ohmygosh! Is he there? Is that Josh? Spencer! How could you?" The phone clicked, and Charlie was gone.

"My life sucks." Josh let his head fall onto the table with a thud.

"Mine, too. Emily's going to hear about that phone call and give me a dressing down. Why do women make everything so complicated?"

"It's our punishment as men. We have to suffer because Adam took that apple from Eve."

"I hate that guy," muttered Spencer, and Josh nodded in agreement.

*****

Emily loved watching her mom and Steven together. He was so devoted and sweet. She was truly happy her mom had found love again after being alone for so long after she was widowed. They never acted jealous or mistrustful. They had absolutely no doubts about each other's fidelity. She was actually a little envious.

She and Spencer were having lunch with her parents in the back room at Papa's Place in celebration of Anne's first day back at work. Her mom looked happier and healthier than she had since the last fateful lunch at Papa's.

"So, I'm not a hundred percent back to normal, but I can take oral antiemetics and vitamins and antihistamines now. And we've finally found a combination that works pretty well." She munched happily on a stuffed baked potato, having not been brave enough to attempt eating the spicy special of the day. "And, I can start exercising again."

Steven frowned at this. "But you're not supposed to overdo it."

Anne waved him off. "I'm dying to get outside and do something. I thought we could go do some little easy hike next weekend."

"Hmmm… I think you're speaking at that HER fundraiser Saturday night. Are you sure you're going to want to hike Saturday morning?"

"That's next Saturday? I forgot. What am I supposed to say? How long do I have to speak?" Her face was as white as her napkin.

"Just twenty minutes."

"Ughh! I'm nervous already."

"Perhaps I could pretend to have appendicitis," Steven suggested playfully, referencing a ploy he used to help distract her from her nervousness during a presentation.

"I guess I'll give Henri a call, so he'll be there to comfort me afterwards," she teased.

"I still don't like that guy." Steven scowled.

"Who's Henri?" asked Spencer.

"He's this French jerk that went after Anne and tried to steal her from me. I was insanely jealous."

"Not any more jealous than I was of Michelle or Ellen," declared Anne.

"Which is ridiculous, since you were the one who wanted me to date Ellen. But that's another story."

"This is crazy," said Spencer. "I've never heard this stuff."

Emily twirled her sphaghetti on her fork. "How did you decide you could trust Steven, Mom? After all, he had quite the reputation in the social columns and tabloids."

"Let me answer that." Steven took a drink of water. "You know, I never minded those rumors, and they were mostly true in the early days. But even though I'd pretty much given up that lifestyle ten years before, my reputation made it hard for Anne to really trust me."

"It was really hard for me to believe he loved me," her mom admitted. "I didn't feel special enough for him to choose me. I was nobody."

"No. You were amazing. You're still amazing." Steven raised her hand to kiss her knuckles. He turned back to Emily. "But it took a lot for me to convince her she was the only one for me."

"You guys are so sappy," said Emily.

"I need to talk to both of you about something serious," said Steven. "It's about Becca. There's evidence she may've been the person who drugged your wine, but not enough evidence to get a conviction. And the District Attorney who handled the case warned me he thought she might try to retaliate."

"What else could she do?" asked Spencer. "I mean, do they think she's violent? Would she try to kill Emily or something?"

"I don't think so. But I really think you should be on guard. I don't trust her."

"I can't believe she did it," said Emily. "She doesn't seem that mean. Kind of ditsy maybe, but not cruel. Are you sure she was even at the bar that night? I didn't see her."

"You didn't see her?" Spencer asked incredulously. "She's the one who invited me to go. She's the one who took the picture of you cozied up to Denning."

"What picture?" asked Emily. "Nobody told me about a picture, and I never cozied up to Asher Denning."

Spencer pulled out his phone and showed her a photograph where she was indeed leaning against Asher. She felt a surge of nausea and blinked at sudden tears.

"I don't even remember doing this. I'm so embarrassed. I wish you'd get rid of this picture."

"He can't," said Steven. "We might need it as evidence some day."

"Okay," Emily sniffed. "I guess she really isn't a nice person. I don't see why you ever liked her."

"I didn't ever like her," Spencer insisted.

"But you dated, didn't you?" She pinned him with narrowed eyes. "According to Best Family Dating Rules?"

"Definitely not. I never kissed her. I never bought her anything. I told you that before. That hike we all went on together was the closest we've ever been."

"Really? But she told me—"

"She lies. Why would you believe her over me?"

Anne put her hand on Emily's arm. "From experience, I'll tell you it was easier to believe Steven was in love with someone else than it was to believe he was in love with me."

Emily's face was scalding hot. Spencer had never used the word love. Grace had said she thought her brother was in love with Emily. But he hadn't said it. Would he ever say it? Would she believe him if he did? She dared a sideways glance at Spencer. His face was equally red. What did that mean? Did he really love her? Or maybe he didn't, and he was embarrassed her mom had mentioned it.

Anne broke the awkward silence. "Uhmm... Are y'all planning to go to Sam and Tanner's wedding? They're planning a big bash. They're going to have dinner and a live band and dancing."

"That sounds so fun. I got my invitation today. We're going together, right Spencer? I mean... If we're still dating in six weeks."

"Of course we'll still be dating in six weeks," he pouted. "We can go, although I don't really dance."

"Oh," she tried to hide her disappointment. She loved dancing—all kinds of dancing, not just ballet. She'd hate to sit around while everyone else was dancing. But she didn't want to hurt Spencer's feelings, so she didn't say anything.

Her mind wandered as her mom continued to chat excitedly about the wedding, bragging about her part in playing matchmaker between the two. Her eyes rested for a moment on Spencer. He raised his arms to stretch, and she watched his muscles flexing through his shirt. She felt a familiar stirring as she admired his form, realizing she'd never seen him with his shirt off, although she'd seen him in a tank top. She wondered how his back would look if she could actually see the muscles. What would his chest look like? What would it feel like? Why hadn't they ever gone swimming before? She should suggest it.

"Emily? Are you in there?" asked Anne.

"I'm sorry. I was thinking... about uhmm... Charlie. What did you ask me?"

"I asked if you'd heard from Charlie this weekend?"

"Well, she called me Friday night. She was a little upset about something that happened with Josh." She gave Spencer a stern look, and he had the grace to look away.

"Is she still giving Josh the stiff-arm?" asked Anne.

"Yes, but he's been pretty persistent. She still thinks he's too much of a player to ever change." Emily looked at Spencer, raising one eyebrow to get her point across.

"He's pretty depressed about it," said Spencer. "He mopes around all the time, and he quit going out to bars altogether. And he evidently follows Grace and Brad around like a lost puppy."

Emily couldn't help feeling sorry for Josh, but he wasn't the first guy to pine for her sister. Maybe she'd put in a good word for him with Charlie, although it probably wouldn't make a difference.

"But she starts class in a couple of weeks, and she's pretty excited."

"I still don't see why she won't let me pay her tuition. It's ridiculous." Steven muttered as he stabbed at his stuffed chicken breast.

"It's her pride," explained Anne.

"*Pride*. If you ask me, you Best girls have way too much of it."

"We should go swimming," Emily blurted without preamble. Then her face flamed. She couldn't stop thinking about seeing Spencer without a shirt on, and the idea burst out of her mouth before she could stop it.

Anne and Steven stared at her in confusion, but Spencer smiled, flashing his dimples. "Great idea. I was thinking the exact same thing." His eyes wandered briefly down from her eyes before he forced them back up again, and she felt a little shock. Maybe he *had* been thinking the exact same thing.

*****

Spencer was having a great day. Lunch had a few uncomfortable moments, but making plans to swim with Emily made everything else worthwhile. Although he wasn't allowed to kiss her, at least he'd be able to feast his eyes on her body. Of course, this meant other guys could also see her, but hopefully there wouldn't be any other single guys around. Steven had offered to let them swim at a hotel owned by Gherring Inc.

He'd also decided he had to learn how to dance before the wedding in six weeks. He saw the disappointment in her eyes when he admitted he couldn't dance. He might be able to fake it if it was only going to be fast dancing. He could sway a bit and watch Emily dance. But Sam and Tanner told him to expect all kinds of dancing, including waltzes and tangos. So he was planning to ask around and secretly take dance lessons. He must really be in love, if he was willing to take dance lessons simply to make her happy.

Who could he ask to find a good dance teacher? Josh and Brad hadn't lived in town long enough. He couldn't bear the thought of the teasing that would come from his sisters, so that option was definitely out. He thought of his other buddies. Landon might be a good source—he had a couple of sisters that might know of a dance teacher.

"Yo, Bro." Landon answered the phone call. "What's up? You going on the hike this weekend?"

"I'm not sure—I'll know later in the week. But I was hoping for a favor."

"Anything... Well, as long as it isn't illegal. Or if you promise we won't get caught."

"Nothing illegal. I just need to learn how to dance so I can dance with Emily at a wedding in six weeks."

"Sorry, buddy. I'd love to teach you, but my dance card is full."

"I'm heartbroken. But I'd really like for you to ask around, maybe ask your sisters, and see if they can recommend a good dance teacher. I need to learn everything—even ballroom stuff like waltzes, tangos, whatever."

"Will do. Can I get back to you this weekend? I'm having dinner with the family Saturday night."

"Outstanding."

"YackAtchaLater."

With those plans in the works he turned his mind to more important matters. He needed to buy an engagement ring. He'd determined it was the only way to convince Emily he wasn't going to move on to another relationship. His plan to earn money parking cars at one of the local hotels would take up most of his spare time, but he wasn't getting any alone time with Emily anyway. He should be able to save enough for a good down payment on a ring in four weeks.

His other option was to admit the truth—that she was the first and only girl he'd ever dated. But he'd waited so long to tell her, she might not believe him. Besides, it was embarrassing. And he couldn't help being pleased at her acceptance he was well versed in physical matters. His greatest fear had been she would suspect his inexperience—that she would judge him as inept. So his ego somehow wouldn't allow him to insist he was unsophisticated and unskilled. No, his best choice was buying a ring.

*****

"I invited Grace and Brad to come swimming with us. That's okay, right?" Emily had decided she'd be less uncomfortable parading around in a swimsuit if there was another girl along.

Spencer frowned. "I guess. Is Josh coming, too?"

"I don't think so."

"Good. I mean, I feel sorry for the guy, but I don't really want him ogling you in a swimsuit. I don't really want Brad ogling you either, but I guess he'll be busy ogling my sister." Spencer looked a bit ill at this thought. "I may need to beat him up, either way."

"It won't be a problem," said Emily. "I'm only planning to watch; I'm wearing jeans and a long-sleeved shirt."

Emily couldn't suppress a laugh. "Ohmygosh! You look like I just killed a kitten. I'm kidding. I'm going to swim."

He grinned. "Awesome. Let's go."

The pool was practically deserted on a Monday night. "This is beautiful!" said Grace. The area surrounding the pool had planter boxes with lush greenery and the pool itself was made to simulate a lagoon, complete with a waterfall. They claimed four lounge chairs and the guys immediately stripped off their shirts and made for the water. Emily had always been a bit modest, but Grace had no such qualms. She pulled off her outer dress to reveal a cute red bikini and raised her eyebrows at Emily as she stood awkwardly by her chair.

"Come on, you can do it. You're worse than Hannah."

Emily turned her back to the pool as she shed her shorts and shirt, tugging and pulling to make sure everything was in place. She wasn't as amply endowed as Grace, and she hoped Spencer wouldn't be disappointed. She had on a two-piece suit, but had added a pair of short black board shorts over her swimsuit bottom. Convinced she was as secure as she could be while swimming, she turned around and headed to join the others in the pool.

Brad was talking to him, but Spencer couldn't concentrate on his words. He had watched Emily slowly divesting herself of her garments with her back to him, and it might as well have been a striptease. And now, he was waiting for her to turn around. He must have been holding his breath, because when she turned around, he released it and almost passed out. She looked like she belonged in a James Bond movie. Her legs were long and slim, yet she was firm and muscular from years of dancing. She'd unbound her long brown curly hair, and it fell across her shoulders and down her chest. Doubtless, she was attempting to use her hair to obscure his view of her slim torso, but the hair and the flimsy material was an ineffective shield. She glided, as she always moved, smooth and floating, mesmerizing, to the side of the pool and dipped a single toe into the water.

He felt a slap on the back of his head. "Put your tongue back in your mouth." Grace laughed.

His face heated at having been so thoroughly exposed in his frank admiration. But the hotness in his face was nothing compared to the fire that burned in the rest of his body. Why had he thought this would be a good idea? Now, he wanted to kiss her more than ever. And not only kiss her lips, but kiss every part of her. He swallowed convulsively. This was like torture, pure agony, to see her and not to be able to touch her. He tried to think of a way they could elope. Perhaps next week...

Emily's face flamed as she moved toward the pool. Spencer was staring at her, and not in a casual way. He was gaping. She made an awkward attempt to move her hair to cover her chest. She gingerly tested the water, relieved the temperature was comfortable. She hurried to slide into the water and moved to join the other three, relieved at the protective covering of the pool water.

Grace suggested a game of chicken fight. The girls would sit on the shoulders of the boys, trying to push or pull one another off their shoulders. Emily was really glad she'd shaved again right before coming, since Spencer had to hold onto her legs to help keep her secure. She soon became engrossed in the competition and forgot to admire the strong broad shoulders she perched on. She and Spencer had a height advantage, and the first few attacks, she managed to easily leverage Grace from Brad's shoulders. There was a lot of laughing and screaming and splashing involved.

Spencer thought the guy who invented chicken fight was a genius. He loved this game. Even when he was relegated to the deeper end of the pool to even out the height advantage, he didn't mind a bit. He had Emily on his shoulders. Her enticing thighs were clutching against his cheeks. He had his hands on her legs, caressing her smooth skin. And it was perfectly acceptable. It was merely part of the game. He wanted to play this game forever. Every day. He swallowed some water as Grace pushed Emily over, her tightly clamped thighs pulling his head under the surface. He didn't care—it was worth it.

Emily was becoming weary, but Spencer seemed indefatigable. Even when Grace called out she was ready to give up, he slipped underneath her and lifted her out of the water with ease. He must be amazingly strong. He carried her on his shoulders to stand next to Grace who was treading water next to Brad, arguing about the score of the game. She suddenly became acutely aware of Spencer's fingers on her calves. His fingers shifted slightly as if adjusting his grip, and then slid along the length of her shin sending shivers up her entire spine. She realized her thigh pressed so intimately against his cheek she could feel the roughness from the beard that had but a few hours of growth.

"Let me down," she said, unable to control the quiver in her voice.

Spencer obeyed Emily's command, albeit with a great deal of regret. They stood in four and a half feet of water, so most of her body was under the surface, but she could still stand easily. His sister, being shorter, was hanging onto Brad's neck and he was holding her in his arms. He suddenly wished Emily weren't quite so tall.

"Why don't we move to the shallow end, so Grace can stand up?" said Spencer.

Brad raised an irritated eyebrow, and Spencer grinned at him. In the shallows, much more of Emily was exposed, although she still attempted to wrap her arms to conceal herself. He decided he could be bold enough to drape an arm around her. He didn't think she'd object, since they were in such a public place kissing wouldn't be a danger.

Spencer's body was amazing. He had muscles everywhere, and no fat whatsoever. Every time he moved, his muscles flexed and rippled under his skin. His chest was well formed, with a bit of hair that seemed to make him that much more masculine. When he put his arm around her, she was conscious of his strength and power. She felt warm and protected, but that's not all she felt. She also felt a different sort of heat. A sizzle that trickled from the place where his fingers toyed with the skin on her arm, spreading through her body, and settling to burn in her core. She found herself closing her eyes and losing awareness of the thread of conversation as she struggled to maintain her composure.

Brad said something while looking right at her. She tried to focus her eyes on him and listen to his voice, but she couldn't quite understand him. Then he laughed and pulled Grace toward him and kissed her full on the lips. Emily was thinking she ought to be shocked at that public display, but she couldn't quite remember what her objections were.

Spencer enjoyed the way Emily relaxed and molded her swimsuit-clad body against him. He felt the scalding contact of her bare skin against his. He let his fingers play lightly against the smooth skin on her arm, while they discussed what they wanted to do after swimming. Grace suggested renting a movie and watching it at Brad's apartment. Then Brad asked Emily what she wanted to do. When she didn't answer him, he chuckled. "I think I know what you'd like to do," he said, "and it doesn't involve watching a movie."

Brad drew Grace into a hearty kiss. Spencer felt a surge of brotherly protest, but tamped it down. Glancing at Emily's drunken expression, he decided to follow suit instead. He bent his head down and lightly touched his mouth against hers. When she immediately moaned softly and parted her lips, his mouth sought hers with unrestrained hunger, and she responded with equal fervor.

"Eh-hem," said Grace. "You guys ready to go?"

Spencer released her lips slowly, reluctantly, and turned to his sister with a contented smile. "Yes, I believe we are."

Emily's lips protested his departure. She felt bereft of the warm caress of his mouth. She opened her eyes and forced them into focus, blinking rapidly. She reddened at Grace's laughing perusal. But before she could decide what to do, Grace locked arms with her and urged her out of the pool, talking and chatting.

"I'm so glad you and Spencer are dating. This is great fun. What movie do you wanna watch?"

The full realization of her very passionate kiss with Spencer slammed into her head. She'd kissed him. She'd kissed him hard. Right in front of Grace and Brad. She stammered, "I... I can't believe we... we..."

Grace gave her a firm elbow in the ribs. "Shut up, Emily. You think too much." She whispered in her ear. "It was just a kiss. Okay? And Spencer's a really great guy. He deserves a girl like you."

The boys were following behind them as they gathered their things and went to change in the dressing rooms. When they were alone in the girls' room, Emily said, "That's why I don't let him kiss me anymore."

"You don't let him kiss you? It sure looked like you let him kiss you," she chuckled.

"Yes, but I didn't mean to."

"Why not? I really don't get it. I'm not teasing you."

"I'm losing my heart to him," said Emily. "And he's going to break it someday." She looked at Grace through a film of unshed tears.

Grace gave her a hug. "Why are you so sure he'll break your heart? I told you he loves you. Hasn't he told you yet?"

"N-no. He... He hasn't."

"Well, he will. But he's afraid to say it unless he knows you love him back."

Emily pondered her statement. It was possible. Maybe he really did.

"So, do you?" Grace asked.

"Huh?"

"Do you love him back? Or are you going to break *his* heart?"

Chapter Fifteen

SPENCER DRAGGED HIMSELF into work on Friday. He'd gotten valet parking shifts two nights in a row. The tips had been great, but his shift lasted until two a.m. He'd taken a cold shower and had drunk two cups of coffee, but still felt bleary-eyed. He was planning to work as many shifts as possible, but he hoped to spend some time with Emily over the weekend. She'd already agreed to give him the entire day on Saturday. He'd love to take her to see a musical, but he was saving his money for a ring. So their current plan was to picnic in the elevated park and rent a movie to watch with Grace and Brad.

"Hey, Spencer." He jumped as Emily spoke from close behind him. "What're you working on?"

"Just a report that's due today," he yawned. "But, I'm looking forward to spending Saturday together."

"Me, too. Uhmm, I wondered what you're doing tonight?"

He felt his stomach twist. He'd already accepted a valet shift tonight. He'd have to lie to her. How could he explain his need for the extra job and still keep the ring a secret? Suddenly it occurred to him, he might buy the ring, ask her to marry him, and she might say no. He'd assumed she'd agree. How could he find out for sure, without actually asking her?

"Uhmm, I actually have to help my father on a project tonight. I'm sorry."

She looked disappointed. Well, it was good she was disappointed, right? At least that meant she wanted to spend time with him. But he needed to keep her from suspecting anything, and it would be even more difficult when he started taking dance lessons. Maybe he could think of some plausible story to tell her.

"It's okay. I may just rent a movie."

"Okay. See you Saturday."

Confusion reigned in Emily's head. Since that fateful Monday night at the pool when Grace had insisted Spencer loved her, she'd been fighting her emotions. Certain he would eventually move on to another girl, she'd done everything possible to avoid falling in love with him. But what if Spencer really loved her? Would he be able to break his old habits of flirting and dating multiple girls? And he was obviously more experienced than she was physically. Would he tire of her rule restricting their physical contact? Would he be so overwhelmed with need he sought relief elsewhere? She had no idea how long guys could actually go without having sex. The movies implied they couldn't wait for long without having physical pain, but she didn't know if that was true. And she was too embarrassed to ask someone. If he did find relief with someone else, how would she know? She simply couldn't bear the thought of him with another girl.

But then to further confuse matters, he'd been acting a little strange since Monday night. Instead of calling constantly and asking to spend time with her every night, he'd only made plans for one or two nights that week. Granted, she'd been mostly turning him down when he asked for more time, but only to avoid the temptation that came from being alone together. Especially since she'd proven to herself she had absolutely no ability to resist him. But now she saw him less and less. She couldn't help but wonder if he was already getting tired of her or tired of all her dating rules. Further adding to her suspicions, he hadn't been available to answer his cell phone the past two nights. He'd called her back within thirty minutes, but it was unusual for him not to answer.

She really needed to talk this through with someone. But who? She considered asking Grace, but she was too defensive of her brother to ever believe he was up to something. She could ask her mom, but she was actually afraid her mom would be too frank with her. Steven and her mom already managed to embarrass her on a regular basis with their overt affection. She could talk to Charlie. But her sister was in a real funk over her relationship with Josh, determined to make a clean break with him before he ever had a chance to disappoint her. Charlie seemed to end most of their phone conversations in tears, a habit highly unusual for her carefree sister. Maybe she could talk to Steven. What was she thinking? She must be getting desperate.

Her cell phone chirped. "Hey, Josh. What's up?"

"Hi, Emily." He drug her name out, using the miserable voice he seemed to have adopted permanently. "I wondered if maybe I could hang out with you and Spencer tonight? Brad and Grace are getting tired of me lurking around, and all my single friends just want to go out and party."

Her heart went out to him. Charlie had broken plenty of hearts, and she seemed to have done an extra special job on Josh. Secretly, she thought Charlie was wrong not to give Josh a chance to prove himself.

"Spencer's busy tonight, but you could watch a movie with me at my place."

"Really? That would be so awesome. I'll pick up a pizza and a movie. What do you want to watch?" He actually sounded almost happy. Poor guy.

"Anything that's not raunchy. I've hardly seen any movies, so I'm sure whatever you pick will be fine. I'll pay you for half so we're officially just hanging out instead of going on a date—according to house rules."

"Good idea. I need to make sure Charlie can't accuse me of dating her sister. That is, if I can get her to talk to me."

"Didn't y'all have a phone conversation last week?"

The glum tone came back to his voice. "Yes. It was about ten minutes of me saying over and over I'd changed and I wasn't ever going to be with another girl, while she insisted that was impossible and it would never work out anyway."

"Oh... Sorry."

"I promise not to spend the whole evening moaning about Charlie." Then he added, "But probably part of the evening."

*****

Anne was excited to be going by herself to a routine pregnancy monitoring appointment. Her first week back at work had gone well, except she was extremely fatigued. But she guessed that was to be expected. She couldn't really remember how tired she was with Emily and Charlotte—it had been way too long. The oral medications seemed to be working well to control the nausea. She was certain she'd gained, and soon she'd be at least back to her normal weight.

The doctor was listening for the heartbeat, and Anne noticed her brows pushing down over her eyes.

"Is everything okay?" Anne's tongue felt thick and wooden. Was the baby dead? Was she going to miscarry?

"No, everything is fine. But I'd like to do an ultrasound today."

"But I thought you weren't going to do an ultrasound until twenty weeks? Is there something wrong with the baby's heart?"

"No, I promise. The heart sounds healthy. Please don't be concerned. But there's no harm in doing an ultrasound to confirm everything is progressing normally."

"Okay, but we decided we don't want to know the sex. We want to be surprised."

"That's fine. We may not even be able to determine the sex at fourteen weeks. But if I can, I won't say anything."

Anne was terrified as the doctor performed the ultrasound, despite her assurances. The doctor turned the screen away from Anne's view at her insistence so she wouldn't accidentally find out the sex. She watched the doctor's expressions, but her face remained very neutral. "This is taking a long time. Do you see something? I mean is something wrong?"

The doctor smiled. "Anne, I can't detect anything wrong. I only needed to confirm what I heard with the Doppler. You're still at high risk for birth defects. We won't know for sure there aren't any abnormalities just from an ultrasound. But so far, everything looks fine, the heart looks fine, and everything is progressing normally."

"So the baby looks healthy so far?"

"Yes, so far everything looks good." Then she moved over to hold Anne's hand between both of hers. She smiled, nodding her head. "With both of them."

Anne paced across the apartment floor, glancing to the door every few minutes. She'd declined the doctor's offer to call Steven and give him the news, choosing to impart the information herself. But now she was regretting her decision. She was afraid to tell him.

Not because she thought he wouldn't be thrilled, but because he was already so overbearingly protective. What would he be like now? He'd have a thousand questions she wouldn't be able to answer. She should have let him find out from the doctor so he could grill her until he was satisfied.

She heard the door opening and froze in place. Wait... She had to look normal. If she looked upset, he'd notice right away. He could read her like a book.

"Hi, Sweetheart. How was your day?" She put on her best happy face.

"My day was fine. You were with me for most of it, so you should know. How was your..." He turned toward her, and suddenly his face turned white. "What's wrong? You look like something's wrong. Is it the baby? Is something wrong?"

"No. Nothing's wrong. I promise."

He fairly flew across the room to wrap her in his arms. "What is it? What happened at your appointment today? Don't lie to me."

"I'm not lying. I promise. Nothing's wrong. But I'd like for you to sit down with me and talk to me for a minute."

He swept her to the couch and pulled her onto his lap. "Talk to me, Anne."

She sighed. Might as well simply say it. She wanted to find some funny way to surprise him, but he knew her too well. "The doctor did an ultrasound today."

"She did? She wasn't supposed to do that yet. Did you find out the sex? Is that what happened?"

"No. She heard something when she was listening for the heartbeat, and decided to do an ultrasound. But everything's fine. It's just..." She choked. She couldn't make the words come out.

"It's just what? Anne! What is it? We can handle anything together, but you have to tell me."

"There're two!" she gasped.

"There to what?"

"There are two! Babies! Twins!"

For a long moment, he was silent. When he finally spoke, his voice croaked. "Twins?"

"She said women over the age of forty-five have about a one in five chance of twin pregnancy. And women with multiple pregnancies are more likely to have hyperemesis gravidarum, too. She missed seeing it on the first ultrasound, but today she thought she heard two heartbeats." She paused to take a breath. "And it turns out she did hear two."

She could see the wheels turning in his head. He opened his mouth to speak, but she stopped him. "Before you pepper me with endless questions, let me tell you this—she said we don't need to do anything differently at all. At least not right now. You can call her on Monday and ask all those questions that are churning in your head."

"But you have to answer a few questions tonight." He leaned down, kissing her cheek. "Will they be identical or fraternal?"

"Most likely fraternal."

"So we could even have a boy and a girl at the same time?"

"Yep. Or two boys or two girls."

"And are you going to get really big?"

"She said I'd only need to gain an extra ten pounds, but I'll probably look pretty big."

"I think this means I'm especially virile. Right?" His dimples danced.

"There's never been any doubt about that," she chuckled. "But I really think it just means I'm old."

"I have one more important question." He nuzzled her neck, sending a little thrill down her spine. "Is it okay to celebrate being pregnant with twins? I mean, is there any chance we might accidentally create a few more babies in there?"

"There's no danger. In fact, I'm almost certain the doctor recommended it."

*****

Emily was glad to not be spending the evening alone, but Josh was still pretty glum when he arrived. They decided to eat first, as neither one was really in a movie-watching mood, despite their plans.

"Has Charlie said anything about me?" asked Josh hopefully. "Wait. If it's bad, I'm not sure I want to know."

"She still doesn't trust you, Josh. She's been hurt before. I know how she feels—I feel the same way. It's no fun. I don't want to do it again."

"If it feels anything like this, I totally understand. I never knew a girl could make me feel so miserable. I almost wish I'd never met her. No, that's not true. As long as there's a chance, it's worth it."

"Let me ask you Josh, why should she trust you?"

"It's true enough she doesn't have any reason to trust me. But I'm willing to prove I've changed."

Emily suddenly realized Josh could provide some of the answers she'd been looking for. "Can I ask you some questions? And will you promise not to laugh at me?"

He grinned. "I'll do my best. But I can't even imagine what you're going to ask. Go ahead."

"So... Uhmm... How long can a guy go without having sex?"

A chuckle escaped before he could stop himself. "I'm sorry. But that's not what I expected. Are you serious?"

She nodded, knowing her face must be bright red.

"Well, you're probably asking the wrong guy. I've never really had to go without before. But, let's see. How long ago did I meet your sister? Like four weeks ago? I can say for sure a guy can go four weeks." He laughed, and then laughed louder at what must be a horrified expression on her face.

What if Spencer couldn't wait? Maybe he already hadn't waited?

"Hold on, I'm teasing you. Don't get upset!" His smile disappeared. "A guy can go a lot longer than that. We just usually don't want to, but we won't die from going without. I'm prepared to go without for a long time to prove myself to Charlie."

But exactly how long was a long time?

Josh interrupted her thoughts. "You're not very experienced are you?"

"Not very."

"And Charlie? Is she like you? Innocent, I mean?"

"Josh I don't think I should talk to you about Charlie."

He groaned, "She is, isn't she? No wonder she doesn't want to have anything to do with a guy like me." He closed his eyes and rubbed his temples. "I'd go back and change my past if I could. Do you think it's a lost cause? Will I ever be good enough for her?"

"What would you do if I told you no? If I told you tonight there was absolutely zero chance she'd ever come around and be able to trust you, what would you do?"

He leaned back in his chair and closed his eyes, rubbing his forehead. He sat forward and caught her gaze, all the humor gone from his face. "I'd do exactly what I'm doing now. That man is gone, the one who slept around, going out with women only for sex. I won't be able to sleep with a girl I'm not in love with—one I'm not willing to commit to. Not now. I know Charlie doesn't believe it and you probably don't either, but I love her. I decided I love her and once I make a decision I stick with it."

"But, Josh. She might never even give you a chance. I'm sorry. I'd love to tell you she'll finally listen to you some day, if you wait long enough. But she might not."

"Then some day, I may really be able to answer your question about how long a guy can go without sex," he said with a smile that didn't quite reach his eyes.

Josh felt his heart die a little. Charlie was innocent and he didn't deserve her. How could he even ask her to be with him?

"Josh... Do you think a player really can change? Can he really stick with one girl? Or will he eventually revert to his old ways?"

Emily was watching him intently, chewing on her lip. "You're not asking about me and Charlie, are you? You're asking about Spencer. Right?"

She looked down. "Yes," she whispered.

"He'd be stupid to want to be with anyone besides you, and I don't think he's that stupid. And he can wait a lot longer than four weeks. He'll wait as long as he needs to. Okay? Feel better?"

"Okay," she agreed. But he could tell she wasn't really convinced. If Emily wouldn't trust Spencer, what chance did he have of ever getting Charlie to trust him? Did it matter? Could he ever actually be good enough for Charlie Best?

"By the way, Emily? Does Spencer know I'm here tonight? I'm a little surprised he was okay with it."

Her eyes widened. "I... I didn't think. Do you think he'll mind? Surely he won't care."

"Of course not. But, I don't want him to beat me up because he thinks I'm chasing you again."

"Ohmygosh! You're right. I should call him now. I don't want him to think I'm hiding something."

He nodded and watched her pull out her phone to call Spencer. She waited and then her face fell when it went to voice mail. "Uhmm. Hi, Spencer. It's Friday night, and I know you're helping your dad with some project, but call me if you get a chance. Josh came over to keep me company." After a pause, she added, "And so he could moan about Charlie, of course. Anyway, call if you get a chance. Bye."

"How was that?" she asked, screwing her face to one side.

"I guess we'll find out. If he comes over with a gun, I think I might be grateful. He could just put me out of my misery."

Spencer cursed under his breath. He'd missed a call from Emily at eight o'clock. It was already after midnight, way too late to call her back. He listened to her message, and cursed a little louder. He didn't want her hanging out with Josh when he wasn't around. But how could he insist she sit around alone when he was secretly working? And now, she was going to wonder why he didn't call her back.

Rather than risk waking her, he sent a text. "Sorry I missed you. Accidentally turned ringer off. Project went long. Call you in the morning."

He'd had a great night in tips so far. One Friday or Saturday night was probably worth two weeknights. But he couldn't give up many weekend nights with Emily, or she'd get suspicious.

"Hey, Spencer! Can you get this one?"

Every car was one step closer to getting a ring for Emily. "I'm coming!"

*****

Becca scanned the hiking group, searching for Spencer. She was totally frustrated. He hadn't come on a single hike in a month, not since the day he'd come on the hike looking for Emily. What did he see in her? She was so flat-chested she barely even looked like a girl. All the guys appreciated Becca's assets and let her know about it. She was very popular, except with Spencer. She hadn't been able to get his attention, and it really bothered her. Now her phone calls went straight to voicemail, and he never called her back. He seemed to be really angry with her, and it wasn't even her fault.

It was all Emily's fault. All she'd done was let him know Emily was going out with another guy. She'd never cheat on Spencer like Emily had. Emily claimed they were only friends, so she was obviously leading him on. She didn't deserve Spencer. And then Mr. Gherring filed charges against her for slipping a ruffie in Emily's wine. It was a good thing she'd gone home and flushed the extras down the toilet after he made some remark about her attempting murder. She wasn't trying to kill Emily. Granted, she put three in the wine glass instead of one, but Emily wouldn't drink the whole glass of wine. It took her over an hour to drink the first glass. And it wasn't that dangerous, either—she'd used them herself and always had fun. Emily had probably faked being sick to get attention from Spencer.

Becca knew she could have any other guy in the hiking club, but now she was determined to have Spencer. Maybe after they'd been together a few times, she'd drop him, just to let him know what rejection felt like. It was almost time for the hike to start, and he still hadn't shown up. Then she heard Landon mention his name to a group of girls.

"Yeah, Spencer needs a dance teacher so he can dance at some wedding in a few weeks."

"What kind of dancing?" asked Marsha.

"He said everything, even ballroom dancing."

"Oh," she replied, "I don't know of a teacher for that. Our place has like a hip hop class."

"Me, neither," said Leah. "But I could ask around."

Spencer wanted to take dance lessons? Becca felt like she'd been given a gift—a second chance. "I know a place," said Becca. "The studio where I take jazzercise has ballroom dance classes on Mondays and Wednesdays."

Landon scrunched up his nose. "I thought you and Spencer weren't speaking to each other."

Becca adopted her most unfairly injured look; "He accused me of something I didn't even do, but I don't hold it against him. Some day I hope he'll find out he was wrong about me, but I'll just give you the information. He doesn't have to talk to me or even know it was me that helped him out."

"Okay, sure. What's it called?"

"Brooklyn Ballroom Dance and Zumba," she said. This was a perfect opportunity. Now to make the most of it...

*****

Spencer and Emily were already walking on the Highline Park when Landon called with the information about the dance class. "Okay, thanks for the info, Landon. I appreciate it. Yeah, maybe next week." Everything was falling together nicely. He was quickly saving up a nice nest egg for the ring. Charlie said she could help him pick out a design Emily would like. Now he had a place to take dance lessons, so he could surprise her at Sam and Tanner's wedding. There was still one tiny little problem. He needed to be sure she would say yes when he asked her.

"What did Landon call about?" asked Emily. "Were you supposed to go on a hike today? You don't need to miss just because of me."

"I'm not anxious to go on another hike when Becca might be there. Your dad said we should watch out for her."

"I don't know. I still think he's over-reacting."

"Don't be naïve, Emily."

"Don't lecture me—I'm not naïve."

Of course she was naïve. She'd trusted Becca enough to call her for information about that hike, and couldn't believe Becca had drugged her wine. But he wisely clamped his mouth shut, and searched for a way to change the subject.

"So how was your date with Josh last night?" He couldn't help the jealousy that crept into his voice. He didn't trust Josh alone with Emily, no matter how much he swore he liked Charlie instead.

"It wasn't a date. We split the cost of a pizza, and he certainly didn't kiss me."

"I don't trust him," he pouted.

"It sounds like you don't trust me."

"That's not it. I don't... I don't like to think of you alone with him—with any other guy. Wouldn't you feel the same way? I mean, what if I spent an evening alone with Candace or Becca or Leah?"

"Who's Leah?"

"She's just a girl in the hiking... That's not the point. The point is, wouldn't it bother you if I spent an evening alone with another girl?"

"No," she said stubbornly. Then she grinned, "You could spend an evening alone with Grace or Olivia or Hannah or Claire, and it wouldn't bother me at all."

"Then I won't be bothered when you spend an evening with any of your brothers, either." He grinned until she laughed.

"Fine, I won't be alone with Josh again, but it really was completely innocent. And he really is miserable. He told me he's in love with Charlie."

"Has he told her that?"

"I hope not. She's definitely not ready to hear that from Josh."

Spencer swallowed hard. "Why wouldn't she want to hear it? You'd think she'd like knowing Josh loved her."

"She won't believe it because they haven't known each other very long. She'll think it's a line." So much for his plan to declare his love to Emily today. She might not be ready for it. How long had they been together? It had only been a couple of months since Emily arrived in New York. But if he counted the time since they first met, it could total eight months. On the other hand, they'd only been officially dating for about four weeks.

"I don't think there's a set length of time you have to know someone before you can love them," he argued. "If it's the right person, it doesn't take long before you know."

"Maybe. But she might think he was saying those words to get her to... to behave in a certain way."

"Behave in what certain way?"

Emily's face turned beet red. "You know. Guys who are experienced, like you and Josh, might say they love a girl just to get her to sleep with them."

So now she was putting him and Josh in the same category. "That's not true... Well, it's not true for me. I'd never do something like that. A guy who did that would be a real slime-ball."

"But how could she know for sure one way or the other?"

"Maybe she doesn't know Josh well enough to know. But you know I'm not like that. Right?"

Spencer held his breath as Emily hesitated. "Even if a guy wasn't purposely trying to manipulate a girl, he might do it subconsciously. Especially, a guy like... like Josh, who's been with so many girls. He's kissed Charlie now, and maybe he thinks he's in love, but it's really only a physical attraction."

Spencer frowned. She hadn't actually answered his question. And now... Was she really talking about Josh, or was she talking about him? "Well, I don't know about Josh, but I've found when you're really attracted to a girl on the inside, you're really attracted to her physically as well. At least, that's how I am with you."

He waited an eternity for her response. "But Josh has been with so many girls. Why would Charlie think she was any different from the others? Even if he thinks so right now, he could change his mind. How would she know if she could trust him?"

"Maybe Josh hasn't been with as many girls as you think."

"Oh, he has. He admits it. But he says he's changed."

"Well, I can't speak for Josh. But as for me, I'm only interested in you. I don't even look at other girls any more."

"Yeah... That sounds exactly like what Josh said about Charlie."

"I think I really hate that guy," he muttered.

"Well, he did try to defend you, if that makes you feel any better. He said you'd be stupid to want to be with anyone else."

"You talked to him about me?" he asked, a little louder than he intended.

Emily's guilty face spoke volumes. "I... I didn't mean to. I was asking general questions about things like how long a guy could go without sex—"

"You talked to him about sex?" This time his voice was loud enough the couple walking in front of them turned to gawk.

Why hadn't he killed Josh that first Sunday morning when he was so tempted?

Emily turned her face to the side to hide her blush. Somehow, her evening with Josh sounded much worse in the retelling. She didn't want him to be on the defensive today. It would make it that much harder to talk to him—to find out the truth. Had he really been helping his dad last night? Why would he lie to her? She could really only think of one reason—he was getting bored and frustrated with her.

She shouldn't have let him kiss her at the pool. But he'd been so tempting, with his arm draped around her, sans shirt, his sinuous muscles flexing in his chest, his hand playing havoc with the nerve endings in her arm, which were evidently connected to every other nerve in her body.

Originally she thought if she didn't kiss him anymore, she wouldn't fall any harder for him. But in reality it was too late. If she was honest with herself, she knew it was true. She was in love with him. It was a tragedy, because she knew it was only a matter of time before he broke her heart.

Then a wonderful thought occurred. There was a bright side to this realization. She might as well kiss him as much as she wanted. Why deprive herself? At least she could enjoy him while she had him. But she had to be careful—she had to hide her feelings. After all, he never claimed to be in love with her. Grace claimed it was true four weeks ago, yet Spencer had never said it. Surely he would have told her by now if it were true.

And at least she could enjoy kissing him until they broke up—as long as they were in a semi-public and safe place where they couldn't get carried away. One thing was certain… When they kissed, her iron willpower turned to jelly, along with her mind and her muscles.

Stopping on a large green lawn area, he spread out the contents of his backpack. They had a blanket to lie on and all the makings for a great picnic, including grapes, cheese, bread, and summer sausage. He'd even included some brownies for dessert.

"Why are you smiling?" Spencer asked.

"I… uhmm… I was thinking how perfect this is. A great picnic on the grass and a book to read. This is such a cool park, up in the air on an old railroad track. It's genius."

"I'm glad you like it." He leaned over her on his elbows as she stretched out gazing up at the clouds. He was close, so close. Was he going to kiss her? She closed her eyes and waited, sensing the nearness of his lips to hers, feeling his breath on her cheek.

Abruptly, he sat up and pulled off his t-shirt, rolling it carefully. She stared hungrily at his rippling muscles as he moved. He smiled as he lay down next to her, propping his head on his shirt.

"No fair. You've got a pillow," she teased.

"Just take off that shirt, and I'll make you one, too." He flashed his even white teeth in a grin.

"I think that wouldn't be wise. I didn't come prepared to sunbathe today." She noted a number of other girls on the park lawn had the forethought to wear swimsuits. "When did you make brownies?"

"I got up early this morning before I picked you up." He yawned, stretching his arms above his head, and she appreciated the display.

"Wow. After you were up so late last night? I saw you texted me after midnight. What project were you working on with your dad?"

"Uhmm, bathroom. You know, uhmm... plumbing and stuff. We were replacing a vanity and sink."

"Oh. Sounds hard. Maybe you could show me at dinner Sunday night?"

"Uhmm, yeah. Well, that's the problem. The new one didn't fit, and we had to put the old one back. That's why it took so long."

"Oh. I see." He was lying. She was almost certain of it. Her heart broke a little. But maybe there was another explanation. She didn't confront him because she didn't want to know the truth. She was in love with Spencer, and right now they were together.

He was sweet and caring and protective. He was the type of guy she'd always wanted—the kind who'd love you so much they'd risk their lives for you. Maybe he really did love her, but he was too insecure to say it. Maybe if she shared her feelings just a little, he'd find the courage to tell her. She steeled her nerves before she spoke in a timid voice.

"Spencer, you know... I really like you a lot. I mean, more than I've ever liked a guy before. And... And I don't know, I just wanted you to know. Because I know you saved my life even after I went out with Asher, and I know I hurt you. And I'm sorry. I don't know if I've ever told you how sorry I am. Except I'm glad I almost died because you saved my life, and that's how I found out how special you are. Well, that and when you kissed me..." She paused, waiting for his response. But he was quiet. Had she said something wrong? Had she hurt his feelings?

"Spencer?" She sat up and leaned toward him, searching his face.

He was sound asleep.

Chapter Sixteen

SPENCER KNEW HE had to talk to his parents and enlist their help. It was Sunday, and family dinner was looming. If only he hadn't used his father as an alibi for Friday night. He groaned. Even if his father agreed to back up his story, his sisters might say something to give away his lie. How could he have been so stupid? He should've made up a different story. Sighing, he decided to face his parents first. He could hear his mother and father in the kitchen.

"Hey, Momma. Papa. Uhmm... Can I talk to you guys?"

His mom immediately got that oh-my-gosh-something-terrible-must-have-happened-tell-me-now-before-I-die look.

"Sure, Son." Joe took his time, filling a glass with water before he sat down at the table with Spencer.

"I got myself in trouble with Emily, and I need you guys to help me out."

"You got Emily in trouble?" Connie asked with wide eyes.

"No. *He's* in trouble," said Joe. "Calm down, Connie. You always overreact."

"I do not. I'm more sensitive to the underlying emotions. You, on the other hand, have the sensitivity of a shoehorn."

"A shoehorn? Where on earth did that come from? That doesn't even make sense."

"Have you ever met a sensitive shoehorn? Of course not. That's what I mean—you're not very sensitive."

"I still say that doesn't—"

"Momma! Papa! Can you argue later? Emily will be here in an hour."

"Sorry, Son. What is it?"

"Well, I told Emily I was helping you with a bathroom project Friday night."

"I see," he said, his eyes narrowing. "And what were you actually doing on Friday night?"

"I was working. I got a job doing valet parking to earn some extra money."

"Are you having trouble making your rent?" asked Connie. "I thought your internship at Gherring Inc. was paid."

"It is. I make enough to pay rent, which is better than a lot of my friends. But I don't make any extra."

"What do you need the extra for? To take Emily out? Wouldn't she understand?"

"Well... I'm trying to save money, and I didn't want her to know. For a ring."

"I knew it! I just knew you were in love with her. You see." Connie punched Joe on the shoulder playfully. "It's because of my sensitivity—that's why I knew before you."

"Have you two talked about this? And have you talked to her dad?" asked Joe.

Spencer gulped. He'd forgotten about talking to Mr. Gherring. "We haven't exactly talked about it. But I'll get around to it before I actually buy the ring." He hoped that was true. He still hadn't figured out how to broach the subject. Saturday had been like torture. He'd been so close to kissing her multiple times, but he'd held himself back. Just barely. He hadn't wanted to upset her, but it was so hard to resist when her lips looked so kissable.

Joe stood up and clapped Spencer on the shoulder. "She's a wonderful girl. We'll love having her in the family. I hope she doesn't mind being swallowed up by your sisters. I'll cover for you this time, but you need a better story if you're going to keep this up. When are you going to ask her?"

"I don't know yet. As soon as I can afford to buy the ring and think of a good way to ask her." He hesitated, "So the other problem is my sisters—in case Emily mentions something about me being here Friday night."

"You're really lucky. All the girls but Grace were at a movie."

"And Grace? Was she out with Brad?"

"Nope, he was working Friday night at the hospital, and Grace didn't feel like going to the movie. I'm afraid she was here Friday night," said Connie.

"Ughh! I'm going to have to bribe her, and she's going to make me pay."

"Sorry, Son." Joe laughed. "You might as well get used to it. Once you're married, it seems they spend all their free time thinking of ways to make you pay."

"Hey," Connie said in mock outrage. "Watch what you say, you old shoehorn!"

"Hi, Gracie. You look nice tonight." Spencer stood in the doorway of her room, wearing what he hoped was a sincere expression.

"Oh boy. You want something really bad, don't you?"

"Can't a guy compliment his gorgeous sister without having an ulterior motive?"

Grace rolled her eyes.

"Okay. I need a favor. I need you to back me up in case Emily asks anything about Friday night. I told her Papa and I were tackling a bathroom project."

"I'm listening."

"I was actually working, but I didn't want her to know I got an extra job."

"Why can't she know you got an extra job?"

"She... She might think it's because Mr. Gherring doesn't pay me enough."

"Hmmm. Nope. That's not a good enough reason. I think you should just tell her the truth."

"Gracie!"

"Forget it."

"Okay... Fine... I'm working to buy an engagement ring."

"I knew it! I knew it! I knew it!"

"You did not."

"Of course I did. You're so gone over Emily. When you're with her I could absolutely sweep you up in a pan and toss you over the wall, and you wouldn't even notice. I take it you finally talked about it? You told her you love her?"

"Well, not exactly."

"Spencer! You haven't told her yet?"

"I'm waiting for the right time."

"But when I talked to her Monday night at the pool she still thought you were some player who was bound to leave her for another guy."

"I told her I wasn't going to leave her."

"But she still thinks she's the last in a very long line of girls you've kissed and more than kissed?"

"The important thing is she knows she's the last—the very last."

"Why didn't you tell her the truth? That she was the only one? She'd feel a lot more secure."

His stomach churned. "It's too late to tell her that now. I don't even think she'd believe it."

"Well, well, well! Are you such a hot kisser she couldn't possibly believe she was your first?" Her voice rose in laughter.

"Maybe I am. It's not funny."

"Oh, yeah—it's funny. But you're getting yourself in big trouble because of your ego, brother. You better swallow it, and tell her the truth. If you're not careful, you're going to have a great big beautiful ring and no one to give it to."

"Shut it. Okay? You haven't told me yet if you'll back up my story."

When she smiled at him, he could have sworn she'd sprouted red horns and a forked tail. "Of course I'll help you, dear brother. We'll discuss your payment at a later time."

Emily marched in the Marshall's front door with a plan. Saturday, after she'd admitted to herself she was in love with Spencer and decided to end the kissing hiatus, he'd missed several obvious kissing opportunities. Either he was finally going along with her earlier no-kissing plan, or he'd lost interest. So tonight, she was going to get him alone and figure out what was going on. She wanted to tell him how she felt about him, stopping just short of saying she loved him. But she wasn't going to say anything at all until she was positive he was still attracted to her. If Grace was right and he really did love her, then surely he would let her know.

She'd even stepped up her game in an effort to make herself a bit more difficult to resist. She had on a cute short skirt with some heels that made her long legs look even longer. Her top was tight enough to accentuate her slender figure although it wasn't extremely low cut. Why bother with a plunging neckline when she didn't have any cleavage to show off? She couldn't compete with Betty Boobs. She'd even added a touch of mascara and some flavored lip-gloss. So her eyes looked enormous and her lips looked... Well, she hoped they looked irresistible.

She was disappointed when Grace met her at the door. She'd hoped Spencer might answer the door alone, and she might be able to use her allure to steal a quick kiss before dinner even started. Since she decided kissing was no longer against the rules, it was almost killing her not to do it.

"Hi, Emily." Grace grabbed her arm, pulling her into the apartment. She gave her a speedy once-over. "You look great. Perfect, in fact. Absolutely perfect. Let's go show you to Spencer."

Before she could think to protest, Grace dragged her into the kitchen.

"Look, Spencer. Emily's here," announced Grace, pushing her toward him.

He turned around from the stove where he was sautéing onions and bell peppers. She was pleased to note his eyes widening as he surveyed her legs. "Hi, uhmm... Hi."

"Good job, Cyrano." Grace poured on the sarcasm. "I can see why you're still waiting for the right time." He glared at her as she departed the kitchen, her laughter trailing behind her.

"The right time for what?" Emily asked when she left them alone.

"Uhmm, she's just being Grace. Giving me a hard time as usual. You... You look fantastic tonight. I mean, not that you don't always look great. But tonight you look even more great." His voice trailed off to a mumble at the end, his cheeks reddening.

"Your veggies are burning, I think."

He whipped around. "Shoot! Oh, man! I guess they'll be okay. Not all of them are burned." He scraped the onions and peppers where they were blackened and adhering to the bottom of the pan.

"I'll eat the burnt ones—I like them with a little char. Sorry I distracted you. Can I help?"

"Sure. Can you stir the beans while I get the fajita meat sliced? And then can you get out the sour cream and pico de gallo and serving spoons."

"This is so great. Mexican food makes me feel like I'm home in Texas."

"Do you miss it a lot?" His brows furrowed.

"Yes. I love Mexican food," she teased.

"Yes, but do you miss Texas a lot?"

"I miss the grass and the trees and the wide open spaces. And strangely enough, I miss driving. I used to get a lot of thinking done while I was driving. Commuting on the subway somehow doesn't lend itself to deep contemplation."

"Solving the world's problems?"

"Yes, and listening to TED talks."

"What about the weather?"

"Well, the summers are much nicer here. We had temps in the upper nineties and over a hundred for most of June, July and August. But, we only had a bit of snow. I'm afraid I'm going to be in for a shock when winter gets here."

"We need to get you some good warm clothes. I'll take you shopping in the fall."

"I hate shopping."

"How could I forget? But somebody has to take care of you."

Emily warmed inside. That didn't sound like a guy who was ready to move on to another girl. Maybe he loved her after all. Maybe tonight he'd tell her so. If he said the words, she was ready to say them back.

Abruptly the kitchen door opened and they were inundated with Spencer's sisters, complete with talking, yelling, and laughter. Marshall family dinner had begun.

Spencer was so distracted he could hardly eat. Why had she worn that outfit to the family dinner? She looked good—too good. He had a hard enough time controlling himself around her, without seeing those amazing legs in that short skirt. And when she sat down next to him, he noticed that it inched up a little further. She caught him checking her out and smiled. That's when he realized the truth. She was teasing him, on purpose. First she'd told him they couldn't kiss, and then she'd worn this super short skirt, simply to test him. Well, two could play at that game.

He returned her smile. And on pretense of adjusting his napkin, he slipped his left hand under the shield of the tablecloth to rest on the soft smooth skin of her thigh. His fingers traced tiny circles on her skin with the lightest of touches. He was pleased to see her struggling to keep her eyes open, breathing shallowly. She clamped her hand over his to hold his fingers still. He maintained a neutral expression, forking a bite of black beans into his mouth. She pushed his hand away, attempting to cross her legs, but bumped her knee on the table.

"Ow!" she cried.

"What did you do to her?" asked Grace.

"It wasn't him. I tried to cross my legs, but these heels make my legs too tall to cross them under the table."

"I love your shoes," said Olivia. "Actually, I love the whole outfit."

"Don't we wear the same size shoes and skirt? You could borrow them any time."

"No!" He must have spoken a bit too loudly, because his entire family was staring at him. "I don't... I don't think it's a good idea."

Grace grinned, "He means he doesn't want his sister looking that hot. Right, Spencer?"

"She's too young," he objected.

"Give me a break, Spencer. I'm twenty-one." Olivia turned back to Emily. "I've got a super cute skirt and shoes that match. We can trade sometime."

"That's a great idea," said Hannah.

"Hannah likes to steal my clothes," explained Olivia.

"Not steal—borrow."

"Except, I have to go digging through your drawers and closet to get my things back."

"Claire's worse than I am," defended Hannah.

Grace told Emily, "At least I'm safe from the marauders."

"That's not really true," said Olivia. "Since her clothes don't fit, we all steal her jewelry."

Spencer was relieved the attention had been drawn away from him. He eased his hand back onto Emily's leg and resumed his ministrations to her soft skin. When she failed in her attempts to remove his hand, she stood up swiftly, forcing him to withdraw.

"I'll get dessert." Emily ripped him to shreds with her eyes. His gaze followed her all the way to the counter and back. When she bent over to throw away her napkin, he almost choked. He quickly grabbed his water and gulped it down

"Grace, don't you have papers to grade?" he asked.

"Oh, no. I got it all done Friday night, when I was here at the house. Don't you remember, Spencer?"

He glared at Grace, trying to imagine his revenge. But she held all the cards right now, and she knew it.

He kept his hands to himself during dessert, rehearsing his speech in his mind. If only he knew for sure Emily felt the same way about him, it wouldn't be so intimidating.

When the family had attacked and eliminated all traces of the Ginger Crinkle cookies Emily had brought, Spencer began to clear the table.

Grace grabbed the plates from his fingers. "We'll get the dishes. Why don't you and Emily go sit on the porch so you can talk?" She ushered them outside and the door clicked shut behind them. Spencer resisted the urge to check to see if she'd locked it as well.

"It seems they don't want us inside. Shall we sit?" He eased onto the glider and patted the space beside him.

Emily sat down cautiously, tugging her skirt to cover as much of her legs as possible.

"I really like this skirt." As Spencer moved his hand toward her exposed thigh, she locked fingers with him. He chuckled. "Oh, so it's look but don't touch? That's fine, I'll be good... for now."

"I'm beginning to wish I'd worn something that covered a bit more."

"Seriously, I'll behave." He opened his mouth to speak, choked, coughed, and cleared his throat a few times. "I... uhmm... How's your mom?"

"She's fine, I guess. I haven't actually talked to her this weekend."

"Oh."

Emily squirmed a bit in the uncomfortable silence. How could she start the awkward conversation about their feelings? Maybe with a question. "So, how long do you think we'll date?" She held her breath, waiting for his answer.

"I wanted to talk about that, too." Spencer smiled, squeezing her hand. I mean, I was thinking maybe a year. Maybe less. Even a year seems like a really long time to me. But, I thought, since I graduate in December. Then I'd get a job and save some money. But, you know, I might not even get a job here. It's all sort of complicated."

Her heart turned upside down. He was planning to give her a year, and even that seemed like a long time to him. She should be glad. That was probably longer than he'd dated any other girls. But somehow, talking about how it would be over after he graduated and got a job, made the end seem so certain. So, Grace was wrong after all. He didn't love her. And she'd done exactly what she'd tried not to do. She'd fallen in love with a guy who didn't love her back.

She struggled to stop the flood of tears. She shouldn't be crying—she was going to ruin the time they had left. Hadn't she decided she was going to enjoy him while she could? And who knew—maybe if they dated for that long, he might fall in love with her, too. Or maybe he was in love with her, but didn't realize it.

His eyes were huge. "What's wrong? Why are you crying?"

"I don't know," she sniffed. "A year... I guess a year is good. I was actually hoping for longer."

He turned to her and picked up both of her hands in his, tenderly lifting them to his lips. "It can be two years if you want. I'm willing to wait."

That's right. She'd forgotten he'd be going without having sex for as long as they dated. No wonder he only wanted to date for a year. She took a long shuddering breath. It was too late now—she'd lost her heart to him. So if he offered her a year, she'd take it. And when it was over, if he hadn't fallen in love with her, she'd pick up the pieces of her heart and move on.

He reached with one hand and brushed a tear off her face. "I know you think I'm a big player, but that's more reputation than truth. I'd never cheat on you. You believe me. Right?"

"Even if..." She hesitated. She had to get this question off her chest. "Even if it means no sex the whole time we're dating?"

"I'm not dating you for sex. I know you don't believe in sex before marriage. That's fine with me. But..."

"But what?"

"But, I'm hoping you'll let up on the no-kissing thing now that we've talked."

"Actually, I decided to change that policy yesterday."

"Yesterday?" he groaned. "Why didn't you tell me?"

"I don't know. I thought you'd guess somehow. You kissed me on Monday, before I lifted the hiatus."

"I think maybe we need to work on our communication skills." He shook his head.

"Well, at least we talked tonight."

"Yes," he smiled. "Yes, we certainly did." His hand moved under her chin and tilted her face up to his. Then he leaned toward her and bent down to touch his lips lightly against hers. He kissed her upper lip and then her lower lip, sucking it gently into his mouth. "You taste so good."

"It's Ginger Crinkles," she said.

"No, it's you. You taste good. You smell good. I love everything about you." He returned his mouth to hers, gently kissing her lips. She felt an ache in her heart. He'd almost said he loved her—almost, but not quite. Then her mind became a blur as he deepened their kiss, tasting the inside of her mouth with his tongue, sending electricity down her spine. He played with her tongue and enticed it into his own mouth. She could hear her heartbeat in her ears and feel the thud in her chest. Abruptly, he broke the kiss and pulled away.

"I don't know if I can make it a year," he teased. "I'd really like to do a lot more than kiss you."

Her face must have looked as stricken as she felt at his words, because he quickly backtracked. "I'm just kidding. I can wait. Please don't cry."

He bent down to kiss her again. His lips caressed hers gently. "Emily..." he moaned and then he was kissing her forcefully, bruising her lips with his passion. "Emily, I..." he breathed the words across her lips.

The door cracked as Claire flung it open, and they sprung apart, sporting guilty expressions. "We're gonna play charades," she announced. "Come on."

Spencer rubbed his elbow where he'd slammed it against the arm of the glider. "I guess our talking time just ended." Then he whispered in her ear, "But I enjoyed it while it lasted."

*****

Anne watched Emily pushing her food around on her plate. She and Steven had decided to keep their news a secret from the general population for a while. But they'd agreed to tell the family members when the time seemed right. Anne had thought tonight might be a good time to tell Emily, so they'd invited her up for dinner. It was Wednesday, and they hadn't had a chance to chat since the previous week. But now, watching her distracted movements, she knew they needed to talk about other things instead. There was something wrong, and it was probably an affair of the heart.

"So, how're things with Spencer?" she probed.

"Fine. They're fine."

"You've been going out a lot lately, right?"

"Well, we had been until recently. But he's been busy every night this week." Her voice whined even as she attempted to appear nonchalant.

"What's he busy doing?"

"How should I know? He doesn't tell me," she snapped.

"Sorry. I just wondered."

"Can't you ask him what he's doing?" asked Steven.

"Oh. He always has an excuse. Tonight, he's volunteering at a homeless shelter. But when I offered to go with him, he didn't think it was a good idea."

Steven frowned. "Well, it might not be safe for you. He's pretty protective."

"No. He's lying to me. I know he is."

"Are you sure?" asked Anne. "That doesn't sound like Spencer."

"I didn't think so either, but I think he's changed."

Steven couched his words in a stern tone. "I don't like this at all. If he's lying to you, you should definitely break up with him. You deserve better. Do you want me to talk to him?"

"No, I'm in love with him—at least, I think I am. Why else would I feel this miserable?" Her lower lip trembled.

Now Steven started laughing. "As best I can recall, you're probably right. It made me pretty miserable at first. And that probably also means you're jumping to all kinds of wrong conclusions."

"He's right, Honey," said Anne. "You two probably need to talk. I'm sure he's in love with you. He sure looked it when you were in the hospital."

"But we talked, and he didn't say he was in love with me."

"He said he wasn't in love with you?"

"No, but he said he didn't want to date any more after he graduated and got a job. Because he might not even get a job in New York and he might have to move."

"That doesn't make any sense to me," said Anne.

"It does to me. He doesn't want to commit because the future's uncertain. And I respect that. I guess there's always a chance he might decide he loves me before then. But now... Now I think he's getting tired of me. He's avoiding me a lot. Why else would he lie to me?"

"How do you know he's lying?"

"I just feel it."

Anne shook her head. "I know you think this is trite, but you can't depend on your feelings. Especially when you're highly emotional. You'll get all kinds of misinformation sent to your brain."

"Let me talk to him," suggested Steven. "If there's one thing I'm good at, it's getting information out of people. I'll find out what he's up to."

"No, because if he's going to hurt my feelings, you'll probably kill him."

"No, I wouldn't—"

"Yes," said Anne. "You probably would. I'll talk to him."

"No, neither of you are going to talk to him. I'll handle it myself. Let's change the subject." She turned her attention to her mom. "How are you feeling?"

"Pretty good. I'm developing a little pooch." She stretched her shirt around her belly. Emily studied it, cocking her head to the side.

"That's great, Mom. I'm sure you'll start actually showing soon."

"Yes, I'm certain I'll be showing. Eventually, no one will doubt I'm pregnant." She laughed. "I almost wanted to wear a fake belly when I spoke at the fundraiser on Saturday."

"Oh, I forgot you did that. How did it go? Were you petrified?"

"Not at all." Steven's eyes crinkled in a satisfied smile. "I teased her so much about not being believable because she didn't look pregnant, she waltzed right through her speech."

"I can't believe I fell for it. He suggested multiple times I shouldn't even speak because people would think I was faking the whole pregnancy and illness."

"She was so ticked off she wouldn't speak to me all the way home. Even after she did a great job on the speech and I confessed I was only trying to distract her."

"Well, it will never work again. Next time, I'll know you're distracting me."

"Maybe you should take a sedative next time," suggested Emily.

"Oh no," Steven said. "Her body overreacts with any type of drug. Evidently this is true for all of you Best girls."

"I feel like taking something now." Emily dropped her head into her hands. "Maybe Steven can think up a distraction for me."

"I have an idea for a distraction. Why don't we see if we can get Charlie on Skype?" Steven raised questioning eyebrows to Anne.

She nodded at him. "Let's do it."

"I don't want you to tell her what I told you. Okay? She's too sympathetic to Spencer for some reason."

"We won't, but it will be fun to talk to both of you together," said Anne. "You'll see."

Their luck held and Charlie was on the computer screen in minutes. "Hey, Mom. Let me see your stomach."

Anne smoothed her shirt over her small baby bump.

"Tsk, tsk, tsk," said Charlie. "Next time, I want to see some real progress. What's going on up there? We had a fantastic rafting trip today. The water was up high and fast. Out of seven rafts, mine was the only one that didn't turn over. You should have seen the video."

Anne watched Emily brighten a little at her sister's enthusiasm.

"Yay, Sister! And all the other guides were guys?"

"Yep, every single one. And all of them bragging before we started." Her voice tinkled with laughter. "I said, 'We'll see—may the

Best woman win.' And I did, of course. And now I get to pick my crew for the next week."

Steven laughed. "All men should beware when a Best girl decides to compete."

"I've kind of beaten the odds myself," said Anne.

"Yeah, Mom. Made it to the second trimester," said Charlie. "Good job. You'll make it all the way now, for sure."

"She's done more than that. Or she's going to do something more than that." Steven's dimples danced with excitement.

Emily's brows furrowed. "What are you talking about?"

"Can I say it?" Steven begged.

Anne laughed at her husband's eagerness—sometimes he seemed like a little boy. She nodded.

"*Twins*," he said. "Can you believe it? We're having twins!"

There was a moment of stunned silence before Charlie said, "I'm gonna be afraid to talk to you on Skype anymore. Ohmygosh! Are you kidding?"

"No way!" screamed Emily, as she rushed to give her mom a hug. "How on earth are you so tiny?"

"Don't worry. I won't be tiny for long," Anne said around Emily's head.

"How on earth could you be pregnant with twins?" Charlie asked.

Steven answered before she could respond. "Women over forty-five have about a one in five chance of having multiples. And," he boasted, "I'm obviously extraordinarily masculine."

"Ughh!" Emily groaned, swiping at Steven's head while he ducked, laughing.

"You make it sound like being extraordinarily masculine is a good thing," said Charlie.

Anne's face broke out in a contented smile, watching her family laugh and interact. But her heart broke for Emily. She knew the misery of loving someone when you thought they didn't love you back.

*****

Spencer struggled with the complicated dance steps. The first night had been relatively easy. He'd quickly conquered the waltz, practicing with a variety of partners, many old enough to be his mother. Then they'd moved on to the cha-cha. He figured he could be passable at this dance after a couple of weeks. But this time the class was all about the tango, a much more intricate and difficult dance.

"I'm never going to get this," he complained to the teacher.

"It's your first time to try it," she said. "It's a hard dance. You'll be able to do the basics by the time the wedding rolls around. Why don't you have your fiancée with you?"

"Oh, I'm not engaged—not yet. But I'm taking my future fiancée to this wedding in five weeks. She loves to dance, so I wanted to surprise her."

"I think that's really romantic. When are you planning to ask her to marry you?"

"Soon, I hope."

"Do you realize you've been doing it? You've been dancing the tango the whole time you were talking to me."

He stumbled in surprise. "Shoot! I'm never going to get this."

"You'll get it." She laughed, clapping her hands for attention. "Okay, class is over. You can find pictures on Facebook tomorrow. Good job, everyone. Next Monday, we'll tackle the salsa."

*****

It was only nine o'clock, and Spencer wasn't tired. He was hovering on cloud nine where he'd been floating since Sunday night when he talked to Emily about the future. They were going to be married. Someday. He'd said a year. She'd said longer. But, he could wait a long time. Why not? He'd already waited twenty-five years. And, he was going to get her a ring, maybe even faster than he thought. If he worked one or two more Friday nights, he'd have enough money. Spencer thought Emily might still be at her mom's apartment. He could surprise her. He decided to check there first and go down to her place if she was gone.

He rang the bell, pacing to calm his nerves until Gherring opened the door. "Hi! Is Emily still here?"

"No, she just left. But come in for a minute."

"I don't want to intrude. I only wanted to surprise Emily."

"That's okay. Come in. We should talk."

"Uhmm, okay." Something in Gherring's tone made him uneasy. "Hi, Mrs. Gherring. How're you feeling?"

"Great. Thanks for asking. How's your mom? Is she enjoying her new job? I really miss having her around."

"She's good, and she loves her job. Thanks, Mr. Gherring, for helping her find it."

"We owe her so much," said Gherring. "I'll always be grateful."

"So, Spencer... What were you doing tonight? Emily said you were working at a homeless shelter," Anne questioned, her stare intense.

The blood drained from his face. "I, uhmm, I wasn't really at a homeless shelter. But, it's a secret. Promise you won't tell Emily?"

"What's going on?" Gherring's voice thundered.

"I'm taking dance lessons."

"What did you say?" Anne's mouth hung open.

"Dance lessons. I'm taking ballroom dance lessons so I can dance with Emily at the wedding."

Gherring began to laugh, and the sound was infectious. Soon all three of them were laughing. Anne had tears in her eyes.

Gherring caught his breath. "Dance lessons? That's awesome. Emily thinks you're losing interest in her, and you're really taking dance lessons for her benefit."

"Wait. She thinks I'm losing interest? She told you that?"

"I'm afraid so," said Anne with more sympathy than her husband demonstrated.

"How could she think that after we talked about—" He barely stopped himself in time. He'd almost said they'd talked about getting married, and he hadn't asked Gherring for permission yet. He gulped. And he wasn't ready to do it tonight. He needed to be prepared to answer questions about how he was going to support her and take care of her. He needed to think about it and rehearse his answers.

"Well, you're either going to have to tell her the truth or be a lot more convincing when you lie," said Anne.

"Oh, man. Thanks for the heads up. I guess I could tell her, but I thought it'd be such a fun surprise."

"Maybe I could help you think of something," said Anne.

"Are you kidding?" Gherring scoffed. "You're the worst liar in the world. He needs a master like me to help him conjure up a good lie. Now, the best lies have an element of truth. Why don't you say you're doing some type of exercise? You could be playing pickup basketball or something like that."

"Yeah, that might work. And my excuse could be I'm not hiking on the weekends anymore."

Anne frowned at Gherring. "You're just a little too good at thinking up a quick, plausible lie. Maybe I should be worried."

"I used my ample skill to snag you. It's too late to worry about it now."

"Wish me luck," said Spencer as he left them, still arguing playfully. He hoped Gherring's lie worked better than his.

Emily heard a knock on her door. She was already dressed in a sleep-shirt and shorts, hair flowing, face freshly scrubbed and ready for bed. She couldn't imagine who'd be at the door at nine thirty. She peeped through the hole and spied Spencer. What was he doing here? She pulled back and looked at herself. She was decent enough to open the door.

"Hi. Uhmm, what're you doing here?"

"I wanted to drop by and see you. I missed you."

"But I just saw you at work."

"And it's been hours since then." Her insides warmed at his words. Maybe he wasn't cheating on her after all. "Can I come in? Only for a minute?"

"Well... Okay. I'm actually dressed for bed."

"That sounds enticing," he teased as he slipped in past her. "But we really shouldn't."

"That's not what I meant."

He laughed. "But a guy can dream, right?"

"Spencer!"

"Okay, sorry." He didn't look the least bit contrite as he plopped down on her couch. She sat down next to him, eyeing him cautiously.

"How was the shelter?"

"I have a confession. I wasn't at the shelter." She held her breath waiting to hear the truth. "I've been playing basketball. I'm sorry I didn't tell you. I was dying for some exercise, but I thought the shelter sounded better." He turned his face up to hers, staring with dark brown puppy dog eyes. How could she resist him? He wasn't losing interest; he only wanted some exercise. She loved his fit body, and she certainly didn't begrudge him the time he spent doing sports and exercising.

"I'm sorry. Forgive me?" He leaned in and stole a kiss.

She jumped up in alarm. "Oh! You can't do that. I mean, not here. I mean, not on the couch."

He bounded up and examined the offending couch. "Why not?"

"It's against the rules. *No unsupported kissing.*"

"What are you talking about?"

"Well, the first rule is: *No private kissing*. That's one Mom gave us back in high school. That means you shouldn't kiss in a place where you have too much privacy—like here, in the apartment. But then the backup rule is if you do kiss in a private place, you have to be supporting your own weight. You know—standing up. Not sitting or lying down. So... No unsupported kissing. It's a rule to help you not have to depend on your willpower to stop, uhmm... to stop doing stuff."

"Exactly how many of these dating rules do you have?"

"You think they're stupid, don't you?"

"No, I don't. It's just I don't know the rules. I know you have rules to define what a date is. Are there other important rules I should know?"

She hesitated, aware of the heat radiating from her face. "There's one that might be important. It's *save the white parts.*"

"What does that mean?"

"It means... well... certain parts don't ever get a suntan, so they're white. And you save those for your husband."

It was his turn to blush. "So you haven't ever... I mean, you've followed the rules?"

By now her face must be glowing red. "Yes, I have. And I intend to keep following them. So, if that makes a difference to you, tell me now."

"It does make a difference." He wrapped his arms around her, kissing the top of her head. "It makes you more special." He rubbed his hands gently up and down her back. "I'm glad to know the rules, and particularly glad you have a nice little tan on your back and your legs."

"Spencer..." He smothered her protest with another kiss.

"It's okay, we're standing."

She relaxed and reveled in the heady feeling that always overwhelmed her senses when he kissed her. His lips traveled down to her jaw. As her head fell back he moved his mouth below to the side of her neck. Her knees trembled. Her head was dizzy, and she would have slumped without his strong arms holding her weight.

He halted his assault and hugged her close again. "I think I like these rules, just fine."

"Yes," she whispered breathlessly. "But this borders on unsupported. Don't you think?"

"I'll check with the legal department tomorrow if you want. But we're definitely standing up."

"I don't think the purpose of the rules is to encourage you to test their limits," she chuckled, regaining the strength in her legs.

"That's how I've always treated rules." He grinned at her. "It's too late to change now."

Chapter Seventeen

"So he quit calling you?" Emily was actually surprised Josh had given up. He'd seemed determined to pursue Charlie as long as it took.

"Well, he still calls once a week and leaves a message, but I don't answer and I don't call him back. And now he sends me an email every day and a snail-mail letter once a week."

Emily smiled. That sounded more like Josh. "And you're still refusing to even consider giving him a chance?"

"Remember, I don't want advice—only sympathy."

Emily sighed. "Okay. But I was only trying to clarify the situation."

"How can I give him a chance? We live across the country from each other."

"But you could talk to him on the phone," Emily argued.

"Sympathy only," reminded Charlie.

"Fine. I do remember how irritated I was when Spencer kept calling and texting when I was in Texas."

"Exactly. And if you hadn't moved to New York, y'all wouldn't have ended up together."

"And we still probably won't be together in the end."

"You're planning to break up with him?"

"No. But he's definitely planning to break up with me, in a year or so."

"That's ridiculous. No he's not."

"No, really, it's true. We talked about it. He doesn't want to commit to anything because he graduates in December and he doesn't know where he'll get a job."

"Emily, he's in love with you. I'm sure of it. Haven't y'all talked at all about maybe getting married?"

"No, we haven't. And he's really gotten into playing basketball lately. The past few weeks, I hardly see him in the evenings. We mostly do stuff on Saturdays during the day."

"He's giving up time with you to play basketball?"

"I know, it sounds bad, but he loves to exercise. I'm trying not to complain about it—I don't want to be a whiny girlfriend. He's so sweet when he's with me. And then there's the kissing."

"Are you sticking to the rules, Sister?"

"I am, but it's not easy. I've been thinking I need to maybe be more sporty, so he'll want to spend more time with me."

"I think he likes you just as you are."

"But maybe if I could play some sport, we could play together."

"Okay, why don't you try racquetball? You get to play inside—you should like that. And it's got a pretty easy learning curve. You'll pick it up in no time."

"If I could find someone to teach me, I could practice while he's playing basketball. Then I could surprise him."

"I'm sure Steven could teach you. And maybe even Josh... I wondered... Have you seen him lately? Josh, I mean? I was just curious."

Emily smiled to herself. So Charlie had some feelings for Josh after all. "No. None of us have seen him lately. Brad told Grace that Josh has dropped all of his old friends, and he doesn't go out at all anymore. He used to hang around with Brad and Grace, but now he spends all of his spare time, such as it is, volunteering at the free clinic."

"Oh. So that part, at least, was true. But I still can't trust him."

"Brad said he's totally sworn off women."

"I'm sure that won't last."

"Well, I'd argue with you, but you could be right. I know even Spencer will eventually move on to someone else."

"Sister, Spencer is nothing like Josh. Believe me. He only wants to be with you." Emily knew her sister had a blind spot where Spencer was concerned. She was almost as bad as Grace.

"I thought I asked for sympathy, too."

"Nope, you didn't ever specify. So I gave you advice."

"Thanks a lot," Emily said sarcastically.

"That's what sisters are for."

*****

Spencer went to the men's room one more time before riding up to the Gherring's apartment. Everything was proceeding according to plan. He'd saved enough money to buy a ring. Well, enough to pay probably two-thirds of the cost and pay the rest off before they got married. Next, he was planning to call Charlie and find out about ring styles, but first he had to ask for permission from her parents. He was so nervous he was tempted to go back down the elevator to the men's room again.

Would they think it was too soon? Would they agree to an engagement before he'd finished grad school? Would they believe he could support her before he'd even applied for a job?

He rang the doorbell with a vague hope no one would answer.

"Spencer. Come in." Gherring stepped back from the open door, gesturing with his hand. "We were just having ice cream. Would you like a bowl? Actually, Anne was having ice cream. She had a craving for chocolate chip mint ice cream, so I had to go buy some."

"Uhmm, no thank you." he mumbled, shuffling through the door.

"Is something wrong? You seem upset."

"No, uhmm... No sir. Everything's fine. But I wanted to talk to you."

"Come in. Have a seat." Gherring guided him to a chair near the couch and sat beside Anne.

When Spencer finally looked up, both were staring at him with wide expectant eyes. He tried to speak, but discovered his tongue was sticking to the roof of his mouth.

"Eh-hem. Excuse me," he croaked. "Could I get a glass of water?"

"Sure." Gherring disappeared, returning quickly with the promised water.

He gulped down a few swallows, looking everywhere in the room but at the Gherrings.

"I... uhmm... I wanted to ask Emily... I mean... I wanted to ask you if I could ask Emily... to... uhmm... to marry me." He closed his eyes and cringed. He felt the blood pounding in his head. That was awful. Were they laughing at him? He couldn't even bring himself to look.

Suddenly, he heard Anne make a funny sound. He looked up and she was giggling with her hand over her mouth. "Steven, was it that hard for you when you asked my dad?"

"Ten times worse," he admitted with a grin. "And your father grilled me before he gave me an answer."

They really were laughing at him. Did that mean they were turning him down? Gherring walked over to shake his hand. "I'm sorry, Spencer. We shouldn't tease you. We've been hoping for this, son. You already have our blessing."

"Really?" He stood up, feeling a weight lifted from his shoulders.

"Of course. We know you'll take good care of her—you already have." Anne rose and hugged him.

"I was afraid you'd think I shouldn't ask while I was in school."

Anne grimaced. "That's because you don't know I married the first time when I was still a sophomore in college. I'm sure you'll do fine. I assume y'all talked about this a little?"

"Yes, we talked a few weeks ago. She wants to wait a long time. I'd rather not wait so long—a year at the most. But, we'll work it out."

"Are you sure y'all talked about it? I'm surprised she didn't say anything to me. The last time she talked to us, she still thought you were losing interest in the relationship." Anne chewed her lip.

"No. We talked about it after Sunday night dinner a few weeks ago. Maybe she's still unsure, though. Maybe she didn't want to tell you until I'd asked her formally. After I give her the ring, she'll feel better. I know I'll feel better to make it official."

"And your mother and father know?" Gherring asked.

"Yes, sir. They love Emily. And my sisters like her better than me."

Anne said, "I have a ring that belonged to my mom. I'd love for you to use the stones in her ring. You don't have to, but it's going to be hers someday. The ring that belonged to Tom's mother is going to Charlotte."

"That would be awesome. Charlie's going to help me chose a setting for her. But she seems so sentimental—I bet she'd love having the stones from her grandmother's ring."

"When are you going to ask her?" Anne asked.

"As soon as I can get the ring and come up with a cool way to ask her. I've been working nights parking cars and saving up the money. I've hardly seen her the past couple of weeks, between parking cars and dance lessons. But it'll all be worth it in the end."

Anne disappeared into the bedroom in search of the heirloom ring, and Gherring was left alone with Spencer.

"Spencer, I have a bit of advice about these Best girls. They get a notion in their heads, and it's hard to convince them otherwise. Are you positive Emily knows you're in love with her?"

"I'm sure. But even if she had doubts, she won't have them after I give her the ring. Right?"

"Yes, the thing is... Well, I almost lost Anne between the time I bought her ring and when I actually asked her to marry me. I really don't want you to make the same mistake."

If Gherring wanted to scare Spencer, he'd accomplished his goal. How was he going to make sure he didn't lose her? "Okay. Thanks for the advice."

"Here's the ring," said Anne, handing him a small box.

"And let me hook you up with my jeweler," said Gherring. "He owes me. He'll take care of you and give you top priority."

"Thanks so much. This wasn't nearly as awful as I thought it'd be."

Anne laughed again. "Glad we weren't as frightening as you thought."

*****

Becca had been very methodical in her planning. She knew she might only have one opportunity to talk to Spencer. Since she'd taken the ballroom dance classes in the past, she was aware of the schedule. This Wednesday would be the tango roundhouse dance, where every man would rotate dancing with every woman. He'd have to dance with her if she went, unless he wanted to cause a scene. Becca had an in with the dance instructor, who'd already informed her Spencer was talking about getting engaged soon. She had to act fast, to keep him from making the biggest mistake of his life.

She was dressed to entice, in a skin-tight black dress with a deep v in the front that displayed her assets well. The slit on the side of the dress went all the way up to her hip so when she lifted it, her entire leg was exposed. She had on five-inch platform shoes that made her legs look longer. She was certain when he saw what she was offering, he wouldn't be able to resist. And all she had to do was get a picture with him taking advantage of her, and the uptight, virginal Emily would drop him like a hot rock. The dance studio photographer was in on the plan, although he didn't know her intentions. She'd only told him she was going to get dirty with Spencer, and she wanted some pictures. She was more than willing to make it worth his while to do her a favor and give her copies of the pictures. Even if Spencer turned her down, she might be able to use one of the pictures with them dancing together. And the photographer was willing to text the picture, so Emily wouldn't know it came from her.

 She wanted Spencer, but she wanted to hurt Emily even more. She was so angry with Steven Gherring for filing charges against her. The search warrant and police questionings were frightening and humiliating. And it had cost her a lot of money to hire an attorney. Granted, her parents had paid for the lawyer, but they'd cut her allowance afterward. Overall, Gherring had made her life miserable for a while, and she'd almost been caught red-handed. She could have been sent to prison. She wanted revenge, and the only way to hurt him, was to hurt Emily. She'd come to despise the sickly sweet girl who'd taken Spencer's attention away from her. Emily Best didn't deserve him, anyway.

 She peered into the studio where the teacher was explaining the rules for the roundhouse tango. She spied Spencer across the room. She was a little disappointed he hadn't dressed up. Most of the women wore nice dresses on roundhouse night, and a lot of the men wore slacks and dress shirts. But Spencer was clad in jeans and a sport shirt. Of course, he still looked hot. Nothing could prevent that. But the pictures would have been so much better if they'd both been dressed up.

 Alumni were always invited to roundhouse night, so there were a number of other girls that'd returned for the opportunity to practice the tango. Sizing up her rivals, she only found one girl who presented real competition. She was tall, with long blond hair, but her dress was nothing spectacular. Satisfied in being the most alluring girl present, she flung the door open and sauntered across the floor, deliberately ignoring Spencer. She planned to adopt an air of total surprise when she saw him.

Spencer studied his feet while the teacher clarified the rules for the evening. He had to switch partners, dancing with all the women present. A number of extra women and a few extra men from previous classes had joined for the reunion dance. He noticed a lot more girls nearer his age. The thought of dancing with them made him even more nervous than dancing with the older women that were normally in his class. He wiped his sweaty palms on his jeans.

Glancing up at a late entry, he spotted a young girl in a skimpy black dress. He returned to the obsessive contemplation of his shoes, but heard the guy next to him murmuring something about the new girl. He peeked under his eyebrows at her, and felt a heavy rock in his stomach. It was Becca.

His mind raced. She was listening to the teacher and hadn't seen him yet. Maybe he could slip away without causing a scene. But the teacher clapped her hands, couples paired up, and tango music blared.

Maybe he could manage to avoid dancing with Becca. If not, he could at least refuse to speak while they danced. His first partner was one of the younger alumni. He was shocked when she danced much closer to him, repeatedly rubbing her body against his.

"Spencer." He heard the teacher's amused voice over his shoulder. "Now you see how you really dance the tango. It is the dance of love. Don't look so frightened."

He recovered from his shock enough to finish the dance and moved to the next partner, who was an older woman, a newbie, like him. He was grateful her dancing was much more tame in comparison to the first girl.

Then Becca was in his arms.

"Spencer?" Her eyes were wide and innocent, but he didn't believe it for a second. "What are you doing here?"

"Taking dance lessons."

She danced with him like the other younger girl had, maybe even more suggestively. "Spencer, let's get together after class. I've got some great moves to show you." She twirled in his arms and lifted her leg high, totally exposed by the slit in her dress. Then she pushed her body against his and slid down his leg, before rising again just as suddenly to fling her arms around his neck. He flinched and closed his eyes, as she pressed her lips to his.

"What are you doing?" He peeled her arms away and gave her a furious shove. "What are you doing?"

"Only the tango." She pushed her lower lip out in a pout. "But we could do more, if you want." She lifted her arms toward him.

"Stop it, Becca. I'm not interested in anything you're offering."

"What do you mean?" Her voice was indignant. "I'm talking about dancing the tango. What are you implying?"

"I'm not implying anything. I'm telling you straight out I'm not interested in you. I'm in love with Emily."

"I don't know what you see in that skinny witch!" she spat out.

He felt rage building inside and struggled to control himself. Other people on the dance floor had stopped to listen to the angry exchange. How he wanted to punch her in the face. But instead, his voice trembling with rage, he told her, "You aren't worthy to be in the same city with her. Not even to be in the same state or country!"

He spun around and stomped out the door. His dance lessons were over.

*****

Emily tried to concentrate on the little ball she was supposed to hit with her racquet. But the noises were so loud, echoing in the room, bouncing off the walls, reverberating in her head. With every loud bang of the ball on the racquet or hitting the wall, she flinched, closing her eyes. Invariably, she swung and missed, often being pummeled by the ball as it bounced off the wall. She wanted to curl up into a small lump and hide in the corner.

Josh shook his head as she jumped and squealed, rubbing her leg where the ball had bruised her. "Emily, I don't think this is working. Tell me again. Why are you trying to learn to play racquetball?"

"Because I thought Spencer and I could play together if I learned how."

He chuckled. "Why is it you're always injuring yourself in an effort to please Spencer when it's absolutely unnecessary?"

"That's not true," she said, annoyed at the petulance in her voice.

"But it is true. Did he ask you to learn how to play racquetball?"

"No."

"So, it was all your idea. Right?"

"No. Charlie suggested it." His face contorted with pain, and she regretted saying her sister's name. "I'm sorry. I wasn't going to talk about her."

He grimaced. "As much as it hurts, I'm still hungry to hear about her. Is she... Is she okay? Is she dating someone else? I really need to know."

"Josh, I shouldn't talk about her."

"Please," His eyes dropped, and his shoulders slumped in defeat. "She won't talk to me or write me back. Does she hate me that much?"

"Josh. I'm so sorry. She doesn't hate you. But I told you she might not give you a chance. I know it's not fair."

"So, you think I should simply forget about her? Move on with my life?" His face was incredulous, as if the very idea was preposterous.

"Probably so. I don't think there's much chance she'll change her mind. At least not as long as you're separated by half a country"

"Will you promise me something?"

"Sure, if I can."

"If she ever moves here, even if it's a year or two from now, will you tell me?"

"Sure, Josh. But don't you think you'll have another girlfriend by then, or maybe even be married?"

His eyes met with hers and held them fast in a piercing gaze. "No, I don't think so. I'm not giving up hope unless I find out she's married to someone else."

She broke off from his intense regard. "Okay. I don't think that's wise, but it's your life."

"So I have a great idea. Instead of staying here and collecting more bruises, why don't I walk you back to your place? You can tell me why you think you need to learn how to play a sport for Spencer, and I can talk you out of it before you kill yourself."

"Do you really think I'm that hopeless?"

"You're far from hopeless, but you need to pick a quieter sport. And whatever it is, you need to wear padding from head to toe. You just get hurt too easily." His green eyes danced with laughter. "And after I convince you not to hurt yourself anymore, you can tell me a few stories about Charlie. I only want to hear what she's doing. Tell me about her rafting, about her signing up for classes and what she's going to take. I'll be happy with any news at all. I'm starved for it."

"Okay," she agreed, secretly happy her racquetball career had met an early demise.

Spencer paced in the lobby of Emily's building. He'd gone straight from the dance class, hoping to talk to her. He wasn't even sure what he was going to tell her. He still hoped to surprise her at the wedding, so he couldn't really reveal the events of the evening. But he felt almost dirty at the memory of Becca's touch, and his ears burned from her remark about Emily. He just needed to hold her. He needed to tell her he loved her. He'd said it before. Hadn't he? He wasn't sure. But Gherring had warned him he could lose her. He needed to reassure himself. And he needed to reassure Emily.

But when he'd arrived at her apartment, she wasn't home. And she hadn't been upstairs at her parents' place. And she hadn't answered her phone. So he decided to wait for her. He'd wait as long as it took—all night if he needed to. And so, he paced.

He heard her voice before he saw her face. Her laughter rolled through the lobby. His heart lifted at the sound.

"Emily!" He turned toward the door with a longing smile. But the smile melted from his face when he saw whom she was with. "Josh."

"I can explain," she cried, rushing to him. "Josh was teaching me to play racquetball."

"It's okay. You're free to date him if that's what you want." He didn't mean those words, but he was so angry he could barely control himself.

"This wasn't a date." Tears spilled from her eyes.

"Look Spencer. I promise I wasn't trying to make a move on Emily." Josh reached out to put a hand on his shoulder, but he shook it off.

"You know what? It's been a long night, and I'm going home. We can talk tomorrow." To his intense embarrassment, he felt tears building in his eyes. He wanted to say something more. To clear the air. To hold her and kiss her and somehow make up. To begin again. But instead, struggling to hide his wet face, he hurried to the lobby exit and slipped into the warm night air.

*****

"Emily, I'm so sorry. I should've known. I would've been just as jealous. I was so bent on hearing about Charlie I didn't think about what might happen."

"It's not your fault. I knew he was upset the last time we were together. I should have asked Steven to teach me, instead."

"He'll be okay tomorrow. We didn't do anything wrong. Deep down, he knows that. He's only being a guy, you know."

"I know. It's just so stupid—and all for nothing. I was terrible at racquetball."

"Uhmm, yes. You were pretty bad." He bit his lips trying not to laugh. "I'm sorry, I really am. Look, I'm going to text him and explain the whole thing."

"That's not your responsibility."

"Of course it is. What if he says something to Charlie? I can't afford a single black mark in her book, even a false accusation could mean the difference between a slim chance and none at all."

"Okay. I'm going to try to call him. But Josh, thanks for trying, anyway."

"Are you sure you're okay?"

"I'll be fine. Eventually. After we talk."

Josh departed while Emily rode the elevator up to her apartment. Before she'd managed to fumble her way into the apartment with her gym bag, her phone beeped with a message. She ripped her phone from her purse, anxious for a word from Spencer. But the message was from an unknown caller. Curious at who might be texting her, she opened the message and was immediately confronted with a picture.

The image made her stomach contract, and she felt bile rising in her throat. Spencer, with his eyes closed, embracing a girl in a sexy black dress. Her arms were wrapped around his neck, and they were kissing. Unable to tear her eyes away, she enlarged the photograph. It was unmistakable. The girl was Becca. And the picture was taken tonight. Spencer had been wearing the same clothes in the lobby.

Her heart broke cleanly into a million tiny pieces.

Chapter Eighteen

SPENCER DIDN'T GET far. He walked for about twenty minutes, trying to clear his head. Why was it always Josh? Maybe it really was an innocent thing—she'd said something crazy about learning to play racquetball. But he really didn't trust Josh. He seemed to be really in love with Charlie, but what if he gave up and decided to go after Emily again? How could he ever compete with Josh, the handsome, athletic doctor?

Then he got a text. He pulled out his phone, hoping it was from Emily. But the text was from Josh.

Spencer, Emily wanted to learn a sport so she could play with you. She said you play basketball every night. She thought if she could play racquetball, you would spend more time with her. She said it was Charlie's idea. I was only trying to teach her. That's all. Josh P.S. If you stay mad at her over this, you deserve to lose her.

What was he doing? He loved Emily. He didn't want to lose her. He had to swallow his pride and go back to her apartment to talk to her. He had to tell her he loved her. Clearly. In no uncertain terms. He could tell her he was giving up basketball. He'd saved enough money he didn't need to park cars any more, and he wasn't going back to dance lessons after tonight. He could make do with the lessons he'd already taken.

It was only nine o'clock. They had plenty of time to talk it out. They might even have a nice kissing make-up session. He allowed himself a little smile at this thought. Why did love have to be so hard?

A few minutes earlier, he'd felt like his life was over. He couldn't think rationally where Emily was concerned. She made him happier than he'd ever been. But she also made him crazier than he'd ever been.

Once he made the decision, he couldn't get there fast enough. He found himself jogging down the street toward her complex. He rushed into the lobby and onto the elevator, pushing the button multiple times in an effort to hurry it along. He exited on her floor and almost knocked someone down in his hurry to reach her apartment. Then, with his heart still racing, he knocked on the door.

*****

Emily stared in shock at the picture as a sob escaped her throat. She felt a blackness closing in on her. The image swam before her eyes as her tears shimmered and fell onto her shirt. She had to go. She couldn't stay here, but she had nowhere to go. If she were home in Texas, she would get in her car and drive until her head cleared. But she wasn't home. She was in New York City. So she headed to the only place she could think to go... Grand Central Station.

She turned off her phone as she walked to the subway station. There was no one to talk to. The only people she knew to call—her mom, Charlie, Grace—would all side with Spencer. They'd defended him every time she talked to them. "Spencer loves you," they'd said. "He just hasn't told you. He won't ever break up with you. He would never leave you." How wrong they'd all been.

He'd obviously come to the apartment to break up with her, having just been with Becca. Her stomach churned as she pictured him kissing her. She remembered Becca's words, "He always comes back to me." She would never have believed Becca, now she knew the truth about her. But no matter how she tried, she couldn't think of a single innocent scenario that would result in the picture she'd been sent.

He'd acted angry about Josh, but he was probably glad to have an excuse to break up with her. Maybe he was tired of her restrictive rules. Or maybe he realized he preferred a more voluptuous figure.

She rode the subway to Grand Central, and found an unoccupied bench to sit on. Unseeing, she stared at the people herding past her like busy ants, on their way to do important things. They exuded excitement and happiness, while she felt lonely and desolate. She reveled in her wretchedness, letting her tears fall freely down her face, amazed someone could be so alone in the midst of the New York City crowd. No one noticed her crying on the bench as they hurried past her to their destinations. She was as isolated as she would have been on a desert island.

After midnight, the crowds were thinning, and she needed to find a place to go. But she couldn't go home. The only person who might be on her side was Josh. He'd understand her misery. On their walk home from racquetball, he'd actually broken down in tears over Charlie. He'd been angry and embarrassed over his loss of control, but she'd sworn never to tell anyone. Josh would understand, but he was scheduled to work in the emergency room all night. Still, instinct drove her to go to the hospital. She could talk to him when he got off work in the morning. She left the haven of her bench, and headed to the subway train.

*****

Spencer knocked on the apartment door, shifting from foot to foot, knowing she'd look through the peephole before she opened the door. When she didn't answer, he knocked louder. She was probably angry, refusing to open the door, denying him the opportunity to talk to her. He knocked again, louder still. "Emily!" he said. "Please! I just want to talk to you." Still no answer. He put his ear against the door, but detected no sound from inside the apartment.

He pulled out his cell phone and called her, but it went straight to voice mail. She'd apparently turned her phone off, and she wasn't home. With dread, he realized she must have gone upstairs to her mom's apartment. He had no other choice but to find her and talk to her, even if it meant facing her parents.

He rang the bell at the Gherring's apartment, wondering belatedly if he should have called first. When Gherring opened the door, his face was creased with concern. "Spencer? What are you doing here?"

"I'm... I need to talk to Emily. Is she here?"

"No, we haven't heard from her tonight. She's probably out with friends, although it's late for a weeknight. She wasn't with you tonight?"

"No, I was at a dance lesson. My last dance lesson." He didn't bother to hide his bitterness.

Spencer's mind was reeling. Who would she go to? She didn't have many friends in the city. Maybe she left with Josh. Or maybe she was with Grace. "Uhmm, okay. Sorry to bother you."

Back at her apartment he knocked again, in a vain hope she would answer. Then he leaned his back against the door and banged his head against it in frustration before he let himself slide down to the floor. He pulled out his phone, and called Grace.

"Hey, Brother. What's up?"

"Is Emily with you?"

"What? No. Why would—"

"Have you heard from her?"

"No. What happened? Did you have a fight?"

"No. Well, sort of. She was coming back from playing racquetball with Josh, and I saw them together in the lobby and kind of lost it. So I stormed out. But I came back thirty minutes later, and she was gone. And she's turned her cell phone off."

"She's probably upstairs."

"I checked already. I think she must have left with Josh."

"I doubt it. Josh and Brad are on the night shift in the emergency room tonight. You could call, I guess, but he won't answer his phone if his shift has started."

"Where could she be?"

"I don't know, but if you got her upset, she might be walking around on the street somewhere."

"But that's not safe."

"Seriously? This is Emily we're talking about. Since when do you think she wouldn't do something hazardous? She's cautious and afraid about things that are actually safe, and totally oblivious with actual danger, like she doesn't have any common sense."

He groaned at the constriction in his chest. She could be walking around in a daze by herself on the streets of New York City at night. "What should I do?"

"I take it she's not answering her phone?"

"She turned it off, unless it's dead."

"You call Charlie and see if she has any ideas. And give Josh a call, in case he hasn't started his shift yet. I'll call Brad, too. And I guess you'd better wait there in case she comes back. She'll probably walk back inside any time now, and you can straighten this whole thing out. But you better let me know the minute she comes back, because I'm really worried."

He disconnected, attempting to tamp down the feeling of dread in his stomach. Gherring's words kept coming back to haunt him. "I almost lost her. I don't want you to make the same mistake." He hadn't even talked to Charlie or taken her grandmother's ring to the jeweler yet. He'd lost her before he even purchased the ring. He felt the small lump of the little ring box wedged in his front pocket. He'd thought he might have a chance to go to the jeweler today on the way to dance class, but found it closed.

He pulled the box out, opening the lid and gazing at the old-fashioned ring. He imagined how it would feel to have Emily's actual engagement ring, to give it to her, to see it on her hand. He tried the ring on himself, but it would barely slide onto his little finger. It was a sweet, old-fashioned setting. There was one central round diamond in a gold carved background that made it appear as a flower. On the side, going down the band were tiny little round diamonds, four on each side. It was probably only half a carat in total, but it would add nicely to the diamond he intended to buy for her. If he ever got the chance.

He tucked the ring safely back into his pocket and called Charlie.

*****

Josh was exhausted. The emergency room had been extraordinarily busy, probably because it was a full moon. Everyone said the full moon brought out the crazy people. There were stabbings and gunshot wounds, car accidents, women giving birth. One guy, who'd gotten his hand stuck inside a glass jar, had to wait for four hours because there were so many other more pressing emergencies.

He and Brad walked back to the residents' room to retrieve their things. When he turned on his phone, he found several phone messages and texts.

Brad, who was checking his phone simultaneously, said, "Emily's missing. Did you get a text about her?"

"Yes, and I think I know where she is."

"Where?"

"She left me a message to pick her up in the maternity ward waiting room."

"Are you kidding me? She's been here all night? We better let everybody know. They're all crazy worried."

"No, don't. Not yet. Her text is begging me not to tell anyone where she is. Let's go talk to her first."

When they reached the waiting room, they spied her at once, curled up on a hard plastic loveseat, asleep, with her head resting awkwardly on her purse.

Josh sat down next to her and gently shook her awake while Brad stood by, watching.

"Hey. What on earth are you doing here? Everybody's worried about you."

She frowned and spoke grumpily as she sat up, stretching her stiff limbs. "I saw their texts last night. I sent a text to Mom and Grace and Charlie and told them I was safe and not to worry. And I already called work and left a message I'd be out today because I'm not feeling well."

"And then what? You turned your phone back off and spent the night here?"

"Yes. I didn't have any other place to go."

"Look Emily, I sent him a text and explained about racquetball. He's not mad anymore. He's going crazy looking for you."

He glanced up at Brad who rolled his eyes and mouthed, "Women!"

But her eyes filled with tears that began to roll down her cheeks, rewetting the salty streaks that had previously dried there. She silently took out her cell phone and turned it on, ignoring all the new messages. She opened a photo and handed it to Josh.

He recoiled in astonishment at the image on the screen. "Okay. That looks bad, but there has to be an explanation. That could have been taken last year." He handed the phone to Brad whose eyes bugged as he let out a low whistle.

"That's what he had on last night. It's the same clothes. The picture was taken yesterday."

"Okay. But still, there's got to be a reasonable explanation," Josh insisted.

"Can you think of one?" Her voice was dead.

"Uhmm... I don't know. Brad? You got anything here?"

Brad shrugged and returned the phone.

"Still, your whole family's worried about you now. They asked both of us to tell them if we found you."

"Please, don't!" She looked up through wet lashes.

Josh stood and walked to the hallway, speaking with Brad in a low voice. "What do we do?"

Brad pulled out his phone. "I forwarded the picture to my cell. I'm going to send it to Spencer."

"Only to Spencer? Not Grace or Charlie?"

He shook his head. "Just him. As guys, we owe him that much. We can't let him get blindsided with this, no matter what he did. Let's take her to our apartment and let her crash on the couch while we're sleeping. We'll make her send out one more I'm safe message. Tell everyone she's spending the day in Central Park. When she wakes up and she's good and ready, she can leave on her own."

*****

Spencer was sitting stubbornly in the hallway outside Emily's apartment where he'd spent the night, listening to Anne and Gherring arguing with him.

"It's ridiculous for you to stay here waiting," said Gherring. "I can't believe you slept out here all night. She obviously found a place to stay last night. And, she's already called in sick to work. So she probably won't be back anytime soon."

Anne said, "I'm still worried. I don't understand what could've gotten her so upset. Are you sure nothing else happened? She didn't kiss Josh, did she?"

"I hope not." Spencer rubbed his throbbing head.

Anne and Gherring received simultaneous text messages. "Is it Emily?" asked Spencer. "What did she say?"

"She says she's spending the day in Central Park," said Gherring.

"She didn't happen to mention where in Central Park, did she?"

"Sorry, Spencer. No such luck." Anne shook her head.

Spencer's phone received a text. His hope surged. Maybe she'd finally responded to him. At this point, he'd rather have her scream at him than continue to avoid communicating. When he opened the text, he noted with disappointment it was from Brad. He opened the attached photo.

"Oh god! Oh god! This can't be happening!" He blinked furiously at the tears that rose in his eyes. The picture blurred, but he could still see it clearly in his mind. Brad's message was brief. *Someone sent her this picture.*

"What is it?" said Anne. "Is it something about Emily?"

"It's Becca! Oh god! I've lost her. It's just like you said would happen. I've lost her." He felt a surge of nausea.

"What happened?" demanded Gherring.

"Someone sent this to her." He handed his phone to Gherring. "It happened at dance class. But it's not what it looks like. Becca was there, and I had to dance with her. She practically attacked me and then I left. That's it. That's all that happened. I ran out and came straight here. And that's when Emily came back with Josh, and I got angry."

He couldn't bear to look at their expressions. The picture was bad—they wouldn't believe him. Emily would never believe him.

"Who took this picture?" asked a grim-faced Gherring.

"There's a studio photographer at every class. They put pictures up on Facebook the next day."

"Well, this certainly explains a lot." Anne put her hand on Gherring's arm. "What can we do?"

"You were right," Spencer told Gherring. "You told me this would happen."

"I wasn't making a prediction. I was giving you a warning. But I didn't actually lose Anne, and you're not going to lose Emily either."

"What can I do? She'll never believe me."

"Of course she will," said Anne. "If she knows you love her, she'll believe you. You just need to tell her again. And again. We have to hear it a lot of times."

"I'm not exactly sure I ever said the actual words, but I implied it when we talked about getting married."

Gherring raised his hand before Anne could respond. "Spencer... Son, we need to talk, man-to-man."

*****

Emily slept for four hours but by noon she was awake, haunted by her own thoughts. She could hear soft snores emanating from the bedrooms. Having slept in her clothes at the hospital, she felt sticky and dirty, and she couldn't wait to bathe. When she slipped quietly into the bathroom to shower, she noticed a set of drawstring scrubs with a note on top. *For Emily*. Relieved at the prospect of changing into clean clothes, she stripped and stood under the water, letting the warm torrents pound on her stiff muscles. She toweled off and put on the soft clean scrubs, chuckling as the drawstring bunched the large amount of excess material. The top also hung loosely on her thin frame, but at least she wasn't wearing her old dirty clothes. She looked in the mirror at the wild mass of long, wet, curls, belatedly realizing she didn't have a brush. She attempted without success to comb them with her fingers. She'd have to borrow a hat.

She was poking around in the kitchen, looking for food, when Brad walked in. "Hey. Good morning. Feel free to eat anything you can find. It may be sparse."

"I'm sorry. Did I wake you up?"

"No, we've both got to be back at work at two thirty today. It's already one o'clock."

"Wow! They don't give you much time to sleep."

"No. But we get used to it. Sometimes our schedule's more normal. Occasionally, we get a whole day off, or even two." He grinned at her. "You look much better in those scrubs than Josh does."

"You're right about that," said Josh as he entered the kitchen, playfully ruffling her wet hair.

"I'm taking a shower," said Brad, disappearing into the bathroom.

Emily found a bowl and cereal, and Josh helped himself to a bowl as well. They ate in companionable silence for a while. Josh spoke around bites. "Did you sleep okay?"

"Much better than at the hospital. Thanks for the couch. And the scrubs. And the shower. And the cereal."

He smiled and nodded.

She added, "And also, thanks for not telling anyone where I was. I don't think I could've handled seeing him."

"And now? Can you handle it?"

"I'll have to. We work at the same place. I'll talk to him with other people around, but I don't want to talk to him alone. He'll just manipulate me with my emotions, and I'll end up forgiving him and giving him another chance." She shook her head, lecturing herself. "I let myself fall in love, knowing he would eventually want to be with a different girl. But I told myself I'd never give him a second chance if he was with someone else. Anyway, I feel sure he wasn't going to date me much longer. He was probably planning to break up last night, anyway. Seeing us together just gave him an excuse."

"You know, a player really can change. I don't ever want to be with another girl besides Charlie."

She put her hand on his arm. "I know. I'm not talking about you."

She jumped at a loud rapping on the door. "Who's that?"

Josh peered through the peephole, and then turned back to her, grimacing. "It's Spencer."

Spencer fidgeted while he waited for someone to answer the door. It had finally occurred to him Brad must have seen Emily or at least talked to her if he got a copy of the picture. He might know where she'd actually gone.

After a long pause, he was about to knock again when the door opened. Josh stood in the doorway, wearing shorts and no shirt. "What do you want?" he asked, his body blocking the entrance. His body language told Spencer he wouldn't be invited inside.

"I'm... I'm looking for Emily. I just wanted to talk to Brad for a minute. I thought he might know where she is."

"Why do you want to know? Haven't you hurt her enough already? By the way, you look terrible. Did you sleep in those clothes last night?"

"Look, Josh," he snapped. "It's none of your business, but that picture was a set-up. I love Emily, and I'd never be with another girl—especially not Becca."

"Really? A set-up? How's that? It sure looked like you had your arms around her and your lips locked."

"I was at a dance class. Okay? A stupid ballroom dance class, because I wanted to surprise Emily. And I didn't even know Becca was going to be there."

"So, let me get this straight. You were trying to learn to dance for Emily while she was trying to learn to play racquetball for you? And you got mad at her and walked out. And then she got mad, and she'll never forgive you?"

A small voice behind him said, "Okay, let him inside."

Josh moved out of the way and made a grandiose gesture for him to enter. He walked through the door, frantically searching for the source of the voice. Then his eyes focused on her. She was sitting alone on a stool, clad in oversized scrubs, with her hair splayed around her face in loose flowing curls, emphasizing her huge eyes—her huge angry eyes.

Emily observed from her perch on the barstool as Spencer entered the room, blinking his eyes as they adjusted from the bright sunlight. The moment his eyes met hers, he started her direction.

"No. Don't come any closer. You can sit over there on the couch."

His face revealed his hurt, but he obediently moved over to sit on the edge of the couch. From this position, she looked down on him. It felt powerful, and she liked it. She was strong. He'd hurt her, and he'd lied to her. But he'd never do it again.

"Can we talk alone?" he begged her, glancing at Josh.

"No. We can't."

Josh grinned and picked up his cereal bowl and spooned a mouthful, munching with noisy abandon.

"Look Emily. I wasn't with Becca. I didn't kiss her. I really was taking ballroom dance lessons, so I could dance with you at Sam and Tanner's wedding."

Josh laughed out loud, and Spencer shot him a furious look.

"I can prove it. There are pictures of the class on Facebook by now. You can see, it really was a dance class."

"Spencer," she said, blinking tears back. "Even if it wasn't true this time, it'll be true another time. I'll always be waiting for it to happen. I thought I could settle for a year or however long you'd give me, but it just hurts too badly. I can't go through that again."

He blinked a few times, his mouth hanging open. "I don't even know what you're talking about. I mean, when we talked about getting married, didn't you know I meant—"

"Getting married? We never talked about getting married."

"Of course we did. How could you forget? We were sitting on the glider on the porch—"

"We didn't talk about getting married—we talked about breaking up. You said you only wanted to date for a year."

"Yes, because I wanted to get married as soon as possible."

"You didn't say that!"

"Yes, I did!"

"Spencer," Josh interrupted with obvious amusement. "When you're arguing with a woman about what was said, she will always be correct. Women have little digital recorders in their minds. They remember every minute detail. She will remember the exact words, the inflection of your voice, and what you were wearing at the time."

"Can he leave us alone now?" asked Spencer, clenching his teeth.

"No."

Josh's mouth stretched in a broad smile as he poured another bowl of cereal.

"The point is," Spencer squeezed out the words, "I do want to marry you. I love you and I think I told you that."

Emily frowned and shook her head.

He sighed. "Okay, well I meant to tell you. But I thought I was showing you. That's why I was taking dance lessons."

"Even if you think you love me, Spencer, I think you might be fooling yourself. You could get tired of me at any time. You're used to excitement and variety."

He groaned. "I can't believe I'm doing this." Just then, Brad came out of the shower and proceeded to pour a bowl of cereal and sit down to observe.

"Please, Emily. Can't we talk alone for just a minute?"

"She doesn't want to be manipulated by her emotions," explained Josh with a grin. "So you'll just have to talk with an audience."

"This is great," said Brad between mouthfuls. "What did I miss?"

"Let's see," said Josh. "He was taking ballroom dance lessons when someone snapped the picture with Becca. And he thought he'd asked her to marry him, but he'd really asked her to break up in a year. And he didn't tell her he loved her when he thought he did. But he took dance lessons instead."

Brad laughed so hard he almost spit out his cereal, and Emily struggled to suppress a grin. Now was not the time to forget her anger. She had to be firm and make a clean break.

She added, "And I've just explained it's not just about the picture. Even if it turns out to be faked, it only shows how vulnerable I am. I don't want to be in a relationship with someone where I'm constantly waiting for him to move on to the next girl. Or go back to the last one."

Spencer covered his eyes and muttered crossly. "There is no other girl. There never will be another girl. There never was another girl."

"Of course there were others," said Emily. "I'm not that naïve, you know. I know what you were like before we started dating."

"There were no others." His voice was flat, like a computer was talking.

"What are you saying?" she asked.

Brad chuckled. "You were the first, Emily. He's saying you were the first one."

She blushed painfully to her roots. "We didn't ever... I mean... We haven't ever done that."

Josh grinned. "Then neither has he."

Spencer moaned and buried his face in his hands.

Emily was flabbergasted. "I don't believe it. You're lying. You're just saying that to make me believe—"

Brad's laughter cut her off. "Oh no, Emily. There's no way he's saying that in front of us unless it's the truth. He's really and truly a virgin. Pretty remarkable these days."

Josh bit back his smile. "Seriously, Spencer. I know you may not believe this, but I'd give anything right now if I could take back my past and say something like that to Charlie." Then he chuckled. "But not in front of two other guys."

Emily sat in stunned silence, contemplating this new information while Josh and Brad put their bowls in the sink, moving toward their rooms.

Before he disappeared, Josh turned back with a wink. "Emily. I think you've humiliated him enough now. He loves you, and you can trust him."

Then his face lost its joking façade. "Just one thing, though. I need you to remember what this feels like. Both of you. Because this is how I feel right now about Charlie. All the time. Every day. So, I'd appreciate it if you'd put in a good word now and then." He spun and slipped through his bedroom door.

*****

Spencer debated his options, deciding he didn't have any. If she still didn't believe him, still didn't trust him, what could he do? He could find the pictures on Facebook and try to prove he wasn't with Becca. But Emily claimed it wouldn't make a difference, anyway. Telling her the truth about his experience level was his final shot. If she turned him down now, he didn't have anything else to offer.

But at least they were finally alone, without an audience—for a few minutes, anyway. He'd simply have to declare his love to her, and face refusal if it came. It would be easier not having Josh and Brad witness his rejection.

He moved to kneel in front of her while she sat motionless, regarding him with wary eyes.

"Emily..." He reached out for her hand, but a loud knock interrupted his words.

"I wonder who that could be." She leaped to the door, squinting through the peephole. "It's Grace and Olivia."

He attempted to hide his annoyance as she jerked the door open. His sisters exclaimed when they spotted their friend.

"Emily!" Grace wrapped her in a bear hug. "I'm so glad you're okay. We were all worried. I didn't even know you were here. I just came over to talk to Brad before he left for work."

"Why did you run off like that?" asked Olivia. "Spencer must have done something worse than he said."

Grace spied Spencer on the floor and stomped over to stand before him with hands planted on her hips. "And there he is on his knees. I hope he's begging for forgiveness. What did you do?"

He moaned, bending over to bang his head on the floor in total frustration. "I didn't do anything. It was a set-up!"

Brad walked out from his bedroom. "Hey, Grace. You need to see the picture Emily got. I have to say it's pretty convincing."

Spencer glared at him, but Brad laughed. "Why are you on the floor? Are you groveling?"

He was climbing to his feet when Josh came out of the back, carrying his laptop. He handed it to Spencer and smiled, clapping him on the back.

"Here you go, buddy. Prove your innocence."

"Grace, will you lock up when you go? We've got to head for work. I'll call you after if it's not too late." Brad gave her a quick hug and a kiss.

"Grace and Olivia could go with you. Emily and I will be glad to lock up the place," suggested Spencer, as he searched madly for the dance studio's Facebook page.

"That's okay," said Grace. "We'll just stay a while. I want to see this picture Brad's talking about."

As Brad and Josh left the apartment, Emily pulled out her phone, displaying the picture for Grace and Olivia, who both gasped audibly.

"Spencer!" said Grace. "When did this happen? You told me you hadn't dated anyone before Emily."

"Becca framed me. Look! Look at these pictures. It was a dance class."

"You were in a dance class?" asked Olivia, looking more astonished than she had at the image of Becca's passionate kiss.

Grace took the computer, and the three girls studied the pictures.

"Oh yeah. There he is dancing with an older lady. Here he's with another pretty girl. I'm not sure this proves anything except you were dancing with other girls."

"Look at this one, where I'm dancing with Becca. Can't you tell I don't want to be with her?"

"Well he does look pretty disgusted in this one, where she's kind of hanging on his leg." Olivia chuckled.

A giggle escaped from behind Emily's fingers. "And this one, right after the kissing picture."

"Oh yeah," Grace agreed with a grin. "His face is a little nauseated. That's really not a good look for you brother."

"And what were you doing in a dance class?" asked Olivia. "And why wasn't Emily with you?"

Spencer tried futilely to keep the exasperation from his voice. "I wanted to surprise Emily because she loves to dance. I knew she wanted to dance at Sam and Tanner's wedding."

"I guess it was kind of sweet," admitted Emily.

"When did you have time to take dance lessons?" demanded Grace. "I thought you were working to buy her a ring."

"You knew about that?" said Emily. "Why didn't he tell me he wanted to get married?"

"Spencer!" Grace scolded. "You were supposed to talk to her."

"It was only a misunderstanding... But we could talk right now if you two would leave us alone."

"You bought the ring?" asked Grace with excitement.

"Not yet. But I did ask her parents for permission. And Charlie was going to help me pick out a setting."

"So you pretty much talked to everybody but me." Emily's eyes flashed with resentment.

"I told you... I thought that's what we were talking about—"

"Well did you at least tell her you loved her? Did she know you hadn't dated anyone else?" Grace turned to Emily. "You know, he had all of us fooled on that one. When we found out he'd never even kissed a girl before—"

"He'd never kissed a girl before? He didn't tell me that. He just said he'd never *been* with a girl."

Grace frowned at Spencer. "Am I right brother? Tell the truth."

"Why not? Total humiliation seems to be the order of the day."

He turned to face Emily with his face burning. "Here it is. I'd never kissed a single girl before I kissed you. None at all. I was always waiting for a special girl to come along, and it just took twenty-five years for that to happen. So there you go. I'm a nerd. I'm totally inexperienced. I'm a fake. Oh, and by the way, in case I didn't make it clear before, I'm totally head-over-heels in love with you."

He squeezed his eyes shut and waited for the sound of her laughter. After a few seconds of silence he cracked one eye open to see what she was doing. She was standing stock still, staring at him, her huge almond-shaped blue eyes brimming with tears.

"I'm sorry—I always say the wrong thing. Please, don't cry. I'll leave you alone. I promise. I won't bother you anymore."

He fought the urge to pull her into his arms and comfort her. How had he made such a mess of things? He clenched his eyes, reaching up to pull his hair in frustration. He flinched as he felt her surge against him, wrapping her arms around his waist and wetting his shirt with her tears.

He let his arms fall around her and rubbed her back, squeezing her against him and nuzzling her damp curls. He was totally confused. Did she like him or did she despise him? Was she angry or had she forgiven him? Did she believe him? Why would she cry and then hug him? This must be some type of farewell hug. She was crying because they were breaking up. He closed his eyes and willed it to last as long as possible.

"Too bad you don't have that ring, Spencer," sniffed Grace. He opened his eyes in confusion to find Grace and Olivia both crying and hugging each other. Girls were so weird. Why were they all crying?

He was thinking it was a good thing he hadn't already bought the ring or destroyed her grandmother's ring. He guessed he could give it back to her since he wasn't going to use the diamonds. He refused to let himself think about another guy making it into an engagement ring for her. He pulled one hand down to reach into his pocket and pull out the ring box.

"Here," he said, holding out the box. "I guess I won't be needing this."

Emily pulled away and gazed at the ring box balanced on his fingers. She picked it up with trembling hands and opened it.

"Oh!" she cried. "It's my Grandmother's ring! I've always loved this ring!"

She pulled the ring out of the box and slipped it on her left hand. It fit perfectly. Then she started crying afresh, throwing herself back into Spencer's arms. This time Spencer kept his eyes open, patting her back and watching in bewilderment as his sisters went on another crying-hugging spree.

Grace furrowed her eyebrows. "Kiss her, Spencer—she accepted."

"Accepted what?"

"You're engaged, you idiot." Grace laughed. "Congratulations!"

Chapter Nineteen

EMILY THOUGHT IT WAS a perfect day. Oh, the wedding hadn't been perfect. Her new shoes made a blister on her toe while they were taking pictures, so she'd discarded them to make her way down the aisle barefooted. The flower girl, one of Spencer's cousins, had run all the way to the altar without throwing any petals, while the ring bearer had refused to take a single step down the aisle. Throughout the ceremony, Josh had been smiling and waggling his eyebrows at Charlie who vacillated between spearing him with her glares and refusing to make eye contact at all. Her sister had been furious with Spencer for choosing Josh as his best man, resulting in their pairing during the wedding ceremony. But over the last four and a half months, Spencer and Josh had become amazingly good friends. Spencer somehow credited Josh with helping him get engaged by providing the computer to prove his innocence, although secretly, Emily knew she would have believed him anyway.

But when Spencer squeezed her hand under the tablecloth, she felt a marvelous joy. She was married to an amazing boy, no—an amazing man. He was not only handsome and smart, but he adored her in every way. He'd already proven he'd do anything to protect her and care for her. And she knew with absolute confidence he loved her and would always love her and only her. And she returned that love with all of her heart.

Parts of the wedding had been storybook perfect. The beautiful classical music emanating from the grand piano. Walking down the aisle with Steven. Standing before the stained glass windows that decorated the front of the church with Charlie and all four of

Spencer's sisters as bridesmaids. Her mother, crying and hugging her, radiantly beautiful despite being eight months pregnant with twins.

And she definitely looked pregnant now.

Steven's Gram, the tiny, feisty, ninety-six-year-old, held hands with Gus while describing her recent marriage to the ninety-one-year-old as robbing the cradle. Gram had insisted on buying Emily's wedding gown, arguing she loved buying dresses for her granddaughters. It had cost way more than Emily was comfortable with, but wearing it made her feel like a fairy princess.

Altogether, it was an amazing day.

Spencer pulled up her left hand and kissed it, gazing fondly at the new band nestled next to her grandmother's ring. "I still can't believe you didn't want a new engagement ring. I think you deserve a bigger diamond."

Emily rolled her eyes. They'd had this discussion so many times. "But I don't like big, flashy diamonds. And this is exactly what I wanted, plus it's sentimental. Anyway, you put plenty of diamonds on the wedding band."

"Yes, but none of them are very big."

"Size isn't important."

He grinned impudently, whispering in her ear, "It will be tonight."

"Spencer!" She knew her face was flaming, as if the entire group of guests could hear.

*****

Josh laughed and joked with the rest of the wedding party, but his heart wasn't in it. His mind was on the tall, beautiful maid of honor with the big golden eyes. He'd thought she was beautiful before, but he'd never seen her in a dress with her hair down. His breath caught in his throat whenever he looked at her. His eyes drank her in as his chest constricted so tightly he was certain his heart wasn't beating.

He'd hoped when they saw each other on the wedding weekend, Charlie would... What had he hoped for? That she would suddenly decide she was in love with him? That she would decide to transfer to NYU in the spring so they could be together? No, he hadn't really even hoped she would start accepting his phone calls. He'd hoped when they were together, he could talk to her. That he could convince her to give him an opportunity to prove himself. That he could show her how much he'd changed. That she would see how different he was. That she would give him a fighting chance.

The band was playing, and guests, young and old, were having fun on the dance floor. When Bohemian Rhapsody played, even Anne Gherring was dancing, swearing she couldn't possibly sit down for this one. There was a variety of music, including oldies, current songs, waltzes, salsas, and tangos. Spencer and Emily had taken more dance classes together, and were showing off their talents to the guests. Josh noticed Charlie was sitting down during a waltz, with a wistful expression, and he moved to stand in front of her.

He held out his hand. "May I have the pleasure of this dance, my fair lady?" He tried to appear confident and suave, but his heart was hammering in his chest. He knew she would turn him down.

His twinkling eyes dimmed as she hesitated. "Josh, I really don't think it's a good idea—"

"Please? It's a waltz. You barely have to touch me."

"I'm really not that graceful."

He laughed. "I'm graceful enough for both of us." He could see her waffling in her refusal. "Come on, you know you want to dance. It'll be fun, even with me."

With a sigh, she took his proffered hand. Regrettably, he noted it was probably sweaty, since he was incredibly nervous in her company. What was it about this girl that made him so uncomfortable in his own skin?

They twirled smoothly around the dance floor. He'd intended to keep up a merry banter to entertain her, but the scent of her hair and the movement of her waist beneath his fingers distracted him. Her right hand trembled slightly in his grasp, but her face remained serene. He pulled her close to him when they turned so she brushed lightly against his chest. He enjoyed the contact so much he turned them as often as possible, until they were both stumbling a bit from dizziness.

Forced to abandon the wild spinning, he smiled unrepentantly. "Sorry. I got a little vertiginous, but it was worth it."

"Vertiginous?"

"Like vertigo—it means dizzy. But turning is fun, don't you agree?" When she didn't respond, he tried a new approach. "Spencer and Emily look very happy together, don't you think?"

She pressed her lips together in a firm line, refusing to engage. He decided to bait her a bit. "It's nice to see you in a dress. You look like a real woman."

"I beg your pardon! Wearing a dress has nothing to do with being a woman. I happen to think it's demeaning to insist women wear dresses."

"Oh, I would never insist you wear a dress. *Au contraire*. I'd be perfectly happy if you wore nothing at all."

"And I'd be perfectly happy if you wore nothing. In fact, I wouldn't even notice."

"Ow! That hurt." He grinned, glad for any attention, even if it was negative.

The song switched to a slow dance, and Charlie moved as if to leave. But he held onto her hand. "Please... Can't we talk, only for a minute?"

"There's no use, Josh. Why do you keep pursuing me?"

He pulled her back to him, lifting her hands and placing them on his shoulders, and setting his at her waist. "See, nothing indecent—just a dance and some conversation. Tell me about school."

"It's fine."

He waited for further comment, but none came. "Charlie, I don't understand why you won't even give me a chance."

She was silent for a moment, and he thought she wouldn't respond. But then the deluge came.

"We're too different, Josh. We live in different states, we have different dreams, and we have different beliefs and values. You believe in casual sex, and that's fine for you. But I'm the absolute opposite of that. Can't you see? There's no hope."

"There's no hope because you refuse to allow it. I'm changing. I've already changed. I'm not the same man you met six months ago, but you won't give me an opportunity to prove it."

"Why are you trying to change into something different to please me? You were fine and happy before you met me. There were obviously lots and lots of women who liked you just the way you were. Why try to change into something you're not?"

"But that's the thing. I wasn't fine and happy before I met you. I was miserable, and I didn't even know it. And now I've met you, so I know I could be really happy if I changed and you loved me. But, you won't give me a chance, so I'm still miserable."

"So, you're saying meeting me took you from being blissfully ignorant about how miserable you were to consciously aware of how miserable you are."

"You're twisting my words." He ground his teeth together, searching for something to say, anything to break through her barriers. "Charlie... Don't you miss me, even a little? Don't you ever think about that kiss?"

She was quiet for a moment. "Josh... Okay, I'd be lying if I said I wasn't physically attracted to you. There. Are you happy? But, that's not enough to build a relationship on."

His mind was spinning. This was his moment, his only opportunity. She'd finally at least admitted to an attraction. If that attraction was all he had to work with, he'd have to improvise.

"So, physically, you could see yourself being married to me? I mean, if I was a different guy with this body and this face, you could love me?"

Her cheeks were so red, he thought she might be in pain.

"I... That's... Okay, yes, I mean, if you were someone else. But—"

"So, what's he like? This other guy? This someone else you're going to marry someday?"

"I... Honestly, I don't think he exists. I don't think there's a guy I'm willing to give up all my independence for. I don't really need a guy, anyway."

"But if he did exist, what would he be like?"

"I don't know. I don't spend time thinking about it." She frowned, pursing her lips. "I guess he'd be a partner. I don't need someone to take care of me like a parent. And... He'd have some cool job, like, I don't know... Maybe he'd be a fireman. Someone brave and adventurous who helps people. Not someone who spends his whole life working to make more money. And he'd be the sort of guy who only wanted to be with one woman for the rest of his life. I don't want to constantly think I'm being compared with someone else—and probably coming up short."

Josh was quiet for a moment, contemplating her words. "Thank you. At least I understand what you want, and how you see me." He couldn't hide the hurt in his voice.

"Josh, I'm sorry—"

"No, it's okay. It's my fault. You hit closer to home than you realize. That's pretty much who I was, but not who I am, and not who intend to be." He took a deep breath and blew it out through his lips. "But let me ask you one thing. You don't think you could ever love a doctor? Not even an adventurous doctor who wanted to help people?"

Charlie felt her face flushing again. She had so little control around this man. It was one of the reasons he made her feel so uncomfortable. When he'd asked her the first question, she'd tried to come up with a description he couldn't possibly fit. It probably wasn't even true. She had no idea who she wanted to spend the rest of her life with or who she could ever be in love with. She only knew her attraction to Josh made her lose the ability to think logically. When she was with him she always lost the upper hand, and she needed that advantage to compete. What was she supposed to say to his question since he was making it specific? What was a safe thing to say?

She was distressed to find tears flooding her eyes. What on earth was wrong with her? She blinked furiously, but a few escaped onto her cheeks. "I don't know," she answered truthfully, pulling her hands away, attempting to escape before he noticed her tears.

"Wait, I'm sorry. I didn't mean to make you cry." He pulled her back against him and wrapped his arms around her. The floodgates broke. She'd been working so hard to be independent and not accept any financial assistance from Steven. But her workload, along with classes and studying, had been overwhelming. And she'd felt so alone and isolated in Colorado with her family across the country in New York City, but she hadn't wanted to admit it to anyone. She hated admitting she was wrong. She'd always hated it. She was so incredibly stressed, but refused to let anyone know. She didn't want to burden her pregnant mom or her sister who was planning a wedding. Now, wrapped in the Josh's arms, she realized how much she missed feeling cared for and comforted. The tears kept coming, even while she tried desperately to stop them.

He led her back to her chair and handed her a clean napkin. Then he knelt down in front of her, peering intently into her eyes as she sniffed. She noticed for the first time his green eyes had little flecks of blue in them.

"Charlie. I'm not going to do this to you anymore. I love you, and I want to be with you. But, I want you to be happy even more. I can't stand that I made you cry. I'm really sorry. I won't bother you any more. But, please... If you ever change your mind, please come find me." Before she could react, he leaned in and brushed his lips lightly against hers. And he was gone.

*****

Anne was enjoying playing mother-of-the-bride. She even had old friends from college who'd made the trip to come and see Emily get married. They'd laughed and talked about old times, and harassed her mercilessly about being pregnant.

"This is a pretty desperate move just to make your boobs bigger," teased Alice.

"I think she did it to get out of exercising," said Katherine.

Anne chuckled. "Really, I was sad because all my old stretch marks were fading, and I missed them."

"So, where are they going on their honeymoon?" asked Debbie.

"They're staying in the city until Monday, and then leaving for Switzerland for ten days. Steven's wedding present."

"Will they be back before the babies come?" asked Alice.

"I hope so. I'm due in four weeks, but I guess they could come early."

"And you don't know what the sexes are?"

"No. We wanted to be surprised. We're only praying they're healthy. But we're trying to be mentally prepared in case they have health issues."

Steven interrupted. "Emily's going to throw the bouquet."

Anne laughed as all the girls pretended to push and shove to get closer to the bride and catch the bouquet. Charlie had been dragged into the foray by Spencer's sisters, but made an obvious show of not raising her hands. When Emily tossed the flowers, they tumbled through the air, almost knocking Charlie in the head. But when she ducked, they fell into Grace's grasping fingers.

As the young men lined up to vie for Spencer's garter, Anne noticed Josh had lost his animated smile. He'd been so excited to see Charlie again, but Anne suspected she'd already broken his heart. He'd become a true friend to Spencer and Emily, but no amount of discouragement seemed to be effective in quelling his focus on Charlie. She worried about her youngest who seemed to be so afraid to admit she needed anyone's help or advice. Perhaps she was also frightened to acknowledge she needed love.

The garter flew out and hit the floor, as no young man seemed bold enough to reach for it. But somehow it ended up in Brad's hands, and he was pushed forward to have his picture taken with Grace.

Although she was having a great time visiting with friends and hated to see the celebration end, the long day was taking a toll on Anne's body. She'd developed a terrible backache, and longed to soak in a hot tub of water. Steven noticed her pained expression.

"Are you okay?"

"Yes, but my back is hurting. And my feet are awfully swollen. My toes look like little sausages."

"Well, the kids are ready to leave. Here comes Emily to tell you goodbye."

Anne hugged her eldest, letting her tears fall freely. "Mom, I'm surprised you aren't totally dehydrated. You've cried buckets."

"I can't help it," she sniffed. "My daughter got married, and my hormones are all messed up. It's a terrible combination. I'm so happy. Y'all have a wonderful trip."

"We will. But call us if the babies come early. Steven said that's why he's sending us on his jet—so we could fly home anytime we need to. I don't want Charlie to see them before me."

"If they come quickly, I'll still get to see them first," declared Charlie. "It takes a while to fly back from Europe."

"I'm not due for another four weeks, so it won't be a problem." She made a face and bent forward with her hands on her back. "But I've got to get home and soak in a hot tub. My back is killing me."

Josh, who was chatting with Spencer, overheard her statement. "Uhmm, excuse me. Mrs. Gherring? Is your back hurting regularly? Could it be contractions?"

"Oh, I don't think so. It's too early, and it didn't feel like this with Emily or Charlie."

"Okay, but I'm sure your doctor told you they might come early."

"Maybe we'll stop by the hospital on the way home, just to be sure," said Steven.

"Let's get the kids on their way. I'll cross my legs until the limousine's gone."

Spencer was ready to go. It wasn't that he didn't like the wedding part or the reception part, but he was ready for the part that came next. Especially after the last four-and-a-half months of sheer torture. It seemed once Emily agreed to marry him, she became incredibly interested in kissing. But like a good accountant, she stuck firmly to the rules. They'd kissed while alone in their apartments, but only standing up. After almost falling to the ground multiple times, she'd finally agreed to let them lean against the wall. He'd argued successfully the wall was only supplying balance, not support, so it wasn't *unsupported kissing in private*. In the end, he was incredibly happy he didn't have to wait a year or more as he'd originally claimed he was willing.

He was also ready to have the first night behind him, so Josh and Brad would quit teasing him. At least he hoped they'd stop. It seems his forced confession was a source of constant amusement for them, even after four months.

"Haven't you got anything more interesting to talk about?" he'd asked them.

"Hmmm, I don't know. Brad, can you think of anything more interesting? Maybe someone who had a heart attack or got a leg cut off or something?"

"Uhmm, yeah. Well, I had this guy who got an ice pick in his eyeball."

"Nahh. That's boring. Let's talk about when Spencer confessed to Emily he wasn't the world's greatest lover."

"Yeah, that does sound more fascinating."

"I'm so glad I'm here to provide a constant source of entertainment," Spencer had quipped.

But his torture and teasing were about to end. And his new life was beginning... With Emily. That is, if he could find her. *Where is she? It's time to go.*

Emily hugged her mom one last time before turning to find Spencer and head for the limousine. Everyone was smiling at her and waving and blowing bubbles. She grabbed Spencer's hand and started outside. Charlie gave her a hug and a kiss. Steven embraced her and kissed the top of her head. Brad and Grace were blowing bubbles and yelling. And Josh was... frowning. Who was he looking at? Was it Charlie? She followed his eyes. He was frowning at... her mom. Her mom, who suddenly didn't look very happy at all.

"Mr. Gherring!" Josh called, "Anne needs you. I think you might need to go."

Steven was at her side in an instant. "Is this it?"

Anne nodded her assent.

Emily tugged on Spencer's hand. "Sorry Spencer. Looks like we may have a slight delay."

His face was that of a man who'd been sentenced to death. Josh approached the couple, obviously amused. "Hey. You guys are staying in town, right? Just go. We'll call you when it's time."

"But we can't just leave," Emily objected.

"Emily, your mom doesn't want you to spend your wedding night at the hospital. Go. We'll call." Josh pushed them toward the car.

"But I'll be worried about Mom."

Spencer dragged her into the waiting limo. "Let's go. I promise I'll distract you."

The door closed and the car started moving. "I don't know. I'm worried." She squealed as he pulled her into his lap. "What are you doing?"

He lifted her chin with his hand and captured her lips with his, sending a familiar tingle down her spine. "I'm distracting you," he said, with his hand trailing down her neck and feathering across her chest, tracing the sweetheart neckline of her dress.

"And guess what?" He wore an impish grin on his face as he kissed her neck and stole her breath.

"What?" she whispered, feeling slightly dizzy.
"No rules!"

*****

Six hours later, Charlie sat in the waiting room with Grace and Brad and Josh. He'd kept himself carefully apart from her. Not once had he spoken to her in any personal way, although he'd been polite. He was keeping his promise—he wasn't bothering her anymore. She'd been so irritated with him before, when he was desperately trying to get her attention. Why wasn't she relieved now, since he was leaving her alone?

She chuckled as Emily and Spencer came rushing in, panting from effort.

"Are we too late? Did we miss it?" Emily wrung her hands together.

"No, Sister. You're just in time. The last report was it would be any minute now." She pretended to study Emily's neck. "Is that a hickey?"

Emily clamped her hand over her neck. "Ohmygosh! Really?" Her face turned crimson, while Charlie burst out laughing.

"I'm kidding. He probably put them where I can't see them."

"Shut up!" Emily gave her sister a shove.

Josh joined them and slapped Spencer on the back. "Buddy, you seem a lot less tense. I've gotta say I'm glad. You were getting pretty grouchy these last few weeks."

She noted with astonishment Spencer only laughed and pulled Emily against him, planting a possessive kiss on her lips. He didn't protest the comment or give the slightest indication of a blush, instead strutting and proudly showing off. While Emily, on the other hand, was flushed from the base of her neck to the top of her forehead.

Suddenly, the waiting room doors opened and Steven appeared, holding a small bundle in each arm. "They're here!" His smile split his face while his dimples danced. "And they're healthy, and Mom's doing great."

Charlie and Emily ran to peer closely at their new siblings. "What are their names?" Charlie asked.

"This is Ellis, and this is Micah." With their little green knit caps, the two looked identical.

"Ellis and Micah? Are they boys or girls or one of each?" asked Emily.

Steven grinned. "Emily, Charlie... Meet your brothers!"

From the Author

Thank you for reading *Best Dating Rules*. I hope this book gave you a fun break from the pressures of real life. If you enjoyed the story, please take a moment to leave a review. Your feedback is invaluable to me and reviews are precious.

Best Dating Rules has been through several professional edits for content and format. However, we are not infallible. You might catch a spelling error or other mistake and, if you do, I would really appreciate it if you let me know. You can contact me at tamiedearenauthor@gmail.com.

Sign up for new release announcements and monthly gift card giveaways at *http://TamieDearen.com/Newsletters*

Follow on Facebook: Tamie Dearen Author

Follow on Twitter: @TamieDearen

Read on for a short peek at the next book.

Best Laid Plans

Book 3 of The Best Girls Series

JOSH STOOD INSIDE the church foyer and peered through the small window, gazing down the aisle at the wedding party, already standing in place for the rehearsal. His eyes found her immediately. He felt a huge rock in the pit of his stomach. After all this time, he'd hoped she wouldn't look as beautiful as he remembered. But she did. He'd wanted to discover his memory of her was flawed, that he'd built her up in his mind. But if anything, she was more striking than he remembered.

Her long brown hair was cascading around her shoulders almost to her waist in soft curls, framing a face with the most exotic golden eyes he'd ever seen. She was tall and thin, but not fragile looking. She had the muscles of an outdoor fanatic. Although, she looked thinner than he remembered. Was she okay? Had she been neglecting herself because of the pressures of going to school while working to support herself? What was he thinking? She wasn't his to worry about. And she never would be.

He cursed under his breath. He'd once thought he could win her love by becoming the kind of man she wanted, but after she'd remained aloof for such a long time, he'd finally given up. He'd changed from a swinging single guy, constantly sporting one beautiful girl after another, to a totally celibate man who never dated. He'd thrown himself into his work at the hospital. And in his spare time he volunteered at the free clinic, keeping such late hours he sometimes fell into bed exhausted without eating dinner. He woke early to work out every day without fail, determined to beat his body into submission. He hoped his mind would submit also, so he could forget that Charlie Best had ever come into his life.

After he'd given up on her, he'd tried to date again, but he couldn't find anyone who appealed to him. No matter how smart, talented, or attractive the girl, he couldn't rake up one iota of interest. He'd had plenty of offers, though. It seemed every single girl he met wanted to date him, but they were only interested in his money and his title—Dr. Josh Branson. So he'd abandoned dating altogether, concentrating solely on his work. When he'd heard Charlie was moving to New York, he'd allowed himself a tiny spark of hope he could give it one more shot, despite the fact she'd totally rejected him for two years. But all of that changed today.

Today he'd discovered he needed a wife, and he needed one fast. For once in his life he had to be totally self-sacrificing. He'd been thinking and agonizing about it since he'd received the news that morning, and he'd made a decision. So now, instead of vainly attempting yet again to start a relationship with Charlie, he had to marry someone else, right away. He'd considered all of his alternatives and come to the conclusion there was only one girl who would understand and agree to marry him in such a short time span—Olivia Marshall.

Made in the USA
Middletown, DE
29 July 2019